S AND PENNANTS

NUMERAL PENNANTS

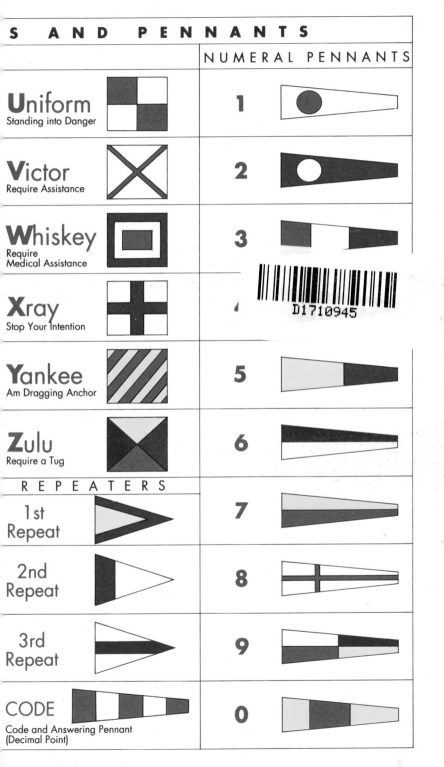

Uniform
Standing into Danger

1

Victor
Require Assistance

2

Whiskey
Require
Medical Assistance

3

Xray
Stop Your Intention

Yankee
Am Dragging Anchor

5

Zulu
Require a Tug

6

REPEATERS

1st
Repeat

7

2nd
Repeat

8

3rd
Repeat

9

CODE
Code and Answering Pennant
(Decimal Point)

0

D1710945

Boating Etiquette

CHAPMAN'S
Nautical Guides

Boating Etiquette

by Queene Hooper Foster

HEARST MARINE BOOKS
New York

Recognizing the importance of preserving what has been written, it is the
policy of William Morrow and Company, Inc., and its imprints and affiliates to
have the books it publishes printed on acid-free paper, and we exert our best
efforts to that end.

Pages 107-117 reprinted courtesy of the New York Yacht Club.

Library of Congress Catalog Card Number: 89-81526

ISBN: 0-688-09457-0

Printed in Italy
First U.S. Edition
2 3 4 5 6 7 8 9 10

Book design by Mary Moriarty
Edited by Lucy A. O'Brien
Produced by Smallwood and Stewart
9 West 19th Street
New York, NY 10011

CONTENTS

CHAPTER ONE

REASONS FOR BOATING ETIQUETTE

B oating etiquette is more than tipping your hat to the commodore. Harbor manners, an important part of this book, are the operational component of boating etiquette and relate directly to safe boat operation in crowded waters. Manners are more important today than they were in the Gilded Age of yachting, because our waters are more congested with a wide variety of watercraft. Good harbor manners are the product of long experience: the skippers with the best manners are those who have been on the water for many years. To those mariners, most of what is in this book will seem like common sense, and something they have always known. The boat operators with the worst manners are often those who just wrote out the check at the boat show, and are testing the limits of their new toys on the water. To them, a book on etiquette might seem silly or arbitrary, perhaps a little stuffy in its emphasis on what is polite or proper. But good manners are not the stuff of late-night boasts around the cabin table or sea stories at the yacht club bar; good manners in crowded waters are a true mark of good seamanship and they deserve the highest level of respect and attention from all mariners. There are many books on the topics of storms at sea, emergency repairs, and man-overboard equipment, as there should be, but there has been little written on the safest way to enter a crowded channel, on passing a small boat with the least distress, or on giving up your right-of-way to a larger vessel.

At a time when operator licensing is a topic of much discussion throughout the boating world, we hear little discussion of how one should actually behave on the water, with or without legislation. Good manners are not subject to regulation and have rarely been identified. If everyone who ventured on the water had a better understanding of good manners, which are really a part of good seamanship, then further legislation might be avoided.

Flags, another chapter herein, are often the first identifying marks on a boat, and as in the great age of sail, they are the first thing you can "read" about a vessel. Is she friendly? In distress? Is the owner aboard? Is she well kept-up? Proper flying of flags can communicate a great many things, as the following chapter on flags will show. Incorrect flying of flags is much like graffiti—it communicates nothing, and offends the eye. It also offends anyone who understands the value of communication by flags, and the tradition thereby represented. Observance of "colors" is a way of proclaiming: "Boating is fun, and I know how to play the game." And since flags snapping in the sunlight can be truly beautiful, it is a way for one boat to add to the beauty of the sport with color, tradition, and ceremony.

Ten Rules of Good Boating Etiquette

1. *Scrupulous observance of the Rules of the Road (see chapter 3)*
2. *Common sense at the helm and throttle*
3. *No wake in harbors or near other boats*
4. *Sensible anchoring practice*
5. *Proper disposal of ship's refuse and sewage*
6. *Quiet operation*

7. *Appropriate communications*

8. *Clean topsides and waterline*

9. *Observance of colors (flags)*

10. *Taut ship: i.e., no flapping laundry out to dry, no flapping halyards or other loose lines, no droopy awnings and sail covers, no fenders adangle*

CHAPTER TWO

FLAGS, OR
OBSERVING COLORS

On the huge, reborn J-class yacht *Endeavour,* the burgee is a flag measuring four feet on the hoist and six feet on the fly. It is secured to an aluminum "pig stick" (the masthead flagstaff), which was formerly a sailboard mast, about eighteen feet long and three inches in diameter. When the flag and pole are raised to the masthead on the 330-foot flag halyard, a brave man or woman in a bosun's chair, on another halyard, accompanies the cumbersome apparatus aloft to be sure it clears the masthead instrument array. It must clear four sets of spreaders, six antennae, and two separate sets of running backstays on its way to the top of the 165-foot mast. Furthermore, the wind direction and strength at the masthead may be quite different than on deck, sixteen stories below, complicating the maneuver even more. The captain has been known to spin the 130-foot boat in circles under power, eyes aloft, to the consternation of the spectator fleet always in attendance, just to help the burgee clear the obstacles on its way aloft. It represents a tremendous effort on a daily basis to observe colors and it indicates a great deal

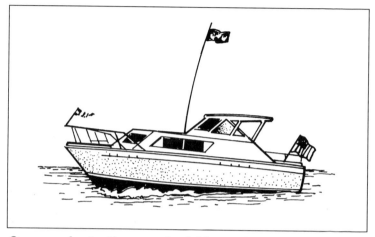

On a powerboat with a mast, the club burgee flies at the bow, the private signal at the masthead, and the ensign on the stern.

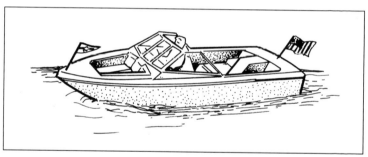

A powerboat with no mast carries the club burgee or the private signal on the bow, and the ensign on the stern.

about that yacht and how she operates. Surely lesser vessels can observe colors without complaining that it's too much work.

Flags constitute a language conveying information to those who speak that language. Before the era of radio, telephones, or Morse code, a vessel could still signal a great deal about her nationality, her owner, and even her intentions to any captain for miles around,

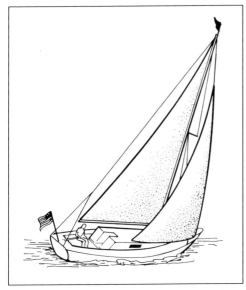

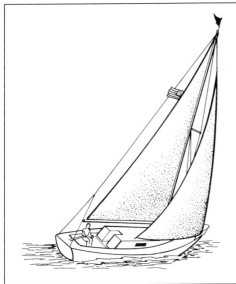

because the language of flags was understood. Since it was vitally important for a captain to know if an approaching vessel was from a friendly nation, in the naval or merchant service, or even a pleasure boat, and useful to know many other things about her, the language of flags became the international language among ships. An explanatory book "intended to cater primarily to situations related to safety of navigation and persons, especially when language difficulties arise" was published by the British Board of Trade in 1897 and

A sloop flies the club burgee or private signal at the masthead, and the ensign on the stern or on the leech of the sail.

distributed to all maritime powers. The 156-page book, *International Code of Signals, H.O. Pub. No. 102*, is still available (revised since the original) to any captain who wishes to say, among other things, "I am abandoning my vessel which has suffered a nuclear accident and is a possible source of radiation danger" (with the two flags, AD). In fact that book, along with a complete set of code flags, is required safety equipment on any yacht competing in the Newport to Bermuda Race. It would permit a yacht to communicate emergency or medical information to Norwegian and Russian ships (presumably standing by) simultaneously, without using either language.

If flags represent the components of a language, their correct placement on the vessel represents the grammar of that language. The right flags flown in the right places and at the right times of day mark the skipper as one who speaks the language of flags. It is not a crime to misuse the language of flags, any more than it is a crime to sing out of tune. But among those who know the difference, it is an unwelcome sight.

Just as there are great debates among language experts about correct word usage, so there are many heated discussions in print and at the dock about correct flag usage. There are rigid schools of thought (the burgee comes down at sunset), and time-honored expediencies (the burgee stays aloft twenty-four hours a day), proponents of new slang (the burgee flies under the starboard spreader), and revisionists (the burgee flies above the bow pulpit on both sail- and powerboats). For the most basic, everyday use, flag etiquette is simple and easy; raise the national flag in the place of honor at 8:00 A.M., take it down at sunset. If you do no more than that you are doing fine. Yacht-club burgees, private signals, Union Jacks, code flags, and pennants are seemingly less well understood, and their location and hours aloft seem to vary, but they are also fairly simple to use correctly, once you decide to set up the necessary halyards and clips and make it a part of your daily shipboard routine. While there are those who might debate the particulars of what is outlined below, it remains the accepted standard of flag etiquette, taken from *Chapman Piloting: Seamanship & Small Boat Handling* (Elbert S. Maloney, Hearst Marine Books), the United States Power Squadrons (USPS), and the New York Yacht Club yearbook.

The United States Ensign

The flag of the United States, the thirteen stripes and fifty stars, is called the national ensign when it flies at the stern of a vessel. It denotes the nationality of the vessel or of her owner. It is distinct from the yacht ensign, mentioned below, which has the fouled anchor and thirteen stars in place of the fifty stars. Even the skipper who cries bah-humbug to flag etiquette and tradition should know the proper display of the national ensign.

The ensign should be flown from 8 A.M. until sunset when the vessel is in commission, though it may be flown when entering a harbor at night for identification purposes. It should be the first flag raised in the morning, sharply at 8 A.M., when yacht clubs may fire a cannon to waken the fleet, and is followed promptly by other flags, burgees, private signals, and so forth. Not so many years ago, ladies who might be aboard the yacht were not permitted to go on deck before colors, because the gentlemen might be enjoying their morning swim over the side, in the nude. The ensign should be the last flag brought in at sunset, again often to the signal given by clubs or flagships, except on Sunday, when no cannon is fired. It should be hoisted smartly, and brought in ceremoniously.

The national ensign should be flown in the place of honor on the boat. Traditionally the captain's domain, the stern of the vessel is still the place of honor, as is the peak of the raised gaff, if you happen to have a gaff-rigged vessel. Whether on a powerboat or sailboat, the flag should be raised to the peak of the gaff when under way. Marconi-rigged sailboats can fly the flag from the leech of the aftermost sail, about two-thirds of the way up the sail, where the gaff would be if the boat were gaff-rigged. When at anchor or at the dock, or when the sail is doused, the flag should be hoisted at the stern. When the sailboat is actively racing, no flags are shown, except identifying flags specified by the race committee or sponsoring club.

The term "colors" technically applies only to the flag at the stern denoting nationality. In practice, however, it has come to mean all the flags flown, all the snapping banners of color, and their timely display.

Rules for All Ensigns

T he size of the ensign is determined by the length of the vessel: one inch on the fly (the longer dimension) for every foot of over-all length. (The ratio between the fly and the hoist is usually 3:2.) That means that for a thirty-nine-foot boat, the flag should be at least thir-ty-nine inches long. Since standard sizes for flags offer only a thirty-six-inch flag and a forty-eight-inch flag, choose the larger flag; better to err with a flag that's too big than one that's too small. An oversize flag rippling over the water can be a beautiful sight.

Some larger boats prefer to secure the flag to the staff with a tiny halyard, to permit the dipping of colors, and to leave the staff in place, bare, when the flag is lowered. Sailboats with overhanging booms may rig the flag from the boom to the rail, and dispense with the staff entirely. Sportfishing boats, which cannot fly a flag on a stern staff, as it interferes with the fishing lines over the stern, have evolved a prac-tical routine of flying the ensign from the tuna towers.

If some obstacle, such as a boarding ladder or an overhanging boom, should interfere with the centerline placement of the flagstaff, it should be located slightly to starboard of the centerline.

When flown upside down, the national ensign is an unofficial but effective distress signal.

It should hardly be necessary to say: the flag should be kept clean of grease and exhaust fumes, neither torn nor badly frayed, and it should be kept taut along its hoist.

Here are a few more pointers to spare embarrassment to neophytes on the water:

The U.S. flag should never be flown from the starboard flag hoist (under the starboard spreader) unless the vessel is under foreign ownership and is visiting U.S. waters.

If you are leaving the vessel before sunset, for example to go ashore for dinner, and won't return until after colors, take the ensign in before you leave the boat.

Don't fly the ensign from the backstay; while it is handy, the angle of the backstay will not allow the flag to fly freely.

Don't fly your state flag at the stern. It may be flown from the starboard spreader, if you need it.

Don't dry the mop in the bracket for the flagstaff.

The Yacht Ensign

Traditionally, only yachts documented with the federal government could fly the yacht ensign, the one with the red and white stripes and the thirteen stars and fouled anchor. Now, however, any yacht, documented or not, may fly the yacht ensign in domestic waters, in place of and in the manner of the national ensign. Designed in 1848 by the New York Yacht Club at the request of the Secretary of the Navy, it was intended to differentiate yachts from commercial vessels, as they might otherwise look the same in those days. It should not be flown on any yacht in foreign waters, where the stars and stripes is the only recognized national standard.

The Power Squadrons Ensign

T he ensign of the United States Power Squadrons may be displayed only by enrolled members of the USPS. Their flag has blue and white vertical stripes, and the upper left corner (or canton) comprises a red field containing a white fouled anchor encircled by thirteen stars.

The Power Squadrons credo reads: "It is an outward and visible sign that the vessel displaying it is under the charge of a person who has made a study of piloting and small boat handling, and will recognize the rights of others and the traditions of the sea. The Squadrons' Ensign also marks a craft as being under the command of a man or woman who has met certain minimum requirements and is so honored for meeting them."

While its preferred location is under the starboard spreader, the USPS ensign may be flown in place of the national ensign on smaller powerboats without masts.

The Yacht Club Burgee

Y achts enrolled in a yacht club are entitled to fly that club's burgee, except when they are under charter to a nonmember. The burgee (pronounced: "brr, gee it's a cold night") is flown from the forward-most truck (the tip of the masthead), or, lacking masts, from the bow staff. It is usually a triangular flag and should be a half-inch on the fly for every foot of the tallest mast. Powerboats should fly burgees roughly five-eighths of an inch on the fly for every foot of overall length. It is raised at colors (8 A.M.), when (or soon after) the ensign is raised, and it is lowered at sunset. However, every club has its own routine for flag display, and members should follow their club's guidelines. Members

of the Cruising Club of America, for example, fly their burgee twenty-four hours a day.

Be careful not to fly your club flag upside down by mistake; if it has a star, that star should point up.

A big problem with the burgee at the masthead is that it interferes with all the new gear that

On a yawl or ketch, the club burgee flies at the mainmast head, and the private signal at the mizzen masthead.

On a schooner, the private signal is on the mainmast, and the club burgee on the foremast.

sailboats seem to collect at the top of the mast. Antennae and anemometers are delicate instruments, and they sprout right where the burgee should be, flying free above the truck. Such instruments are easily damaged by a whipping burgee with a long stick attached. The trick is that the pig stick must be long enough and light enough to lift the burgee above the instruments when it is raised to the fullest. A wooden dowel or an old broom handle works well, or an aluminum pole for the high-tech yacht. Make it longer than you might think necessary, up to four or five feet long, with most of its length above the knots of the halyard. The flag halyard should go up the starboard side of the mast, and should be cleated at the shrouds or the chainplates, where it will not chatter against the mast in a breeze.

It will take practice to be able to raise the burgee efficiently, plus what may seem like hours of straining your neck and staring into the sun. The worst part is just before the burgee breaks into clear air above the masthead, when it hangs up on the shroud tangs or on the mast crane and seems to want to knock out the antenna. It whips the antenna at high frequency and snarls itself in a knot around it. This is where you curse flag etiquette in general. Then the flag breaks free above the truck, clear of gear and fluttering smartly for all to see. You may be tempted to nail it there and leave it up day and night, once it is up and flying.

Commodore Frank V. Snyder of the New York Yacht Club once said, in exhorting the assembled skippers at the club's annual cruise to observe proper use of the club's flag, "If you don't know where the top of your mast is, don't fly the burgee."

Powerboats have an easier time with burgees; theirs is set on a short bow staff above the bow pulpit, flying freely over the foredeck.

Private Signals

T he private signal (also called the house flag, in the manner of the merchant shipping lines) is a flag designed by the owner to identify his or her vessel. It is flown from the aftermost mast (or the mainmast on vessels with more than two masts), or in place of the club burgee on single-masted vessels. On powerboats with no masts, the private signal may replace the club burgee at the bow staff. It can be triangular, swallow-tailed, rectangular, or pennant-shaped; its size is about the same as a yacht-club burgee. Even though *Lloyd's Register of American Yachts,* which included a register of private signals, no longer exists, private signals are still helpful in distinguishing a yacht from her sisterships at a distance, and in cases of more than one owner, in indicating which partner is aboard. Private signals may give a hint of the owner's name by an initial, a color, or shape. They may be flown by day only, or day and night.

The Union Jack

I f the blue canton with the fifty white stars could be cut out of the yacht's national flag and become a flag itself, it would be the Union Jack. While U.S. naval vessels display the Union Jack at the bow when at anchor, yachts should fly theirs only between 8 A.M. and sunset on Sun-

This documented two-masted vessel flies a Union Jack at the bow, a meal pennant on the port spreader, a club burgee on the mainmast, a private signal on the mizzen, a USPS ensign on the starboard spreader, and the yacht ensign on the stern.

days and holidays, and only at anchor, never when under way. (At a mooring or at the dock is acceptable, too.) It is flown at the bow, either on a jackstaff or secured vertically to the forestay. Be sure to fly it right side up, stars pointing up, in the "shed water" position.

Other Flags

The Owner Absent flag is a rectangular blue flag displayed under the starboard spreader, at anchor or under way, whenever the owner is not on board. (If guests or family members are aboard without the owner, the guest flag, a blue rectangle with a white diagonal stripe, should fly instead.) While not frequently seen, these flags remain useful to signal the owner's friends that the vessel may be under charter or on a delivery trip.

The owner's meal flag, a white rectangular flag, flies at the starboard spreader at appropriate times on large yachts. A red pennant under the port spreader signifies crew mealtime.

The Night Hawk, a long blue pennant or windsock, flies in place of all other flags on sailboats at the masthead, after colors (at night). It allows the night watch to check wind direction easily.

A Homeward Bound pennant, rarely seen today, is a long, skinny (15:1) flag that was flown by fishing vessels and merchant ships on their homeward passage. It is horizontally divided into two halves, red and white, with a blue canton with stars.

A single code flag flying from the bow pulpit or from the backstay indicates that the boat is actively engaged in racing. It represents the class number of that boat, assigned to her for that race by the Race Committee.

Other commonly used single code flags are the red code flag B, used to initiate a protest in sailboat racing; the yellow code flag Q, to request customs clearance in foreign ports; and the tricolor T flag,

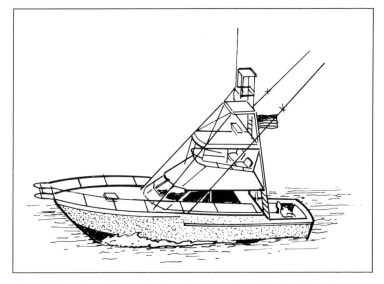

Sportfishing boats have developed the custom of flying the ensign from the tuna tower.

hoisted at the starboard spreader when launch service is requested.

Sportfishing boats fly special flags to signify their catch, and the yacht club officers fly special flags in place of their club burgee to denote their rank in the club. These are prescribed in the club's bylaws.

The red rectangular flag with the white diagonal stripe denotes "diver down" and is flown by boats actively attending a diver under water. While the official diver's flag is a "rigid replica" of code flag A, the red flag is generally recognized as the diving flag. It should not be flown by a boat going to and from the dive site.

While not actually a flag, the black anchoring ball should be displayed above the foredeck of larger vessels at anchor. At night it is replaced by the anchor light, a 360-degree white light over the foredeck or on the masthead.

The Courtesy Flag

T he courtesy flag is the national flag of the nation the yacht is visiting. It should be flown from the forward starboard spreader hoist as soon as customs are cleared and the yellow Q flag comes down. It should be flown both under way and at anchor or dockside, and should be about half the size of the national ensign. Mastless vessels may use the bow staff for the courtesy flag.

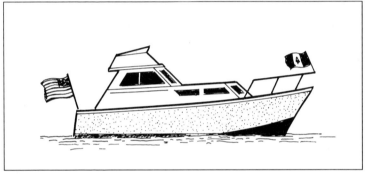

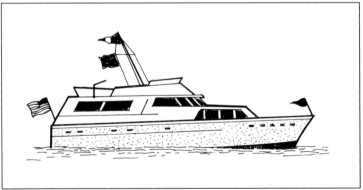

On a boat with no mast, the courtesy flag flies at the bow. If available, the starboard spreader hoist is the best location for the courtesy flag.

On a vessel with two or more masts, the courtesy flag flies under the forward starboard spreader.

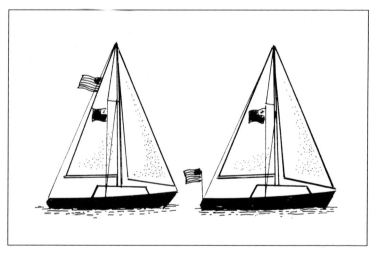

Sailboats should fly the courtesy flag under the starboard spreader, whether under sail or at anchor.

Dressing Ship

Most yachts use their set of code flags only to dress ship for holidays and special events. The International Code Flags are a time-honored and much under-utilized form of communication among vessels. The forty small, colorful flags comprise twenty-six rectangular letter flags, ten pennant-shaped numeral flags, three pennant-shaped flags called first, second, and third repeaters, and the "answering pennant." Their use is described in the *International Code*

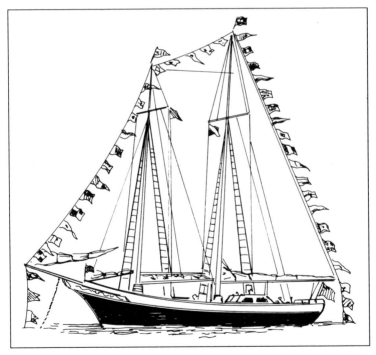

Dressing ship, the signal flags encircle the boat from waterline forward, to masthead, to waterline aft.

of Signals, H.O. Pub. No. 102, mentioned earlier, and they are still used in ship-to-ship communications.

For national holidays, special occasions, and launchings, yachts may "dress" while in port between 8 A.M. and sunset. All code flags (without flags such as burgees or the Union Jack) are strung together and raised to the masthead(s) and out to the boat's fore and aft extremities, whether it be the tip of the bowsprit or the overhanging boom. The line of flags should "encircle" the boat, from the waterline forward, aloft to the top of each mast, and down to the waterline aft; a flag or two should hang off the bow and off the stern, held secure by small weights.

The order of the flags is not important since they carry no more than a festive message, but they look best when they alternate two letter flags with one numeral pennant. A handy sequence is: AB2, UJ1, KE3, GH6, IV5, FL4, DM7, PO third repeater, RN first repeater, STO, CX9, WQ8, ZY second repeater.

The ensign, the burgees, and the Union Jack may be hoisted in their proper locations at the same time. A yacht should not get under way while "dressed" unless she is in a parade or on her maiden or final voyage.

CHAPTER THREE

HARBOR MANNERS

T here is a legend in the history of automobiles describing the first car accident. The first two cars in Ohio, the only two cars in Ohio, arrived at an intersection at the same time. Neither one wished to give way to the other. The drivers weren't use to it; they were used to being almost the only car in the state, and proceeding unimpeded. So, lacking the common sense that two horses might have shown at the same intersection, they collided.

Fortunately, boating is not quite as unregulated as those two cars in Ohio. We have the Rules of the Road, a marvelous, thoroughly tested body of rules that allows boats of many descriptions to navigate the same waters at the same time, in safety. It is just about impossible for two vessels to collide if each skipper knows and understands the Rules of the Road.

Though there is no substitute for a thorough reading of the Rules of the Road (see chapter 5 of *Chapman Piloting*, "Rules of the Road: Right-of-Way and Sound Signals"), a few of the most important rules bear repeating at every opportunity. These guidelines are from the Steering and Sailing Rules, which are almost identical for the U.S. Inland Rules and the International Rules.

Vigilance

T he first rule of the sea is constant vigilance. In practice, the person at the helm of a pleasure boat becomes the lookout, but the skipper or watch captain, or the person with the greatest experience, must keep a lookout, too. This is probably the greatest failing in pleasure boats: the person at the helm leaves the wheel for a soda, hoping the boat will stay on course; an inexperienced operator panics at the wheel and turns into another boat; the autopilot lulls the person at the helm into forgetting to look ahead as the boat plows steadily onward; or the sails prevent a clear view to leeward. It is easy to let vigilance slip, especially when few boats or hazards are around and the eyes on deck get complacent, or when everyone is concentrating so hard on some task at hand.

When visibility is less than perfect, every means available should be used to keep up vigilance. Listen for other boats, use the radar, and make systematic observations of anything that appears on the screen, and assign someone to do nothing but watch. In extremely low visibility, be sure to do everything you can to be seen by other boats: sound the horn in foggy conditions, use the correct navigation lights at night, and carry as big a radar reflector as you can. (Don't forget the old remedy of balled-up aluminum foil and empty soda cans wrapped up in a plastic garbage bag and hoisted aloft, or as high as possible, if you find yourself without a reflector in poor visibility.)

Don't rely on your instruments, no matter how sophisticated they might be. Boats with accurate loran sets can hit the navigational buoy they intended to round; two boats with operating radars can collide as they misjudge the other's speed or course. Keep a lookout at all times: constant vigilance.

A useful method for determining when the risk of a collision exists is the rule of constant bearings. Say you are at the helm of a small boat under power and see a big powerboat proceeding toward you on your starboard bow. You visually line up the powerboat with a lifeline stanchion or a fixture near the rail of your boat, say a cleat, without changing course. You watch the bearing, the line-up between the other boat and the cleat, as the powerboat gets closer. If the powerboat stays in line with the cleat as it approaches, then there is a danger of collision. The bearing has remained the same. The Rules of the Road then come into play, and your boat must give way, altering course or speed. This is a particularly useful trick to tell to neophytes at the helm because it helps them concentrate on the potential for collision, to maintain a constant watch on a boat in view, and to give useful information to the skipper on the risk of collision.

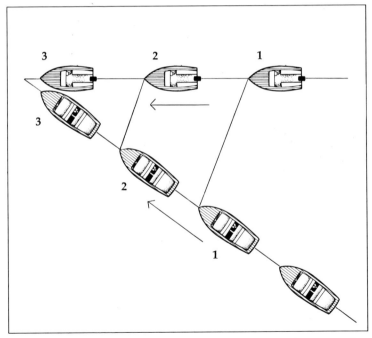

A risk of collision exists if the relative bearing between boats remains the same.

Keep an eye out on behalf of your neighbor on the water, too. If you see a boat dragging something over the side, such as a swimming ladder, a dock line, or a bathing suit, tell them; the people on board will probably be glad to hear about it before it is lost overboard. Point it out if you see a boat dragging her anchor, chafing her mooring lines, or rubbing against a piling. Point out hazards in the water, such as half-submerged logs, to boats following in your wake. Generally look out for the other guy's well-being at the dock and under way. Turn it around the other way: You would be happy to know if you were about to lose gear overboard, if your boat smelled of explosive gasoline fumes, if your tender broke loose or your lines nearly chafed through, before bad things actually happened.

Safe Speed

E very vessel must proceed at a safe speed at all times. As simple as this important rule is, it does not tell you what a safe speed might be. One boat's idle speed might be another boat's breakneck speed, and what was a safe speed yesterday is not necessarily safe today. Here is where the skipper's experience and judgment come into play. The Rules provide some guidelines for determining a safe speed in given conditions.

Visibility:

In heavy rain or fog, or at dusk or night, your boat's speed should be slow enough to allow you to see any boat ahead of you, and to allow you time to change course safely. Boat speed should also factor in any limits on visibility placed by the boat itself, for example a high bow obscuring the view forward, or a rain soaked windshield.

Traffic Density:

If the waters are crowded, you have to drop down from cruising speed. You may need to reduce speed just to figure out who has the right-of-way between you and every boat approaching you. A slow speed will give you and all the other skippers enough time to calculate what is going on. You may think you have it under control until the boat next to you surprises you with a quick change of course. If evasive action is necessary or if you are the "give-way" vessel (the "burdened" vessel in the old parlance) a change of course to avoid one vessel will put you in danger of collision with another.

Most harbors have a posted speed limit, marked by small buoys with "5 MPH" on them or with a big sign on land. Some busy stretches of water are designated as speed zones, comparable to a school zone on land. Florida waters in particular have many miles of speed zones limiting boat speed or designated as no wake zones. Tickets and fines can be issued. On one narrow stretch of the Intracoastal Waterway in the Carolinas where local children in small boats play near the channel, a stiff fine is due and payable at the time of the violation, which means that the harbormaster's boat comes alongside and waits for the cash, presently about eighty dollars. The speeder is hauled into the dock if no payment is forthcoming. This hard-nosed enforcement policy has evoked a lot of criticism, but boats move through the area at greatly reduced speeds.

Whether posted with speed limits or not, few harbors are able to enforce their speed limits as effectively as they should. State and local governments are always quick to cut monies for the harbor patrol from their budgets, and their many other duties often prevent harbormasters from lying in wait for speeders. It is too often left to the skipper's judgment (and willpower) as to how fast his or her boat should go, and when you have paid big bucks for a boat that can do fifty MPH, and no one is standing by to tell you otherwise, it gets tempting to just lean on the throttle and go. Therein lies one of the biggest hazards on the water, the boats that can't seem to slow down in congested areas. The Rules of the Road require a "safe speed," but don't say what it is, the harbormaster is too busy to give tickets to all the speeders, and most boats are designed to do many times the speed limit. What to do? It is up to the individual skipper to judge and maintain a safe speed, to consider the safety and comfort of all the boats nearby, and to set a good example to skippers with less experience and less judgment. Lives are lost and property damaged when judgment fails.

Maneuverability:

Your own vessel's maneuverability will help determine your speed. A big heavy vessel must proceed at a speed slow enough to allow for a quick stop or turn in spite of her way and momentum. Even more important, your boat's maneuverability is limited by how well the person at the helm can handle the vessel. If he or she doesn't realize that the stern is going to swing much wider than the bow in a tight turn, it's better that this be learned at a slow speed.

Consider the sea conditions in determining your speed. Choppy seas will make the boat pound unnecessarily, while a slower speed will allow most boats to ride easily over the same seas. Speed is one of the most important elements in storm tactics and in safe boat-handling in rough conditions. Control of the boat's speed in rough weather is one of the most difficult aspects of good seamanship, whether for sail- or powerboats, and whole books are written on the topic. And remember: For many smaller boats, rough conditions may be the product of a passing boat or two, not only a passing squall.

Navigational Hazards:

Keep in mind the depth of the water, and your draft. Obviously, it is better to run aground at half speed than at full speed. Most boats fitted with depth sounders have a readout at the helm to record how much water is under the keel: they are often fitted with alarms to warn of shallow water. But if you are going too fast the alarm will do you no good, as you won't have time to change course; you'll just hit bottom as the alarm sounds.

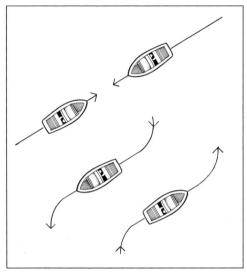

Course changes should be large enough to be noticed early.

Specific rights apply to every vessel meeting other vessels.

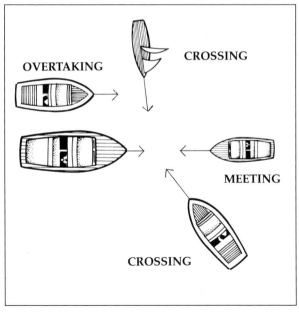

OVERTAKING

CROSSING

MEETING

CROSSING

35

No Wake

Y ou are responsible for any damage caused by your wake. Big rolling wakes are one of the most troublesome aspects of speed. Wakes are not mentioned in the Rules of the Road, but a safe speed at all times is an important part of the Rules, and wakes are a function of speed. Minding your wake by controlling your speed is of great importance to the safety of all vessels. Even a tug with barge can sustain damage when a big pleasure-boat wake rolls in, sending the barge crashing into the tug.

You never know what damage your wake might be inflicting on other boats. Being rolled about by a wake is not merely annoying, though it is that, too. It can be dangerous to very small boats that can be quickly swamped, sending their occupants for an unexpected swim. It is almost as though every speeding boat leaves storm conditions for the boats behind her, kicking up waves usually reserved for a gale and sending them from shore to shore. A big wake can roll boats of any size into the pier or against their lines, causing damage to the lines, the boat, the pier, or even the people who may be fending off the pier. Particularly in otherwise calm waters, a wake can cause distress and discomfort. A quiet marina can turn into an instant maelstrom with all the boats pitching, masts tangling, and drinks flying when a thoughtless powerboat steams down the channel nearby, pulling too big a wake.

Whistle Signals

I n a crowded commercial harbor where tugs and ferry boats criss-cross the channel and oilers and tankers glide close by one another, the radio is often filled with cryptic communications on navigational matters. "Pass you on one whistle, skipper" or "Coming up on your stern with two whistles." Whether these coded messages are exchanged on VHF channel 13 between bridges, or delivered by the horn blasts themselves, they refer to the sound signals.

Sound signals are required by the Rules of the Road for all powered vessels approaching within one-half mile of one another. Too few pleasure boats take the time to observe the simple signals properly; their value is underestimated. Like the use of flags on a yacht, proper use of signals marks the skipper as a courteous observer of the traditions of the sea, and as a knowledgeable communicator. Unlike flags, the use of signals can add a great deal to the safety of the vessel that uses them correctly, which is why they are prescribed in the Rules of the Road.

There are only five signals you need to know. The most important is the Danger Signal—five or more short blasts on the horn. It means "Stop your intentions!" or "Danger ahead!" It is sounded whenever one skipper considers another skipper's actions dangerous to either skipper's boat. If you hear five blasts on the horn, slow down immediately until you can determine what the perceived danger might be.

Three blasts on the horn means "My engines are in reverse." This might mean that the boat giving the signal is going backward, or it might mean she is stopping suddenly. Three blasts are given when a boat backs out of a slip, warning boats nearby of the maneuver.

One short blast on the horn means "I intend to leave you on my port side," or in the International Rules, "I am altering course to starboard," which is really the same thing if you think about it. Like two cars on a narrow roadway, boats customarily pass port side to port side whenever they meet head on, making the appropriate course change to starboard as they approach one another and sound one short blast. They communicate and agree on this simple maneuver when one boat sounds a short blast (either boat may initiate the exchange) and then the other boat answers with the same single short blast. If either skipper sees danger in this intended action, the danger signal of five blasts is sounded. Neither vessel should proceed until a new agreement is reached through further signals or through VHF radio channel 13 on one watt of power, or through channel 16.

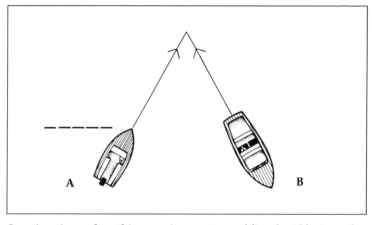

In a situation such as this, a mariner must sound five short blasts on the horn (represented by the dashes) to indicate danger: stop your intentions.

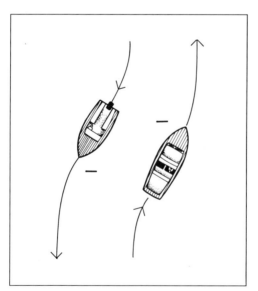

Both boats sound one blast and both alter course to starboard.

Two short blasts on the horn (in the Inland Rules) means, "I intend to leave you on my starboard side," which amounts to the same thing as the International Rules definition of "I am altering course to port." It should be answered by two short blasts from the approaching vessel, resulting in an orderly starboard side to starboard side meeting, or passing

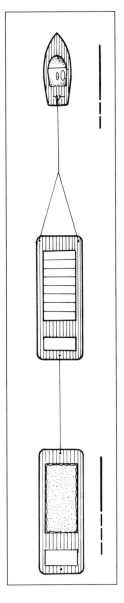

The vessel being towed sounds one long—three short blasts in reduced visibility immediately after the towing boat sounds its own signal.

a slower vessel on her port side.

One long blast should be sounded by a vessel entering a channel from a berth to alert other vessels in the channel of her action. A vessel entering a channel has no right-of-way over boats already in the channel, just as cars entering the highway must give way to the cars already proceeding along the highway.

Unfortunately for sailboats with their engines turned off, sound signals are not used between two approaching boats under sail. This omits a valuable means of communication from their repertoire. Of course, sail–

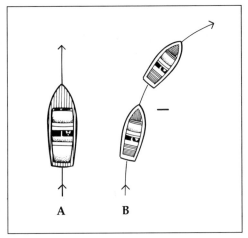

In the International Rules, course changes are signaled, but the signal is not returned by other vessels.

boats using their engines are considered powerboats and can make use of the signals above.

Note that these sound signals are to be used whenever vessels are clearly in sight of one another, at one-half mile apart and closing. They are not to be used in fog or at night, when the signals for reduced visibility are used.

The basic signal given in fog is one long blast about every two minutes when under way. A vessel restricted in her ability to maneuver, and that includes boats under sail, tugs pushing barges, vessels constrained by their draft, and vessels engaged in fishing, all sound the same signal: one long blast followed by two short blasts. Other signals indicate other types of vessels in poor visibility, for example, a vessel being towed (or the last barge in a string) should sound one long blast then three short blasts right after the towing vessel sounds her signal of one long and two short blasts. These and other signals are given in detail in chapter 5 of *Chapman Piloting.*

Where signals are concerned, the International Rules of the Road differ slightly from the Inland Rules. The International Rules require the one and two blast signals whenever a vessel plans to change course, as described above, but these signals need not be answered by other vessels, unless the approaching vessel will be taking a similar change of course, as happens quite often when two boats agree to make a port-to-port meeting.

Passing Techniques

W hen one boat overtakes another, there is a simple procedure that allows both boats to cause the least possible disruption to one another's progress and that makes the maneuver more comfortable for both boats. The procedure was developed and perfected in the Intracoastal Waterway, the 1,200-mile stretch of protected water that runs the length of the Eastern seaboard where hundreds of boats proceed at different speeds down the same channel. The passing procedure is needed because of the problem that arises when a faster boat, say a trawler proceeding at eight knots, wishes to pass a sailboat motoring along at six knots. The trawler pulls a big wake at eight knots, yet cannot slow down to reduce her wake and still maintain a passing speed. The passing maneuver takes a long while with only a two-knot speed differential, and the big wake rolls the sailboat the whole time. The sailboat skipper shakes his or her fist because the boat rolls mercilessly, and the trawler captain is furious because so much time is spent at the edge of the channel. It happens to each boat ten times in a day.

The slower boat can show good seamanship, as well as the utmost courtesy and graciousness, by initiating the procedure: The sailboat's skipper drops the boat's speed down to dead low or even idle just as

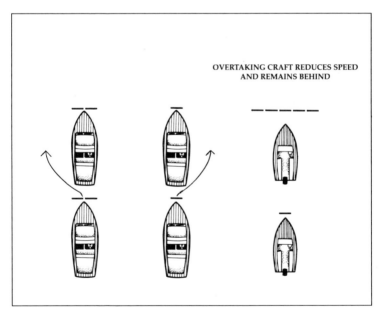

OVERTAKING CRAFT REDUCES SPEED
AND REMAINS BEHIND

An orderly exchange of horn signals clarifies a passing maneuver.

the faster boat nears the stern. The overtaking boat will be able to drop her speed down to where there is no wake, yet maintain sufficient speed to pass quickly, say at five knots in our example. The whole maneuver takes only a minute, then both boats resume their cruising speeds, with their skippers in a much happier frame of mind. The time or momentum lost in throttling back briefly is easily rewarded by the quickness of the whole passing maneuver. The overtaken boat is not rolled around, and the overtaking boat is soon back in center channel at normal speed.

Right-of-Way

A boat approaching on your starboard side has right-of-way, and you must alter course to go astern or adjust your speed to get out of her way. The other boat, the "stand-on" vessel (also called the "privileged" vessel), should maintain course and speed while you maneuver around her. (Note the courtesy mentioned earlier in which both boats reduce their speed to expedite a passing maneuver.)

All vessels, under sail or power, give the right-of-way to fishing vessels when they are actively engaged in fishing and to any vessel with limited maneuverability, including very large vessels, tugs with barges, even pleasure boats too large to make a quick course change.

Right-of-Way for Sailboats

Sailboats have the right-of-way over boats under power that are not engaged in fishing and not limited in their maneuverability. This needs some clarification, because sailboat skippers think that when under sail they have the right-of-way over all other vessels. It just isn't so.

Sailboats with their engines on are considered powerboats in the Rules. It isn't enough that the sails are up and drawing, that the boat is heeling nicely or getting most of her speed from the sails. If the engine is on, the sailboat is considered a powerboat and loses all rights as a sailboat. She must steer clear of other sailboats without their engines on, and is subject to the Rules of the Road like any other powerboat.

If a sailboat is overtaking a boat under power, even if she is under sail alone, she must give right-of-way to the powerboat. This happens frequently in the cases of fast catamarans and sailboards.

If the boat under power is less maneuverable or is constrained by her draft, then the boat under sail must keep clear. This should prevent the little twenty-four-foot sailboat from sailing across the bow of a tugboat, or even in front of a large pleasure boat in the channel. All too often, the small-sailboat skippers give themselves the right to interfere with the larger boat's passage when in fact the larger, less maneuverable vessel should be allowed to proceed under the Rules.

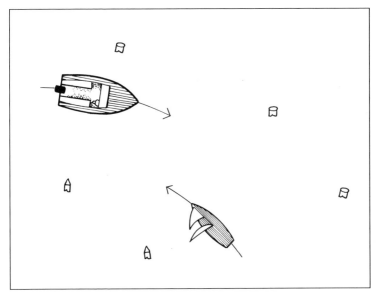

The boat under sail must keep clear of a boat confined to the channel.

More Rules for Sailboats

Between sailboats under sail, there are special rules to prevent collisions. They are arbitrary and should be memorized by every sailboat skipper and anyone else who may take the helm.

The vessel on the starboard tack, that is, with the wind crossing her starboard side first (with the starboard side "up" if the boat is heeling), has right-of-way over the boat on the port tack.

When both boats are on the same tack, the boat to leeward (the boat that gets the wind second) has the right-of-way.

When you are on the port tack and are approaching another sailboat, but you cannot tell what tack she is on, you must assume she is on the starboard tack and that she has right-of-way.

Finally, a whole book of rules for sailboats during a race is available from the U.S. Yacht Racing Union in Newport, Rhode Island. Racing sailboats need to carry a copy of these rules on board.

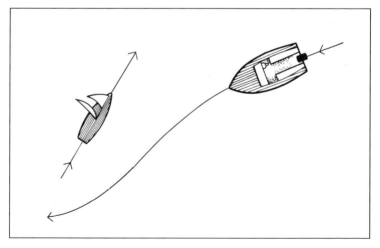

The powerboat alters course to avoid a boat under sail.

Sailboat skippers have to realize that nonsailors have no idea why sailboats have to zigzag so much, or why their course changes so frequently. To nonsailors, sailboats seem like the rudest boats on the water because they sail slowly down the center of the channel, capriciously change course 90 degrees, and vary their course this way and that as though avoiding logs. When a sailboat is the stand-on vessel, which she frequently is, she is under obligation to maintain her course and speed, so other vessels can plan their maneuvers around her. Skippers of racing sailboats frequently annoy other skippers with their self-absorbed maneuvering: You go out of your way to avoid the sailboat, which then changes course to get in the way again. And then the skipper rudely shakes a fist at you. Those skippers must realize that they are subject to the Rules of the Road during the race, even if it is not to their tactical advantage to be the burdened vessel.

The Gracious Gesture

In very congested waters, where pleasure boats of all descriptions are changing course this way and that to avoid one another, some understanding between boats beyond the basic navigation rules becomes essential. Radio communication may not work to clarify all the maneuvering necessary, whistle signals would fill the air with blasts from every direction, and all vessels, even a vessel with the right-of-way, would have to slow down and consider all the turmoil.

While it is so important to know the Rules of the Road yourself, and to handle your boat accordingly, it is equally important to know that the skipper on the boat approaching you knows the rules, too. How do you know this? You observe the other boat carefully. You watch her course, check that the person at the wheel or tiller sees you coming, adjusts the boat's course early if appropriate, or maintains his or her course while observing your course carefully. Knowledge and constant vigilance are required.

There is a courtesy on the water not prescribed in the Rules of the Road, but of great use to nonprofessional mariners. It is a means of communication not generally available to large vessels, but it accounts for much of the safe maneuvering among small (under forty feet) pleasure boats. This is the gracious gesture of "After you, captain." It may be a friendly wave across the water at an approaching vessel, and the simple acknowledgement that the other person sees you coming, or it may be a timely change of course to avoid a developing right-of-way situation. When a big powerboat motors slowly down the channel, the small-sailboat skipper might gesture with an arm to indicate that the powerboat, which might well be the give-way vessel, should proceed on course while the sailboat makes a small course-change. It happens all the time, in a manner similar to two people passing through a doorway at the same time. And so a better understanding develops between boats, and a better day—not to mention a safer day—on the water is had by all concerned

The Courtesies of Anchoring

W hen you set an anchor in the modern boating world, you have instant neighbors, often quite close by. In addition to securing a big enough anchor to an appropriate rode, giving it enough scope to dig into the bottom at an effective angle, and choosing a clear stretch of water with sufficient swinging radius (all of which is covered in detail in *Chapman Piloting*'s "Anchoring" chapter), you must consider your new neighbors. They will be carefully considering you. In many crowded anchorages, the hazard in the night is as likely to be your neighbor's boat as storm winds, high tide, low tide, or a change in the weather. It may also be a neighbor who shouts to waken you and tell you that you are dragging, which is much better than waking to the rudder grounding on a lee shore.

If every skipper practiced the rudiments of an effective anchor set, there would be less occasion for the exercise of good manners at anchor. Unlike a car, which stays when you put it in park, a boat will slither around on even a well-set anchor, and even the largest anchor and the most far-traveled skipper may drag from time to time. Knowledge, seamanship, and good gear should keep most boats out of trouble most of the time, but good manners may be needed when these are not enough to keep boats from "mixing it up" with one another late at night.

The dragging anchor must be hauled up and reset. If your boat is backing out of control into other boats, admit it at once. Don't argue; don't wait for the anchor to dig in. You'll save yourself time and trouble. Haul up the anchor and reset it promptly in another location and/or anchor with heavier gear.

The boat that anchors second must haul up and reset her anchor should she interfere with a boat that anchored earlier. The boat that anchored first has the right to stay where she is, assuming her own anchor has not dragged. Often the boat that put her anchor down first assumes that she need not reset it, even when she drags into another boat. That is when you hear the screaming match: "You were there, I was here." "No, you were there, I was here." Note that the first rule is that the dragging anchor must be hauled and reset.

Don't anchor among moored boats. Boats that are moored may be "at home" and unattended, or they may be paying good money to the owner of the mooring or the harbormaster to lie on that mooring in safety. In either case, they will have different swinging radii from that of anchored boats, and the anchored boat must move if there is trouble.

Don't anchor among empty moorings either. Their owners will probably return, and they have a right to ask for their full swinging room. The anchored boat has to move again.

Don't anchor close by another boat if you can comfortably anchor further away.

Use an anchor light or a 360-degree white masthead light to show your presence to other boats under way. This is part of the Rules of the Road and is a very good practice too often forgotten. A bow light, masthead tricolor, or masthead strobe will not do as an anchor light: They signify you are under way, or in distress. If you feel you need additional lights at night for safety, leave the cabin lights or the spreader lights on; they have no legal significance or meaning and effectively show your presence to other boats.

Keep the noise down on your boat: Loud music, partying, generators, children, dogs, and snapping halyards can be annoying to people who have gone to extra trouble to anchor just to get away from the hubbub of shore life.

Be mindful of local town ordinances that apply to anchored boats. Though not always adequately posted or charted, restrictions on the length of time you may remain at anchor, whether you may live aboard, whether two or more boats may raft up, or whether overboard sewage discharge is permitted, may affect your visit. These restrictions have sprung up as a result of abuses over the years and can seem rather strident; they may or may not be enforced. Keep in mind also that you may be asked to pay a fee to marinas for services ashore which might be free to paying dockside customers, such as dinghy tie-up, garbage disposal, fresh water, car parking, and, of course, showers. Marinas and other waterfront establishments may have tremendous costs associated with these services, though they may seem minor to you, and it is only fair to pay them a small fee for the use of their facilities.

Rafting-up

T he rafting of friendly yachts, one next to the other, is one of the joys of convivial cruising, and in clement weather, can increase the capacity of a small harbor, as well as the deck space available for a party. The procedure for rafting-up is about the same as making an approach to a dock, except that the dock is swinging back and forth, and may have a swaying mast which can tangle dangerously with other masts at the spreaders. The use of spring lines becomes especially important.

Except in harbors like Cuttyhunk, off the coast of Massachusetts, where boats are assigned three to a mooring (each paying its own fee) by the harbormaster, rafting is usually by mutual agreement between skippers, or by a mothership tending to the needs of a smaller or racing vessel. Boats may raft on a mooring or on the largest boat's anchor, but if more than one anchor is needed, consider making another raft. When more than one anchor is used, they may tangle or drastically alter the strains on all the lines as the boats turn.

Rafting is safe only if all vessels in the raft are attended at all times: A capable person must be aboard each boat in case the anchor begins to drag and the raft must break up promptly. Every boat should be prepared to depart the raft and take care of herself should the weather change. If a change is expected, the raft should break up while it is still light, before darkness makes anchoring more difficult.

Even rafted among friends, crew should ask permission to step aboard, or to cross the deck to another boat, before doing so for the first time. Privacy is harder to maintain in a large raft, and so it is all the more precious: Cross the foredeck rather than walking through the cockpit, tread lightly as you cross the deck to minimize the noise and reduce the rolling of the boat.

CHAPTER FOUR

DOCKSIDE MANNERS

Approaching the Dock

Any landing that causes no damage is a successful landing. Beyond that there are a few courtesies, mentioned below, that will make a happier landing. Chief among them is that you must be sure your boat is welcome where you choose to tie up.

Reservations

A friendly hail across the water should secure a dock for smaller vessels, but radio contact via VHF radio works best in large harbors and for larger yachts. Many busy ports are booked up months in advance. These marinas should be phoned by landline as soon as you know when you plan to be there. A good source of marina phone numbers is the *Waterway Guide*, an annual guide published by Communication Channels. This publication also gives the VHF channel normally monitored by a particular marina, usually 16, 68, or 09.

Whether you have reservations or not, contact the marina only when you are within clear radio range. Don't clog the airwaves by trying to raise a marina which is still beyond range. In fact, many busy marinas prefer that you wait until you are within visual range so they can direct you to the appropriate pier right away. The marina should be able to tell you what side to place your fenders and docklines on, in preparation for docking. You should be able to tell them your departure date, fuel needs, water and electrical service, and repair needs.

Dockage rates often cannot be discussed over the airwaves. They may change from week to week, season to season.

Keep in mind that every marina, even the most decrepit one, is sitting on prime waterfront real estate, and that there are probably weekly pressures to build condos under the travellift. The people who own the marina could make a lot more money by selling out to developers. Operating a profitable marina is difficult at best; give the owners their due.

Private Docks

A small private dock in Newport has a sign reading, "Any boat left on this dock will be taken away and sunk at owner's expense." Not all private docks post such a sign, but you should steer as clear of private docks as if they did.

Docking

Making a good landing is not so much a matter of courtesy as a function of knowledge and forethought. Tidal current, wind, engine configuration, talent on the foredeck, and talent on the pier are factors almost as important as the handling at the helm, and must be carefully considered by the skipper. Good seamanship is shown by the skipper's careful coaching of everyone on the boat before the docking maneuver begins. Even the skipper of a small boat should inform the crew as to which slip they intend to enter, or what side of the boat will be at the dock. All fenders should be in place, at a height even with the dock, and evenly placed along the widest section of the hull. Docklines should be led clear of lifelines and staunchions, coiled neatly, then laid on the deck or held by a crewmember ready to throw them ashore. Fenderboards should be placed, if necessary, after all lines have been snugged up, so that the boat will rest stationary alongside the piling.

Handling a Line

Crew members should understand where each line on the boat is intended to go on the dock. Is this a forward spring or a stern spring? They will probably have occasion to tell someone taking the line which way it is supposed to go. If they don't know, they can ask the skipper. If the skipper doesn't know, consult the chapter on "Power Cruiser Seamanship" in *Chapman Piloting*. Crew members can tell the dock attendant not to snub up too quickly (the cause of many a botched landing), to put the eye splice around a certain piling, or to cleat it fast to ease the boat alongside. It is the skipper's job to see that this is all understood and carried out without much yelling. A good skipper never blames the crew or the current for a botched land-

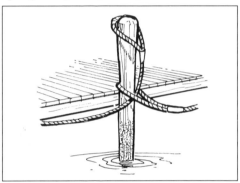

One eye can be passed through another on a piling so that either can be removed easily.

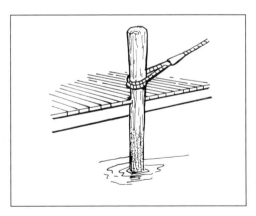

An extra loop around the piling prevents slippage up or down.

ing; it is the skipper's failure to communicate the vessel's needs to the crew or a miscalculation of the conditions that will botch things up. The more discussion that goes on before docking, the better the chances for a quiet and orderly maneuver.

Anyone handling a dockline should learn how to throw it properly, extending its full length and reaching its destination. Learn to coil a line quickly, in big, even coils, in case it should fail to reach the dock on the first throw. Separate the line roughly in half, holding half of the coil in each hand. Throw the first half high across the dock, in a big sweeping gesture, almost like bowling in the air, and let the remaining coils follow. Coil quickly but very carefully if it falls short; more throws are spoiled by fouled line than by late timing. And do the dock attendant a favor; don't throw the wet, heavy line in his or her face. No one would be able to see it coming, much less catch it, while shielding the face for self-protection. Aim the line to land on the dock, at the feet of a grateful attendant.

Fenders

Fenders, too frequently called bumpers, are simple and useful devices, yet they are so often sloppily used that they have become a mark of poor nautical etiquette all by themselves. The rule for fenders is: A boat under way should never be seen with its fenders over the side. When she is dockside, naturally she will use all fenders necessary. As soon as she is away from the dock, a yacht's fenders should be pulled up as promptly as is humanly possible, so that at no time could a shoreside onlooker see a boat under way with fenders adangle.

If you should see a boat that has failed to ship the fenders, and they are dangling and banging over the side in the bow wave, point it out to the skipper politely. If the skipper responds that the boat will soon be docking, or has just come from the dock, ask the skipper if he (or her husband) leaves his fly undone on the way to or from the bathroom. The affront to good manners is about equal.

Pets Aboard

T ake your dogs and cats, monkeys and birds aboard with you wherever you go. Animals are usually well-liked on the water and they make good cruising companions. Unfortunately, too many dogs go unchaperoned, making a mess on the pier or up on the yacht-club lawn, or yapping at dawn. Many marinas have posted rules or have prohibited pets entirely; it is easy to understand why if you have ever met a growling Chesapeake Bay retriever on the dock beside your cockpit. It shouldn't take a book on boating etiquette to tell people to curb their dog when ashore, leash it if it is fierce, and keep it from trespassing on other boats.

Noise

I t doesn't take a book on nautical etiquette to tell anyone that excessive noise is offensive. On the water it is a particular nuisance because sound travels great distances, offending the ears of many. Muscle boats, sounding like a jet plane right overhead, are big offenders when it comes to noise. Like motorcycles a decade ago, these boats despise mufflers, and they are responsible for their own bad reputations. Some townships have attempted to regulate the noise level on their waters, in addition to regulating speeds, although noise regulations are difficult to enforce.

Use of electrical generators can be annoying to neighbors late at night or early in the morning. Particularly at quiet anchorages, generators generate complaints.

Sailboats can be big offenders in the noise department, too. A very slight breeze can set halyards to tapping on the mast in the most irritating rhythm. No amount of tightening will cancel this rat-a-tat; the lines must be pulled away from the mast, either by securing them to the bow pulpit or lifelines, or by the use of gilguys, light line used to tie halyards out to the shrouds and away from the mast. Jon Wilson of *WoodenBoat* magazine has pointed out that a slapping halyard is just as offensive when it slaps on a wooden mast as on an aluminum mast, and that it may remove varnish, too. The Concordia Yard boatyard replaces the short gilguys on the Concordia yawls in their care every year, so that they will always be in place, ready for use, and to keep the yawls tidy.

Gilguys should tie off the halyards whether there is a breeze to make the halyards slap or not. It may be long after the owners have gone home that the breeze builds enough to set the halyards slapping, and that's when the boat in the next slip will start complaining about the noise. A modern equivalent to the noisy halyards is the noisy furling slot appearing in new rigs. It will howl like an empty soda bottle when you blow on it, yielding an unearthly low whistle. Ask your sailmaker for a stopper at the masthead if this noise emanates from your boat.

Noise in the form of loud music is as offensive in crowded harbors as it is from across the street, perhaps moreso because sound carries so well across the water. It is even worse in uncrowded harbors. Treat your maritime neighbors as you treat your neighbors ashore, or perhaps better than that.

Keep in mind that, because sound travels so well across the water, normal conversations carry much further than you may expect. This can be embarrassing when the subject of your conversation raises his or her head out of the companionway wearing a scowl.

CHAPTER FIVE

RADIO MANNERS

Misuse of the VHF radio is a real problem on busy waterways, where frequencies with specified uses are overcrowded with idle chatter between boats. The FCC has strict regulations for the use of VHF radios, but these regulations (given in *Chapman Piloting*, chapter 22, "Electronic Equipment: Communication") are not sufficient by themselves to keep the airways clear, and too many skippers seem unaware of the regulations anyway. Skippers must know the regulations, and have the courtesy to observe the intent of the regulations as well, particularly these:

1. Use Channel 16 for distress and hailing only.
2. Keep conversations as short as possible.
3. Use minimum power (one watt) whenever possible.
4. Listen before transmitting so you don't "step on" other calls.

Keep in mind the assigned purpose of the different VHF channels. Channel 16 is the most important one: It is the distress, safety, and call frequency. It is also the most abused channel. It should be monitored by all vessels whenever the radio is turned on but not actively in use. Transmissions should be brief in the extreme. "*Moonfleet, Moonfleet, Moonfleet.* This is the yacht *Saphaedra,* WJZ 1234. Come in please. Over."

"*Saphaedra,* this is the yacht *Moonfleet,* WYX 3212; switch and answer channel 72, channel 72."

The reply: "Switching to channel 72."

End of transmission on channel 16. If no reply is heard, wait two minutes before hailing again. If there is still no reply after three tries, hold off for fifteen minutes: Your party is not listening or is not within range. ("Over" may be omitted when the reception is good.)

Channel 6 is for the intership safety communications, with the emphasis on safety. Along with channel 16, all radios are required to have channel 6 (also given as 06).

Noncommercial craft, that is pleasure boats, have five assigned intership channels: 68 (the most popular), 69, 71, 72, and 78. To select a working channel, determine which of these is free of traffic before raising another vessel on channel 16, then switch to that channel as soon as contact is made.

Channel 70 used to be a common working channel but has been designated as a distress and safety calling channel for digital selective calling only. This will be a new high-tech transmission (not yet on line) that will broadcast special safety announcements.

Noncommercial boats should use channel 9 (or 09) to communicate with commercial vessels and with commercial shore facilities such as marinas and yacht clubs.

Channel 13 is for navigational matters between ships (large vessels must monitor channel 13 in addition to channel 16) in constricted waters, and an approaching barge can often be raised on channel 13. Army-operated locks and drawbridges usually monitor channel 13, too. It should always be used with only one watt of power.

The Coast Guard delivers safety messages on channel 22(A), which is also used by pleasure boats to converse with the Coast Guard, although it is basically reserved for the U. S. government.

Channels 25, 26, 27, 28, and 84 are the Marine Operator channels used to patch VHF radio calls into the local landlines, i.e., for ordinary phone calls home. On a Saturday evening in the boating season, these channels are nearly impossible to use because of the long waiting lists of callers, and the interminable listening you have to do while you wait your turn to make a call. You can wait for an hour by the radio to make your call and find out that nobody is home at the number you are trying to reach. Your calls are not private and cannot be made at a specific time due to the traffic. Cellular phones are a better alternative for the skipper who frequently needs landline service.

Skippers who want to contact another boat can plan ahead by pre-arranging a VHF channel to monitor at a certain time of day, or a certain time during every hour (such as twenty minutes after every hour). Most new radios can monitor two or more channels at once, so skippers can monitor a predetermined channel and channel 16 at the same time. This plan can free up channel 16 for other uses.

When you use your VHF radio (other than for calls through the Marine Operator—landline telephone calls) imagine that a small boat far away is in distress, sinking, or with someone overboard, and is trying desperately to contact someone on channel 16. Her batteries are low and her signal is weak. The distress call needs to get through, even more than your call to reserve a slip at the marina. Listen for that call before you key the mike. Think of that distress call trying to get through during your conversation about the size of bluefish, and keep your conversation short, even on a working frequency.

Think of that distress call when you blast away at full twenty-five-watt power to another boat close by, sending your signal much further than it needs to go and interfering with other calls. If you have ever made a distress call, or heard a distress call transmitted over the air, it is easier to remember the courtesies mentioned above, and the reasons for them. They are all directly related to safety on the water.

CHAPTER SIX

MANNERS ON THE RACECOURSE

acing brings out many of the best and most knowledgeable sailors all at once in an organized group. The best boat handling, the best boats, the sharpest crews, and the most experienced skippers convene in high concentration on a racecourse. They know the racing rules like sea lawyers, can handle adverse weather and sea conditions like veterans of ocean wars, and know the bearing and "distance off" of every boat in the fleet. Yet some evil mood often accompanies racing fleets, causing fine sailors to forget their own kindly natures, their good manners, and something more important as well: The skipper at the helm of a racing sailboat sometimes seems to forget the Rules of the Road, which apply to them just as much as they do to other boats of varying types enjoying the water.

Good Manners for Race Participants

In addition to the bonds of good fellowship set by the other competitors, and the level of sportsmanship established by the sponsoring club or committee, racing skippers should be bound by their knowledge of the Rules of the Road. This would seem fairly obvious, but it is too often forgotten in the heat of close competition. Racing sailboats have no special rights of way; they are not mentioned in the Rules of the Road, except as sailboats. They rarely qualify as "least maneuverable vessel" or as "restricted in her ability to maneuver." They are usually highly maneuverable; their skippers just don't want to give an inch. Somehow the skippers see only the competitors in their own fleet; other boats are almost invisible. They often seem surprised by the close proximity of a nonracing boat and are not prepared to change course. They certainly won't alter speed to avoid a confrontation, but will keep up their racing trim. In the highest levels of racing, where the skippers should know the Rules well, manners may be just as bad as those in the junior racing program, or perhaps much worse.

The Rules say nothing about a boat stealing wind from the sails of another boat; so why is it that a cruising boat passing within five boatlengths of a racing boat is subjected to contemptuous shouts of rage as if he had stolen the trophy? The Rules do not permit a sailboat to cross slowly in front of a tug and barge coming down the channel; yet many tugboat captains in Long Island Sound have premature gray hair from leaning on the throttle in hard reverse to avoid a tiny self-righteous sailboat. The Rules do not suggest that the give-way vessel can become the stand-on vessel by dint of rude and offensive exclamations designed to intimidate the privileged vessel into altering course immediately. The racing boat, like every other boat, must consider her right-of-way as outlined in the Rules of the Road and then act accordingly. Even if the racing boat does have the right-of-way, she cannot alter course (e.g., tack or jibe, or bear off sharply) while another vessel is maneuvering around her. As well as studying the Racing Rules (to see, for example, who has a "mast abeam" or an overlap), racing skippers should know the Rules of the Road cold.

And if nonracing boats should have the courtesy and good manners to stay out of a racing boat's wind, and throw no wake to shake the sails, and if tugs and tows should cross clear ahead, the racing sailboat must consider herself lucky, although there will be no good excuse to lose the race.

Good Manners for Spectators

R acing requires tremendous concentration by the participants, and precise courses are set not to the compass, but to the shifting wind direction. In a breeze the boats will be on a fine edge balancing crew weight with sail area, and a gap in the concentration of the person at the helm can spill the occupants out of the boat in a second. The skipper and crew on the rail will be all too aware of their fine balance, and perhaps nervous about it. They may react badly when their balance is threatened. The smaller the boat, the greater the chance for a swim, and the more enraged the skipper will be if his or her balance is disturbed by the presence of another boat. For the sailor who has never raced a boat, it can be difficult to understand the seemingly capricious behavior of a serious racer; it behooves the nonracing boat to courteously avoid the racing boats altogether.

If you see a bunch of similar sailboats all pointing in the same direction, you may assume that they are engaged in a race, and that they would prefer that a nonracing boat stay clear of the fleet as a whole. If it is possible to alter course or speed to circumnavigate the fleet, then do so before any conflicts of course cause the racers to lose their concentration, and before any right-of-way situation arises. Take the stern of the last boat in the fleet. Even the straggler will be irate if you cross the bow and throw a wake.

By calculating which buoy or marker the fleet may be aiming for, you may be able to determine the turning mark of the racecourse, and avoid the fleet as a whole again after they change course and head the other way. Race courses are usually triangular, like the America's Cup

Course or the Olympic Course, with all marks of the course left to port, but they may be any shape the Race Committee signals to the fleet at the start. It may be nearly impossible to determine the progress of the fleet around the course, or even what mark they are headed for. Watch the first boat in the fleet to see the new direction of the course.

A fleet of large sailboats may be so spread out that each competitor looks like a lone cruising boat out for a sail. If the sails are carefully trimmed, and look like spider webs of high-tech ribbon, and if the crew is perched on the rail as though on the bleachers, then the boat may be part of a long-distance race. If it is calm, a boat in the thick of a race may look like a baking beach party, with sails flapping like laundry out to dry, going nowhere with the crew asleep on the foredeck. That crew may be just as mad when a wake rocks the boat and shakes what little wind there is out of the sails, and kills hard-won momentum.

Outside busy yacht harbors such as Annapolis, Marblehead, or San Francisco, there may be many, many fleets of gnatlike sailboats darting every which way. You will have to cut across one fleet or another in order to get anywhere at all. You must run the gauntlet of shouting racers as quickly as possible, observing the right-of-way rules and running no boats down. Wait a minute at idle speed to let the fleet pass if you have time; you may learn something about racing by observing the difference in sail trim or crew concentration on the first boat in comparison to the last boat. As in any congested harbor, every boat has to accommodate the other boats using the same waters by reducing speed, altering course, and sometimes signaling graciously for another boat to pass on her way across their course.

CHAPTER SEVEN

GUESTS ABOARD

A guest's work is never done.

Visiting at a friend's summer house for the weekend, you might expect to sleep late in the morning, enjoy a leisurely breakfast on the porch with the newspaper and the puppy, venture out to go antiquing or to pick apples for a pie, perhaps take a dip in the pool, drinks and a video after dinner. No work, no cleaning, no tidying up. Minimal exertion, maximal leisure.

A guest's function on a boat is usually as crew, and crew is expected to be active and keep busy. There is always more to do on a boat; and about the only chance you get to sit around and be idle is when you take the time to say "let's just sit for a minute" to watch the sunset, or to scrutinize another boat's anchoring detail nearby. Otherwise, all crew can expect to be on the go almost all of the time.

Even before the boat leaves dock, there are chores to do. If you are on a big powerboat, the windows on the bridge may need a freshwater rinse, the case of wine may need to be brought aboard and stowed, and the shore power cord may need to be coiled and stowed, all before the voyage begins. On a little sailboat going out for the weekend, the ice needs to come aboard at the last minute and the food stowed above it, and the duffles need to be jammed into the foot of the bunk. None of this kind of work requires great seafaring experience, so neophytes need not be idle; lots of chores that the skipper can and should delegate to the weekend guest always crop up. Of course if you are visiting Malcolm Forbes on the 130-foot *Highlander,* the uniformed crew serve hors d'oeuvres, and polish the brightwork for your inspection.

A good crew makes the skipper look smart, though the truth may be otherwise. They know where to stow their own gear (with a little hint) and where much of the ship's gear should be. When called upon to handle a piece of equipment, they know the general routine from stowing the docklines to operating the loran. They can make a line fast to a cleat without making one hundred turns to bury the cleat. They can show a less experienced crew member how to use the winch handle and how to put it back after every use.

Crew who have been on the boat before and are returning for more are the best crew to have, whether you are racing in the top levels or cruising across the bay. Perhaps they can recall glorious moments of past voyages, and therefore understand the boat's idiosyncrasies and how to deal with them. They know where the Phillips-head screwdriver is and how the icebox works; they might know the skipper's idiosyncrasies, too. Crew members such as these are a boat's greatest asset. They make a boat safer than the best safety equipment, faster than the latest new sail, and easier to handle than all the short-handed cruising gear put together. If and when you find a crew who enjoy the boat and the voyages you take together, bind them to you with bonds of love, money, or the promise of adventure; whatever works to guarantee their return. As good care as the skipper takes of the engine, the sails, the topsides, or the brightwork, he or she should take even better care of the regular guests.

Inexperienced crew can be almost as helpful as the expert, sometimes more helpful if their enthusiasm results in a willing hand. Skippers can become jaded about some of the simple pleasures of being on a boat, like the sounds of the boat, the change of light across the water, the novelty of the loran, or the power of the canvas. New crew help old crew to see again some of the mystery and excitement of boats; the skipper might for a moment forget the leaky sump tank and the prop wobble. It doesn't matter if the skipper didn't order the new sail or the latest electronic device, the guests are thrilled by how the boat throws a wave aside. It may help the skipper to see that something has gotten unnecessarily complicated, like using all the interfaced electronic devices to find the home mooring on a clear day.

Neophyte crew have to observe carefully how the experienced crew handle the boat, then ask questions about everything they don't understand. Much of basic boating, sail or power, is just common sense. On a well-run boat, there is a good reason for every esoteric device and procedure, though it may not be apparent. When the time seems right, ask why. If the skipper seems too busy to bother with too many questions of "What is that?", ask anyone else on board who seems knowledgeable. If you find yourself in the troubling situation of being the most experienced crew member and still not knowing what to do, ask the skipper directly, and hope for a good answer.

Guests can spend time practicing things which may come in handy later on. Try tying bowlines and rolling hitches in spare time. Figure-eight knots are very nautical and easy to tie and untie. Practice using your judgment of the right-of-way situations as they develop between other boats, and see how the skipper is judging his or her own boat's maneuverability and speed.

"All aboard? Let's go."
"Ready on the bow line? Fend off."
"All fenders on deck? Bring them aft."
"Got the docklines aboard? Coil them up."
"Got them coiled and ready to hang up? Stow them below."

"Got them stowed? Stow the fenders."

"Are they dirty? Clean them off."

"Got them clean? Take the docklines out again and put the fenders in first."

Endless.

Cooking

G uests may be asked to help prepare food in the galley, and no one needs to shirk this duty, even if they categorically refuse to enter a kitchen when ashore. It is quite a different job on a boat. (Dishwashing remains about the same as its shoreside equivalent, or worse, without the dishwasher, without the running hot water, practically without any water.) Cooking aboard is always a creative endeavor, challenging available foods to go together, preparing favorite dishes without the regular ingredients, and preparing greater quantities of everything.

The quantity of the food prepared is always more important than the complexity, and it may be more important than the quality. Hungry crew will only complain about the cooking if there is not enough food; they'll rarely complain otherwise. Happily, a decent cook gets a disproportionate share of praise and affection, usually deserved and always appreciated.

If the menus are kept simple, cooking can easily be done by any willing guest. The cook can often collar other hapless crew to peel potatoes, set the table, or slice the bread, and the work gets spread around as needed. On a longer voyage, assigned cooking chores spread the work load more equitably; however, someone must be given full responsibility for the galley and the orderly distribution of its contents.

Cleaning

C leaning jobs may be pleasanter on board a boat because the space to clean is always smaller than its landside equivalent. However, boats get dirtier than you might imagine even on short voyages. Cleaning chores need to be assigned or else they won't get done; no one ever volunteers to clean the head. Daily chores are mentioned in pages 87–89, in the section on the ship's daily routine. They need not fall to the guest all the time, though it may seem that way to the guest. At the end of a passage, guests should always help with the end-of-trip cleanup, which includes a wipe down of all surfaces below deck, particularly the head and galley, and a thorough sweeping up of the whole boat. Guests should not shirk this duty or slip away with this simple job undone.

The Skipper's Responsibility to Guests

I f the guests have to work hard to earn their keep on board, the skipper has an even greater responsibility to each guest. It falls to the skipper to make sure that every guest has a minimum of knowledge about safe procedures on board and actions and equipment to use in any kind of emergency. Guests may not know to ask for simple instruction on where the flares are stowed, where the fire extinguisher lies, or where their own life preserver is stowed. The skipper has to point out the safety equipment with care and sufficient emphasis that the guests will consider the possibilities of danger and remember where the equipment is stowed should it be needed in a hurry. The skipper is the one who stows the equipment and checks its operation, but it may be the guest who gets it out and uses it.

The skipper must also see that no hazards considered routine to experienced crew take a green sailor by surprise. Gear such as jibing booms, gimballed stoves with hot food, or luffing sails, can be deadly if their power or danger is not anticipated; lesser gear, such as cabinets that suddenly swing open, fishhooks near at hand, hot coffee spilling, and lines subjected to sudden strain can cause serious injury. The skipper must do his or her best to alert (or perhaps just remind) every guest to all these hazards on a boat, and be ready with a real first-aid kit and a medical book when trouble arrives.

In the skipper's mind should come first the safety and welfare of the crew, second the safety and welfare of the vessel (where it differs from that of the crew), and third the efficiency of the voyage or race.

Ship's Routine

W hile most experienced sailors have a good idea of what special rules relating to the personal habits of the crew should be observed on board a vessel, these are different for every boat and for every skipper. The fifty-foot wooden schooner *Mya* was almost lost when a cantaloupe seed jammed her bilge pump open, and for years thereafter her skipper would not permit a cantaloupe on board under any circumstances. Such rules may differ on different types of voyages, too.

Based on bad experiences in the past, a skipper may establish very strict rules on smoking below deck, stowage of personal gear, stowage of cameras or other heavy gear, drinking before a certain hour, talking to whomever has the helm, use of the navigator's station or the charts, handling of expensive or dangerous equipment (loran, the sextant, stove, kerosene lantern), having glassware on deck, or other potentially dangerous practices which may seem harmless to less well-traveled mariners. Such rules may be different for every vessel. The old sailor's wisdom of "different ships, different long splices" still applies.

There may be more idiosyncratic ship's regulations dealing with such things as stowage of seaboots, tidy bunks, opening the icebox for snacks, treatment of wet socks (thrown overboard), potato chips consumed on teak decks, shore shoes carried aboard, etc. These should not be considered on a par with safety regulations, like those suggested above or outlined in many books on the topic; they are rules to make living close together easier. While the skipper has to make all shipboard rules known in advance if they are to be followed scrupulously by all concerned, he has to maintain a fine balance between too many rules and fun. The rules may be posted somewhere below deck, or just mentioned from time to time as needed.

"Happy Hour"

S kippers are always responsible for the safe operation of their vessels, and are therefore responsible for the sobriety of their guests whenever the boat is under way. Heavy drinking and boating have a long and troubled history together, dating to even before the days when dead-drunk sailors were shanghaied from the bar onto a sailing ship, where they awoke the next day far out to sea, on the start of a three-year voyage. Drinking continues to be a problem on the crowded water today; most boating accidents are caused by excessive drinking by the vessels' operators. Drinking is often unwittingly encouraged by the stuffiest of yacht clubs and by the saltiest of sailors, who consider themselves great proponents of safety at sea. Skippers should think long and hard about how much liquor is served to themselves and to the guests on board their yachts.

Note that the new federal policy of Zero Tolerance makes a vessel subject to heavy fines or confiscation by the Coast Guard if illegal drugs in any form are found on board.

The House Gift

Normally, etiquette would suggest that a guest bring a small gift to the host for the weekend, maybe some wine or an offer to bring a dinner or to buy dinner in a restaurant. Guests and skippers should be aware that the Coast Guard has ruled that gifts to the operator of a vessel, even the purchase of a tank of fuel, may constitute a charter fee, and may subject the vessel to the licensing and operating requirements for "carrying passengers for hire." The fine print in insurance coverage may affect liability in such a case, too. While it probably isn't the intent of the Coast Guard to make all guests arrive for the weekend empty-handed, the skipper and guests might keep this definition of "carrying passengers for hire" in mind.

Clothing

If you go out in a boat once or twice a year, the chances of having only bathing suits in your duffle when it is blowing a gale and forty degrees, or of having full foulies and gloves when it is baking hot, are good, especially after the skipper has told you to bring only what you will need, and in a small dufflebag. Having the right clothes at the right time on a boat is as chancy as predicting the weather, because it is the same thing.

A marvelous array of new fabrics makes clothing selection a highly subjective and personal matter. You can spend a great deal of money on self-drying, brightly colored, high-tech clothing, from wicking underwear to Arctic hats, breathing storm pants, and fingerless gloves. It has made the chance of being warm and dry and stylish at the same time a high probability.

Clothing is always a topic of much on-board discussion. (The only topics generating more discussion and thought than clothing on a boat are the weather and the food.) Even—or perhaps especially—in the highest levels of offshore competition, one's clothes can become an obsession: what is wet, what is still dry, what is lost in the bilge, what is loaned to every watch, what wears best, what is really waterproof, what is worth the great sums of money spent on it, and what isn't. You might feel you have to spend the money for top-of-the-line, all-weather clothing, and then find that people who go out every weekend have low-tech clothing from ten years ago, and that they don't seem uncomfortable at all. The big racing boats with crews of twenty people often give out complimentary clothing with the boat's name emblazoned on it; while this may be partially for harmony in photographs, it may be more to relieve the crew's mental energy from the strain of discussing the pros and cons of the various types of clothing they each brought aboard, allowing them to concentrate on more important jobs at hand.

The only solid guideline for clothing is that it should be closely guarded, not so much because it might be borrowed as because clothing easily gets out of control on a boat. All clothes, from hats and sunglasses to wet socks and cast-off sweaters, should be carefully stowed and out of sight when not being worn. It may be tempting to ask someone who is going below to hand up your jacket or sunglasses; it may be tempting to stash your sweater in a corner of the cockpit when the sun comes out and then forget about it, but this is how clothing becomes a problem on a boat. Some skippers of the old school used to make a practice of throwing overboard every article of clothing left unattended, to teach the uninitiated to keep their possessions to themselves. This shouldn't be done any more, since even a pair of socks costs as much as a steak, but crew should guard their clothing as though that were still the practice.

Care of the Seasick

I f there were a cure for motion sickness, NASA would have found it for their astronauts. Millions are spent preparing each space-shuttle crew for the rigors of weightlessness, and NASA has probably tried more cures for nausea than are generally available to the boating public, but none has emerged as more effective than others. The nausea, lethargy, and loss of appetite of motion sickness still visit 30 percent of the humans who orbit in outer space. It is the same affliction that visits the weekend sailor crossing the Chesapeake Bay to St. Michaels on a windy Saturday. Even the newest and most high-tech remedy, the medication-releasing round patch worn behind the ear of a sailor the day before departure and throughout the voyage, works only for some people, and sends others into a fantasy land with a dry mouth and a poor idea of which way is up. Then they get sick anyway. Pills, patches, acupressure bracelets, herbs, mantras, crackers—none works as well as lying quietly under a tree. And none works consistently better that the oldest remedies, which include:

> A chair suspended from the deckbeam, hanging like a
> canary cage
> A gimballed saloon*
> Tight corsets to keep the gut from surging
> Colonic irrigation
> Belladonna plasters over the solar plexus
> Constant flow of Champagne

The orator Cicero preferred certain death to seasickness. He had taken refuge from Poplius (Marc Anthony's sicair), who had placed a price on his head, on a vessel, but he preferred to jump overboard and swim ashore into the hands of his enemies, and was assassinated. Such may seem to be the only relief for the victim of seasickness.

---

* The *Bessamer,* a 350-foot paddle steamer, was built in England in 1875 with an entire first-class saloon suspended on gimbals in the middle of the ship.

The greatest sailor of all time, Ulysses, had his moments with *mal de mer*, Homer tells us. Lord Nelson suffered with "Heavy seas, sick to death," and a popular America's Cup skipper is known to suffer from it. Seasickness does not exclude one from the ranks of the finest sailors the world has ever known. What might exclude you from these ranks is a failure in your ability to carry on in spite of the discomfort of nausea. The sailor who honestly admits to occasional bouts of seasickness, but who knows he or she can do the job nonetheless, is far preferable a crewmember than the sailor who swears to never suffer any nausea; the boaster may never have been tested, and may be the one to lie in the cockpit or a bunk and groan while others take over the watch.

Seasickness makes you lethargic, weak, down at the mouth, and hopeless, in addition to dizzy and prone to vomit. It makes you want to roll through the lifelines and slip into the waves to end the horrible condition that flesh is heir to. You may not care if the fuel needs checking, the sails need trimming, or the navigation needs updating. It can make you furious with yourself for being out there at all; so furious that you don't care if you are wet and cold, hungry and dehydrated, or drifting into harm's way.

Neophyte victims of seasickness need care and attention; though they may not get it if things are really rough. Never ask someone with a pale face if he or she feels sick; you can tell by the frown and quiet nature, if not by the sudden trip to the lee rail (the rail that is down, and downwind). Sometimes just thinking about seasickness can rock the boat just a bit more and cast the victim into a sea of despair. People who are seasick should be encouraged to participate actively in whatever is going on on deck, encouraged to drink something (soda or broth is best), and to eat something bland, even if it comes up later. Give the seasick an active job on deck, such as trimming a sail, steering, or watching for a buoy. The less said about being seasick, the better. If the wolf of *mal de mer* knocks on the door, pretend that you do not hear. If you answer the door, the wolf will come bounding in.

If trouble looks inevitable, direct the seasick crew to the lee rail.

Often they will feel much better after a few moments leaning over the rail and clearing out the stomach, and will soon be ready to get on with their duties. Give them a moistened paper towel and a very small glass of water. This small courtesy has a surprisingly helpful effect in bringing the victim's spirits up quickly.

If someone's really in the grip of the wolf and feels unable or unwilling to help manage the vessel, you must send him or her off watch, to a bunk below and amidships (the most comfortable part of the boat) to lie down with a blanket. Once down, though, it may be harder than ever to return to the deck. Stricken crew may say they feel more comfortable huddled in the corner of the cockpit, under a blanket, staring out at the unbalanced horizon, but they get in the way of active crew there, and should be encouraged to wait out their suffering down below, with their eyes closed. It will be warmer, quieter, and easier to get some curative sleep. Lee cloths or leeboards should be set up for sick crew to keep them from tumbling out of the berth in the roll of the waves, but sick crew either forget or don't know what lee cloths are, or what might be the most comfortable berth for them, so the skipper or another active crew member should help to get the sufferer comfortable and safely tucked away.

Plutarch, in his *Treatise on Natural Causes*, said that sleep, either natural or artificial, is the best antidote for *mal de mer* because it relieves the mind of its burden of fear. While not many experienced sailors or scientists would agree that fear is the only cause of seasickness, Plutarch was right about sleep. If the vessel can be operated without them, let the sick crew go to sleep: Send them below and pack them into a berth for the duration of the bad weather. Oral medication may stay down and be more effective when accompanied by a heavy dose of sleep. Even the sickest neophyte may feel better at the next watch.

If the watch below has enjoyed a pleasant sleep, a critical transition occurs when they are called on deck to relieve the on-watch. The brief minutes between lying warm and rested with eyes closed and reaching the deck all dressed and ready for action can be rough moments for any stomach. Anything that the skipper can do before the voyage to speed those seconds will be appreciated by crew making the difficult dash between bunk and deck: snacks to grab from the galley on the way up, for instance, or special stowage areas for things like boots, flashlights, harnesses, or other items that might make the watch on deck more comfortable and safe. Trying to get any task accomplished below deck is sure to worsen whatever queasy feelings someone already has—the less time spent fiddling with things below deck, the better the chance for active recovery.

The skipper might consider a slight change of course or speed to relieve the problems for the crew. Sometimes a very small course adjustment can change a boat's angle to the seas and moderate her motion, perhaps in the lee of an island, or a bit off the wind. A slightly slower speed can ease the pounding of the hull and allow the boat to glide more comfortably over the seas. Though not always possible, such considerations can make the voyage a great deal more pleasant and safe, and not necessarily any longer in the end.

If seasickness continues, it quickly becomes a medical problem and must be taken very seriously indeed. While people don't die of seasickness, they can die of dehydration associated with it. If the victim of seasickness lies below in a seeming coma, oblivious to the activity on deck for over a day, the skipper should consider the person ill, and in need of care and attention. Consult a medical book. It is part of the skipper's job to keep the crew's welfare uppermost in mind and to do everything possible to hasten the end of the trial by waves and bring on the return of good health.

Often enough, when the boat rounds the breakwater and begins to steady her motion in flat water, the sick will rise from their bunks and feel miraculously better, hungry for missed lunches and full of the energy they have built up sleeping, while the other crew members are exhausted from the extra work they have put in. Most people forget their misery entirely after eating a little something. The boat can be cleaned up and a real meal contemplated. Seasickness is perhaps the only disease from which full recovery is just about guaranteed (eventually), though it seems to have a side effect of mild amnesia. That is why people return to sea even after suffering a cruel bout of seasickness, during which they swear never to go near a boat again; they quickly forget how bad it feels to be seasick.

CHAPTER EIGHT

BOAT MAINTENANCE

T he condition in which a boat is kept by her owner is an important part of boating etiquette. Surprisingly, a boat's appearance need not be a function of the dollars spent on her at the boat yard, although that helps a good deal. Here is a checklist of details that might be considered by the owner who loves his or her boat and wishes to show the boat off to the greatest advantage at all times.

The Hull

A clean and bright hull might be the first indication of a boat's true nature. Faded dark colors on a fiberglass hull make an otherwise fine yacht look tired and unkempt. On a wooden boat, the seamless glossy coat of paint makes the boat look like she is on her way up, whether the garboards are spongy or not. Glass boats might need a new gelcoat after several years; even white hulls lose their shine eventually. Annual waxing and frequent wipe downs with a mild cleaner keep the hull gleaming from week to week. If your engine exhaust outlet leaves a stain along the hull from drips or exhaust fumes, wipe the hull down frequently, especially after a long day under power, to keep it from getting permanently stained.

On inland passages, where boats churn through the rich, brown swamp waters, a telltale brown "moustache," or bow-wave stain, appears along the waterline at the bow. You can spot boats that have made the long trip up or down the Intracoastal Waterway by the "Waterway smile" they wear at the bow. That moustache is OK while you are making the trip, but when you get where you are going give the boat a "haircut and a shave" to indicate that you have "arrived" after a long trip. The brown stain will make a permanent mark on the gelcoat if left on too long. Oddly enough, blue toilet-bowl cleaner seems to take this stain off neatly without harming the gelcoat or paint underneath.

When the aged leaky steel hull of the J-boat *Endeavour* was pulled from her mud berth of forty years, the first thing the owner, John Amos, did after securing the leaks was to slap a coat of paint on the rough topsides: Endeavour Blue, the color named for the original color of the boat in 1934. This was to signify that the boat had come alive again, and indeed she had.

The single best thing you can do for your boat's appearance is to make the hull shiny and bright.

The Waterline and Boottop

The colored band around the boat just above the surface of the water on the hull is called the waterline, and the second decorative band of another color (if there is one) is called the boottop. Even sitting at the dock, the waterline and boottop will pick up a brown scumline, a bathtub ring of harbor dirt. But these bands are usually of a harder type of paint, so they can withstand abrasive scrubbing. Boat owners should take advantage of this feature and scrub the waterline and boottop frequently with a stiff brush or abrasive pad.

Deck and Cabin

T eak decks are not absolutely necessary in order for a vessel to be considered a "yacht," but they help. Care of teak decks remains a topic of debate among the most knowledgeable charter skippers and big-yacht owners. To scrub or not to scrub, whether to keep the teak golden and oiled with biannual chemical cleaning and scrubbing (and eventual deterioration of the deck) or to leave them "bone," a weathered gray, with eventual drying and cracking of the wood. For teak decks to look their very best, they will take as much work as varnished surfaces. A large expanse of such a deck is a wonder to behold, particularly if you have tried to maintain one in its oiled and golden condition.

Just as teak decks are not really required on a boat, neither is the bright gold teak color mentioned above. The deck can be cleaned when necessary, at least once a year, and allowed to weather evenly without getting too gray or too dry. Mud brought aboard by the anchor or from shore on shoes should be hosed away before it dries in the grain, and grease from spilled food or repair projects should be rinsed out with a teak cleaner and flushed with water. Teak oil can be applied to protect the wood from drying out. The teak will retain all its nonskid properties indefinitely, and look shipshape for many years.

For boats with nonteak decks, there is no excuse for anything but a sparkling clean deck. Hose it with water, fresh or salt, and scrub the waterways. Keep the scuppers or deck drains free of leaves and shells from the mud brought aboard by the anchor. Rough deck surfaces, intended to keep the crew from slipping, collect dirt; they need special attention with a brush if they are not to look like a brown repair patch on the white deck.

Cabin sides don't get very dirty in the course of a season so they tend to be ignored. Keep an eye out for "tear stains" in the cabin from the portholes. Keep the portholes themselves wiped clean with fresh water and a soft cloth if they are easily scratched Plexiglass™, particularly if they are large and afford a view from below. White salt residue makes the surfaces dull.

Clutter

O n long voyages, many sailors like to lash extra equipment all over the deck and cabin top: gerry cans of extra fuel and water, coiled lines, sails, awnings, dinghies, sailboards, etc. At the dock, boats acquire folding chairs, buckets for fishing or beachcombing, uncoiled water hoses, hanging black shower bags, and bicycles. The whole boat begins to look like a backyard full of discarded gear. This is questionable seamanship (a big sea can carry off this heavy gear along with the lifelines it is tied to), and there is no question that extra gear lying around the deck detracts from a boat's appearance. Yacht designers stake their careers and their artistic merit on the careful drawing of a yacht's sheerline. It is too bad if the proud owner then clutters it up by storing gear on the deck and festooning the lifelines with major equipment. A boat should be "clean" in the largest sense of the word, the decks "clear for running," and the curve of the sheer and of the cabin uncluttered.

Awnings and Covers

Awnings should be taut and as close to horizontal as possible. A droopy sunshade makes the whole boat look as though it were melted by the sun. A breeze will catch a loose awning and shake it mercilessly until it rips or tears out its grommets. A tight, well-fitted awning will withstand more wind (though perhaps not a gale) because there is no loose, flapping material subject to a sudden gust. Most sailboat awnings set best when hoisted and tensioned fore and aft then secured at the edges and corners evenly. This should avoid the doghouse look of the awning peaked in the center.

Sail covers are necessary to protect the sail from the ultraviolet rays of the sun whenever the sails are left unused in bright sunlight. While sail covers may be made to fit snugly or loosely around the furled sail according to the sailmaker's style, they should be stretched tightly fore and aft with as few vertical or diagonal stretch-marks as possible. This assures that the after end of the furled sail is covered and protected.

Ship's Laundry

Boats generate a tremendous amount of laundry, from wet towels to blue jeans that never dry because of the salt in them. When a sunny day comes along, it is tempting to hang out all the ship's laundry, all the towels and foul-weather gear that need air. Lifelines seem to be made to string up clothing, and a certain amount of public airing of the laundry may have to be done, but it is a terrible thing to do to a boat's appearance on an otherwise lovely day. Besides, clothes have a way of drying slowly all day, then just as they dry, flying away and landing in the water. Hang things below and allow a breeze to blow through to dry them on the good days when the crew will all be up on deck. Send everything out to the laundry right from the marina or yacht club; it comes back the same day, all dry and neatly folded. The boat's appearance has not suffered a bit.

Garbage Disposal

P raise and congratulations are due to the crew that totes lots of garbage bags ashore after a short cruise. It means that the garbage did not go over the side into the bay.

In the old days a vessel could return from months at sea with nary a garbage bag to tote ashore. Now even a very small boat returns from a weekend trip with several large plastic bags of refuse. While marinas may grumble as they order larger dumpsters, mariners should be thankful that the garbage is not circulating around the cruising waters.

Unless you spend a great deal of time at sea, far from land, you should bring everything back to the dock with you. Follow the old rule of wilderness camping: What you carry in, you carry out. This applies first and foremost to plastic of any kind. Styrofoam coffee cups, beverage-can rings, plastic packaging, and plastic soda bottles last far longer than you will, and they don't just visually pollute; they kill wildlife for years when discarded in the open. Don't use these items on board, or if absolutely necessary, plan to load them off the boat into dumpsters ashore.

Glass bottles, aluminum cans, and paper garbage—routinely cast overboard when the vessel is way out at sea—do not present the same environmental debacle that plastic presents. But this type of garbage should never be jettisoned when you are anywhere near land. Bob Ballard was disgusted to see a fresh beverage can lying on the bottom of the North Atlantic, at twelve thousand feet, when he discovered the wreck of the *Titanic*. The can was from his own vessel, in defiance of ship's rules.

Organic material is also routinely thrown overboard: dinner scrapings, mildewed fruit, stale bread. Usually it makes fine chum for sea-gulls and ducks, and later for fish and other marine life, but too often such refuse finds its way to shore, where it fouls a beach or lays up alongside another boat. Think carefully before discarding any organic material, even bread crumbs. How would you feel if that material washed up alongside your boat, or lay on your waterfront property, rotting slowly and drawing flies?

Marine Sanitation

The matter of marine sanitation is an important one for a book on boating etiquette to address. It is a matter of common decency and courtesy to comply with the law, and with the intent of the law. While not well understood, or even discussed in yachting circles, sewage disposal is a matter of growing urgency in the marine world. Technology does not permit an ideal solution to the problem of sewage disposal on boats (or on land for that matter) and as a result, even the most environmentally conscientious skipper may have thought up a list of excuses for not installing or not using installed equipment for sewage disposal on board. Instead of thinking up excuses, a concerned skipper might try to think up ways to improve compliance with the law and to speed up technological development of on-board treatment systems so that safe, economical, odor-free, and practical sewage systems become the standard in the marine community. Keep in mind that some communities, such as the towns of New Shoreham (controlling Great Salt Pond on Block Island), Cuttyhunk, Avalon on Catalina Island, and many on the Great Lakes are preparing to restrict their waters to boats with holding tanks only. For a group of people who appreciate the beauties and cleanliness of the marine environment, mariners are very slow to clean up their own house, and thus lead the way in the nation's concern for clean water.

CHAPTER NINE

SHIP'S DAILY ROUTINE

F irst thing in the morning: start water for coffee. Turn off the riding light if at anchor. In fair weather, wipe brightwork (all varnished wood and polished brass) with a chamois cloth and the available dew. Check anchor rode or mooring pennant and freshen the nip (i.e., adjust the pennant or rode a few inches so that any small cut or pressure on the line at the chock is relieved). Inspect tenders alongside or astern for rainwater or leaks. Bail if necessary. Wipe down the hull with a damp, soapy sponge, or swab the decks with a mop and sea water. Open the hatches and portholes for ventilation. Calculate weather and tides and begin charting a course for the day.

At 8 A.M. raise colors at the cannon's report, first the ensign on the stern, followed by the personal signal and/or the club burgee at the masthead(s), or at the bow on a powerboat. On holidays, the code flags are raised to encircle the boat and dress ship. On Sundays, the Union Jack is raised (stars pointing up) over the foredeck. The Union Jack and the code flags are all brought down before getting under way. Breakfast may be well along, depending on the day's plan. Breakfast dishes should be put away before any open water is encountered.

Throughout the day under way, the skipper is constantly mindful of the presence of other boats and their relative position in his or her boat's course. Whenever a risk of collision is present, the appropriate Rules of the Road come into play, and the skipper decides which boat is the give-way vessel, and which the stand-on vessel. If a change of the course is required by the Rules, the change made is both significant and early, so that all boats in the vicinity understand the action. Whistle signals are used whenever appropriate: One blast signals a turn to starboard, and two blasts signal a turn to port when under power. If traveling in inland waters, these signals are answered by the same signal when understood and agreed to by the approaching boat.

Speed and wake are kept way down whenever other boats may be affected. Powerboats drop down from cruising speed when passing other boats or when entering congested waters. Racing fleets are avoided as a whole; tugs and commercial ships are avoided long before a right-of-way situation develops. Active fishing vessels are avoided, with special consideration given to their nets and lines.

When within range, a VHF radio call can be made to the day's destination, perhaps a marina or harbormaster. Before keying the mike, the skipper listens on the predetermined channel for any radio traffic. The marina or harbormaster may be talking to another boat, but the skipper waits until they are finished before trying to raise them, to let them know his or her ETA and the boat's needs.

Approaching the marina, the skipper discusses the docking maneuver with the crew, detailing the location of the fenders, the most critical lines ashore, and safety precautions, such as not using your feet to fend off the pier. On the approach, if the skipper has nothing further to tell the crew members, who are standing by with lines coiled and ready to throw, he or she can concentrate on calculations of the current, the wind, and the throttle.

With the boat secured at the dock, the departing crewmembers help in a whirlwind cleanup of the vessel below decks, wiping down the head and galley and sweeping the sole. Sails are folded and put away. Sail covers and awnings are set up taut. The boat is hosed down and cleaned as needed. Garbage is taken ashore in sealed bags and deposited in a dumpster. The skipper completes arrangements with the dockmaster or marina office.

At sundown, the flags are brought down from the masthead and off the stern. Sundown is marked by a local cannon report or is determined by consulting a table of sunsets in an almanac or local newspaper. Docklines are checked again to determine the effect of the tidal rise and fall. Hatches are closed against the cool night air and the weather report is reviewed again, for the chance of a storm or rain.

CHAPTER TEN

THE YACHT-CLUB CRUISE

P lanning for the yacht club's summer cruise begins almost a year before the first rendezvous on the water, when the officers of the club hash out an itinerary for the week of cruising. The club officers must plan to visit harbors other than those visited the previous year, commodious enough for their entire fleet (which could be two hundred boats), and hospitable enough to service the needs of perhaps two thousand people on the move. Shore transportation, car parking, groceries, hardware, access to medical facilities, and shoreside accommodations, as well as fuel docks and repair services, must be available. Local yacht clubs, marinas, and harbormasters will have much to say about the fleet's intended visit in their harbor. Scheduling must not conflict with local events, other clubs' cruises, or holidays.

Harbors are selected with sufficient depths for the club's largest boats, requiring maybe ten feet at low water, and with swinging room in the anchorage for 150-footers. They must be sufficiently close that even the small boats can move quickly and safely on to the next harbor in fog or severe weather. And the cruise must be sufficiently scenic or interesting to attract the membership to join it in the first place. Although called a cruise, most such annual outings include a heavy schedule of racing every day, usually point-to-point races to help the fleet get quickly from one harbor to the next. Most of the fleet joins the races daily.

The event may begin with the Captain's Meeting on Friday at 1800 hours; captains only are expected to attend. The commodore gives some welcoming remarks and any news, and introduces local dignitaries or host-club commodores, who also make some remarks. Cautionary notices, scratch sheets, and a hefty booklet are distributed to each captain. The fleet roster gives each boat's name and hailing port, the owner's name, the names of the entire crew (this could be twenty-eight names), and the boat's rating according to a United States Racing Union Racing Certificate supplied by the owner. A big cocktail party begins right after, with old friends from previous years meeting again, greetings to the arriving crew, and the loading of cartons of supplies.

This is a busy time for launches that shuttle people to and from the yachts assembled in the harbor. The launches may be local boats chartered for the event or the club's own launches, brought along for the duration of the cruise. The launch drivers are busy responding to requests for service on the VHF radio and watching for code flag Tango flying from a starboard spreader, indicating a request for transport. New yachts in the fleet are ogled and inspected, old regulars are remembered for their winning ways, their great beauty, or their recent mishaps. This is the time to have your boat all spruced up; for some yachts, this is their finest hour: gleaming bright and clean, in racing trim (as far as possible with all the stores for a full crew for a week aboard), sail covers bent on tight, and flags snapping. No orange jerry cans of extra water tied to the lifelines, no stains dripping from the rusting chainplates, no moustache under the bow from the swamp water of the Intracoastal Waterway, and no laundry drying on the boom. All boats have clean waterlines, their teak decks are golden, and their varnishwork glistens an even color gold. At another time she might have baggywrinkles and banana stalks in the rigging and sailboards on the foredeck. Now she appears as though posing for her formal portrait on the cover of a magazine, clean and neat, gear stowed away, flags flying. And always she should be able to add grace and splendor to whatever harbor she visits. Which is one of the things a good boat should do best, on the yacht-club cruise or not.

The boat manufacturers, dealers, and designers appear in their newest creations, eager to show off their boat's cruisability, racing ability, or good looks. While they don't put up the bright logo banners in the rigging as they do at the boat shows, they make their presence known to those around who might be interested in seeing the new boat. Raft-ups, cockpit gams, and visiting in general begin in earnest.

Colors are observed whether or not the captain is aboard the yacht. At sunset and the report of the cannon on the flagship (the commodore's vessel) or from the clubhouse, the owner's signal and the club burgee are brought down from their masthead locations on every boat, and the national flag is brought in from the stern. Courtesy flags on foreign vessels are left flying under the starboard spreader. (No U.S. registered boat should fly the U.S. flag under the starboard spreader at any time.) The fastidious traditional boat might raise her Night Hawk, to give the crew a wind indicator aloft throughout the night. All vessels at anchor raise and light the riding, or anchor, light.

Parties ashore and aboard may continue for much of the night but in the morning all boats observe colors promptly at 8 A.M., at the flagship's report (no cannons on Sunday). At 8:30, the yachts of each flag officer of the club raise in concert the signal flags indicating the day's destination. The flagship may also announce on a predetermined VHF channel: "The fleet should be advised that the flagship is flying code flags Echo Kilo Uncle Golf." The skipper of each boat in the fleet has to thumb through the club yearbook to see that EKUG means, "The squadron will get under way for Stonington, Connecticut." When each yacht has deciphered the message, she raises her answering pennant (part of every code-flag set) to the starboard spreader to indicate that she has understood the commodore's signals.

Then the parade begins. No vessel precedes the flagship out of the harbor. Your anchor is up and secured, dinghies are aboard, and the engine is on, but you wait courteously for first the flagship, then the other flag-officers' vessels to pass in order of rank before you fall in behind the lead boats. The fleet follows in a disorderly file. On foggy mornings, which you often find at such an hour, it can be very helpful to follow other boats along, especially since they are going to the same place. If it is too foggy or stormy to start a race, the flagship may fly code flag Lima, meaning simply, "Follow me." Usually, the fleet proceeds to the starting line for the race of the day; the answering pennant is doused.

At the starting line, the race committee begins its work of evaluating the weather conditions, anchoring for the starting sequence, and establishing the first leg of the course. All flags on boats planning to race come down, except the class flags attached to the backstay. Spectator boats leave all their flags flying, indicating that they do not plan to race. They stay clear of the boats' maneuvering and racing, and proceed at will to the destination of the day.

Racing takes up the best part of the day. Courtesies are observed during the race that you might expect from people who will be spending the next five consecutive days in friendly proximity, and who have been racing against each other for perhaps several years. Large boats might pass other boats in smaller classes to leeward, leaving the smaller boat with clear air. Yachts guilty of fouling another yacht should drop out of the race immediately by leaving the course and raising their flags, before a protest proceeding need be initiated. All yachts should complete the race if they can, even the ones in dead last place. At the end of the race, the apparent winners are congratulated, the losers are challenged to do better tomorrow. These courtesies do not mean that the racing is not as serious as the best sailors in the fleet can make it.

In the evening, before colors (sunset), the race committee delivers the computer-generated race results to each yacht in person. Invitations for parties to be held later in the cruise are also delivered by hand. Rafting, visiting, and partying continue. Yachts may depart the cruise at any time, signaling their departure by hoisting the code flag Whiskey, to indicate, "I intend to leave the fleet," and notifying the fleet captain by VHF radio; in theory, the club officers are looking out for the welfare of every boat in the fleet.

The yachts have to look shipshape despite a week or more of hard use. Exhaust fumes are scrubbed from the topsides if they make a stain, and the hull is kept generally clean, if not polished. Brightwork should be rinsed with fresh water if salt spray dries on it, and windows (on large boats) and brightwork chamoised every morning. Sails are neatly furled every evening, and the jibs are bagged and put away. Awnings are taut and clean.

Halfway into the week's cruise is the scheduled lay day, when the fleet remains at anchor and "dresses ship" from 8 A.M. to sunset. Special races, shore activities, extra provisioning, and visiting between yachts fill the day. The balance of the week continues with racing every day. Awards are not formally given until the club's annual awards ceremony, usually in the fall.

Ship and Yacht Names

A vessel's name conveys a lot about how the owner thinks of his or her boat. How do you think a boat with a name like *Marauder* will negotiate a crowded channel? Most jokes get old with constant retelling; how does a name like *MAL de MERried* sound after a few years of ownership? How effective will your radio transmissions be to the boat called *Let's Do It!?* ("*Let's Do It!*, *Let's Do It!*, *Let's Do It!*, this is *Why Knot?*, come in on channel 68." "*Why Knot?*, *Let's Do It!*, negative on Channel 68, try 72.")

Choose boat names with care; people often know owners by their boats, and boats by the choice of their names.

The following list of names from the last four centuries is provided to inspire new yacht owners, who may be seeking a name that will wear well over time, and which may even enhance the value of the boat.

Early Names of Ships and Yachts
WITH APPROXIMATE LAUNCH DATES, WHERE KNOWN

Jupiter, Dutch ship, 1639
Constant Reformation, English ship, 1648
Royal Charles, English ship, 1660
Henry
Mary
Expedition

Charles, English yacht, 1663
Merlin, English yacht, 1673
Cleveland, English yacht, 1673
Adventure, English ship, 1673
Princess
Revenge
Kitchen, English yacht, 1675

Names of the First American Squadron of Ships
LAUNCHED IN 1775

Alfred, warship
Andrew Doria, brigantine
Cabot, warship

Columbus, warship
Providence, warship

American Ships in 1776

Baltimore Hero, privateer
Betsy, brigantine
Lady de Graaff, privateer
L'Indien, warship

Randolf, frigate
Ranger, warship
Smack, brigantine

Clippersships of the 1850s

Arrow
Blessing of the Bay
Carrier Dove
Celestial
Champion of the Seas
Chariot of Fame
Dashing Wave
Expounder
Flyaway
Flying Arrow
Flying Fish
Forward Ho

Golden Light
Grey Feather
Herald of the Morning
Highflyer
Kathay
La Superior
Lightfoot
Northfleet
Ocean Telegraph
Pampero
Pride of the Sea
Race Horse

Seaman's Bride
Stag Hound
Stornaway
Sultana
Sunny South
Susquehanna
Three Bells
Westward Ho
Witch of the Wave
Wylo
Ziba

Names Considered Suitable for Yachts in 1877

Abeona, Goddess who protected voyagers.

Achilles, Bravest and most handsome of the Greeks.

Avosit, A long-legged bird.

Bella Donna, Beautiful woman.

Bellona, Goddess of war and a charioteer.

Circe, Daughter of the sun.

Corrina, Poetess of Thebes.

Czarina, Empress of Russia.

Daedalus, Inventor of masts and sails for ships, in addition to the well-known wings.

Dione, Ocean nymph.

Duen, Master.

Fortuna, Goddess of happiness and misery.

Gemma, Jewel.

Griffon, Creature with the head and paws of a lion, and the body and wings of an eagle.

Hotspur, Fiery.

Ivanhoe, Title character in Sir Walter Scott's novel of twelfth-century England.

Jaseur, Talker, chatterer.

Juno, Queen of heaven.

Minotaur, Mythological figure, half man, half bull.

Nada, Nothing, a term of endearment.

Nikoma, Victory

Nimrod, The first great hunter.

Nooya, Silver gull of Canada.

Norna, German sea nymph.

Oberon, King of the fairies in medieval folklore and Shakespeare's *A Midsummer Night's Dream*; one of the five satellites of Venus.

Onda, Wave.

Ondina, Little wave.

Paragon, Something excellent.

Phosphorus, Morning star.

Piccola, Little one.

Pomona, Godess of fruit trees.

Queen Mab, Fairy queen who rules dreams of men; poem by Shelley.

Saphaedra, Goddess of tides and currents.

Satanella, Small female devil.

Speranza, Hope.

Sylph Graceful nymph.

Syren, Singing sea nymph.

Titania, Queen of fairies; wife of Oberon in *A Midsummer Night's Dream*; one of five satellites of Uranus.

Una, Heroine of legend.

Undine, Water sprite.

Vacuna, The goddess of leisure and repose.

Vanda, Polish princess.

Varuna, Mythical deity.

Vera, True.

Verve, Dash, spirit.

Virago, Female warrior; bold, furious woman.

Volage, Fickle, inconstant.

Vol-au-Vent, Fly to windward.

Vril, The new force.

Waveny, A river.

Welle, Wave.

Zamba, Wild doglike animal with horse's head.

Zenobia, Courageous and beautiful queen of Palmyra who led 700,000 men into battle.

Zephyrina, Female version of the west wind.

Zigan, Gypsy.

Names of Early Ocean-Racing Yachts

The following list of ocean racers—through 1946—gives the names of yachts that were well known at the time. Many are still known by knowledgeable sailors of today for various reasons. Many are still sailing under their original names.

Actaea, 61-foot Stephens cutter
Ailsa, 127-foot Fife yawl
Alcyone, 40-foot Casey yawl
Amaryllis, 63-foot yawl
Amberjack, 41-foot Alden schooner
Amorita, 99-foot Smith schooner
Apache, 198-foot Reid bark
Asta, 88-foot Watson yawl
Astarte, 76-foot Herreshoff ketch
Atlantic, 185-foot Gardner schooner
Avanti, 55-foot Stephens yawl
Ayesha, 46-foot Rhodes yawl, still sailing
Baccarat, 46-foot Pouliot cutter
Bagherra, 65-foot Crowninshield schooner
Barlovento, 64-foot Cox and Stevens schooner
Baruna, 72-foot Stephens yawl, still sailing
Belisarius, 54-foot Herreshoff yawl, still sailing
Benbow, 71-foot Clark sloop
Blitzen, 55-foot Stephens cutter, still sailing

Bloodhound, 63-foot Nicholson yawl
Blue Goose, 70-foot Hand schooner
Blue Water, 55-foot Alden schooner
Brilliant, 61-foot Stephens schooner, still sailing
Cambria, 108-foot Ratsey schooner
Caroline, 64-foot Lawley schooner
Chubasco, 67-foot Stephens yawl, still sailing
Coronet, 133-foot Poillon schooner, extant
Curlew, 65-foot Alden schooner
Cygnet, 58-foot Cox and Stevens schooner
Dauntless, 120-foot schooner
Dervish, 85-foot Crane schooner
Diablo, 60-foot Herreshoff schooner
Dorade, 52-foot Stephens yawl, still sailing
Dragoon, 66-foot Ford and Payne ketch
Edlu, 68-foot Stephens yawl, still sailing

Elena, 136-foot Herreshoff schooner

Elizabeth McCaw, 63-foot Stephens yawl

Enchantress, 136-foot Smith schooner

Endymion, 135-foot Crane schooner

Escapade, 72-foot Rhodes yawl, still sailing

Fandango, 84-foot Burgess schooner

Fearless, 54-foot Alden schooner

Foxhound, 63-foot Nicholson cutter

Gesture, 57-foot Stephens sloop, still sailing

Golden Eye, 41-foot Rhodes yawl, still sailing

Good News, 64-foot Stephens yawl, extant

Grenadier, 59-foot Alden schooner

Guinevere, 195-foot Swasey schooner

Gypsy, 50-foot Paine sloop, still sailing

Hallowe'en, 70-foot Fife cutter, still sailing

Hamburg, Watson schooner

Hamrah, 54-foot ketch

Hawaii, 70-foot Crowninshield schooner

Henrietta, 107-foot schooner

Highland Light, 62-foot Paine cutter, still sailing

High Tide, 70-foot Alden schooner

Hokuloa, 36-foot Alden sloop, still sailing

Hother, 46-foot Rhodes cutter, still sailing

Ilex, 50-foot Nicholson yawl

Islander, 34-foot yawl

Isolt, 62-foot Burgess cutter

Jolie Brise, 56-foot Paumelle cutter

Kirawan, 53-foot Rhodes cutter

Ladona, 81-foot Hand schooner

Landfall, 71-foot Herreshoff ketch, still sailing

Land's End, 38-foot Crocker ketch, still sailing

Latifa, 69-foot Fife yawl, still sailing

Lexia, 64-foot Shepherd cutter

Lurline, 86-foot Turner schooner

Magic Carpet, 38-foot Atkin ketch

Maid of Maltham, 48-foot Giles cutter

Malabar, various Alden schooners to 58 feet, many still sailing

Malay, 45-foot Roue schooner

Mandoo, 71-foot Alden schooner

Mariner, 107-foot Burgess schooner

Maruffa, 67-foot Rhodes yawl

Mary Ann, 41-foot Alden schooner

Memory, 59-foot Herreshoff cutter

Meridian, 72-foot Alden schooner

Merry Widow, 52-foot Alden schooner

Miladi, 32-foot Herreshoff cutter

Mist, 38-foot Lawley schooner

Mistress, 60-foot Hoyt schooner

Mohawk, 60-foot Alden schooner

Mustang, 45-foot Stephens sloop, still sailing

Nam Sang, 66-foot Paine ketch

Narwhal, 40-foot Rhodes cutter

Navigator, 78-foot Burgess schooner

Neith, 52-foot Herreshoff cutter, still sailing

Nimrod, 44-foot Casey yawl

Nina, 59-foot Burgess schooner, still sailing

Nordlys, 71-foot Roue schooner

Nordwind, 78-foot Gruber yawl

Northern Light, 45-foot Roue schooner

Patience, 68-foot Nicholson cutter

Peter von Danzig, 59-foot Gruber yawl

Pinta, 57-foot Alden schooner

Restless, 40-foot Lawley schooner

Revenoc, 45-foot Stephens sloop

Rofa, 50-foot Herreshoff schooner

Roland von Bremen, 58-foot Gruber yawl

Rose of Sharon, 52-foot Burgess schooner, stillsailing

Rugosa, 59-foot Herreshoff yawl

Santana, 55-foot Stephens schooner

Scaramouche, 41-foot Schock schooner

Seafarer, 91-foot Crowninshield schooner

Sea Witch, 54-foot Alden yawl

Señora, 70-foot Mower schooner

Skal, 48-foot Rhodes cutter

Spookie, 45-foot Stephens cutter

Starlight, 44-foot Stephens cutter

Stella Maris, 54-foot Steele ketch

Stiarna, 63-foot Nicholson cutter

Stormy Weather, 53-foot Stephens yawl, still sailing

Suluan, 44-foot Luders yawl

Sunbeam, 157-foot Byrne schooner

Surprise, 44-foot McManus schooner

Svaap, 32-foot Alden ketch

Talayha, 102-foot Herreshoff cutter

Tamerlane, 38-foot Huntington yawl

Teal, 53-foot Alden schooner

Teragram, 58-foot Alden schooner

Thistle, 150-foot Wintringham schooner

Tigress, 56-foot Hand schooner

Trade Wind, 57-foot Alden schooner, still sailing

Tradition, 60-foot Alden schooner, still sailing

Two Brothers, 43-foot Alden schooner

Utowana, 190-foot Webb schooner

Vagrant, 76-foot Herreshoff schooner

Valkyrie, 73-foot Alden ketch

Vamarie, 70-foot Morgan ketch

Vega, 47-foot Eldridge-McInnis schooner

Venona, 65-foot Smith schooner

Vesta, 105-foot Alden schooner

Volante, 52-foot Alden schooner

Voyager, 44-foot Stephens yawl

Water Gypsy, 59-foot Alden schooner

Whistler, 61-foot Hand schooner

Windigo, 71-foot Stephens yawl

Zaida, 57-foot Alden yawl, still
    sailing
Zeearend, 55-foot Stephens yawl

Zodiac, 126-foot Hand schooner
Zoriada, 56-foot Kemp cutter
Zuhrah, 84-foot Lawley schooner

How many of today's yachts' names will be known after more than forty years? Those marked as still sailing or extant may not be the only ones. Research is ongoing.

COMMON MISTAKES IN USAGE

Wrong: "Pass to *port* of the lighthouse."

Right: "Pass to *the south* of the lighthouse" or "Leave the lighthouse to *starboard*."

Neither a lighthouse, a pier, a buoy, nor a sandbar has a port or starboard side, but they do have a south, north, east, or west side, a windward or leeward side, a seaward side, and a deep-water side. Only a boat has a port and a starboard side.

Wrong: "Put the *bumpers* over the side."

Right: "Put the *fenders* over the side."

Bumpers are on the front of a car; fenders protect the side of a boat.

Wrong: "The boat is at the end of the *dock*."

Right: "The boat is at the end of the *pier, wharf,* or *float*."

The dock is where the boat lies; either in the water or in a dry dock. The pier, wharf, or float is where you walk to get on the boat while the boat is in the dock.

Wrong: "We are doing eight *knots per hour.*"

Right: "We are doing eight *knots,* or eight *nautical miles per hour.*
The term "knot" is a measure of speed, not of distance. It means "nautical miles per hour."

Wrong: "The *tide* runs at two knots" or "The *tide* was against us."

Right: "The *current* runs at two knots" or "The *current* was against us."
Tides are the rise and fall of the water caused by the gravitational pull of the moon and sun. The tide goes up and down, and generates the current, which flows horizontally.

Wrong: Flying the U.S. flag under the spreader.
The U.S. flag is always flown from the place of highest honor on U.S. registered ships and boats. It is flown between 8 A.M. and sunset.

New York Yacht Club Signal Code

The signals in the Yacht Code consist chiefly of signals for inter-communication between vessels of the squadron.

Racing and Special Signals	D to Z
Other Racing Signals	AI to AY
General Signals	BA to GT
Designating Signals	HA to HN
Days of the Week	IQ to IZ
Hours of the Day	JA to KY
Names of Places	NA to WI

A yacht signaling another yacht in a Club Code should fly as the first flag in the hoist the Club Burgee of the Club whose Code is being used.

When operating as a squadron, however, the Club Burgee may be dispensed with if so specified by the General Orders or the Sailing Instruction.

A yacht signaling another yacht in the International Code may opt to fly the Code (Answering) Pennant either as the first flag in the hoist or a separate hoist.

No designator is used when signaling merchantmen, naval vessels, etc. in the International code.

When several flag hoists are displayed simultaneously they are to be read in the following order: (a) Masthead, (b) Triatic stay, (c) Starboard yardarm or spreader, (d) Port yardarm or spreader.

When more groups than one are shown on the same halyard, they must be separated by the tackline and be read in the numerical order of their superiority.

When more hoists than one are shown at the same yardarm or spreader, but on different halyards, the outboard hoist is to be read first. When more hoists than one are shown at the triatic stay, the foremost hoist is to be read first.

A signal is said to be superior to another when hoisted before, either as regards time or hoist. It is said to be inferior when it is after, either in point of time or hoist.

All vessels to which signals are addressed shall hoist the Code (Answering) Pennant partially (at the dip) as soon as each signal is observed, and full up (two-blocked) when such signal is understood.

The signal of execution for all signals is the hauling down of the signals.

When additional signals are needed, they will be authorized by general orders and should be entered in club books.

See H. O. 102 for proper procedure in making signals and for complete Emergency and International Codes

Racing and Special Signals

D	Do you assent to postponing the race until later in the day?
E	Do you assent to calling the race off for the day?
T	Send Club Launch.
W	Permission to leave squadron is requested.
X	Permission to proceed at will is requested.
Y	Leave all marks to starboard.
Z	Leave all marks to port.

Other Racing Signals

A I   Finish—This yacht will take time at finish.
A J   Finish—Will you take time at finish?
A K   Finish—Yachts will take their own time at finish.
A N   Race Committee—Is Committee on Board Committee boat?
A O   Race Committee—Report is ready.
A P   Race Committee—Report on board this vessel at —.
A Q   Race Committee—Do you agree to race tomorrow?
A V   Start—Race will be sailed on —.
A W   Start—Race will be sailed today at —.
A X   Start—Race will be sailed tomorrow at —.
A Y   Start—When will race be started?

General Signals

B A   Anchor—Are you going to anchor at —?
B C   Anchor—at —.
B D   Anchor—at will.
B E   Anchor clear of the channel.
B F   Anchor for night at —.
B G   Anchor—intend to anchor during fog.
B H   Anchor near me.
B I   Anchorage should be shifted; you will be aground.
B L   Assistance—Do not require further assistance.
B M   Assistance—Do you require assistance?
B N   Assistance—Do you requre a tow?
B S   Assistance—send anchor.
B T   Assistance—send hawser.
B U   Assistance—send tow boat. (See also "Emergency Signals" for International Code signals requesting assistance.)
C A   Boat(s) adrift—please pick up.

C B Boat(s) from all yachts report to Flagship for instructions.
C D Boat(s) from this yacht return immediately.
C E Boat(s) cannot be sent.
C F Send boat alongside.
C G Send boat ashore.
C H Send boat to Flagship.
C I Boat will be sent for you.
C J Will you send a boat for me?
C P Captains and guests are invited on board Flagship at —.
C Q Captains and guests are invited on board this yacht at —.
C R Captains' meeting will be held on Flagship at —.
C S Captains report on board Flagship on coming to anchor.
C T Captains' meeting will be held on board —.
C U Code—Have no International Code book.
C V Code—Will (or will you) use the International Code Signal?
C W Code—Captains' meeting will be held at —.
C X Colors—Morning colors.
C Y Colors—Evening colors.
C Z Congratulations, well done.
D A Engagement—Previous engagement prevents.
D C Mail for you ashore at —.
D D Mail—Is there mail for me?
D E Mail—Please bring or send mail.
D G Power yachts will take sailing yachts in tow.
D H Power yachts will tow sailing yachts after finish.
D J Signal annulled.
D K Signal cannot be complied with.
D L Signal—Do you understand my signal?
D M Signal for me should be repeated.
D N Signal should be shifted to more conspicuous hoist. (See **ZL** under "Emergency Signals" for "Signal not understood.")
E A Squadron—Anchor at —.
E B Squadron—Divine service will be held on Flagship on Sunday at —.
E C Squadron—disbanded.
E D Squadron—disbands at —.

E F   Squadron—disbands on —.

E G   Squadron—dress ship at —.

E H   Squadron—dress ship at colors on —.

E I   Squadron—get underway.

E J   Squadron—get underway at —.

E K   Squadron—get underway for —.

E L   Squadron—get underway tomorrow at —.

E M   Squadron—illuminate on night of —.

E O   Squadron—not to get underway at present.

E P   Squadron—not to get underway today.

E Q   Squadron—Proceed at will.

E R   Squadron—Proceed at will to —.

E S   Squadron—Will join the squadron at —.

E T   Squadron—Will you join the squadron at —.

F A   Supplies—Alcohol is needed.

F B   Supplies—Food is needed.

F C   Supplies—Fuel oil is needed.

F D   Supplies—Garbage boat is needed.

F E   Supplies—Gasoline is needed.

F G   Supplies—Ice is needed.

F H   Supplies—Water is needed.

F I   Taxi—order one taxi cab for me.

F J   Taxi—order two taxicabs for me.

F K   Thank you.

F L   Weather—calm.

F M   Weather—clear.

F N   Weather—foggy.

F O   Weather—heavy wind.

F P   Weather—moderate sea.

F Q   Weather—rough sea.

F R   Weather prediction—Good weather.

F S   Weather prediction—Small yachts should make harbor.

F T   Weather prediction—Stormy weather (from —).

F U   Weather prediction—Watch ground tackle.

F V   What is the weather outside?

F W   What is the weather prediction?

F X   When did you leave — (or pass —)?
F Y   Where are you bound?
F Z   Where are you from?
G A   When do you go ashore?
G B   Will be on board at —.
G C   Will not go ashore.
G D   Will send a reply.
G E   Will you and guests come aboard at —?
G F   Will you and guests breakfast with me at—?
G H   Will you and guests dine with me at —?
G I   Will you and guests lunch with me at —?
G J   Will you come aboard at —?
G K   Will youbrealfast with me at —?
G L   Will you dine with me at—?
G M Will you lunch with me at —?
G O   Will you meet me ashore at —?
G P   Will you meet me at club at —?
G T   Wish you a pleasant voyage.

Designating Signals

H A	Commodore	**H G**	Fleet Surgeon
H B	Vice Commodore	**H J**	Race Committee
H C	Rear Commodore	**H K**	Club Station
H F	Fleet Captain	**H N**	Fleet Chaplain

Days of the Week

I Q	Sunday	**I V**	Friday
I R	Monday	**I W**	Saturday
I S	Tuesday	**I X**	Today
I T	Wednesday	**I Y**	Tomorrow
I U	Thursday	**I Z**	Yesterday

Hours of the Day

J A	MIDNIGHT	J N	6:00 "	K A	NOON	K N	6:00 "
J B	12:30 A.M.	J O	6:30 "	K B	12:30 P.M.	K O	6:30 "
J C	1:00 "	J P	7:00 "	K C	1:00 "	K P	7:00 "
J D	1:30 "	J Q	7:30 "	K D	1:30 "	K Q	7:30 "
J E	2:00 "	J R	8:00 "	K E	2:00 "	K R	8:00 "
J F	2:30 "	J S	8:30 "	K F	2:30 "	K S	8:30 "
J G	3:00 "	J T	9:00 "	K G	3:00 "	K T	9:00 "
J H	3:30 "	J U	9:30 "	K H	3:30 "	K U	9:30 "
J I	4:00 "	J V	10:00 "	K I	4:00 "	K V	10:00 "
J K	4:30 "	J W	10:30 "	K J	4:30 "	K W	10:30 "
J L	5:00 "	J X	11:00 "	K L	5:00 "	K X	11:00 "
J M	5:30 "	J Y	11:30 "	K M	5:30 "	K Y	11:30 "

Names of Places

[The New York Yacht Club is the only club to have devised a set of signals for place names.]

N A Absecon, N.J.
N B Ambrose Channel Light Tower
N C Annapolis, Md.
N D Atlantic Highlands, N.J.
N E Bakers Island Light, Me.
N F Baltimore, Md.
N G Bangor, Me.
N H Bar Harbor, Me.
N I Bar Island, North side of Bar Harbor, Me.
N J Barnegat Light, N.J.

N K Bath, Me.
N L Bass Harbor, Me.
N M Bay Ridge, N.Y. Bay
N O Beaver Tail, R.I.
N P Belfast, Me.
N Q Beverly, Mass.
N R Black Rock Harbor, Conn.
N S Block Island, R.I., East Harbor
N T Block Island, West Harbor, Great Salt Pond
N U Blue Hill, Me.
N V Brenton Reef Light

N W	Bristol, R.I.		P C	Cuttyhunk, Mass.
N X	Boon Island, Me.		P D	Deer Island Thorofare, Me.
N Y	Boothbay, Me.		P E	Delaware Breakwater, Del.
N Z	Boston, Mass.		P F	Duck Island Breakwater,
O A	Burnt Coat Harbor, Me.			Conn.
O B	Buck Harbor, Me.		P G	Dutch IslandHarbor, R.I.
O C	Buzzards Bay Entrance Light		P H	Dyer Bay, Me.
	Tower, Mass.		P I	East Chop, Vineyard Haven,
O D	Camden, Me.			Mass.
O E	Cape Ann, Mass.		P J	Eastern Point Breakwater,
O F	Cape Charles, Va.			Mass.
O G	Cape Cod Canal (East En-		P K	Eastport, Me.
	trance), Mass.		P L	Eaton's Neck, N.Y.
O H	Cape Cod Canal (West En-		P M	Edgartown, Mass.
	trance), Mass.		P N	Eggemoggin Reach, Me.
O I	Cape Elizabeth, Me.		P O	Egg Rock, Frenchman Bay,
O J	Cape Henlopen, Del.			Me.
O K	Cape Henry, Va.		P Q	Falkner Island, Conn.
O L	Cape May, N.J.		P R	Fire Island Light.
O M	Cape Poge, Mass.		P S	Fishers Island Sound.
O N	Cape Porpoise Harbor, Me.		P T	Flanders Bay, Me.
O P	Cape Sable, N.S.		P U	Franklin Island Light House,
O Q	Captains Island Light, Conn.			Me.
O R	Casco Bay, Me.		P V	Fort Pond Bay, N.Y.
O S	Casco Passage, Me.		P W	Fortress Monroe, Va.
O T	Castine, Me.		P X	Fox Island Thorofare, Me.
O U	Chatham Lights, Mass.		P Y	Gardiners Island, N.Y.
O V	Chatham Roads, Mass.		P Z	Gardiners Bay, N.Y.
O W	City Island, N.Y.		Q A	Gay Head, Mass.
O X	Cold Spring Harbor, L.I.,		Q B	Gilkey Harbor, Isleboro, Me.
	N.Y.		Q C	Glen Cove, N.Y.
O Y	Clarks Point, Buzzards Bay,		Q D	Gloucester, Mass.
	Mass.		Q E	Gloucester, Eastern Point
O Z	Cranberry Island, Me.		Q F	Goat Island, Me.
P A	Cross Rip Shoal Horn Buoy		Q G	Grand Manan, N.B.
P B	Cutler, Little River, Me.		Q H	Grand Manan Channel, N.B.

Q I	Graves, The, Mass.	R T	Mount Desert Rock, Me.
Q J	Gravesend Bay, N.Y.	R U	Mystic Seaport, Conn.
Q K	Greeenport, N.Y.	R V	Nahant, Mass.
Q L	Greenwich, Conn.	R W	National Harbor of Refuge, Del.
Q M	Greens Ledge Light, Norwalk, Conn.	R X	Nantasket Roads, Mass.
		R Y	Nantucket, Mass.
Q N	Hadley Harbor, Mass.	R Z	Nantucket Shoals Lightship
Q O	Half Way Rock, Mass.	S A	Nauset Beacon, Mass.
Q P	Half Way Rock, Me.	S B	New Bedford, Mass.
Q R	Halifax, N.S.	S C	Newburyport, Mass.
Q S	Hamburg Cove, Conn.	S D	New Haven, Conn.
Q T	Hampton Roads, Va.	S E	New London, Conn.
Q U	Hardings Ledge, Mass.	S F	Newport, R.I.
Q V	Harpswell Sound, N.B.	S G	New Rochelle, N.Y.
Q W	Head Harbor, N.B.	S H	New York, N.Y.
Q X	Highland Light, Mass.	S I	Norfolk, Va.
Q Y	Horseshoe, N.J.	S J	North Haven, Me.
Q Z	Horton Point, N.Y.	S K	Northeast Harbor, Me.
R A	Hudson River, N.Y.	S L	Noyack Bay, N.Y.
R B	Hull, Mass.	S M	Old Field Point Light, N.Y.
R C	Huntington Bay, N.Y.	S N	Orient Harbor, N.Y.
R D	Hyannis Port, Mass.	S O	Orient Point Light, N.Y.
R E	Isleboro, Me.	S P	Oyster Bay, N.Y.
R F	Kittery, Me.	S Q	Padanaram, Mass.
R G	Larchmont Harbor, N.Y.	S R	Pleasant Bay, Me.
R H	Lloyd Harbor, N.Y.	S T	Plum Gut, N.Y.
R I	Mackerel Cove, Me.	S U	Plymouth, Mass.
R J	Manhasset, L.I.	S V	Point Judith, R.I.
R K	Marblehead, Mass.	S W	Point Judith Breakwater, R.I.
R L	Marion, Mass.	S X	Port Clyde, Me.
R M	Mattapoisett, Mass.	S Y	Port Jefferson, N.Y.
R N	Matinecock Point, N.Y.	S Z	Portland, Me.
R O	Monhegan, Me.	T A	Portland Lighted Horn Buoy, Me.
R P	Monomoy, Mass.		
R Q	Montauk Point, N.Y.	T B	Portsmouth, N.H.
R S	Morgan Bay, Me.	T C	Portsmouth, Little Harbor, N.H.

T D	Pretty Marsh Harbor, Me.		**U N**	Tompkinsville, S.I., N.Y.
T E	Provincetown, Mass.		**U O**	Trafton Island, Me.
T F	Providence, R.I.		**U P**	Vineyard Haven, Mass.
T G	Quicks Hole, Mass.		**U Q**	Watch Hill, R.I.
T H	Race Rock Light, N.Y.		**U R**	Wellfleet, Cape Cod, Mass.
T I	Race, The, N.Y.		**U S**	West Chop, Vineyard Haven,
T J	Riverside, Conn.			Mass.
T K	Rockland, Me.		**U T**	West Harbor, Fishers Island,
T L	Rockport, Me.			N.Y.
T M	Roque Island, Me.		**U V**	Whitehead Island Light, Me.
T N	Sag Harbor, N.Y.		**U W**	Wings Neck, Mass.
T O	Sakonnet River, R.I.			(Wenaumet Neck).
T P	Salem, Mass.		**U X**	Winter Harbor, Me.
T Q	Sandy Hook, N.J.		**U Y**	Woods Hole, Mass.
T R	Saybrook Breakwater, Conn.		**U Z**	Wood Island, Me.
T S	Seagirt Light, N.J.		**V A**	Alexandria Bay.
T U	Seal Island Light, N.S.		**V B**	(See Emergency Signal.)
T V	Seguin Island, Me.		**V C**	Buffalo.
T W	Severn River, Md.		**V D**	Charlotte.
T X	Sheffield Island Light		**V E**	Chicago.
	House, Conn.		**V F**	Cleveland.
T Y	Shelter Island, N.Y.		**V G**	Coburg.
T Z	Shinnecock Light, N.Y.		**V H**	Country Club.
U A	Small Point Harbor, Me.		**V I**	Detroit.
U B	Somes Sound, Me.		**V J**	Duluth.
U C	Southwest Harbor, Me.		**V K**	Dunkirk.
U D	Southeast Harbor, Me.		**V L**	Erie.
U E	St. John, N.B.		**V M**	Georgian Bay.
U F	Stamford, Conn.		**V N**	Goodrich.
U G	Stonington, Conn.		**V O**	Green Bay.
U H	Stratford Point Light, Conn.		**V P**	Hamilton.
U I	Stratford Shoal Light, Conn.		**V Q**	Harbor Beach.
U J	Swans Island, Me.		**V R**	Harbor Point.
U K	Tarpaulin Cove, Mass.		**V S**	Houghton.
U L	Tenants Harbor, Me.		**V T**	Lake St. Clair Club.
U M	Thimble Islands, Conn.		**V U**	Mackinac Island.

V W Marquette.

V X Milwaukee.

V Y Nipegon.

V Z Oswego.

W A Port Huron.

W B Presque Isle.

W C Put-in-Bay.

W D Sackets Harbor.

W E Sandusky.

W F Sault Ste. Marie.

W G Toledo.

W H Toronto.

W I Welland Canal.

Emergency Signals

C Yes—(affirmative).

F I am disabled—communicate with me.

N No—(negative).

O Man overboard.

U You are running into danger.

V I require assistance.

A E I must abandon my vessel.

A N I need a doctor.

C B 4 I require immediate assistance; I am aground.

C B 5 I require immediate assistance; I am drifting.

C B 6 I require immediate assistance; I am on fire.

C B 7 I require immediate assistance; I have sprung a leak.

K Q I I am ready to be taken in tow.

N C I am in distress and requre immediate assistance.

Z L Your signal has been received but not understood.

For all other communication with Naval, Coast Guard, or Merchant Vessels, yachts must use the International Code Book (See H.O.102).

GLOSSARY

Aboard in or on a ship or boat

Aloft above the vessel, in the rigging

Anchor rode the rope or chain used to anchor the boat

Anemometer a wind-velocity indicator, usually in the form of three small cups spinning on a vertical spindle

Answering pennant a red and white vertically striped pennant, part of a set of signal flags, hoisted to indicate that a message is understood

Apparent wind the wind as it is perceived on board a boat. It will differ from the true wind by a factor of the boat's speed and course.

Autopilot an electronic compass-related steering aid that maintains a steady course. Sailboats may have a wind-direction sensing component.

Azimuth the BEARING of a celestial body

Backing wind wind changing direction counterclockwise

Backstay a stay supporting the mast from the STERN to the masthead. Running backstays are in pairs (PORT and STARBOARD) and are adjustable with each TACK.

Baggywrinkle fuzzy chafing gear made of old rope, to protect sails from wear and tear against the rig

Bark (barque) a vessel with three masts, square-rigged on the fore and mainmasts, FORE-AND-AFT on the MIZZEN

Barquentine similar to a BARK but FORE-AND-AFT on the main and MIZZEN

Bearing the horizontal angle between two objects. It may be a compass angle or a relative angle.

Beaufort scale a scale of wind conditions in which Force 0 is a flat, glassy calm, and Force 12 is a hurricane

Bend on to rig a sail to mast and boom in preparation for raising the sail

Berth a narrow bed on board a boat

Boottop the second line of color painted around the waterline

Bosun's chair a small seat of canvas or wood used to haul a person ALOFT to inspect or repair rigging or sails

Bow the front end of the vessel

Bow line the dockline that secures the BOW of the boat

Bowline a sailor's favorite knot for making a loop in a LINE; it is strong, easy to untie even after a strain, and it never slips (pronounced bo' lin)

Bowsprit the long spar that extends ahead of the BOW

Breakwater an artificial barrier intended to add protection from heavy seas to harbors or inlets

Bridge the control center on a ship

Brig or **Brigantine** a two-masted vessel, square-rigged on the foremast, FORE-AND-AFT on the mainmast

Brightwork varnished wood or polished brass on deck

Buoy a floating aid to navigation, or a small marking float

Burdened vessel the old term for the GIVE-WAY VESSEL in a right-of-way situation; still used frequently

Burgee a triangular PENNANT or SWALLOW-TAILed flag indicating a vessel's owner or club association

Call sign the group of letters or numbers assigned to a vessel for radio identification

Canton the top, inner corner of a flag

Canvas The general term for all sails set, whether made of canvas or synthetic material

Chafing gear soft wrappings in the rigging to prevent wear and tear on sails or LINE

Chainplates structural supports in the hull for securing the shrouds

Chart a map of the water showing coastline, rocks, BUOYs, and much more

Chock a strong fitting for LINEs passing over the rail

Clean lines an unobstructed visual run of the hull line from BOW to STERN

Cleat a horned fitting used to secure a LINE

Cockpit a well in the deck of a boat where the wheel or tiller is located

Colors the national ENSIGN, often expanded to mean all flags flown with the ensign

Compass course the course steered as indicated by the compass

Current the horizontal movement of water caused by tidal or other forces

Cutter a sailboat with a FORE-AND-AFT mainsail and two or more headsails

Danger signal five or more blasts of a horn or whistle, indicating "Danger! Stop your intentions!"

Depth sounder an electronic depth-measuring instrument

Dip to lower the ENSIGN one-third of the way down the staff to show honor to a warship. *At the dip* indicates a flag one-third of the way down the flagstaff.

Ensign the national flag flown by ships of the nation

Fathom six feet of water

FCC the Federal Communications Commission, the agency governing radio equipment and operation

Fend off to prevent violent contact when coming alongside

Fender a sturdy, inflatable cushion designed to protect the TOPSIDES from rough piers

Fenderboards stout timbers hung horizontally over the side between FENDERs and rough pilings

Flag hoist the position of a flag HALYARD and the flag fully raised, as in the STARBOARD flag hoist, which runs from the deck to a small block attached to the starboard spreader

Fly the longer, horizontal dimension of a flag

Fore-and-aft parallel to the centerline of the vessel

Foredeck the section of the deck at the BOW

Forestay the stay supporting the mast, from the BOW to the mast-head

Fouled anchor (1) an anchor caught up in rope or another entanglement. (2) part of an official seal of high office in maritime administration.

Gaff a spar to which the upper edge of a four-sided FORE-AND-AFT sail is attached

Gale Force 8 on the BEAUFORT SCALE, with winds from 34 to 40 KNOTs (39 to 46 MPH)

Genoa an oversized, overlapping jib used primarily when sailing upwind

Gilguys light LINEs used to tie unused HALYARDs away from the mast, to avoid chafe

Gimballed suspended on two pivot points or concentric rings to permit an object (a table, a compass, a stove) to remain level in spite of the vessel's motion

Give-way vessel the vessel that must alter course or speed to stay clear of the STAND-ON VESSEL; also called the BURDENED VESSEL

Ground tackle a general term for all the gear associated with anchoring

Growler a piece of low-lying ice floating in the sea

Halyard LINE used to haul a sail or flag ALOFT

Head the toilet or toilet room on a vessel

Helm the steering apparatus or steering characteristics

Hurricane Force 12 on the BEAUFORT SCALE, with winds of 63 KNOTs (73 MPH) or higher

Inland Rules the NAVIGATION RULES used inside demarcation lines at the entrance to most harbors, rivers, bays, and inlets. Similar to the INTERNATIONAL RULES but changed to reflect the smaller size of boats on inland waters.

International Rules NAVIGATION RULES used outside the demarcation lines at the entrance to harbors, rivers, bays, and inlets

Jibe to swing the boom across the boat as the wind direction changes across the STERN

Ketch a two-masted sailboat whose MIZZEN is large and placed forward of the rudderpost

Knot a unit of speed equalling one NAUTICAL MILE per hour

Lee the vessel's side (or the coast) which the wind crosses second

Leech the trailing edge of a FORE-AND-AFT sail

Lee cloth a sturdy cloth laced on the edge of a bunk and attached overhead to prevent a sleeper from rolling out of the bunk in a SEAWAY

Lifelines stout wire (often plastic coated) rigged around the perimeter of the boat to serve as a handrail, and to prevent crew from falling overboard

Line rope, when used aboard a vessel

Long splice a splice joining two rope ends which does not increase the diameter of the rope

Loran (from *long range navigation*) an electronic position-finding receiver

Marconi historical name for the modern triangular mainsail of most sailboats

Mizzen the aftermost mast and sail in a YAWL, KETCH, or FORE-AND-AFT-rigged ship

Morse code a signal code comprising dots and dashes permitting communication by sound or electronic signal

Muscleboat the generic term for a class of large powerboats designed for high speed only, characteristically with an oversize engine, flush deck, and tiny COCKPIT

Nautical mile one minute of latitude, or about 6,080 feet

Navigation Rules the RULES OF THE ROAD in the U.S.

Nip a short turn or twist in a rope

Nun a cylindrical red unlit BUOY, with even numbers

Observance of colors the display of the national ENSIGN and other flags from 8 A.M. to sunset

Off soundings in water so deep that a sounding lead would not touch bottom, usually considered water deeper than 100 FATHOMs

Overtaking vessel the vessel moving faster, and therefore required to give way to the overtaken vessel

Pennant a narrow, tapering flag

Pig stick a long, lightweight pole used to raise the BURGEE above the masthead

Port the left side of a vessel, when viewed facing the BOW

Port tack the TACK where the wind crosses the PORT side of a sailboat first; the sails (and boom) are on the STARBOARD side. The port-tack boat is the BURDENED VESSEL and must give way to a boat on the STARBOARD TACK.

Private signal a yacht owner's personal flag, also called the owner's signal or house flag

Privileged vessel the old term for the STAND-ON VESSEL, the vessel with the right-of-way.

Protest a formal objection by one yacht to another yacht's action on the racecourse

Pulpit rigid framework at the BOW supporting LIFELINES

Radar reflector a passive sphere of metal plates that reflect a radar's signals

Relative bearing the BEARING of an object in relation to the vessel's centerline

Riding light the anchor light, a 360° white light shown at night when the vessel is at anchor

Rigging, standing the wire rigging that holds up the mast

Rode the anchor LINE

Rules of the Road a set of requirements to promote safe navigation, including use of navigation lights, steering rules, sound signals, and distress signals. They include the INLAND RULES and the INTERNATIONAL RULES. Also called *72 COLREGS*.

Running Lights the lights required by the NAVIGATIONAL RULES for operating a vessel at night, red on the PORT side, green on the STARBOARD side, plus other appropriate white lights

Sailboard generic term for a sailing surfboard with a small sail held by one person, who is standing on the board

Schooner a vessel with two or more masts, with the foremast shorter than the mainmast

Scope the ratio of the length of the RODE to the depth of the water the anchor is set in

Scuppers drain holes in the deck

Seaway, in a in choppy or heavy seas in open water, causing much motion on board

Sloop a single-masted sailboat with a mainsail and single jib

Stand-on vessel the vessel that has the right of way, the right to proceed unhindered by another vessel; also called the PRIVILEGED VESSEL

Starboard the right side of the vessel, when facing the BOW

Starboard tack the TACK where the wind crosses the STARBOARD side first. The sailboat on the starboard tack is the PRIVILEGED (stand-on) VESSEL.

Stern the back end of the vessel

Storm Force 10 on the BEAUFORT SCALE, with winds from 48 to 63 KNOTs (55-72 MPH)

Swallow-tail a flag having a divided end in the shape of a bird's tail

Tack (1) to change course in a zigzag manner while sailing upwind. (2) a change in course.

Tide the vertical rise and fall of water caused by the gravitational pull of the moon and sun

Topsides the sides of the hull above the waterline

Trawler a popular type of powerboat with the characteristics of slow, steady speed, comfortable living quarters, and long range under power

Truck the wooden circular cap on a traditional mast

Tuna tower a metal armature rising above the BRIDGE on a sport-fishing boat, with a small platform for an observer to stand and scout out fish

Two-blocked hauled all the way up so the two parts meet and cannot go any further

Under way in motion through the water

Union the CANTON of the American flag: the blue field with fifty white stars

Union Jack the blue flag with fifty white stars flown from the BOW on Sundays, at anchor, from 8 A.M. to sunset

VHF radio *very high frequency* radiotelephone with a maximum range of about 25 miles

Warps, streaming dragging heavy LINEs to slow a boat in STORM conditions

Watch captain the person designated by the skipper as the one in charge of the vessel's safety during a specified time, his or her *watch*

Way the movement of a ship through the water, using her own power

Windward side the side the wind reaches first

Yacht a boat designed for pleasure rather than commerce, fishing, or work; one that has amenities suggesting luxury and comfort

Yacht ensign the optional flag flown in place of the U.S. ENSIGN by documented yachts in domestic waters

Yawl a two-masted vessel on which the MIZZEN is small and is stepped aft of the rudderpost

INDEX

Alfa
Diver Down; Keep Clear

Kilo
Desire to Communicate

Bravo
Dangerous Cargo

Lima
Stop Instantly

Charlie
Yes

Mike
I Am Stopped

Delta
Keep Clear

November
No

Echo
Altering Course to Starboard

Oscar
Man Overboard

Foxtrot
Disabled

Papa
About to Sail

Golf
Want a Pilot

Quebec
Request Pratique

Hotel
Pilot on Board

Romeo

India
Altering Course to Port

Sierra
Engines Going Astern

Juliett
On Fire; Keep Clear

Tango
Keep Clear of Me

DATE DUE

APR 1 '66			
APR 18 '66			
MAY 4 '66			
APR 24 '67			
MAR 18			
MAR 28 '68			
MAY 6 '68			
MAY 23 '68			
MAY 26 '69			
MAY 14 '99			
	MAY 14 '99		
GAYLORD			PRINTED IN U.S.A.

perhaps thanks to Robert Browning's reputation and backing, he made some beginnings of a success. But in the meantime the necessity of supplying him with sufficient money to live in the way that he expected involved his father in an uncomfortable situation that he was to regret for many years.

Louisa, Lady Ashburton was a young widow of dark and classical beauty, with a considerable fortune. Like her husband's first wife, she had been extremely devoted to Carlyle. 'A rich and generous presence,' Henry James wrote of her, 'that wherever encountered, seemed always to fill the foreground with colour, with picture, with fine mellow sound and, in the part of everyone else, with a kind of traditional charmed, amused patience.' She was warmhearted and demonstrative, and in the set that Browning frequented she and her friend Lady Marian Alford were leading and most lavish hostesses. He had met her first during her husband's lifetime, and had known her for quite six years when some time in 1871 he proposed marriage. A marriage between a widower of fifty-nine and a widow of forty-two could clearly have none of the romance that he had known with Elizabeth. It was, however, perhaps unnecessarily frank of the poet to say as much in making his proposal. For not only did he make it clear that his heart remained buried in Florence, but he added that it was largely for his son's sake that he contemplated the alliance. Lady Ashburton's indignant refusal was hardly unreasonable, but Browning took it extremely hard, forgiving neither her nor himself for the indignity he had suffered. 'I see every now and then that contemptible Lady Ashburton,' he wrote three years later, 'and mind her no more than any other black beetle—so long as it don't crawl up my sleeve.' So savage a remark is out of

keeping with Browning's character. Possibly he had been genuinely fond of Lady Ashburton, and the worldly interests to which he had ascribed his proposal were intended chiefly to excuse himself in the eyes of his dead wife; perhaps his exaggerated frankness was mere scruple, intended to prevent all shadow of deception. Seldom had Browning made so seemingly insensitive a gesture in any relationship before. He had indeed no enemies, except for the one or two who quarrelled with him at that point, out of partisanship for Lady Ashburton. Those to whom he volunteered an explanation, however, remained his friends. Moreover, Lady Ashburton seems to have alienated her sympathizers by bursting out 'in all the madness of her wounded vanity,' as Browning put it, into calumnies easy to rebut. Later she appears to have made some attempts at reconciliation, but Browning resisted them.

Miss Isa Blagden continued faithful; with her perhaps his bond was stronger than ever it had been with Lady Ashburton, for she had known Elizabeth. But he did not meet her often, since she still lived in Florence; and there in 1872 she died. The poet had now no link remaining with Italy, but in the same year his old friend Alfred Domett returned from New Zealand after nearly thirty years of absence, and the friendship, which had lapsed, was joyfully renewed. In April of that year Domett noted in his diary, which provides much material for this period of the poet's life: 'Browning tells me he has just finished a poem, the most metaphysical and boldest he has written since *Sordello*. He is very doubtful as to its reception by the public.' The poem was *Fifine at the Fair*, and its difficulties arose from the care with which Browning disguised the actual incidents which had called it into being. For Mrs. Orr it is 'a defence of incon-

stancy, or of the right of experiment in love.' She even
views it as a piece of 'perplexing cynicism.' In fact it is
a statement, overcoloured with self-reproach, of the
strong pull of the world against a man's fidelity to his
marriage; *Fifine at the Fair* is not an account of his affair
with Lady Ashburton; there could be nothing in
common between the gipsy girl in the circus tent with

> Sunshine upon her spangled hips,
> As here she fronts us full with pose half-frank, half-fierce,

and the society hostess who had refused him her hand.
But though Fifine is not related except in the most
distant way to the lady whom he had so unsuccessfully
wooed, the poem is the direct outcome of his experience
with Lady Ashburton. For it had brought sharply to his
notice the extent to which the memory of his marriage
was growing dim. He was unwilling, however, to
symbolize by a woman of flesh and blood, the forces
which were deflecting him. That would have been
to admit too much. So it was a creature half-girl, half-
woman, elusive, strange and almost sexless, that he cast
for the role of temptress. Yet even as she is copied
from a gipsy seen at a French fair, she does not fail to
betray her singular fascination for the lonely widower
who created her. The intention of the poem, Browning
told Dr. Furnivall, 'was to show merely how a Don Juan
might justify himself, partly by truth, somewhat by
sophistry.' But, as both Mrs. Orr and Edward Dowden
have complained, it is extremely hard to see where, in
this poem, truth ends and sophistry begins. In justifying
himself to his shadowy wife—or conscience—Elvire,
for his pursuit of the gipsy girl, the husband talks of some
necessary knowledge that can only be gained from the
other sex. Himself he compares in a most involved

K

piece of argument, to the swimmer who in an intro-
ductory lyric has caught sight of a butterfly fluttering
above the sea; now he lies on the water, his head almost
submerged, till suddenly 'sun, sky and air so tantalize!'
that he reaches up his arms to the heavens, and sinks.
So he must live, he concludes, immersed in the things of
the world, but always struggling to reach above them:
a situation which Browning works out in this extended
simile:

> I liken to this play o' the body,—fruitless strife
> To slip the sea and hold the heaven,—my spirit's life
> 'Twixt false, whence it would break, and true, where it
>   would bide.
> I move in, yet resist, am upborne every side
> By what I beat against, an element too gross
> To live in, did not soul duly obtain her dose
> Of life-breath, and inhale from truth's pure plenitude
> Above her, snatch and gain enough to just illude
> With hope that some brave bound may baffle evermore
> The obstructing medium, make who swam henceforward
>   soar:
> —Gain scarcely snatched when, foiled by the very effort,
>   sowse,
> Underneath ducks the soul, her truthward yearnings dowse
> Deeper in falsehood! ay, but fitted less and less
> To bear in nose and mouth old briny bitterness
> Proved alien more and more . . .

To mix further with the world, then, served the purpose of making the world seem increasingly unbearable;
consorting with a hundred Fifines only served to enhance
the value set on a single Elvire. Yet Fifine claims to be
nothing that she is not, and Elvire owes her beauty to
his artist's imagination—a fact that would be truer of a
dead wife than of a living one. Again Elvire stands above
Fifine, therefore Fifine can give him more of the lowly

experience he needs. For Elvire may be trusted; Fifine
teaches one to take care of oneself. The argument of the
poem becomes more and more intricate. Never had
Browning so resolutely refused to speak out. Yet its
conclusion is perfectly plain. Though he may convince
Elvire in argument of the necessity of his meetings with
the gipsy girl, one last meeting with her, and his wife
will be gone:

> I go, and in a trice
> Return: five minutes past, expect me! If in vain—
> Why slip from flesh and blood, and play the ghost again!

So the poem ends. But in its epilogue the wife who,
though betrayed, he has sworn shall suffice, does return
as a ghost, and as a ghost prompts Don Juan, now the
householder of an empty house, in the writing of his own
epitaph:

> 'Help and get it over! *Re-united to his wife*
> (How draw up the paper lets the parish people know?)
> *Lies M., or N., departed from this life,*
> *Day the this or that, month and year the so and so.*
> What i' the way of final flourish? Prose, verse? Try!
> *Affliction sore long time he bore*, or, what is it to be?
> *Till God did please to grant him ease.* Do end!' quoth I:
> 'I end with—Love is all and Death is nought!' quoth She.

Browning remains enigmatically ironic to the end.
For the poem's problem is insoluble; nor was he prepared to state it as frankly as he had stated his problems
before. There is throughout a confusion that appears
almost deliberate about the precise benefits to be won
from the alluring gipsy. Was it knowledge that his Don
Juan was seeking, or diversion? 'An actual Elvire and
an actual Fifine may be the starting points,' writes
Dowden, 'but by and by Elvire shall stand for all that is
permanent and substantial in thought and feeling,

Fifine for all that is transitory and illusive.' In face of Browning's own statement to Dr. Furnivall, and the knowledge that has transpired about his relations with Lady Ashburton since Dowden wrote, one must conclude that his assessment of the poem is over-philosophical. Its merits lie entirely in its descriptive passages. Seascapes and landscapes evoking the flat country about Pornic, the picture of the fair itself and of the carnival in St. Mark's Square at Venice, go some way towards atoning for the critical disquisitions that obscure but do not conceal the fundamental content of the poem.

Fifine at the Fair is not, for all its narration in the first person, a dramatic monologue. The 'Men and Women' had spoken with their own voices and in their own defence, but the personality of Don Juan in *Fifine* is no sooner created than it disintegrates, leaving Robert Browning with a mere ventriloquist's dummy to speak his reflective discursions. The unfaithful husband is among the poet's very few unsuccessful creations, for soon Browning does not even trouble to fit his language to the probable thoughts and viewpoint of the man who is supposed to be talking. Such were the penalties of his reluctance to speak out.

Fifine at the Fair differs from its predecessors in its metrical form. For Browning was never permanently content with the blank verse medium over which he had won such mastery. The six-beat line of *Fifine*, and its division into short sections corresponding to paragraphs, the reintroduction of rhyme and the frequency of anapaests, seem to blur the poem's argument. Much of it indeed appears to have been composed in an emotional undertone.

In *Red Cotton Night-cap Country*, Browning's next poem, he returned to blank verse, and advanced a stage further

towards objective presentation. In this second dramatization of a *cause célèbre*, he touches, perhaps with less reluctance than in *Fifine at the Fair*, on the same problem of self-mastery or self-indulgence, and on yet another of the questions which had exercised him throughout his life, that of belief in the supernatural. In its inception *Red Cotton Night-cap Country* was as deliberate an exercise as *Balaustion's Adventure*. The story of *Fifine at the Fair*, however overstrained, was of the stuff of Browning's own experience. The fascination of a gipsy had long ago promoted 'The Flight of the Duchess' and an actual Fifine had attracted him at an actual fair. *Red Cotton Night-cap Country*, however, owed its origins to a dispute with Miss Annie Thackeray, whom he met at St. Aubin on the Norman coast in the summer of 1872. She had humorously described the district, from the caps of the fisherfolk as 'White Cotton Night-cap Country.' Everything was so sleepy, she implied, that nothing at all ever happened there. Browning however knew of certain melodramatic happenings which had taken place in the previous year and which made 'Red Cotton Night-cap Country' a more fitting name for the district. As the poem opens in this meek, 'hitherto un-Murrayed bathing-place' he reasons with Miss Thackeray on the relative suitability of the two titles. The case which Browning interpreted in his poem was in its origins a simple one: a Paris jeweller who had lived with a mistress on a local estate had killed himself by jumping from a tower. In the tale, as told to the poet by his friend Milsand, the reason for his suicide had been remorse at his unfilial behaviour to his mother, and at the grief his irregular union had cost her. Later, however, when Milsand told him more Browning decided that the man's chief considerations had been religious. The accounts

he then collected locally and from the newspapers confirmed him in this interpretation. The original Mellerio,
a Spaniard, had certainly been a man with a strong vein
of superstition in his make-up; Browning, however, saw
him, in more extreme terms, as a man who had demanded
a miracle. His jumping from the tower had been, as the
poet viewed it, no suicide but a challenge to the Virgin
of a local church to transport him through the air, a
supernatural event which would condone—or even
justify—the uneasy compromise between faith and
immorality in which he was endeavouring to live. The
poem's central theme is the impossibility of this compromise. As it was impossible for the Don Juan of
Fifine at the Fair to divide his life between Elvire and the
gipsy, so the jeweller of *Red Cotton Night-cap Country* is
unable to reconcile the 'Turf and Towers' of its subtitle.
The two symbols recur in the poem with a constancy
unusual in Browning's work, the Tower from which
Mellerio's counterpart Léonce Miranda jumps to his
death standing for the religious life, and the Turf on
which he falls for the life of the world. But the miracle
in which the crazy jeweller comes to believe will
reconcile this duality and solve everything. Nor will its
effects be limited to his own benefit. The news of it will
be the signal for the revival of faith throughout France.
He imagines Renan coming out into the street where he
lives in Paris and burning his book, and Napoleon III,
when he hears of it, resigning his Empire, 'twenty years
usurped,' to the legitimate Bourbon, 'Henry the Desired
One,' who will from that moment reign in France.

> O blessing, O superlatively big
> With blessedness beyond all blessing dreamed
> By man! for just that promise has effect,
> 'Old things shall pass away and all be new!'

> Then, for a culminating mercy-feat,
> Wherefore should I dare dream impossible
> That I too have my portion in the change?
> My past with all its sorrow, sin and shame,
> Becomes a blank, a nothing!

So, like another Master-builder, he stands in the Belvedere he has himself constructed, ready to take flight; in the Belvedere for whose creation his mother has reproached him, viewing it as the overweening sign of his extravagance. For, as Browning drew her, she had advocated an impracticable, mere easy-going compromise between the twin claims of turf and towers, recommending indeed that he and his mistress should live on quietly in the country, inhabiting no grand new apartments but

> the south room, that we styled,
> Your sire and I, the winter chamber.

Browning departs so far from the story as he had first heard it as to make her underline the moral which he had already stated in his capacity of commentator, that man should climb no towers but pick his way 'like a sage pedestrian.'

But Léonce Miranda is not capable of taking a middle path. Like Ibsen's architect, he has built a tower within himself from which he must challenge, not the future generation that treads him down, but the rising tide of unbelief. But this deed will do more; it will restore the innocence of his smirched mistress. The Virgin will join his hand with hers in true marriage; he will worship one and yet love the other. The poem becomes at this point a crazy travesty of *The Ring and the Book*. It is as if the Pope were asked to give his blessing to the carnal marriage of Caponsacchi and Pompilia.

Not only is Miranda crazy, however, but his tower, the tower of the old faith, cannot be rebuilt. His attempt to raise it in the form of a new Belvedere is as fantastic as his appeal to miracle. Here Browning repeats in stronger form his judgment upon the Church of Rome delivered in 'Christmas Eve':

> Disturb no ruins here!
> Are not they crumbling of their own accord?
> Meantime, let poets, painters keep a prize!

The picturesque towers of the old faith might be the stuff of which poems and paintings could be made, but now there were other paths to tread, and not all of them hugged the flat ground. There was a steadier method of climbing now, the method of utilizing doubt long ago adumbrated by the dying Saint John in 'A Death in the Desert,' and Browning's moral for *Red Cotton Night-cap Country* is in effect a secular restatement of that poem's message that:

> God's gift was that man should conceive of truth
> And yearn to gain it, catching his mistake
> As midway help till he reach fact in deed.

It is a judgment of the same weight that Browning was now delivering, ten years later, in his role of commentator, upon the sordid fate of his crazy jeweller. If you are adventurous and climb yourself, he advises his reader,

> Plant the foot warily, accept a staff,
> Stamp only where you probe the standing point,
> Move forward, well assured that move you may:
> Where you mistrust advance, stop short, there stick!
> This makes advancing slow and difficult?
> Hear what comes of the endeavour of brisk youth
> To foot it fast and easy!

Red Cotton Night-cap Country was condemned by R. H. Hutton of the *Spectator* for containing no single line of poetry. In argument he conceded to Alfred Domett a single passage, which does not today seem to stand out from the even texture of the poem. Certainly it is concerned throughout, except where the poet interpolates a passing sketch of Milsand, with the morally sordid. Moreover it bears marks of hasty writing; it took Browning only seven weeks to complete the first manuscript from which it was printed. Yet, despite a few obscure passages, it makes far easier reading than *Fifine at the Fair*, for the verse, though it does not rise to passages of beauty that would be foreign to the purpose of the poem, very seldom falls into flatness. There are indeed few descents in the course of the whole of the poem's forty thousand lines. Browning certainly remained the master of his medium, and was still a superb analyst of motive, but the world about him was growing dark and he was alone. Yet in the ugliness and evil that seemed everywhere to confront him, he found always reflections of sanity and truth, if not of beauty.

In *Aristophanes' Apology*, however, which followed upon *Red Cotton Night-cap Country* two years later, in 1875, Browning returned to the deliberate pursuit of beauty, taking up the tale of Balaustion where he had left it, and using it as a framework for a transcript this time of the *Heracles* of Euripides. The poem as a whole falls below the level of *Balaustion's Adventure*, being rather an archaeological reconstruction in the manner of the prologue he had once given to Artemis than a poem with deep personal associations. It contains however passages of real magnificence recalling the supreme Miltonic invocations in *The Ring and the Book*, passages the more welcome for the poem's position in Browning's

œuvre between *Red Cotton Night-cap Country* and *The Inn Album*. There are few finer affirmations in all his work than Balaustion's on her flight back to Rhodes after the fall of Athens:

> Why should despair be? Since, distinct above
> Man's wickedness and folly, flies the wind
> And floats the cloud, free transport for our soul
> Out of its fleshly durance dim and low—,
> Since disembodied soul anticipates
> (Thought-borne as now, in rapturous unrestraint)
> Above all crowding, crystal silentness,
> Above all noise, a silver solitude:—
> Surely, where thought so bears soul, soul in time
> May permanently bide, 'assert the wise,'
> There live in peace, there work in hope once more—
> O nothing doubt, Philemon! Greed and strife,
> Hatred and cark and care, what place have they
> In yon blue liberality of heaven?

After this the poem's arguments concerning the nature of comedy and the justification for satire seem a little academic. The rest of the verse is clear and good with occasional passages of description as colourful and pleasing as the best in the *Adventure*, but about the whole poem and the *Heracles* translation it contains, clings the air of the study, which was rendered stuffier rather than dispelled by such notes as that informing the reader that the kordax-step was the Greek equivalent of the can-can.

The Inn Album, published in the same year as *Aristophanes' Apology*, draws once more on law reports from the contemporary press. Little though Browning felt in theory that such should be the exclusive subjects of his poems, in this phase of his life they inevitably were. For in this poem, to a greater degree than in *Red Cotton*

Night-cap Country, Browning was obsessed by death. In *The Inn Album* indeed the number of deaths is in excess of the poetic probability. It is perhaps right that the elder woman confronted by her former lover and jolted out of the dead life she had been living, should commit suicide; the murder of that lover by her younger admirer, however, is not very convincing. The characters are right, but the dénouement, owing to Browning's too great addiction to violence, is false. The plot is one of the neatest Browning ever contrived, preserving as it does the unities of time and place. He claimed that it was founded on a story told him thirty years before by Lord de Ros. Whether founded on fact or not, it allowed of far better shaping than had the stuff of *Red Cotton Night-cap Country*. But not only is its story much more compact, it contains also passages of far more concentrated verse than he had written since *Balaustion's Adventure*, among the best a description of a night walk that shows the vigour with which the poet of *Pauline* and *Sordello* lived on in the middle-aged widower who wrote *The Inn Album*:

> 'Twixt wood and wood, two black walls full of night
> Slow to disperse, though mists thin fast before
> The advancing foot, and leave the flint-dust fine
> Each speck with its fire-sparkle. Presently
> The road's end with the sky's beginning mix
> In one magnificence of glare, due East,
> So high the sun rides,—May's the merry month.

But there is no merriment in the hearts of the characters, and the curtain falls on an Elizabethan plethora of corpses upon which an unsuspecting and innocent girl is about to open the door. Edward Dowden compares it with that brief and poignant

dramatization of an earlier murder case, the anonymous *Yorkshire Tragedy*. Certainly its colour is a murky grey relieved only by occasional glimpses of the English countryside in which it is set, and by the charm of the younger woman, whose appearances however are few. The inn itself might be situated in Hell so little hope is there for those who enter there; in that Hell which is described by the elder woman's narrow clerical husband, a place where he expects the wicked to meet:

> After death,
> Life: man created new, ingeniously
> Perfect for a vindictive purpose now
> That man, first fashioned in beneficence,
> Was proved a failure; intellect at length
> Replacing old obtuseness, memory
> Made mindful of delinquent's bygone deeds
> Now that remorse was vain, which life-long lay
> Dormant when lesson might be laid to heart. . .

The picture of man granted the power to know the consequences of good and evil only at the moment when it is too late for him to make use of his knowledge is among the ugliest drawn by any nineteenth-century poet, exceeding even the horror of *The City of Dreadful Night* from which, at least, Thomson believed there was release at death. It is indeed strange, in the light of such a passage, that Browning should still be censured for his facile optimism.

Formally *The Inn Album* is the most perfect of the shorter novels in verse. It is also Browning's final achievement in direct narrative of any length, and marks a final peak in the range he had ascended with his *Men and Women*, a range which looks out over a plain which the poet spent the next nine years in crossing. For, except *La Saisiaz*, a poem comparable in its premonitory

significance to *Christmas Eve and Easter Day*, Browning attempted nothing of the first importance thereafter until his not wholly successful *Ferishtah's Fancies* of 1884.

Since the publication of *Fifine at the Fair* the popularity he had won with *Men and Women* and with *The Ring and the Book* had begun to wane. Soon the old reproaches of obscurity began to appear in the journals, though the critics were not so unanimously against him as they had been in the past; the *Athenaeum* reviewer even considered *The Inn Album* an advance upon *The Ring and the Book*. But Browning had long meditated his revenge on the critics, and in his next volume, *Pacchiarotto, and How he Worked in Distemper*, etc., he was to take it. For he had exhausted the vein he had tapped in *Fifine at the Fair* and could now turn his attention to trivial themes. Now the antagonistic pulls of the world and the ideal, the present and the past, were alike growing weaker. Nor did he still think of love as he had done when he wrote *The Ring and the Book*. In *Red Cotton Night-cap Country* it had been no ennobling passion, and the crazy jeweller's endeavour to make it so had preposterously failed. In *The Inn Album* it was a thing of this world only, an obsession that brought grief to its victims, but no intimations of a higher beauty.

In his new lyrical volume Browning treated the subject as he had treated it in early years, in all its possible combinations and situations but without any close reference to his own case. Such poems as 'St. Martin's Summer,' and 'Bifurcation' are studies of cases as imaginary as those of 'A Woman's Last Word' and 'The Last Ride Together.' The *Pacchiarotto* volume, however, was primarily an attack upon the critics, mild and expostulatory in such short pieces as 'House' and 'Shop'—the first of which has been quoted in the opening pages of this

study—and rumbustiously offensive in the title poem. For this hasty and deliberately cacophonous attack, which singled out the invidious Alfred Austin for a drubbing, Browning returned to the manner of 'The Pied Piper.' His invective is a little too contemptuous to be amusing, his ingenuity a little too provocative to please. He had treasured up his grievances too long for them to pass as mere good fun. But the lyrics of the new volume, even when using up rags and tags of themes already treated, achieve certain new masteries, chiefly in ironic anecdotes which look forward to Hardy, and in cryptic metaphysical statements that seem directly modelled on the short-lined verse in the second part of *Faust*.

> Could I but live again,
>   Twice my life over,
> Would I once strive again?
>   Would I not cover
> Quietly all of it—
>   Greed and ambition—
> So, from the pall of it,
>   Pass to fruition?

This opening of the second of his 'Pisgah Sights' owes everything to Goethe. Yet its claim to compress a lifetime's experience in a few short lines is hardly valid. In fact 'Pisgah Sights' fail to make a statement, chiefly perhaps because Browning was still a long way from having distilled the experience of his life into a single and uniform belief. More typical of his attitude in his sixty-fourth year was his testy demand to be left alone voiced in the poem 'House':

> I have mixed with a crowd and heard free talk
>   In a foreign land where an earthquake chanced:
> And a house stood gaping, nought to baulk
>   Man's eye wherever he gazed or glanced.

The whole of the frontage shaven sheer,
   The inside gaped: exposed to day,
Right and wrong and common and queer,
   Bare, as the palm of your hand, it lay.

With Elizabeth's death the front of his house had indeed fallen, and all had been able to witness his sorrow, but now he wished to live on in private without prayers. He did not care to spend the whole of his life publicly selling his wares either, like the poet he writes of in 'Shop,' the companion piece to 'House.' His intention was to withdraw a little and contemplate life's little ironies from a distance. Deliberately he returned to his study, and in 1877 undertook, in order to please Carlyle, a verse translation the *Agamemnon of Aeschylus*. So literal and awkward was this translation that Alfred Domett supposed him intentionally to have made it as difficult for English readers as the original Greek is said to have been for the Greeks. But his drift towards the academic and towards a greater detachment was sharply checked by the death of a very dear friend.

Miss Egerton Smith, whom he had first met in Florence where she had come on a visit, was a wealthy woman of whom he saw increasingly more as his older women friends forsook him. His sister-in-law Arabella, Miss Isa Blagden, Lady Ashburton, all were lost to him by death or difference, and Miss Egerton Smith had come to take their places. With her he went frequently to concerts when in London, and each season for the last few years she had joined the poet and his sister on their various summer expeditions abroad. In the summer of 1877 she was staying with Robert and Sarianne in a small villa called La Saisiaz four or five miles to the south-west of Geneva, when suddenly she died.

'Browning had been for his usual bathe,' wrote Domett in his diary, having heard an account of the matter from Miss Browning, 'in a pool among trees down the mountainside, and on returning found that Miss Smith had not made her appearance. "All right," he thought, "she is saving herself for the journey" (a walk in the mountains which they had planned for that day). Miss Browning going into her room to look for her, found the poor lady lying with her face downwards upon the floor. She put her arm round her, saying, "Are you ill, dear?", then she saw that she was insensible.'

The shock of this sudden meeting with death sent Browning, on his return to London, to re-examine his beliefs once more. In the resulting poem, *La Saisiaz*, his affirmation is less wholehearted than of old, and stronger in its review of the good things of life he had enjoyed than in its statement of philosophical belief. That he trusted in a future life is clear from reports of his conversations with friends. But in *La Saisiaz* he failed to clothe his conviction in striking imagery. The poem's argument is loose and over-wordy; its best lines are not those which testify to his temperate hope of a future immortality, but those which remember the woman who has died, and portray the Alps among which he and she had meant to walk on the day of her death. In places where an emotional clinch is needed, Browning for the first time proves insufficient master of his medium, and lapses into such diffuseness as:

> So, I hope—no more than hope, but hope—no less than hope, because
> I can fathom by no plumb-line sunk in life's apparent laws,
> How I may in any instance fix where change should meetly fall
> Nor involve, by one revisal, abrogation of them all . . .

Using equally loose metres, Arthur Hugh Clough was able to lend more conviction to his doubts than did Browning to his statement of belief in a future life. Miss Egerton Smith's death had called up a memory, and reminded him of his own mortality. Perhaps it challenged him to look back once more on his own loss. The emotional weakness of much of the poem, however, suggests a refusal to face all its implications. Browning was less ready with answers to his own questions now than he had been when he wrote 'Christmas Eve,' and the only beauties of *La Saisiaz* are the colours of retrospect with which he summons up the vast Swiss landscape:

> There's Salève's own platform facing glory which strikes
>   greatness small,
> —Blanc, supreme above his earth-brood, needles red and
>   white and green,
> Horns of silver, fangs of crystal set on edge in his demesne.
> So, some three weeks since, we saw them: so, tomorrow
>   we intend
> You shall see them likewise; therefore Good Night till
>   tomorrow, friend!

But his friend had not lived to take that walk with its views of Mont Blanc, and Browning was a man of sixty-six who might soon know the answer to the questions his fancy and reason debated in his memorial poem to Miss Egerton Smith.

In his work of the next few years, however, he returned to the lyric and the story. Reflective poetry spoken in the first person he abandoned for ever with *La Saisiaz*. The autobiographical element, nevertheless, was to appear triumphally again.

The Two Poets of Croisic makes a neat juxtaposition of two tales associated with the seaside place where Browning had spent several summers. His first poet,

L

René Gentilhomme, whose mediocre ode is accepted as a prophecy by the superstitious Louis XIII, subsides into what seems to have been a welcome oblivion; the second poet who has for long believed in his entirely fictitious fame decides in the end that the only true glory is that which a man has had no hand in making. In one sense *The Two Poets* is a premature farewell to Browning's own reputation; what matters, as he sees it, is the experience of being a poet, or of having been a poet. In its modesty, and its treatment only of what Browning has felt and known, the end of *The Two Poets* is more successful that that of *La Saisiaz*. There's a simple test, he says, by which to weigh the worth of poets. The one who prevails will be the

> . . . strong since joyful man who stood distinct
> Above slave-sorrows to his chariot linked.

> Was not his lot to feel more? What meant 'feel'
>   Unless to suffer! Not, to see more? Sight—
> What helped it but to watch the drunken reel
>   Of vice and folly round him, left and right,
> One dance of rogues and idiots! Not, to deal
>   More with things lovely? What provoked the spite
> Of filth incarnate, like the poet's need
> Of other nutriment than strife and greed!

> Who knows most, doubts most; entertaining hope,
>   Means recognizing fear; the keener sense
> Of all comprised within our actual scope
>   Recoils from aught beyond earth's dim and dense.
> Who, grown familiar with the sky, will grope
>   Henceforth among groundlings? That's offence
> Just as indubitably: stars abound
> O'erhead, but then—what flowers make glad the
>   ground!

Such verses with their stronger imagery and their closer pattern of alliteration bespeak knowledge greatly in excess of the theoretical philosophizings of *La Saisiaz*. The story of the two poets is pedestrian, but the end of the poem fresh and direct, in its acceptance of the state of doubt which in the earlier poem he had failed to dispel.

The Browning of these late years was an even more solitary man than he had been after Elizabeth's death. Without Miss Egerton Smith he no longer went to concerts. His daily and weekly routine became increasingly rigid. 'He was averse,' writes Mrs. Orr, 'to any thought of change. What he had done once he was wont, for that very reason, to continue doing,' and the way he spent his days was described in detail after his death by an old servant in an article in the *Pall Mall Gazette*.

'He rose without fail at seven, enjoyed a plate of whatever fruit—strawberries, grapes, oranges—were in season; read, generally some piece of foreign literature, for an hour in his bedroom; then bathed; breakfasted—a light meal of twenty minutes; sat by the fire and read his *Times* and *Daily News* till ten; from ten to one wrote in his study or meditated with head resting on his hand. To write a letter was the reverse of a pleasure to him, yet he was diligent in replying to a multitude of correspondents. His lunch, at one, was of the lightest kind, usually no more than a pudding. Visits, private views of picture exhibitions and the like followed until half-past five. At seven he dined, preferring Carlowitz or claret to other wines and drinking little of any. But on many days the dinner was not at home; once during three successive weeks he dined out without the omission of a day. He returned home seldom at a later hour than half-past twelve; and at seven the next morning the round began again.'

It was not a routine conducive to the writing of poetry, but the life of a man who needed human contacts, yet wished to form no new and strong emotional bonds that might cause him to lose his memories of the old ones. Nevertheless in the three hours he spent in his study he composed in the years of his decline the two volumes of *Dramatic Idyls* and *Jocoseria*. The contents of these three books are on a lower level of inspiration than any other group of Browning's poems. Each one of these dozen and a half stories in verse is marred by the Browning mannerisms, and not one of them is brought to life by any urgency in its telling. Monaldeschi's murder fails to arouse the shudder of horror which had been at the poet's command ever since his 'Madhouse Cells'; and 'Ixion' turns on his wheel at no more than a conversational pace. Ned Bratts and his wife brawl excitedly about their conversion, but to no purpose. No reader can care about their fate. The anecdotes might suit a fourteen year old; the method of telling, however, would defeat any but a skilled Browning reader. Here rhymes which had been effective in the aggressive knockabout of *Pacchiarotto* pull the story up short. Nor is Browning any happier in his metres. The six-beat line of *Fifine* takes the place of his characteristic blank verse, and conveys an effect of jocose lightness quite at variance with the poem's purpose. This new awkwardness in Browning's manner bespeaks a growing impatience with anecdote and reader. He will throw his story off as once he threw off 'The Pied Piper,' but now he has lost his skill. Yet among these offhand narratives he dropped occasional short pieces that recalled his long-ago *Dramatic Lyrics*, yet revealed a new art of compression and a live metrical dexterity. Such a piece as 'Never the Time and the Place' amply proves that when

the old poet was moved he could still write as well as he had done then. Indeed he said as much in his epilogue to the last of the *Dramatic Idyls*:

> Touch him ne'er so lightly, into song he broke:
> Soil so quick-receptive,—not one feather-seed,
> Not one flower-dust fell but straight its fall awoke
> Vitalizing virtue: song would song succeed
> Sudden as spontaneous . . .

But the continued spontaneity of his song could hardly have been credible to those who met him in fashionable drawing-rooms. For the picture that he presented in society was a of rather coarse little man, who was sometimes mistaken for a successful stockbroker. In conversation he was given to the aggressive monologue, often laying down the law on subjects he knew very little about. Politics had by now ceased to interest him, but religious arguments fascinated him, as they did Tennyson. 'Whatever he had to consider or speak about, he disposed of in the most forthright style,' wrote W. M. Rossetti. 'Every touch told, every nail was hit on the head.' Another friend describes him 'as a strong man armed in the completest defensive armour, but with no aggressiveness.' It is difficult, however, to credit him with a permanent absence of aggression; the writer of *Pacchiarotto* was not a man to suffer fools. It is probable that with the years he grew less and less able to allow his fellow guests a hearing. Asked on one occasion whether he did not object to the adulation with which he was treated he replied in surprise: 'Object to it! No; I've waited forty years for it, and now I like it!' 'He appeared,' says Mrs. Orr, 'more widely sympathetic in his works than in his life; with no moral selfishness, he was intellectually self-centred.' Defensive armour

is perhaps the most revealing analogy of all. Never to the end of his days was Browning at his ease with his fellow men; always he felt that either by their criticism or their prying they were trying to impinge on his privacy. In private conversation and even in correspondence, he was a great deal more approachable. There exist many of his letters in which he painstakingly explains the meaning of a passage to some correspondent perhaps unknown to him. The stalwarts of the Browning society he treated with ceremonious politeness, which its founder Dr. Furnivall seems to have presumed on. It is seldom perhaps that a scholar has the opportunity of setting an author an examination paper in his own works, and Furnivall certainly took advantage of this privileged situation. Another, even less disinterested, scholar, T. J. Wise, also fastened himself upon Browning with a view to his own profit. Some of his questions in respect to the first publication of such rarities as *Pauline* he was later able to turn to his own dishonest profit. For, some years before his death it was discovered that this assiduous scholar and collector had himself called into existence several 'early' printings of works by the Victorian great. But if the attention of Wise and Furnivall was somewhat self-interested, and if the Browning Society itself was something of an embarrassment, though perhaps an aid to the sale of his books, Browning's friendship with Edmund Gosse had no disadvantageous aspect. It was to Gosse that he handed over the embarrassing box containing the poems and papers of the unfortunate poet T. L. Beddoes, an unwanted legacy, which he had kept for ten years, as Robert Bridges afterwards kept Gerard Manley Hopkins' poems, in doubt as to what he should do with them; and to him he would talk about his own early life and the people he had met. But there is an

occasion recorded by Gosse when Browning launched into a far more exciting topic 'passing from languid and rather ineffectual discussion of some persons well known to us both into vivid and passionate apology for an act of his own Colombe of Ravenstein. It was the flash from conventionality to truth, from talk about people whom he hardly seemed to see to a record of a soul that he had formed and could follow through all the mazes of caprice. It was seldom, even in intimacy I think, that he would talk thus liberally about his sons and daughters of the pen, but that was mainly from a sensible reticence and hatred of common vanity. But when he could be induced to discuss his creations, it was easy to see how vividly the whole throng of them was moving in the hollow of his mind. It is doubtful whether he ever totally forgot any one of the vast assemblage of his characters.' One is reminded of Browning's favourite novelist Balzac, whose characters were more real to him than the men and women he knew.

Gosse had won the old poet's confidence. Usually in society he refused to read his poems or to discuss them. Often he pretended entirely to have forgotten what he had once written. Once indeed he claimed not to have looked at a line of *The Ring and the Book* after it was published. Henry James saw him as a divided personality. The one side which Gosse records, the poet, 'sat at home and knew, as well he might, in what quarter of *that* sphere to look for suitable company.' But the man of the world 'walked abroad, showed himself, talked right resonantly, abounded, multiplied his connections, did his duty.' 'Tennyson,' said some lady, 'hides himself behind his laurels, Browning behind the man of the world.'

In the autumn of 1878, after seventeen years' absence,

the poet went back to Italy, treading once more the streets of Asolo which he had not seen since his earliest visit of all; and from Pippa's town he moved to Venice, where he now stayed each autumn for three years. In England recognition gathered weight. In 1882, Oxford gave him the honorary degree of D.C.L. in celebration of his seventieth birthday, and Edinburgh an LL.D. in 1884. As an outcome of the Browning Society's activities, which in his capacity of a 'new Browningite' he continued to watch with some misgivings—he is said to have asked Gosse not to join it—his old friend Mrs. Sutherland Orr was commissioned to compile her *Handbook to Robert Browning's Works*, a careful piece of exposition, which he characterized in the last year of his life as 'the best of helps for anyone in need of such when reading —or about to read my works. It is done far better than I could hope to do it myself.' It was indeed extremely well done, though not without considerable assistance from Browning himself. Mrs. Orr's interpretations are generally reliable except when she is dealing with Browning's religious beliefs. Here her own theism causes her to underrate his fundamental Christianity. Her *Handbook*, however, which passed through three editions between 1885 and the poet's death, and her biography which appeared in 1891, together with the Browning Society's activities, put the seal on Browning's reputation as poet and philosopher. Whether he subscribed to the legend of himself as philosopher is not clear. Certainly, however, he never disowned it.

Chapter Seven

LAST PARLEYINGS OF A SOLITARY MAN

H AD Browning died at seventy-one, it would have
been concluded no doubt that in the last years of
his life his inspiration had waned, that his subtlety and
mature insight had left him, and that mere technical
ingenuity had survived. His last three volumes, however,
Ferishtah's Fancies of 1884, *Parleyings with Certain People
of Importance in Their Day* of 1887 and *Asolando*, which
was published on the day of his death in 1889, testify
alike to a recovery of his powers and a new deepening
of his experience towards the last. For, confronted with
the shadow of death, he began to take stock of his knowledge and belief, at first with some intellectual delibera-
tion, but latterly in a more emotional way, by calling up
the scenes and feelings of his youth. But *Ferishtah's
Fancies* might seem to have been undertaken as a conscious
counterpart to Goethe's *Westöstlicher Diwan*. The oriental
convention is the same, and here, for the first time
Browning elected to speak as through a mask, to distil
an objective truth for a public which had begun to
look to him, as had the sage of Weimar's public in his old
age, for a philosophical statement. Not only is the
attitude Goethe's but the somewhat elliptical lyrics set
between the more discursive parables also bear traces of
the German master's influence, though less direct
traces than did Browning's deliberate borrowings from

the second *Faust* in his 'Pisgah Sights'. For his Persian
stories he reverted to his familiar blank verse, a medium
whose beat seemed to have weakened a little with time.
Yet there are moments when his rather colourless,
imageless narration suddenly pulses at the old pace.
'Why, hate!' he demands in his 'Pillar at Sebzevar,' a
poem that rates love above the pursuit of knowledge,

> If out of sand comes sand and nought but sand
> Affect not to be quaffing at mirage,
> Nor nickname pain as pleasure. That, belike,
> Constitutes just the trial of thy wit
> And worthiness to gain promotion,—hence,
> Proves the true purpose of thine actual life.
> Thy soul's environment of things perceived,
> Things visible and things invisible,
> Fact, fancy—all was purposed to evolve
> This and this only—was thy wit of worth
> To recognize the drop's use, love the same
> And loyally declare against mirage
> Though all the world asseverated dust
> Was good to drink?

The message that Browning proclaims in *Ferishtah's
Fancies* is something more than a declaration against
belief in mirages. Deliberately he seems to be limiting
his claims, husbanding that minimum of his spiritual
resources in which he could ultimately count. There is
no affirmation as far-reaching as that of 'Easter Day,' none
as positive in its exposition as 'A Death in the Desert.'
The best single poem in the book 'A Bean Stripe; also,
Apple-eating,' limits itself to recommending a with-
holding of judgment, to a stressing of man's ignorance.
No experience is purely black or white. Our very scheme
of goodness is a fiction. But it is a fiction created by God
within the human mind, and of God all we can know for

certain is that He is working there for truth with a force as impersonal as gravity, a force which proclaims itself in the works of great men and in the glory of the stars. The sense within us that we owe a debt does not vouch for the existence of someone ready to take his due. 'See,' he begins in a phrase that was later to find an echo in one of G. M. Hopkins' sonnets,

> See! stars are out—
> Stars which, unconscious of thy gaze beneath,
> Go glorying, and glorify thee too
> —Those Seven Thrones, Zurah's beauty, weird Parwin!
> Whether shall love and praise to stars be paid
> Or—say—some Mubid who, for good to thee
> Blind at thy birth, by magic all his own
> Opened thine eyes, and gave the sightless sight,
> Let the stars' glory enter?

Praise is due not to the glory of the firmament but to the unseen image who gave man the gift of sight. The poem ends with a homely comparison:

> Him
> I thank—but for whose work, the orchard's wealth
> Might prove so many gall-nuts—stocks or stones
> For aught that I should think, or know, or care.

The subject of the interspersed lyrics is human love; each of them is connected thematically with the parable it follows, and each recalls the poet's own experience in the past. For here he abandons his tales of imaginary lovers and speaks of what he has known, reverting in the lyric that follows 'A Pillar at Sebzevar' to the motive of silent adoration, pleading in another for leave to love with his whole being, body as well as soul, and speaking in a third of love as the sure guide through the recesses of another's heart:

You groped your way across my room i' the dear dark
    dead of night;
At each fresh step a stumble was: but, once your lamp
    alight,
Easy and plain you walked again: so soon all wrong grew
    right!

The themes of love recollected and faith reduced to
its very skeleton alternate rather than interlock in the
course of the book. But in the 'Epilogue' they are brought
together in the form of a question he had never framed
before, a question whose relationship to the more discursive searchings of *Christmas Eve and Easter Day* is
demonstrated by the appearance of a familiar simile.
For the intimations he receives of some divine purpose
working in man recall to him that image of the moon
emerging from clouds that had marked his moments of
vision in those early poems.

Only, when I do hear, sudden circle round me
    —Much as when the moon's might frees a space from
    cloud—
Iridescent splendours: gloom—would else confound me—
    Barriered off and banished far—bright-edged the black-
    est shroud! . . .

Then the cloud-rift broadens, spanning earth that's under,
    Wide our world displays its worth, man's strife and
    strife's success:
All the good and beauty, wonder crowning wonder,
    Till my heart and soul applaud perfection, nothing less.

But now, in his old age, he wonders whether even this
apparent certainty is not a subjective experience, born
of his own love rather than vouched for by any external
reality.

Only, at heart's utmost joy and triumph, terror
  Sudden turns the blood to ice: a chill wind disencharms
All the late enchantment! What if all be error—
  If the halo irised round my head were, Love, thine
    arms?

But, it seems, the doubt is immediately assuaged. Even
if the love he had known were the poet's only evidence
of the divine purpose it would be enough. Such is the
sense of his 'Epilogue's' concluding verse. Yet there is
something unsatisfactory about its last line. The tension
rises through the first three lines, the two dull 'ud'
sounds of 'sudden' and 'blood', followed by the falling
away of short 'i' sounds in 'chill,' 'wind' and 'disencharms,' and the repetition of sound from a rising to a
falling rhythm in 'disencharms' and 'enchantment,'
prepare for the shrill and despairing 'What if all be
error?' which finds no answer in the muffled and plethoric
last line. This 'Epilogue' is, I think, the record of a most
profound questioning that did not find an immediate
answer.

Parleyings with certain People of Importance in their Day
was dedicated to the memory of yet another of Browning's lifelong friends, his French critic Milsand, who had
died in the year before its publication. In the year
before that, Alfred Domett, Browning's oldest friend of
all, had passed away. In October 1877 Pen, whose
painting had not won him patrons, and who now at the
age of thirty-eight was still dependent upon his father,
married a wealthy American heiress. Browning's letter
to his son congratulating him on his engagement testifies
to his continued preoccupation with the feckless
fellow's fortunes.

'You are just at the time of life when you may "take a
fresh departure" with the greatest advantage. You can

bring all your acquired Continental knowledge to bear on an English enterprise: take a house and studio here, and try what may be done when your work may have the chances which you never yet enjoyed—of being seen, as you produce them, in your own studio, with the advantage of acquaintance with all the artists you care to know. Miss C. (Fanny Codrington, his fiancée) has spoken to me with the greatest frankness and generosity of the means she will have of contributing to your support— for my part, I can engage to give you £300 a year . . .'

But despite the poet's businesslike provision his son did not make his name as a painter. Miss Codrington's fortune and the royalties from his father's books were to prove sufficient to keep him in elegant and amateurish idleness. Perhaps too much had been asked of him as a child; he seems to have had no talents except a capacity for being unabashed by his own failure.

A month or two before the wedding Browning moved from his house overlooking the Regent's Canal to a larger one in De Vere Gardens. His books sold steadily and, with Pen settled, his obligations were small. A year or two before, he had endeavoured to buy a decrepit Venetian palace, in order that Pen should have 'sunshine and beauty about him, and every help to profit by them.' The old poet was growing exceedingly fond of Venice. There and in St. Moritz and in the Savoy Alps he and his sister spent their summers and autumns. Not till the last did his health seem to be failing; a hale old man, though subject to increasingly heavy colds, he replaced his old friends with new acquaintances; his visitors book read like a page from the *Almanach de Gotha*. Yet among the noble names were still those of the great writers of his time, and of the little personal following of almost professional Browning lovers.

It was his loneliness in the midst of so much distinguished company that the poet turned back to speak with some of his very earliest friends, the men whom he had first met in the books of his father's library. He had a phenomenal memory. Edmund Gosse indeed instances the picturesque account he gave towards the end of his life of a headache he had suffered from at the age of twenty-one. Gosse uses the anecdote as testimony to Browning's phenomenal freedom from illness. But set beside his *Parleyings* and his autobiographical 'Development' in his last volume of all, it tells of an increasing preoccupation in old age with the task of calling up the past. The *Parleyings* are, as was remarked in the second chapter of this study, his *Dichtung und Wahrheit*, a stock-taking as careful as that which had reduced his burden of belief to the minimum in *Ferishtah's Fancies* and its 'Epilogue.' But along with a close examination of the past went an amazing clarity. The people with whom the poet parleys are shadows; only their arguments remain. But in discussion with these, his dead masters of the past, Browning stumbled upon new discoveries, and on one especially that was to be rediscovered independently and much exploited by the psychological theorists of our own century. For in his parleying with the Walloon art historian Gerard de Lairesse, Browning elaborated the thought that mythology, which had once presented the old outward panorama of gods and immortals, had now become inward and psychological:

> If we no longer see as you of old,
> 'Tis we see deeper . . .

he informed his long dead master, in terms that seem to prophesy the subjective interpretations of the old tales that are a principal theme in Rilke's poetry, and that

have lately been vulgarized on the French commercial stage. Lairesse, in his day, could not refrain from using them as a mere embellishment, an error which Browning condoned even as he pointed it out. 'Make it plain to me,' he demanded, 'why you

> poured rich life
> On what were else a dead ground—nothingness—
> Until the solitary world grew rife
> With Joves and Junos, nymphs and satyrs. Yes,
> The reason was, fancy composed the strife
> 'Twixt sense and soul: for sense, my De Lairesse,
> Cannot content itself with outward things,
> Mere beauty: soul must needs know whence there
>   springs—
> How, when and why—what sense but loves, nor lists
> To know at all.

De Lairesse's practice was right in his century. But now the poet's visions are capable of no such pallid embodiments. They are no longer concerned with calling up the past, but with hope for the future.

The *Parleyings* contain other thoughts that extend past the discoveries of Browning's maturity. But the territory into which he was now moving was one that he was never completely to master. There are of course also repetitions, perhaps rather more concise and objective, of early motives: a return, for example, to the theme of *Fifine* in the 'Parleyings with Daniel Bartoli.' Here the widowed de Lassay, failing to remember the wife he had lost,

> took again, for better or for worse,
> The old way in the world, and, much the same
> Man o' the outside, fairly played life's game . . .

while the duke, who had renounced this same woman that had become de Lassay's wife, is haunted by a spectre

of another sort, a more resplendent and less wayward Fifine, whose connection with Lady Ashburton is less carefully concealed than was that of his gipsy temptress, half woman, half girl. The quotation opens with that familiar image which is always a sign of a heightened subjectivity in Browning's thought:

> The duke reviewed his memories, and aghast
> Found that the Present intercepts the Past
> With such effect as when a cloud enwraps
> The moon and, moon-suffused, plays moon perhaps
> To who walks under, till comes, late or soon,
> A stumble: up he looks, and lo, the moon
> Calm, clear, convincingly herself once more!
> How could he 'scape the cloud that thrust between
> Him and effulgence? Speak, fool—duke, I mean!

And the duke speaks:

> Who bade you come, brisk-marching bold she-shape,
>   A terror with those black-balled worlds of eyes,
> That black hair bristling solid-built from nape
>   To crown it coils about? O dread surmise!
> Take, tread on, trample under past escape
>   Your capture, spoil and trophy! Do—devise
> Insults for one who, fallen once, ne'er shall rise!

Suddenly the emotional tension of the poem is as strong as that of 'Childe Roland'. For while intending to call up the harmless ghost of Daniel Bartoli from the day of his childhood, Browning had summoned instead the very incarnation of the world's sway, a figure who could obscure the moon of his own memories, and bring with her something of the chill terror that he had not been able to dismiss by the halting reassurance of the last line of his *Ferishtah* 'Epilogue'—whose weakness, significantly enough, is repeated in the defective last line of the

M

quotation. Perhaps occasionally now Browning's ear was beginning to fail him. But there is a surprising strength of feeling that arises again and again in the *Parleyings*; in the attack on Disraeli in 'George Bubb Dodington,' and in the magnificent and moving land-scapes in 'Gerard de Lairesse,' the eighth and ninth sections of which, with their picture of the storm and the clear morning that follows, have an effect comparable to Beethoven's in his *Pastoral Symphony*. There is indeed a quality about this description that Browning had hardly bettered since the time of *Sordello*:

> But morning's laugh sets all the crags alight
> Above the baffled tempest: tree and tree
> Stir themselves from the stupor of the night,
> And every strangled branch resumes its right
> To breathe, shakes loose dark's clinging dregs, waves
>   free
> In dripping glory. Prone the runnels plunge,
> While earth, distent with moisture like a sponge,
> Smokes up, and leaves each plant its gem to see,
> Each grass-blade's glory-glitter. Had I known
> The torrent now turned river?—masterful
> Making its rush o'er tumbled ravage—stone
> And stub which barred the froths and foams: no
>   bull
> Ever broke bounds in formidable sport
> More overwhelmingly, till lo, the spasm
> Sets him to dare that last mad leap: report
> Who may—his fortunes in the deathly chasm
> That swallows him in silence!

The *Parleyings* contain many passages of this packed alliterative texture. It is as if Browning has at last solved the technical problems that had obscured so many of his lines till now. The verse is compact, yet the mean-ing is clear. But the poems as a whole do not live up to

their surprising best. Nowhere, perhaps, is the argument so tiresomely involved as that of *Prince Hohenstiel-Schwangau*, yet there is a great deal more discursive reasoning than the emotional passages can atone for. None of the poems is an organic whole. For the personages do not come to life, and it is only a framework of human character that can hold a dramatic monologue together. But in parleying with his ghosts Browning evoked old feelings in strange new strength. No longer did he require reassurances; the object of his demands was no 'fresh knowledge' nor

> Fuller truth yet, new gainings from the grave.
> Here we alive must needs deal fairly, turn
> To what account Man may Man's portion, learn
> Man's proper play with truth in part, before
> Entrusted with the whole . . .

Now that death was near, he was confident that more truth would be revealed to him beyond the grave. In his *Parleyings* he seems to be preparing his baggage for the journey, cutting himself down to the minimum of belief and knowledge in order to travel light. At the same time he no longer found it needful to turn his eyes away from any memories; the shadowy, sexless temptress Fifine yielded to the 'bold she-shape' in 'Daniel Bartoli'; and the country took on the vivid colours of a landscape seen for the last time in 'Gerard de Lairesse.' Moreover, his verbal mastery had returned to him now, though but fitfully; only the poet's sense of character had not revived.

Asolando, Browning's last volume of poems, contains little on a level with the best of the *Parleyings* except his final 'Epilogue.' The world was now empty: all that remained was a speculative hope of the renewed presence, beyond death, of Elizabeth Browning. There

is humour in one or two poems and certainly some
strength still in the ironic 'Imperante Augusto Natus
est—,' a poem which treats once more the theme of
'Cleon,' of the classical world's ignorance of the miracle
that was taking place in its midst. But at the last the
poet's vein was retrospective; he looked back on the
intimations he had received, not like Wordsworth in his
childhood, but in his maturity:

> And now? The lambent flame is—where?
>   Lost from the naked world: earth, sky,
> Hill, vale, tree, flower,—Italia's rare
>   O'er-running beauty crowds the eye—
> But flame? The Bush is bare.

Nevertheless, in his 'Epilogue,' despite its halting
rhythms, there is a sense of courage and achievement.
Here perhaps he overstates his case. But he knew that
he had no cause to ask for pity, that he had lived his life
richly and at the end borne his solitariness with dignity
and in hope. But more perfect than his 'Epilogue,' and
more suitable as a final quotation, are the last verses of
'Prospice,' a poem on the same theme of death, which
had appeared in his *Dramatis Personae* twenty-five years
before:

> For sudden the worst turns the best to the brave,
>   The black minute's at end,
> And the elements' rage, the fiend-voices that rave,
>   Shall dwindle, shall blend,
> Shall change, shall become first a peace out of pain,
>   Then a light, then thy breast,
> O thou soul of my soul! I shall clasp thee again,
>   And with God be the rest!

When the time came for leaving England in 1889, his
seventy-eighth year, the poet was more reluctant than

usual to set out. His health was now failing, and he thought that Scotland might be a more suitable place than Italy for spending the summer. But his son was established in Venice and a friend had invited him to stay at Asolo, Pippa's Asolo, which gave its name to his last volume. Here he was happy among his memories, playing on an old spinet, writing to the last and reading aloud from Shakespeare, Shelley, or his own *Ring and the Book*. He no longer talked of serious matters, but gossiped with his hostess and the sculptor Story, who had been his friend for forty years. So charmed was he with the place that he entered into negotiations to purchase a site in the town on which to build himself a house. As winter drew on, however, he left for Venice to join his son and daughter-in-law, and there he caught a bronchial cold and, as he was recovering from it, died of heart failure. On that day *Asolando* was published in London, and on the last day of the year the poet's body was buried in Westminster Abbey.

Chapter Eight

THE UNACKNOWLEDGED MASTER

'I NEVER designedly tried to puzzle people, as some of my critics have supposed,' wrote the poet to W. G. Kingsland, the future author of *Robert Browning: Chief Poet of the Age*, at a time when he was writing *The Ring and the Book*. 'On the other hand I never pretended to offer such literature as should be substitute for a cigar, or a game of dominoes to an idle man. So perhaps on the whole I get my deserts and something over . . .' The early controversies about Browning's poetry centred on its obscurities. Landor, Tennyson, his old friend Arnould, were all puzzled by the congested nature of his line, the causes for which were clearly explained by Swinburne when he observed: 'He never thinks but at full speed; and the rate of his thought is to that of another man's as the speed of a railway to that of a waggon, or the speed of a telegraph to that of a railway.' It was of a piece with his volubility in company, his excitable gestures, his occasional fits of anger. Much of his writing was hasty, many lines still seem needlessly elliptical. But the obscurity of Browning's verse was a lesser problem to succeeding generations than to men of his own time, whom he answered most cogently in a letter to Ruskin dealing with that critic's strictures on *Men and Women*.

'We don't read poetry the same way, by the same law; it is too clear. I cannot begin writing poetry till

my imaginary reader has conceded licenses to me which you demur at altogether. I *know* that I don't make out my conception by my language: all poetry being a putting the infinite within the finite. You would have me paint it all plain out, which can't be; but by various artifices I try to make shift with touches and bits of outlines which *succeed* if they bear the conception from me to you. You ought, I think, to keep pace with the thought tripping from ledge to ledge of my "glaciers", as you call them; not stand poking your alpenstock into the holes, and demonstrating that no foot could have stood there;— suppose it sprang over there? In *prose* you may criticize so—because that is the absolute representation of portions of truth, what chronicling is to history—but in asking for more *ultimates* you must accept less *mediates* . . .'

But many of Browning's critics were far less consequent in their objections than Ruskin, some of them indeed hugging the lowest levels of misunderstanding, and others raising Ruskin's objections in cruder form. One compared the verse of *Strafford* to the staccato speech of Mr. Jingle; another, also turning to Dickens for his analogy, considered Browning to have adopted 'the random style of address of Mrs. Nickleby.' The prize for irrelevant incomprehension, however, should go to the critic of *Fraser's Magazine* whose viewpoint was as perverse as it is now entertaining: 'There are fine ballads,' he says, 'healthy and English, clear of that Italian-esque pedantry, that *crambe repetita* of olives and lizards, artists and monks, with which the English public, for its sins, has been spoon-fed for the last half-century, ever since Childe Harold in a luckless hour thought a warmer climate might make him a better man . . .'

But *Christmas Eve and Easter Day* stimulated miscon-

ceptions which were much more lasting than a critic's
mere objections to that 'indescribable savour of the
Continent,' which *Fraser's* man found in the early
lyrics. These two poems of 1850 founded the awkward
legend of Browning's message, of certain theological
lessons which could be learnt from his poetry. But the
exact nature of his message was far from clear, and discussion of his beliefs very often blinded his readers to
the virtues of his poetry. Was he or was he not a
Christian? The evidence was conflicting. On the one
side he was a very irregular church-goer, attending the
French reformed service with Milsand in Normandy or
the Waldensian chapel in Venice, but seldom visiting any
place of worship in London; and for additional proof of
his apparent unbelief there was his thunderous 'No,' to
Robert Buchanan's categorical question: 'Are you a
Christian?' On the other side there was a letter written
to an unknown correspondent in 1876, who imagined
herself to be dying, and in this there seems to be a fundamental affirmation of Christian faith. But Browning was
clearly an eclectic, accepting some Christian doctrines,
passionately hostile to such ideas as eternal punishment
beyond the grave, which he, nevertheless, envisaged in
The Inn Album. Again, did Browning or did he not accept
the Darwinian theory? To this he gave his own positive
answer; that so much as seemed proved in it he had himself stated, before Darwin, in *Paracelsus*; that in *Luria* he
had postulated 'an everlasting moment of creation, if one
at all—past, present and future one and the same state'—
but that he did not consider what he thought to be
Darwin's case as to changes in organization, brought
about by desire and will in the creature, proved.

Nevertheless, whether Browning stated his beliefs or
left them in doubt, they puzzled and fascinated the

generation of the nineties. Fortunately, however, his puzzling message was not the only quality for which he was read. Perhaps indeed he has never been so well loved as in the decade that followed his death. For the nineties appreciated his vigour, his sense of character and that picturesqueness which his early contemporaries had dismissed as a mere 'savour of the Continent.' All that they failed to detect was the depth of experience that underlay these several surface virtues. However, among critics of that time, Arthur Symons rated Browning second to Shakespeare alone; Walter Pater, who might have been expected to dislike the roughness of the poet's texture, spoke of 'his power of putting a happy world of his own creation in place of the meaner world of common days;' and Wilde did not disagree.

But underlying this vein of true appreciation persisted the stubborn belief that Browning was a philosophical poet, and it is this belief that turned the tide against him early in the second decade of the new century. The blame for this rests largely with the pundits of the then defunct Browning Society. For though many eminent men—Walter Raleigh, Symons, W. M. Rossetti, James Thomson, and Bernard Shaw—belonged to and addressed it, there remained a small and solid core of Browningites who considered themselves the poet's only legitimate expositors; and the Society was bent on expounding the poet's message of faith, even if that entailed the reduction of his poetic statements to plain prose meanings. Chief among the official Browningites was Mrs. Sutherland Orr, the only one who had been on terms of close friendship with the poet himself, and who had been so helped by him in the compiling of the *Handbook* that he would, in later life, refer a questioner to that book rather than attempt to answer him afresh from his own memory.

But this high priestess was herself a theist and, in many of her expositions of the poems, had subtly and no doubt unconsciously contributed to a false picture of a consistently theistic Robert Browning, a figure who failed to attract the next generation of readers. But though Mrs. Orr's unwitting misrepresentations did something to damage her master's reputation, F. J. Nettleship, in many ways a more senstive interpreter, did far more mischief. 'For us today then,' he would demand, 'what is the lesson that the poet would teach?' It was he, more than anyone, who elevated Browning into a prophet. But for all his search for ready-made morals, and calendar tag applications, Nettleship was not so wrong-headed as he seemed. He may have misrepresented Browning but at least he realized that there were deeper meanings to be found in the poetry than critics had yet discovered. Unfortunately he had a disconcerting way of reading into a given poem what theoretically should have been there; it was mistaken of him, no doubt, to go to *Fifine at the Fair* in hopes of a lesson in conduct, and even more mistaken of him to deny Fifine's attraction for Browning, and to dismiss as sophistry those parts of the poem which bore firm evidence to the contrary. But at least Nettleship was in pursuit of psychological significances that existed and could be found. He refused, for instance to accept 'Childe Roland' as a mere fantasy. Furnivall had asked the poet on three separate occasions whether there was any hidden or underlying meaning in 'Childe Roland' and three times received a denial. But Nettleship did not accept Browning's answer, and wrote a paper for the Society in which he not very successfully explored the poem for concealed significances. What is more, anticipating the psychological critics of the next century, he justified himself by quoting George Eliot to the

effect that 'the words of genius bear a wider meaning than the thought which prompted them.' Browning read his article and remarked with a laugh that he supposed the meaning Nettleship found was there in the poem, though he had not known it when he wrote it. The joke seemed to be against the Browning Society pundit, whose interpretations were necessarily wild, being based rather on intellectual than psychological reasoning. But at least Nettleship's persistent search for underlying meanings was more fruitful than the succeeding generation's assumption that the poems were objective creations, and that Browning's characters, though sometimes voicing his own opinions, could not be made to give evidence concerning his true personality, attitudes or interests. Browning had himself made an inconclusive statement on this point long ago in his letter to Ruskin from which quotation has already been made. 'You may be right,' he said, 'however unwitting I am of the fact. I *may* put Robert Browning into Pippa and other men and maids. If so *peccavi*; but I don't see myself in them at all events.' Nor have his twentieth-century readers; and this blindness is one of the root causes of his contemporary neglect. For during the last forty years, at least, there has been an increasing tendency to measure the value of poetry by the intensity of the involuntary psychological confessions that can be read into it. But the statements which could be extracted from Browning's poetry were not those for which critics influenced by psycho-analysis were looking. They tended therefore to view the poet as one who consistently avoided topics that might give him away. Gerard Manley Hopkins gave weight to this accusation in a letter to Dixon, published for the first time in the thirties, in which he spoke of Browning's 'frigidities.' But Hopkins'

objections were based, for the most part, on a very special set of prejudices. He criticized particular images, as Eliot later criticized Shelley's, and found them blurred. How many natural descriptions, however, he might have noticed that are as firm in outline as his own! But what chiefly exasperated him was 'Browning's way of talking (and making his people talk) with the air and spirit of a man bouncing up from table with his mouth full of bread and cheese and saying that he meant no nonsense.' This Chestertonian vice he found, quite inexplicably, at its most intense in 'The Flight of the Duchess.' But this is a mere surface objection, not founded on a consideration of Browning's work as a whole; it could not possibly be made to apply to *The Ring and the Book*. It is, I think, no more than a mere casual cover for a much more fundamental distaste for Browning's protestantism, for his steadfast attempts to see reality not through the eyes of a Church or a tradition, but through those of a man alone, self-reliant yet conscious of a single man's limitations. Browning, moreover, mixes intellect and emotion in a very different way from Hopkins or his master Donne—whom, incidentally, he greatly admired long before his poems were generally read. To Browning the essential experience was emotional, and only its exposition intellectual; Donne and Hopkins, on the other hand, to quote T. S. Eliot's words, felt their thought as immediately as the odour of a rose. This distinction between the intellectual and the reflective poet is, however, a psychological one only, with no importance in the field of values. Hopkins' intolerance of his elder contemporary was based on no serious attempt at value judgment. It was the prejudice of a man of different faith and different attitudes, and a prejudice that he could not always sustain. 'The Brownings are very fine too,' he admitted

once, 'in their ghastly way.' It was a reluctant and half-hearted confession, but no more than was due to the author of *Pacchiarotto*, who in light-hearted mood had prepared the way for Hopkins' own masterly word combinations—for such neologisms as trambeam, rook-racked, arch-especial. Little as Hopkins liked Browning's beliefs—which he condemned as Broad Church —or his reflective attitudes, he had considerable respect for his technique.

But the 'intellectual' line of attack did not develop until Browning's reputation had already slumped. Hopkins' letters were not published till the nineteen-thirties. The real enemy to his reputation was the totally false legend that his characters had very little to do with the poet himself; that they were so many voices invented for the purpose of stating some particular point of view. This 'parnassian Browning, a multiple impersonator, a master of realistic detail and didacticism' seems to Sir Maurice Bowra a sort of sententious grave-digger at the funeral of the last Romantics; better Rossetti with his laudanum and his flowing cloak than that well-dressed dapper old gentleman with a sound taste in Rhine wines. For Professor Tillyard, a representative critic, perhaps, of the other University, Browning is capable of expressing the small social and moral commonplaces, the more quotidian of the human passions, but lacks that obliquity of approach, that knack of saying several things at once, without which, according to the Cambridge school, nothing profound can be expressed.

But alongside accusations of parnassian dullness and petty realism, there run even graver charges of psychological falsity. F. L. Lucas, the chief prosecutor in this court, clearly enjoys certain of Browning's lyrics, but he

is repelled by what he considers the poet's optimistic
misconceptions concerning the world. For Mr. Lucas
likes his poetry to be melancholy and stoical, and more
than suspects those of the Victorian poets who could see
any hope beyond the grave. Browning, for him, is an
insensitive and pompous man who after one burst of
romance, out of which he made his best poetry, 'settled
again into that even tenour' in which he persisted to the
end. Mr. Lucas compares him indeed to his own Bishop
who ordered his tomb in St. Praxed's church, alleging
that they had a great deal in common, both of them being
mighty appreciative of the things of this world. If only
Browning had been content, this most entertaining critic
implies, to rejoice like that half-pagan creature of his
imagination, to enjoy things as he found them, to write
love lyrics and describe the picturesque aspects of the
Italian Renaissance without pointing a moral, how much
better a poet he would have been. But since, for Browning, love was not merely a series of bitter-sweet trans-
ports but an experience carrying with it intimations of
something even higher, and since Renaissance Italy was
at best a background against which he set dramas of the
human mind transcending any historical period; since
the poet was more concerned with Pompilia and Caponsacchi and the Pope than with one half-Rome or the
other, Mr. Lucas was in effect asking Browning to limit
his talents and his insights to his secondary material, a
field of which he had been complete master before he
had any emotional experience at all, before he so much
as met Elizabeth. For the book that this unorthodox
Cambridge critic singles out for his highest praise is the
Dramatic Romances of 1845. Mr. Lucas' attitude to the
mature Robert Browning is that of the poet's own
dispassionately acid *tertium quid*, reporting to his

Excellency the exaggerated and vulgar behaviour of certain people who are in fact living with an intensity of which he is completely unaware. 'Browning,' says Lucas in criticizing the last 'Epilogue', 'calls the theatre of the world to take note how a Browning can live and die.' But of all Victorian poets Browning was most sparing of the first person singular; he put it behind him after *Pauline* and very seldom used it again. When he did it was because the experience he had to describe was one that he knew to be shared by his fellows.

A younger generation view Browning with yet another variety of distaste. John Heath Stubbs in his *Darkling Plain*, a book which follows the fortunes of Romanticism after the death of Byron, Shelley and Keats, gives his reasons for attempting to omit all notice of either Browning or Tennyson. In fact they bob up repeatedly in his book, like unwanted guests at a garden party. Browning, according to him, rendered poetry palatable to the earnest Puritan intellectuals of his day. But his only surviving merit for this most destructive critic is that despite his preoccupation with half-digested thought he possessed a fancy less restricted and more vigorous than Tennyson's, and therein bore a distant affinity to Beddoes. Heath Stubbs singles out 'Childe Roland' as 'a pure exercise in the horrible,' a category of thought which he considers less poetic than 'the terrible,' since it dwells not on moral evil but on sheer physical pain. The imagery of such a poem, in Heath Stubbs' opinion, contradicts the intellectual creed of courage and optimism which was the outward face that Browning turned to the world. He is, in fact, repeating in his own way Lucas' accusation of falsity. For he approaches poetry from a psycho-analytical point of view that presupposes inspiration to arise from the same

'unconscious' level as dreams: a misconception which confuses the two very distant human activities, the one purely mechanical, the other the product of some profounder intimations from a source outside man's common thoughts and feelings, the record of some emotional flash of comprehension that lights for him a universe outside that of his own fears and guilt. Heath Stubbs says that in 'An Epistle of Karshish', 'A Death in the Desert,' 'Caliban upon Setebos' neither intuitive faith nor honest doubt speaks clearly. But that is to judge Browning from a preconceived point of view, to which only the statements of Clough and Christina Rossetti seem valid. In fact there is at man's ordinary level of insight no constant mood of either faith or doubt. There are certain experiences that may serve to strengthen the one, certain aridities that make for the other. It is of these varying levels of certainty and illusion that Browning speaks through his various characters. Pompilia's sleepwalking certainty of right and wrong, the Pope's sudden emotional understanding at the end of a life of intellectual comprehension, and Caponsacchi's despairing cry, are three lightning flashes in a world where one half-Rome slanders and the other half indistinctly senses that something strange is taking place. But the vast panorama of *The Ring and the Book* required a degree of intellectual organization beyond the capacities of any of the later Romantic poets whom Heath Stubbs praises. Far from Browning's merits being, in Heath Stubbs' words, not strictly poetic, they are poetic on a far greater scale than those of Beddoes, Patmore, Christina Rossetti or Hopkins, all of whom certainly spoke with intensity but out of a more circumscribed field of experience.

Somewhat deeper in her incomprehension because

more muddled in her thinking is the advocate of 'subjective universality,' Miss Kathleen Raine, whose ideal visionary poet must 'participate in the unconscious and half-conscious imaginings of the community.' Certainly as a deep level mass-observer Browning is no more successful than as the poet of 'the terrible' which Heath Stubbs would wish him to be. For Miss Raine he is, however, 'a major poet, but a poet only in the lowest sense in which it is possible to use the word at all.' But it is difficult to attach any precise significance to a statement that really says no more than that she does not like Browning, yet is not prepared to say that he is negligible. It serves however as additional proof that contemporary critics are prone to approach Browning with preconceptions concerning the nature of poetry that make it impossible for them to accept him for what he is.

But there is a further obstacle to the appreciation of Browning that looms even larger at the present day than the objection of the psychological critics, and that is the backwash of imagist theory that still informs much poetic criticism. We have come to look too closely at the strength, originality and evocative power of the single poetic image, and to read our poetry, if not phrase by phrase, at least line by line, blind to the importance of large scale poetic organization. Browning, however, like Shakespeare and Milton, built his poems massively. Often, as Sir Maurice Bowra has pointed out, he is careless of individual words; sometimes his ear is defective and his rhythm careless, and like all Victorian poets he finds it hard to solve the problem of poetic diction. His rhythms are spoken rhythms, conceived on a basis of dramatic speech Elizabethan in its influences. His over-compression—Elizabethan too in its way—tends, as Swinburne pointed out, to make his meanings at times

obscure. Never, as a lyricist, is he as certain in his language as a far lesser poet than he, William Barnes. For Barnes in his restricted way solved the problem of poetic vocabulary by returning to an uncontaminated dialect. Put 'Love among the Ruins' beside Barnes 'Fall Time', and you see the advantage of an unworked idiom over one already overrich in associations. Barnes is describing his own Dorset country:

> The rick's a tipp'd an' weather-brown'd,
>   An thatch'd wi' zedge a-dried an' dead;
> An' orcha'd apples, red half round,
>   Have all a-happer'd down, a-shed
> Underneath the tree's wide head.
>   Ladders long,
> Rong by rong, to clim' the tall
> Trees, be hung upon the wall.

The verse, at first sight simple, is elaborately organized with internal rhymes, assonances and half-rhymes. But at least one half of its freshness it owes to the unfamiliarity of its language; 'a-dried an dead,' 'a-shed,' 'be hung' in what Barnes called National English, would seem 'poetical' and trite; and it is just these old forms and inversions that mar Browning's equally well organized and subtly rhymed poem:

> And such plenty and perfection, see, of grass,
>   Never was!
> Such a carpet as, this summer-time, o'erspreads
>   And embeds
> Every vestige of the city, guessed alone,
>   Stock or stone—

Here 'o'erspreads,' legitimate in Dorset dialect, is false in National English, and 'stock or stone' raises an imprecise and literary image that lowers the tension of the verse. Purely as a lyrical poet of mood, Browning is,

as Bowra says, careless in his language. For his idiom is not sufficiently pure for such small-scale purposes.

But Browning's nearest to lyrical perfection, such a poem as 'Love in a Life', contains hardly any of those archaisms and inversions that trouble our contemporary ear.

> Yet the day wears,
> And door succeeds door;
> I try the fresh fortune—
> Range the wide house from the wing to the centre.
> Still the same chance! she goes out as I enter.
> Spend my whole day in the quest,—who cares?
> But 'tis twilight you see,—with such suites to explore,
> Such closets to search, such alcoves to importune!

Yet even here is a slight roughness, no more rasping perhaps than the unexpected jolts that Hardy introduced into his lyrics to remind the reader of fate's asperities, but sufficient to prevent the poem's singing itself, as an Elizabethan lyric does. For unfortunately Browning is never so certain of himself in a light metrical form as in those more loosely constructed poems for which he adapted the double-jointed medium of Hood and Barham. In them his language is more colloquial, his poeticisms appearing, as it might be, between inverted commas. As an example of this mood, which prevails in poems as various in their emotional charge as 'The Pied Piper' and 'The Flight of the Duchess', it is worth quoting a verse from one of the far less well-known 'Garden Fancies.' in which the unfortunate volume of the pedant 'Sibrandus Schafnaburgensis' has just been fished up from a well:

> Here you have it, dry in the sun,
>   With all the binding all of a blister,
> And great blue spots where the ink has run,
>   And reddish streaks that wink and glister

> O'er the page so beautifully yellow:
>   Oh, well have the droppings played their tricks!
> Did he guess how toadstools grow, this fellow?
>   Here's one stuck in his chapter six!
>
> How did he like it when the live creatures
>   Tickled and toused and browsed him all over,
> And worm, slug, eft, with serious features,
>   Came in, each one for his right of trover?
> —When the water beetle with great blind deaf face
>   Made of her eggs the stately deposit,
> And the newt borrowed just so much of the preface
>   As tiled in the top of his black wife's closet?

Here Browning is using a uniform vocabulary in which he can express both his observations and his amused and intellectual comments. It is a verse form which is not capable of filling every purpose, and one reason, perhaps, for the failure of *Fifine at the Fair* was the use in it of such a diction, suitable enough for light-hearted narrative but incapable of carrying any emotional weight:

> So with this wash o' the world, wherein life-long we
>   drift;
> We push and paddle through the foam by making shift
> To breathe above at whiles when, after deepest duck
> Down underneath the show, we put forth hand and
>   pluck
> At what seems somehow like reality—a soul.

The lines convey nothing of the metaphysical discovery they were intended to communicate. Perhaps Browning's reluctance, in that poem, to specify the exact nature of the worldly pulls that tempted him to forget his Elvire, dictated also the would-be almost casual form of the poem. But that side of Browning's talent, so long as it was applied to the writing of poems

within its scope, was more certain in its mastery than was the lyrical side, in descent from Shelley, which too often just fell short of complete mastery.

By far the richest side of Browning's multiform achievement, however, was the verse of his dramatic monologues, of *The Ring and the Book*, *The Inn Album* and the *Parleyings*. This medium is, I repeat, at its loosest and flattest in 'Bishop Blougram' and *Prince Hohenstiel-Schwangau*. For Blougram's lukewarm confession of faith it has a correspondingly plain unemphatic line:

> Well now, there's one great form of Christian faith
> I happened to be born in—which to teach
> Was given me as I grew up, on all hands,
> As best and readiest means of living by;
> The same on examination being proved
> The most pronounced moreover, fixed, precise
> And absolute form of faith in the whole world—
> Accordingly, most potent of all forms
> For working on the world.

The assonances are few and unmarked; the third, fifth and sixth lines slide almost unnoticed from the blank-verse rhythm, and the whole forms an intellectual statement almost devoid of imagery. It is already three-quarters of the way to the completely unobtrusive verse of T. S. Eliot's *Cocktail Party*, to such a passage as that in which Reilly discusses the inevitability of Celia Coplestone's death:

> The only question
> Then was, what sort of death? I could not know
> Because it was for her to choose the way of life
> To lead to death, and, without knowing the end
> Yet choose the form of death.

Eliot's rhythms depart further from those of the five-beat line, and Eliot again would not allow himself the

inversion of Blougram's 'which to teach,' or the ellipsis of his fourth line. But the spoken rhythms of Eliot's play, as indeed much else in modern poetry, owe something to Browning. Ezra Pound indeed, started much under the influence of the 'old mesmerizer' who—thanks to Hood perhaps—had at times half freed himself from the tyranny of poetic diction.

> Cat's i' the water-butt! Thought's in your verse
>   barrel,
> Tell us this thing rather, then we'll believe you,
> You, Master Bob Browning, spite your apparel
> Jump to your sense and give praise as we'd lief do.

Pound's verses are almost a parody, closer in spirit to J. K. Stephens' mocking 'Birthdays' than to genuine Browning. For Pound's attitude to his master was clearly ambivalent. But by way of Pound's influence on Eliot, and Eliot's on Auden, the blood of Browning's verse is still running in contemporary poetry, contributing an hereditary feature here and there, a grotesque twist to Robert Graves, perhaps, and an ingenious rhyme to Edith Sitwell's *Façade*. Recessive rather than dominant, he remains nevertheless an ancestor. But when we compare the quotations from 'Bishop Blougram' to that from *The Cocktail Party* we find one radical dissimilarity. Although innovating, Browning was content, even at his most conversational, to retain in his monologues the mannerisms of the Elizabethan dramatic line; for despite his contemporaneity and colloquialism Blougram is made to speak verse less free than that of 'The Flight of the Duchess'. Nevertheless, Browning's most successful medium is his blank verse line, which Blougram's monologue displays at its flattest level. It is, however, capable of developing a richness of texture to correspond

to the richer thought and greater emotional conviction
inspiring other poems. There is a very great contrast,
indeed, between the unemphatic, imageless argument of
Blougram or the Saviour of Society and the Pope's
language as he gives his interpretation of Guido's plot
against Pompilia:

> 'Tis done:
> Wherefore should mind misgive, heart hesitate?
> He calls to counsel, fashions certain four
> Colourless natures counted clean till now,
> —Rustic simplicity, uncorrupted youth,
> Ignorant virtue! Here's the gold o' the prime
> When Saturn ruled, shall shock our leaden day—
> The clown abash the courtier! Mark it, bards!
> The courtier tries his hand on clownship here,
> Speaks a word, names a crime, appoints a price—
> Just breathes on what, suffused with all himself,
> Is red-hot henceforth past distinction now
> I' the common glow o' hell. And thus they break
> And blaze on us at Rome, Christ's birthnight-eve!

The alliterative division of the first and second complete lines quoted: the three contemptuous dull U
sounds of the fourth; and the repeated hard C's of the
third and fourth picked up again in the seventh and
eighth, and leading to the 'crime' of the ninth and the
'Christ' of the last; the three B's in the last two lines:
all these devices show the contrived complexity of the
passage, which has been constructed as a single block
held together by far more than the logic of its argument
and the comparative regularity of its beat.

But this brilliance of texture Browning preserved long
after the writing of *The Ring and the Book*. It is every bit
as rich, indeed, in such a passage as that from *The Inn
Album* in which the woman reproaches her returned lover
for the ruin he has brought her:

> That moment when you first revealed yourself
> My simple impulse prompted—end forthwith
> The ruin of a life uprooted thus
> To surely perish! How should such spoiled tree
> Henceforward baulk the wind of its worst sport,
> Fail to go falling deeper, falling down
> From sin to sin until some depth were reached
> Doomed to the weakest by the wickedest
> Of weak and wicked human kind?

The dead M's and P's of the first two lines, with the repeated 'IMP' of the second; the three W's of the fifth line, the F's and D's of the sixth, and seventh and eighth, and the repeated U's of the last two reinforce the heavy rhythm of inevitability that informs the whole passage.

Such was his technical mastery, and combined with it there was his sharp, penetrating vision of the external world, a vision that could catch in *Pauline*, in *Sordello* in the monologues and right into his old age, a mood of nature, a cloudscape, or the houses and streets and people of a town. His scenic detail had all its sharpness of outline still when he came at seventy-three or four to his parley with Gerard de Lairesse, an old man still celebrating the midday of his inspiration:

> Noon is the conqueror—not a spray, nor leaf,
> Nor herb, nor blossom but has rendered up
> Its morning dew: the valley seemed one cup
> Of cloud-smoke, but the vapour's reign was brief,
> Sun-smitten, see, it hangs—the filmy haze—
> Grey-garmenting the herbless mountain-side,
> To soothe the day's sharp glare: while far and wide
> Above unclouded burns the sky, one blaze
> With fierce immitigable blue, no bird
> Ventures to spot by passage . . .

Such is Browning's control of verbal sound and

recorded vision. He was, to use his own definition, an objective poet where Shelley was a subjective one. As such his appeal was to the aggregate human mind and his concern with the doings of men. So, though unsuccessful as a playwright, he was, primarily and always the poet of the dramatic situation, and a 'fashioner' before he was a 'seer.' Shelley took only from nature what struck out most abundantly and uninterruptedly his inner light and power. Browning took much more, but not, in parnassian fashion, merely for the sake of the men and scenes and cities he described. He viewed nature and humanity with ceaseless curiosity and sympathy, trying over in his poetry ever fresh combinations of character and landscape, but always with the view of discovering some secret that lay behind them. Had he pursued the course on which he embarked in *Pauline* he would have continued to lay bare his own heart in the hope of discovering the secret there; had he pursued the false trail struck in 'Christmas Eve' he would have ceaselessly argued about the ultimate nature of experience and lost his clue in a welter of mere ratiocination. As it was he embodied ever and again in fresh poetry his flashes of comprehension concerning the relations of the trinity, Love, Knowledge and Faith, which came thickest in his early maturity, but which did not desert him in his long years of outwardly barren living, and which returned with renewed strength in the years immediately before his death. Browning had indeed a philosophical message, though not one of the kind the Browning Society was looking for. The secret, he tells us again and again, is to be found in man's experience, not in abstraction but in the welter and richness, in the violence and colour, in the love and beauty of the world itself.

o

SHORT BIBLIOGRAPHY

This list is intended merely to denote the sources I have used most freely in the writing of this book. It will be useful to any-one wanting to read more about the poet, but it is in no sense a guide to the huge field of Browning studies, nor even a com-plete list of the works that I have consulted.

THE POETICAL WORKS OF ROBERT BROWNING, 2 vols. in one. John Murray.

ROBERT BROWNING: POETRY AND PROSE, edited by Simon Nowell-Smith. Rupert Hart-Davis. Reynard Library.
This contains an interesting selection from Browning's shorter poetry well-printed, the essay on Shelley and a handful of letters, including one to Ruskin reprinted from Frederick Collingwood's *Life*.

LETTERS OF ROBERT BROWNING, edited by Thurman L. Hood. John Murray.

NEW LETTERS OF ROBERT BROWNING, edited by de Vane and Knickerbocker. John Murray.

LETTERS OF ROBERT BROWNING AND ELIZABETH BARRETT, 1845-6, 2 vols. in one. John Murray.

DEAREST ISA, Robert Browning's Letters to Isabella Blagden, edited by Edward Mc Aleer. Thomas Nelson & Sons.

LETTERS OF ELIZABETH BARRETT BROWNING, edited by F. G. Kenyon. 2 vols. The Macmillan Co., New York.

LETTERS OF ELIZABETH BARRETT BROWNING TO HER SISTER, 1846-1859, edited by Leonard Huxley. John Murray.

ROBERT BROWNING'S PERSONALIA, by Edmund Gosse. T. Fisher Unwin.

ROBERT BROWNING, by William Sharp. Walter Scott.

LIFE AND LETTERS OF ROBERT BROWNING, by Mrs. Sutherland Orr. John Murray.

HANDBOOK TO ROBERT BROWNING'S WORKS, by Mrs. Sutherland Orr. George Bell & Sons.

LIFE OF ROBERT BROWNING, by Edward Dowden. Everyman. J. M. Dent.

BROWNING'S BACKGROUND AND CONFLICT, by F. R. G. Duckworth. Ernest Benn.

LIFE OF ROBERT BROWNING, by W. Hall Griffin, completed and edited by H. C. Minchin. Methuen.

BIOGRAPHICAL AND CRITICAL STUDIES, by James Thomson. Dobell.

ROBERT BROWNING'S EARLY FRIENDS, by S. K. Ratcliffe. The Cornhill No. 979. Summer 1949.

NOTE

The following books, which have appeared since the first publication of this one, contain interesting material on the poet:

ROBERT BROWNING: A Portrait, by Betty Miller. John Murray, 1952. This is a biography, somewhat psycho-analytical in tone, but by far the best modern account of the poet.

AMPHIBIAN: A Reconsideration of Browning, by Henry Charles Duffin. Bowes and Bowes, 1956. This contains interesting assessments of many poems, joins issue with some previous critics and devotes a special appendix to refuting Mrs Miller.

BROWNING'S CHARACTERS: A Study in Poetic Technique, by Park Honan, Yale University Press, 1961. This is a very thorough investigation of Browning's sense of character and his technique in the dramatic monologue.

INDEX

his contemporary by buying the acting manuscript of
Colombe's Birthday, which Browning had written out for
Charles Kean, from Bertram Dobell for £10. Other
admirers were Norman MacColl and Dr. F. J. Furnivall,
the Shakespearean scholar, who was later to be joint-
founder of the Browning Society. He was to prove,
however, a rather embarrassing disciple.

Outwardly Browning's life was uneventful. He was
continually entertained, staying at a variety of country
houses, chiefly with members of the nobility, and returning hospitality only sparely, for his household was
not on the scale that permitted of lavish entertainment.
From the time of his father's death, his sister Sarianne
lived with him; and shared with him his annual holidays
on the French coast. Between the pair there was a very
close bond of affection. Penini was a source of considerable anxiety to them both. Shortly before his
going up to Oxford, his father had spoken of his moral
qualities as 'really nearly all I could wish.' He praised
him for his 'truthfulness, and deepness of feeling, and
firmness of mind.' But before he was nineteen Penini
had begotten children on two French girls met upon
holidays. He did not fulfil his father's hopes that he
would get into Balliol, but was accepted by Christ
Church, where according to Alfred Domett, he made
his mark 'more by the skill he showed at rowing and
billiards than by any success at the University subjects
of study.' 'Pen won't work' was his father's comment.
Not only was he idle, but his financial demands were
considerable. Clearly he was very far from the prodigy
that his parents had supposed. He had however some
talents as a draughtsman, and on his coming down from
Oxford, without a degree, his father packed him off to
Antwerp to study painting, a profession in which,

Women, and though there is much in common between the meticulous detail of such a poem as *Sordello* and the background of a Rossetti painting, difference of temperament should have so blinded Browning to Rossetti's qualities as a poet. His own effect on the younger man's development had been so strong that William Michael Rossetti speaks of Browning 'like the serpent rod of Moses' swallowing up, for a time, all other influences: readers of Rossetti's 'A Last Confession' can see the evidence. Swinburne too was a warm admirer of Browning and in his book on George Chapman went out of his way to defend the elder poet's work against the charge of obscurity, a service which earned him an obviously delighted and somewhat embarrassed letter of thanks. Only Alfred Austin remained permanently hostile. He was for Browning a shadowy and contemptible figure whom he saw behind any anonymous review that was in the least critical. Austin himself denied authorship of several of the severer notices, but was certainly responsible for an attack on *Balaustion's Adventure*, in which he took various lines out of their context as 'specimens of Mr. B's inability to write.' But little by little there were gathering around Browning a small group of scholarly admirers, whose questions about his work and the details of his early life he answered with very considerable patience. There was the young Edmund Gosse, whose interest was finally rewarded by a series of interviews out of which grew an article for an American magazine upon 'The Early Career of Robert Browning,' and H. Buxton Forman, then at work upon his edition of Shelley. Browning's correspondence with him was concerned rather with the Romantic poets, about whom he had information derived from Leigh Hunt, than with his own. Buxton Forman, all the same, showed his admiration of

for the 19th'—the customary monthly letter having been
delayed by three days. 'Well, I go with you a good way
in the feeling about Tennyson's new book: it is all out
of my head already. We look at the object of art in
poetry so differently. Here is an Idyll about a knight
being untrue to his friend and yielding to the temptation
of that friend's mistress after having engaged to assist
him in his suit. I should judge the conflict in the knight's
soul the proper subject to describe: Tennyson thinks he
should describe the castle, and the effect of the moon on
the towers, and anything *but* the soul . . . The old
Galahad is to me incomparably better than a dozen
centuries of the "Grail," "Coming of Arthur" and so on.'
Of William Morris's *Earthly Paradise* he speaks in much
the same vein. 'The lyrics were "the first sprightly run-
nings"—this that follows is a laboured brew with the old
flavour but not *body*.' Rossetti he viewed with even less
favour. 'I have read his poems,' he wrote to Miss
Blagden in a letter three months later than that in which
he delivered judgment on Tennyson and Morris '—and
poetical they are,—*scented* with poetry, as it were—
like trifles of various sorts you take out of a cedar or
sandal-wood box. You know I hate the effeminacy of
his school,—the men that dress up like women,—that
use obsolete forms, too, and archaic accentuations to
seem soft—fancy a man calling it a lil', lil'es and so on:
Swinburne started this, with other like Belialisms—
witness his harp-playér etc. It is quite different when
the object is to *imitate* old ballad-writing, when the thing
might be; then, how I hate "Love", as a lubberly naked
young man putting his arms here and his wings there,
about a pair of lovers,—a fellow they would kick away
in the reality.' It is strange that though the Pre-
Raphaelites were among the first admirers of *Men and*

Chapter Six

SUBJECTS CLASSICAL AND SENSATIONAL

'IN English literature the creative faculty of the poet has not produced three characters more beautiful or better to contemplate than these three,' wrote the 'Edinburgh' reviewer of the Pope, Caponsacchi and Pompilia. 'We must record at once our conviction, not merely that *The Ring and the Book* is beyond all parallel the supremest poetical achievement of our time, but that it is the most precious and profound spiritual treasure that England has produced since the days of Shakespeare.' With such uncompromising praise did the *Athenaeum* greet Browning's great poem. Thus established in popular favour Browning embarked on that period of his life when the emotions of the past fell into retrospect and the prospect of death was still a distant one. Each poem that he wrote was sure of an appreciative welcome. There were still, of course, the persistently uncomprehending: Fitzgerald, for instance, who never could read Browning, and Carlyle who made very little of him, and Connop Thirlwall, Bishop of St. David's, who spoke of the Chinese-like condensation of his style. Tennyson found *The Ring and the Book* full of strange vigour and remarkable in many ways, though he doubted whether it could ever be popular.

Browning's own opinion of Tennyson in the *Idylls of the King* is very clearly stated in a letter to his constant correspondent Miss Isa Blagden dated 'March 22nd. '70,' objectivity in his narration was more than a merely formal development. It marked both a further stage in the autonomy of the work itself, and a weakening of the emotional drive that set it in motion. Browning, in the years following Elizabeth's death, was concerned with the single theme of his fidelity to her memory, and such poems as touch upon this problem—*Fifine at the Fair* in particular—reveal a certain tightening of emotional tension. For the rest, between *Balaustion's Adventure* and the *Jocoseria* volume, only *La Saisiaz*, written under the impact of a friend's sudden death shows traces of deep and personal feeling. The virtues of these works of Browning's maturity are narrative virtues, the poet's individual cast of mind appearing rather in his choice of subjects and treatment than in personal identification with the characters he created. With the rough ore of his experience, which he had rounded in *The Ring and the Book*, he was now content to alloy a less precious metal, but the resulting amalgam nevertheless was capable of taking a very fine polish. Only with the work of his old age, written in the prospect of a death which he did not fear, does the proportion of gold in his metal signally increase.

Prince Hohenstiel-Schwangau is perhaps the most contrived and intellectual of all the great monologues. Moreover it is also the only one to display real falsities of presentation. For the Prince's opening, addressed to a young lady of an adventurous type—as Mrs. Orr puts it—whom he has picked up in Leicester Square, strikes an undignified note that the poem is slow to recover from.

> You have seen better days, dear? So have I—
> And worse too, for they brought no such bud-mouth
> As yours to lisp 'You wish you knew me!' . . .

The lady seems hardly a fitting listener to play Gigadibs to his Blougram. Indeed the personality of his curiously chosen interviewer, 'under a porkpie hat and crinoline,' casts a preliminary aura of doubt on the value of the 'once redoubted Sphynx's' confession. At first he appears to be no more than a seedy political adventurer; only as the poem progresses does it become clear that Browning has endowed him too with some of his own qualities. But the passages in which the poet speaks with his own voice are much outweighed by the poem's inconsistencies, its casuistries and tangled argument.

Prince Hohenstiel-Schwangau is probably the least successful of Browning's mature works. Even in its form it is a belated survival from the period before *The Ring and the Book*. For by grouping his twelve dramatic monologues around the single theme of the Roman murder, Browning exhausted the possibilities of his medium. Now he was to advance by stages to a simple narrative presentation along a single time sequence, the contrasting interpretations of his story's facts being suggested, not by fictional characters, but by the poet himself in the role of commentator. But this increased

God takes the business into his own hands
At such time: who creates the novel flower
Contrives to guard and give it breathing-room:
I merely tend the corn-field, care for crop
And weed no acre thin to let emerge
What prodigy may stifle there perchance . . .

Though it may be argued that here Browning is speaking only for a character, and a character indeed who admits that there are moments in the world's history when his timid conservatism is not enough, nevertheless, as his intimate friend Mrs. Sutherland Orr remarks in her *Handbook*, the imaginary speaker here so resembles Mr. Browning himself that we forget for the moment we are not dealing with him. The tergiversations of his Prince may not be Browning's, but this statement of belief certainly is. Never since his abandonment of his Shelleyan enthusiasms had he been a liberal in domestic politics in any respect other than his passionate advocacy of the right of free criticism. Abroad, however, like most enlightened men of his day, he sympathized with the Italians in their struggle for unity, and with the North against the South in the American civil war. But this was ground common to both parties, a mere desire to extend to less fortunate lands the benefits of nationalism and unrestricted trade on which England was prospering. Late in life he composed a sonnet proclaiming 'Why I am a Liberal,' but he never found a place for it in his collected work. For by the time of its writing he had already differed with Gladstone over the subject of Home Rule, and was moving in a liberal-unionist direction. In the spring of 1888, meeting the liberal leader at John Murray's, he was somewhat unhappy at being put beside him. Nobody, however, he noted, could have been more agreeable.

its implications were clearly rather on the side of hostility than of partiality. Even so, Browning had to deny to so intimate a friend as Miss Edith Story that he had 'taken the man for any Hero.' Like other poems whose characters were unsympathetic to the poet, it lacks those touches of natural detail which relieve even the most casuistical of Browning's arguments. The tangled reasoning and the flatness of the verse merely reflected the mediocrity of the Prince whose motives the poet had set out to justify. Compared with the least colourful character in *The Ring and the Book*—Juris Doctor Johannes Baptista Bottinius perhaps—Prince Hohenstiel-Schwangau was disappointingly grey. The poem was far less compelling than any part of Browning's masterpiece. Yet even the monologue of that dubious Saviour of Society contributes features of its own to Browning's self-portrait.

Certainly it provides one more proof, if proof be necessary, of Browning's indeterminate political position. It is a study rather in human motive than in statecraft. Yet its prevailing tone is so far from liberal that it raises doubt as to the genuineness of the liberalism the poet professed. For if the poem has any fixed standpoint it is a preference for the stubborn and muddled conversation of the imperfect and a mistrust for liberal or republican reformism, which seemed to Browning dangerous and chimerical. So at least he states through the mouth of his Prince in what is the core of his defence:

> I saw that, in the ordinary life,
> Many of the little make a mass of men
> Important beyond greatness here and there;
> As certainly as, in life exceptional,
> When old things terminate and new commence,
> A solitary great man's worth the world.

published until 1871, the year after the pinchbeck
Emperor's eclipse at Sedan. There is something of the
spirit of Sludge about this imaginary German princeling
who acts as so fictitious a mouthpiece for the exiled
Bonaparte. Indeed at the opening of his monologue he
is made to voice the fear that his exploits may be compared with the 'stilts and tongs and medium-ware' of
the despised Home. But Browning did not view his
subject with the undivided hostility he had devoted to
Sludge. At his most judicious, he saw the fallen
Emperor as one who had, for a time, done genuine
service to France and to the world, by standing in the
way of those utopian schemes that he so much distrusted.
Napoleon III had wished to build on sound foundations,
and to that extent Browning could approve of his policies,
but fundamentally he found the Bonapartist adventurer
unsympathetic. 'I thought badly of him at the beginning
of his career, *et pour cause*,' he wrote to Miss Blagden
after the poem's publication: 'better afterwards on the
strength of the promises he made, and gave indications
of intending to redeem. I think him very weak in the last
miserable year.' But, only three months before, he had
written with uncharacteristic prejudice that Napoleon
III should be blotted out of the world as the greatest
failure on record, the alleged benefits of his reign being
no more than the extravagant interest which a knavish
banker pays you for some time, till one fine day he
decamps with the principal. A poem written in so
divided a mind could be no more than an intellectual
exercise. So obscure was its moral indeed that the
critics, who were now far from hostile, could not make
out whether it was meant as 'a scandalous attack on the
old constant friend of England,' or as a eulogium on
the Second Empire. It was, of course, neither, though

an air of retrospect about Browning's evocation of the
Greek scene. There are passages in which he seems to
recall rather the timeless world of art evoked by Keats
than the spectacle of a Greek play performed in a Greek
theatre which they are intended to portray. The description of Alcestis' funeral, in particular, has clear
affinities with the *Ode on a Grecian Urn*, whose lines it
seems to echo.

> Wherewith, the sad procession wound away,
> Made slowly for the suburb sepulchre.
> And lo,—while still one's heart, in time and tune,
> Paced after the symmetric step of Death
> Mute-marching, to the mind's eye, at the head
> O' the mourners—one hand pointing out their path
> With the long pale terrific sword we saw,
> The other leading, with grim tender grace,
> Alkestis quieted and consecrate,—
> Lo, life again knocked laughing at the door!
> The world goes on, goes ever, in and through,
> And out again o' the cloud. We faced about,
> Fronted the palace, where the mid-hall-gate
> Opened—not half, nor half of half, perhaps—
> Yet wide enough to let out light and life,
> And warmth and bounty and hope and joy, at once.

So, as in *The Ring and the Book*, life goes boisterously
and carelessly on, heedless of the private grief or the
sudden miracle in its midst. Alcestis is dead, and the
visiting Hercules must be welcomed; tragedy must be
hidden from those who are too obtuse to comprehend it.

After the Mediterranean clarity of *Balaustion's Adventure*, its successor, *Prince Hohenstiel-Schwangau, Saviour of
Society* seems doubly drab and confused. It is the defence
of Napoleon III that Browning had sketched out in
Elizabeth's lifetime, but which was not written and

Hercules, who wrestles with death for Alcestis, and brings her back to her husband in the upper world. Furthermore Browning puts into the mouth of Apollo a magnificent speech in praise of the things of this world, which is a pure statement of the poet's own feelings, His feelings also dictate the form of Admetus' speech over his dead wife, into which Browning puts all his own grief and resignation:

> Since death divides the pair,
> 'Tis well that I depart and thou remain
> Who wast to me as spirit is to flesh,
> So thou, the spirit that informed the flesh:
> Let the flesh perish, be perceived no more,
> Bend yet awhile, a very flame above
> The rift I drop into the darkness by.

Balaustion's Adventure is a reconstruction almost Pre-Raphaelite in its patient detail, yet it is less pedagogically accurate than Browning's first attempt in this vein, 'Artemis Prologizes,' for it is informed with far deeper emotion. Not only has the legend of Alcestis a private significance for the poet. It stands also, in the form that he gives it, as a parable telling of personal salvation by the double forces of love and the creative powers, an idea which had been present in so many of his earlier poems, and which his oblique method of presentation allowed him to show here working on various levels.

The colour of the poem is not Greek, but of the nine-teenth century. Admetus' action in accepting Alcestis' sacrifice is excused and explained, not by the fact that he was obeying the instructions of Apollo, but by his promise to remain faithful to Alcestis after her death and to take no other wife: a justification very far from the spirit of Euripides. There is, moreover, despite the circumstantial way in which Balaustion tells her story,

constant reader of Euripides for many years, and was greatly interested in problems of translation. While engaged in this project he discussed many lines in detail with Jowett. But he was not content, as he was to be in later years when he undertook the *Agamemnon* of Aeschylus, merely to give an English version of the Greek play. There is a passage in Plutarch's life of Nicias in which he tells of the welcome given by the Syracusans to Athenian slaves and fugitives who could recite the verses of Euripides, instancing 'a reporte made of a ship of the city of Caunus, that on a time being chased thither by pyrates, thinking to save themselves within their portes, could not at the first be received, but had repulse: howbeit being demaunded whether they could sing any of Euripides songes, and answering that they could, were straight suffered to enter, and come in.' On this ship Browning places his Rhodian girl, Balaustion, who by reciting the *Alcestis* and describing its actions wins a reception for her countrymen and a husband for herself.

By this oblique method of presentation Browning was able to graft upon Euripides' play an interpretation of his own. For the legend of Alcestis had significances that applied to his own case. There was a parallel, as he saw it, between his own loss of Elizabeth and the widowed condition of Admetus, whose wife had gone down into Hades, leaving him 'with her whole soul entered into his.' Such an idea of a mingling of souls was Shelleyan, though perhaps Platonic in its first origins, and certainly foreign to Euripides' way of thought. This did not prevent Browning from introducing it into Balaustion's commentary on the action, and with it another interpretation of his own, also unvouched for by the Greek original. For in *Balaustion's Adventure* it is Love, and not

weather and clouds are exactly recorded. But he had a profounder reason for his concern with the violences and the subtleties of criminal behaviour. It is on a world full of life and contradictory activity that he believed the lightning flash of revelation would strike. As in a picture where crowds rush hither and thither about their own business while the procession of the Cross passes almost unnoticed towards Calvary, so in a courtroom and a city, preoccupied with the scandal of a *cause célèbre*, the miracle of its central figure is hardly observed. Violence attracted Browning both as a contrasting background and as a catalyst for the beauty he set out to record.

The reviews of *The Ring and the Book* were uniformly favourable. Never had Browning met with such unstinted praise. It passed immediately into a second edition, and what Mrs. Orr has called the fullest decade of Browning's life began, a decade not only productively rich but one filled with even more social activites. In 1867 Oxford had conferred on the poet an honorary M.A. A little later Jowett was instrumental in getting him elected honorary fellow of Balliol. Next year he was proposed as Rector of St. Andrews, but declined. He feared that the office would entail too much expense. All these honours gave him very great pleasure, for he had long laboured under the feeling that he was neglected, if not openly disliked, by his contemporaries. Not so long ago he had described himself to Mrs. Millais—Ruskin's Effie Gray—as the most unpopular poet that ever was. Now he was coming into his own.

Balaustion's Adventure, published two years after the completion of *The Ring and the Book*, was intended in the first place to be a mere transcript from the *Alcestis* of Euripides, which had been suggested to the poet as a subject by Countess Cowper. Browning had been a

very best and subtlest of Browning's blank verse. Nowhere more than here was he the master of variety within a uniform pattern. Other poets in as long a narrative might have resorted to metrical variations, but Browning was able to make each character speak in his own idiom within the limits of a single verse form. There is the broken, nervous defence of de Archangelis, whose mind is half on the case and half at home, where they are preparing a party for his young son. He can have little sympathy with the violence and wounded pride of his client Guido Franceschini, but he makes an eloquent pleading. His opponent Bottinius, on the other hand, puts up a far more rhetorical display, at the expense of Pompilia whose good name he should be trying to preserve. Nothing of this is superfluous. To reduce the poem, as many have wished to, by the five chapters of commentary and pleadings would be to deprive it of its frame. For it is the story of a miracle that happened in the world, a miracle all the more compelling because its witnesses did not cease their worldly activities for it, but continued to be the gossips, the casuists, the sycophants they had always been.

It has been objected, of course, that so commonplace an incident as that recorded in the square yellow book is too trivial a subject for great poetry. Wonder has been expressed that Browning should take such a great interest in murder trials. For, like his father before him, he was minutely familiar with every *cause célèbre* within living memory. Nor was this the only anecdote of its kind that was to give him the idea for a poem. A partial explanation of their fascination for him lies in the sheer wealth of detail a court case offers. He is the poet, above all others, who revels in documentation. In his poems places are exactly described; animals, vegetation,

I

It was not the flowering of love, but an experience akin to the birth of faith in one whose religion had been but a formal practice. Franceschini's transformation, on the other hand, comes to him only when in his last despairing cry he utters her name:

> Abate,—Cardinal,—Christ,—Maria,—God, . . .
> Pompilia, will you let them murder me?

The remaining five sections of the book are given up to opinion and commentary, which serve the purpose of revealing the complexities of the case, of giving the drama body and background, and of acting as a kind of obscene chorus of the blind, probing and poking at the wonder they cannot see. Pompilia's innocence indeed appears the whiter for its handling and mishandling by one half-Rome and the other, and by that judicious third personage, neutral, flippant and indifferent, who sums the matter up for some Highness or Excellency, and in fact gives as objective a view of the matter—for all that it is worth—as anybody concerned with the case. Then there are the lawyers, Juris Doctor Johannes Baptista Bottinius, who succeeds in smirching Pompilia as much by his compromising defence as does his pedantic colleague, the excellent Latinist Dominus Hyacinthus de Archangelis, by his assumption of her adultery. The whole motley assemblage is brought to life by the vigour and subtlety of Browning's verse; the courtroom is full; and Rome and Arezzo and Florence, the scenes of the drama, palpitate with noisy, argumentative passions. In 'Mr. Sludge' and 'Bishop Blougram,' Browning's line has shown signs of a certain drabness, the usual concomitant with him of an English subject. *The Ring and the Book*, however, true to its setting, took on the far greater colour of his earlier Italian poems; indeed it contains the

> This something like a foothold in the sea,
> Although St. Peter's bark scuds, billow-borne,
> Leaves me to founder where it flung me first?
> Spite of your splashing, I am high and dry!
> God takes his own part in each thing He made;
> Made for a reason, He conserves his work,
> Gives each its proper instinct of defence.
> My lamblike wife could neither bark nor bite . . .

His moment of recollection is over; the poison rises once more to his lips. But now he is not despicable; worthless, greedy, envious, embittered, murderous though he is, something has grown in him under the weight of his suffering. Is it the radiance of the lines he is given to speak, or the unquestioning forgiveness of his 'lamblike' wife that has brought it out? From an Elizabethan villain he has become a sinner whose soul may yet be saved. For, in Browning's eyes, no character was evil beyond redemption, and contrasted though Franceschini is with Caponsacchi, both are, in the ultimate, worldlings who are redeemed by Pompilia: Caponsacchi from a successful but wasted life, and Franceschini from damnation.

The transformation wrought in the ambitious priest by his first snatched interview with her is expressed in the language of a miracle:

> In rushed new things, the old were rapt away;
> Alike abolished—the imprisonment
> Of the outside air, the inside weight o' the world
> That pulled me down. Death meant, to spurn the
> > ground,
> Soar to the sky,—die well and you do that.
> The very immolation made the bliss;
> Death was the heart of life, and all the harm
> My folly had crouched to avoid, now proved a veil
> Hiding all gain my wisdom strove to grasp.

> So, let him wait God's instant men call years;
> Meantime hold hard by truth and his great soul,
> Do out the duty! Through such souls alone
> God stooping shows sufficient of His Light
> For us i' the dark to rise by. And I rise.

It was to Caponsacchi, the worldly priest whom her presence had transformed, that she spoke. Yet the words, if put into the mouth of the dying Elizabeth, might be read as a promise to Browning himself and a reminder of the duty he had still to perform; to hold hard by the truth and, by bearing witness to the light he had known, to shed sufficient of his own for others, if not for her, to rise by.

After Pompilia and the Pope, the characters who stand next in recession from the poem's centre are the two active participants, Caponsacchi himself and the sour, avaricious decayed nobleman, Guido Franceschini, who was her murderer. Franceschini is not a mere Websterian embodiment of perversity, yet there is an Elizabethan quality about him. He has confessed to his crime under torture, but unlike Mr. Sludge he does not whine. He fights back with the cornered doggedness of the impoverished representative of a great line he claims to be. There are indeed moments when he too is invested with a human dignity, moments such as that in which he reasons soberly with his judges, with all the strength of one who has suddenly found a certain clarity:

> Come, I am tired of silence! Pause enough!
> You have prayed: I have gone inside my soul
> And shut its door behind me: 'tis your torch
> Makes the place dark: the darkness let alone
> Grows tolerable twilight; one may grope
> And get to guess at length and breadth and depth.
> What is this fact I feel persuaded of—

> Never may I commence my song, my due
> To God who best taught song by gift of thee,
> Except with bent head and beseeching hand—
> That still, despite the distance and the dark,
> What was, again may be; some interchange
> Of grace, some splendour once thy very thought,
> Some benediction anciently thy smile . . .

Here, and in the Pope's speech, and in the statement of the dying Pompilia lies the core of *The Ring and the Book*. Indeed in Pompilia's conclusion, in the blessing she calls down upon the head of Giuseppe Caponsacchi, Browning rises to a height equal to that of Milton's invocation. In bidding farewell to the priest whose devotion to her has been expressed only in selfless service, she states at the same time Browning's own interpretation—in the spirit of Shelley—of the saying that in heaven there is neither marrying nor giving in marriage. For to him Christ's words were a promise that there exists a link in eternity corresponding to that union which in the realm of time is called marriage. 'Marriage-making for the earth,' he concedes in Pompilia's words,

> With gold so much,—birth, power, repute so much,
> Or beauty, youth so much, in lack of these!

But her dying vision is so acute that she can point to a state transcending it:

> Be as the angels rather, who apart,
> Know themselves into one, are found at length
> Married, but marry never, no, nor give
> In marriage; they are man and wife at once
> When the true time is; here we have to wait
> Not so long neither! Could we by a wish
> Have what we will and get the future now,
> Would we wish aught done undone in the past?

moral values, with a great deal of Bishop Blougram remaining in his composition, the Pope sees in this humble victim with her icy resolution, the symbol of a *summum bonum*. Perhaps, indeed, his knowledge of her life may be the one experience left him to attain,

> Just the one prize vouchsafed unworthy me,
> Seven years a gardener of the untoward ground.

In defining the Pope's limitations and his apprehension of higher values lying beyond them, Browning was defining his own state in all but his moments of supreme inspiration. Like the old man, he was for the most part confined to the common levels of experience; his highest aim to view the world without partisanship, to study and present the case of each of his *Men and Women*, trying their merits 'with true sweat of soul,' and reluctant to condemn even a Sludge or a Caliban unheard. But there was a poetry more profound than this forensic dramatization; there were moments of vision; and one of these he expressed in Pompilia, the missing base to the isoscele. The comparison brings us back to the triple pattern of art, love and faith which was fundamental to his experience. By her presence—as by David's at the couch of the sick Saul—the objective study of a Roman murder case, in itself as sordid as the history of Sludge's frauds, though by its Italian background more picturesque, was transformed into an affirmation of faith. For it is the motive of faith that is stressed, with a solemnity recalling that of the Invocation to Light in *Paradise Lost*, in Browning's address to 'lyric love, half angel and half bird,' at the conclusion of the first book. These lines are more than a memorial to his dead wife:

a child
Of seventeen years, whether a flower or weed,
Ruined . . .

For so she seems to that 'Other Half-Rome,' the
spokesman of the gossips who take her part. Certainly
Pompilia is a great deal more than the pathetic
victim Browning read of in the square yellow book.
She is Our Lady of Sorrows, Elizabeth, Pippa and
also—the incarnation of selfless love, of that selfless
love that Robert Browning had long ago tried to
express in 'Cristina,' the love of one content to
serve without hope of reward; to submit herself, as the Archbishop bade her, to the duties of a
loveless marriage, and to flee from that marriage only
at the promptings of a higher duty, for the protection of
her unborn child but for no happiness that she can expect
for herself. The Pope, indeed, skilled in the secrets of
the heart, in whom age has come to irradiate intellect
with the light of intuition, an old man 'with winter in
his soul beyond the world's,' sees her as the incarnation
of that quality which the world so tragically lacks. 'Is
man strong, intelligent and good,' he asks, 'up to his
own conceivable height'—

Is there strength there?—enough: intelligence?
Ample: but goodness in a like degree?
Not to the human eye in the present state,
An isoscele deficient in the base.
What lacks then, of perfection fit for God
But just the instance which this tale supplies
Of love without a limit? So is strength,
So is intelligence; let love be so.
Unlimited in its self-sacrifice,
Then is the tale true and God shows complete.

Unable himself to transcend the intellectual sphere of

sort, a drama for the study, it is true, but one in which the greatest issues of good and evil, and all the intervening greys and half-tones between them would take human shape. Here a tenfold soliloquy would be harmonized into a single celebration of woman's innocence and her redemptive purity. From the mingled ore and alloy of that brutal Roman tale was to be shaped a ring. Then by an artificer's trick the impurities required for its forging were to be spirited away under acid, to leave it pure gold. The ring's symbolism was two-fold. It stood for the marriage of Robert and Elizabeth Browning, to the memory of which the whole poem was dedicated. But it stood also for the marriage of fact and fiction, for the 'pure fact' of unalloyed gold that could be extracted from the raw material of life, by use of an alloy, the poetic imagination. The book was the raw material; the ring the refined, delicately incised product, and his supreme tribute to Elizabeth. For in Pompilia, its murdered heroine, he saw, despite her extreme youth, the figure of his dead wife, a figure who for all her everyday tarnished circumstances, strikes the priest Caponsacchi, who is to contrive her rescue, as the symbol of eternal womanhood at the first moment he sees her, there at the window of her husband's house,

> Framed in its black square length, with lamp in hand,
> Pompilia: the same great, grave, griefful air
> As stands i' the dusk, on altar that I know,
> Left alone with one moonbeam in her cell,
> Our Lady of all the Sorrows.

But not only 'Our Lady of Sorrows,' not only Elizabeth Barrett, have gone to Pompilia's composition. She has the childish innocence of Pippa, too, of a Pippa on whom Monsignor has had no mercy,

At a cursory reading Browning 'knew the whole truth.' The yellow book contained no obliquities. There was no doubt from the start about the innocence of the murdered wife. All the pleadings and counter-pleadings were there, all the depositions of defendants and witnesses, everything but the mystery of human motive and the convolutions of human character which were to be the true subject of his poem when it came to be written. The book immediately seized upon Browning's imagination, and he began to outline a poem which should view these events, now more than a century and a half old, from a variety of angles. 'When I had read the book,' he told his friend R. Lehmann, 'I went for a walk, gathered twelve pebbles from the road, and put them at equal distances on the parapet that bordered it. Those represented the twelve chapters into which the poem is divided, and I adhered to that arrangement to the last.' But he did not begin the writing of *The Ring and the Book* at this point. For within a few months he was offering the story to one friend as the possible plot for a novel, and later suggesting to another that he should write a historical account of the case. It was not until after the publication of *Dramatis Personae* that he set about collecting further documents concerning this 'Roman murder' and embarked on his four years' task.

The Ring and the Book was to be his greatest achievement in the field of monologue, for in it nine personages were to reveal themselves by casting concentric but contradictory lights on the same events, with the poet speaking in person at the opening and the close. Here the weaknesses that had prevented his writing successful plays were to be turned to strengths, the succession of soliloquies combining to build a mighty drama of a new

his future biographer, and F. J. Nettleship were re-examining *Sordello* and proclaiming that its obscurities were not so great after all. But by this time Browning was at work on that masterpiece that took him four years to write, *The Ring and the Book*.

The tale of Browning's discovery and purchase of the square yellow book containing the story of a Roman murder which had been the sensation of the year 1698 is told in the first book of the poem itself. It was on a torrid June day in 1860 that he picked it up for a mere lira in the square of San Lorenzo in Florence, and began to read it before he had left the market, continuing in the words of the poem itself,

> from written title-page
> To written index, on, through street and street,
> At the Strozzi, at the Pillar, at the Bridge;
> Till by the time I stood at home again
> In Casa Guidi by Felice Church,
> Under the doorway where the black begins
> With the first stone-slab of the staircase cold,
> I had mastered the contents, knew the whole truth
> Gathered together, bound up in this book,
> Print three-fifths, written supplement the rest.
> *Romana Homicidiorum*—nay,
> Better translate—'A Roman murder-case:
> Position of the entire criminal cause
> Of Guido Franceschini, nobleman,
> With certain Four the cutthroats in his pay,
> Tried, all five, and found guilty and put to death
> By heading or hanging as befitted ranks,
> At Rome on February Twenty Two,
> Since our salvation Sixteen Ninety-Eight:
> Wherein it is disputed if, and when,
> Husbands may kill adulterous wives, yet 'scape
> The customary forfeit.'

Such progress could no more attend his soul
Were all it struggles after found at first
And guesses changed to knowledge absolute,
Than motion wait his body, were all else
Than it the solid earth on every side,
Where now through space he moves from rest to
    rest.

This is the clearest statement of Browning's belief in all his poetry, a statement the more solemn for the flatness of its imagery, and by the mere hair's breadth that it rises above the prose of that scientific materialism which it so triumphantly refutes. It was such a statement that Tennyson felt empowered to make in his moments of spiritual experience, but which he could never substantiate in poem or discussion. Perhaps Browning owes some of his contemporary unpopularity to his defence of just this pedestrian belief that doubt is far from being the virtue that it is at present assumed to be, that it is a state to be transcended and that God's great gift to man is that he should conceive of truth,

And yearn to gain it, catching at mistake,
As midway help till he reach fact indeed.

Dramatis Personae met, on its publication, a far greater measure of success than had any previous book of Browning's. A second edition was soon in the press. For a new generation was growing up for whom the difficulties of his poems seemed to have diminished. It was particularly in the University towns of Oxford and Cambridge that sales were high. But not only was Browning finding new readers among undergraduates; soon his poetry was to find critics in England as penetrating as his friend Milsand in France. Three years after the appearance of *Dramatis Personae* both Edward Dowden

soaring, is celebrating no more than the C major of *this* life, even though he dwells on the intimations of a deeper reality that come with the practise of art. Ben Ezra, on the other hand, like the David of 'Saul,' completes the triple pattern and proclaims a fuller faith. 'Abt Vogler' might conceivably have been written before Elizabeth's death; 'Ben Ezra' could not have been, for its certainty can only have been plucked from the teeth of dire adversity.

What had been discursive thought in *Christmas Eve and Easter Day* and what had been oblique and objective in the 'Epistle of Karshish' were combined, in the new book, in a single monologue that is perhaps the greatest of all. 'A Death in the Desert,' the third of its major triumphs, is written in Browning's familiar, reflective mood. It is one of the most profound statements of the Protestant standpoint in English poetry, for its certainty also has been gained in a struggle, in this case in a struggle against the forces of both dogma and doubt. It is a record of the last days of St. John, dying in some Syrian cave whither he has been transported to avoid the persecutions that are now beginning, of

> brother John,
> Who saw and heard and could remember all . . .

and who knew that if the times were at hand when there would be no more living witnesses to testify to the truth of the Gospel story, the doubt that must now ensue is essential to the Divine purpose. For

> . . . man knows partly but conceives beside,
> Creeps ever on from fancies to the fact,
> And in this striving, this converting air
> Into a solid he may grasp and use,
> Finds progress, man's distinctive mark alone,
> Not God's, and not the beasts': God is, they are,
> Man partly is and wholly hopes to be.

'I strove, made head, gained ground upon the
  whole!'
  As the bird wings and sings,
  Let us cry 'All good things
Are ours, nor soul helps flesh more, now,
  than flesh helps soul!'

It was a jagged affirmation, one might say, wrung from
recalcitrant experience in a struggle which has impressed
itself on the uneven texture of the lives. Compared to
his own 'Saul' and, even more, when contrasted with
Shelley's 'Lines to a Skylark,' a poem not dissimilar in
metre and mood, 'Rabbi ben Ezra' seems deliberately
rough; the final lines of each stanza appear indeed pur-
posely to hold up the poem's flow, whereas in Shelley's
poem they lead smoothly into the next verse. The Rabbi's
glorification of old age remained a favourite of Browning's
till the last. There was a sense in which he himself had always looked forward to 'the last of
life,' as the fulfilment 'for which the first was
made;' it was with this thought in mind, perhaps,
that he had written off his youth, in that curious
letter to Elizabeth in which he had spoken of having his
mind 'set in ultimate order for the few years more.' Unlike the Romantics, he had set out from the start to write
not the poetry of youth but that of old age. That was why
his desire had been to hasten his maturity and transcend
with all speed the mood he had expressed in *Pauline*.
Therefore it was, in anticipation, that he placed so many
of his profoundest poems on the lips of old men.

'Abt Vogler,' the second of the new book's great
affirmations, flows more smoothly than 'Rabbi Ben Ezra,'
its anapaestic measure suggesting a less impeded optimism
than the Hebrew's broken iambics. But its scope is
smaller. For the musician, with all his orchestral

How many of the *Dramatis Personae* were written before Elizabeth's death there is no means of knowing. Most, however, must have been the product of the poet's early months in London. Indeed, the triumphant unstopping of the full organ, the blaring out of the mode Palestrina in 'Abt Vogler,' 'Rabbi ben Ezra,' 'Prospice' and the 'Epilogue' may well be read as evidences that Browning was indeed beginning to live on in the spirit of his letter to his sister, written after Elizabeth's death; 'living on in the presence of her, in every sense.' For in the person of his learned Hebrew, ben Ezra, he returns once more to the mood of 'Saul,' this time affirming that old age is, as it was in a more limited sense for his grammarian, the fulfilment of life, and proclaiming afresh that sublime resolution of the world's dichotomy that he had reached in 'Saul.' 'Should not the heart beat once "How good to live and learn",' asks the old rabbi, with deeper wisdom than the plodding grammarian had ever attained.

> Not once beat 'Praise be Thine!
> I see the whole design,
> I, who saw power, see now love perfect too:
> Perfect I call thy plan:
> Thanks that I was a man!
> Maker, remake, complete,— I trust what Thou
>   shalt do!'

> For pleasant is this flesh;
> Our soul, in its rose-mesh
> Pulled ever to the earth, still yearns for rest;
> Would we some prize might hold
> To match those manifold
> Possessions of the brute—gain most, as we
>   did best!

> Let us not always say
> 'Spite of this flesh today

He hath watched hunt with that slant white-wedge eye
By moonlight; and the pie with the long tongue
That pricks deep into oakwarts for a worm,
And says a plain word when she finds her prize . . .

Caliban is alive. Mr. Sludge alone is unrelievably drab. Better a savage who knows no god, Browning seems to say, than one who traffics meanly in evidences.

The *Dramatis Personae*, as a whole, is more forthright in tone than *Men and Women*. On the one hand, there are more pieces concerned with human baseness; on the other, at least five poems make greater affirmations of spiritual truth than their more oblique predecessors, 'The Epistle of Karshish,' and 'Cleon.' The least interesting pieces in the new book are a group concerned with life's seamy side, poems for the most part dwelling on love's decay, and ascribing its cause rather to the shortcomings of the lovers than, as in earlier poems of love and loss, to the contrariness of circumstance.

I had dipped in life's struggle and, out again,
    Bore specks of it here, there, easy to see,
When I found my swan and the cure was plain;
    The dull turned bright as I caught your white
On my bosom: you saved me—saved in vain
    If you ruined yourself, and all through me!

It was a vein that was to be worked more succinctly by Thomas Hardy who, lacking belief in an ideal of behaviour from which his characters had fallen, was able to present their circumstances more barely, and to suggest a more potent and indifferent destiny than Browning believed in. Unsuccessful though 'May and Death,' 'Apparent Failure,' and two or three more pieces were, they at least prepared the way for the later poet's more astringent treatment of Life's little ironies.

been reserved for the interviewing journalist was here
the main strand in the character of Mr. Sludge himself.
It is stated in the opening lines:

> Now, don't, sir! Don't expose me! Just this once!
> This was the first and only time, I'll swear,—
> Look at me,—see, I kneel,—the only time,
> I swear, I ever cheated—yes, by the soul
> Of Her who hears—(your sainted mother, sir!)
> All, except this last accident, was truth—

From the outset we are debarred from sympathy with
this whining, fraudulent creature who preyed on the
weaknesses of his clients, but struck treacherously
whenever he thought he could catch anyone at a dis-
advantage. For all the other personages in the great
monologues Browning will play the part of defence
counsel; but against Sludge he appears in person briefed
for the prosecution, thus revenging himself at leisure for
the deceptions Home had practised on his dead wife.
Caliban, too, mocking, fearing and scolding his god
Setebos by turns, is ugly as the personages of *Men and
Women* were not. Yet he is inhuman rather than mean,
the incarnation of what man would be without love, a
creature of primitive intelligence and crude urge for
power, creating his deity by the light of his own limitations. There is a deliberate oafishness about his ungainly
lines, whose accents are thrown hither and thither in
imitation of the slow, jolting action of the creature's
mind. Yet Caliban is almost redeemed by his wry
humour, and by the native poetry with which he describes the denizens of his isle:

> Yon otter, sleek-wet, black, lithe as a leech;
> Yon auk, one fire-eye in a ball of foam,
> That floats and feeds; a certain badger brown

entertained by the very wide circle which he had gathered around him in the past, and which was constantly increased by fresh acquaintances or by the arrival in London of friends whom he had made abroad. His life was for very many years one of ceaseless activity rendered possible only by his buoyant good health. He wrote, he saw his friends, he varied his year by taking long summer holidays at different seaside places on the Breton and Norman coasts. It was the life of a public man, kept in balance by the cult he made of preserving intimacy with Elizabeth's closest friends, with her sister Arabella until her death, with Miss Isa Blagden, with whom he exchanged letters written by her regularly on the 12th of each month, the date of his wedding, and replied to by him on the 19th, and with the Storys. But his greatest responsibility to her memory was the education of their son, which proved no easy task, and over the details of which he brooded with a more than paternal solicitude.

It was not until 1864 that the poet published the successor to *Men and Women*, his small volume of *Dramatis Personae*. The new poems broke no fresh ground. Compared with his *Men and Women* they depended rather more uniformly on the objective anecdote; there were no such pure inspirations as 'Childe Roland.' The most substantial, indeed, of the new monologues, 'Mr. Sludge, the Medium,' adhered very closely to certain recent events, for in it the spiritualist Home, in the very thinnest of disguises, was allowed to attempt not so much his own defence as justification, which took the form of a bitter and penetrating attack on the credulous society people who had encouraged him and his frauds. The poem has the flatness of 'Bishop Blougram' but not the same humanity. For the meanness which in 'Blougram' had

H

Chapter Five

THE ROUGH ORE ROUNDED

'My life is fixed and sure now,' wrote Browning to his sister in the letter in which he described Elizabeth's last days and her death, 'I shall live out the remainder in her direct influence, endeavouring to complete mine, miserably imperfect now, but so as to take the good she was meant to give me . . . I shall live in the presence of her, in every sense, I hope and believe—so that so far my loss is not *irreparable*—but the future is nothing to me now, except in as much as it confirms and realizes the past . . . I do not feel paroxysms of grief— but as if the very blessing she died giving me, insensible to all beside, had begun to work already.' The remainder of Browning's life was passed in the endeavour to live up to the experience of that moment, and all that is important in his later poetry is the record of his success or failure in his endeavour to do so. Immediately he left Florence with his son, first to join his father and sister on the French coast and then to return to England. He felt that he had no longer any business in Italy, now that she was dead. In London he would be near her sister Arabella; in London Penini could be educated; in London the poetry Elizabeth had left behind her could be published, and his own work (still without *Pauline*) collected in a definitive edition of three volumes.

In the summer of 1862 Robert Browning took a house in Warwick Crescent, Paddington, and was soon being

she had heard that Henrietta was ill she had hoped to go to England, but she had not the strength. Yet Browning was not more than usually apprehensive about her health. Indeed he was enjoying a typical Roman winter. He had laid his writing aside, and in intervals between entertainments was learning to sculpt in Story's studio. He had written nothing, indeed, for a year. The news of Garibaldi's success in Naples and Sicily was encouraging, and on a wave of optimism the Brownings were soon discussing the possibilities of a grand meeting in France that summer with Robert Browning senior, the poet's sister and Elizabeth's sister Arabella. But shortly before their return to Florence, Elizabeth fell ill once more, and all they could do was to get back to Casa Guidi. Now the political news was bad, and this affected the sick woman's spirits. But no one suspected that she was so near her end. On June 28th, however, after less than a week's renewed illness, with almost no presentiment and little pain, Elizabeth Barrett Browning suddenly died, leaving her husband after fifteen years of marriage to face a further twenty-eight years of life alone.

to his wife's overestimate of the pocket Napoleon. The news of the peace of Villafranca disillusioned him and brought on a severe attack of Elizabeth's chest complaint, which was rendered more severe by the pains of angina; and, in the midst of his anxiety, Browning assumed responsibility for the aged Landor, who had returned after many years of estrangement to rejoin his family at Fiesole and, after quarrelling with them, found himself homeless.

Next summer the Brownings spent at Siena, with Elizabeth still in an extremely weak condition. There they met the Storys, who had now taken charge of Landor; there, whilst Italy was still in upheaval, Landor wrote alcaics by turns against his wife and against Napoleon III; there Elizabeth Browning corrected the proofs of her *Poems before Congress*, which were still full of uncritical praise of the Emperor, and there, in the evenings they and all their circle sat on their lawn under the ilexes and cypresses, talking over their tea until long after the cool night had fallen, of their hopes and their fears for the new Italy, which was still to be long in taking shape.

Browning at that time proposed to anatomize Napoleon III in a poem, as he was to anatomize that other charlatan Home, about whom he differed so radically with his wife. But *Prince Hohenstiel-Schwangau, Saviour of Society* was not to be published for another twelve years, by which time the Emperor had finally lost his throne and what remained of his reputation at Sedan. Perhaps in the interval that plan of the poem underwent revision; perhaps the pocket Napoleon was allowed to put up a better defence for himself in 1871 than he would have been allowed in 1859.

In the autumn of the next year the Brownings were once more in Rome, and it was here that Elizabeth received news of her sister Henrietta's death. When

poem *Aurora Leigh* while Robert made a further vain endeavour to simplify the recalcitrant *Sordello*, she fell ill again; and no sooner had she recovered than bad news came from England, of the serious illness of their old friend John Kenyon. It was to his offices that they owed their original introduction, and to him too they owed most generous financial help. To England therefore they returned, to stay with him for the last time. On his death in the following winter he left each of them a generous legacy.

The first news that greeted them on their return to Florence for the next winter was of the immediate success of *Aurora Leigh*, a success infinitely greater than that of *Men and Women*. Browning had, however, no spice of jealousy in his composition. Probably he still thought that she was really a better poet than he. Indeed he glowed in his wife's fame, and was continually bringing up good reviews of her poem to show to friends, and recounting the editions that had gone through the press.

Now the Brownings planned to visit Egypt and the Holy Land in the next winter, but Elizabeth's health would not allow it. News that her father had died, still unreconciled to her, had greatly distressed her in the spring of 1857. That summer they joined Browning's father and sister on the French coast, staying in Paris on the way, where they met old friends and Browning gave up writing for a while to try his hand at drawing. Next winter they were again in Rome. Now, in 1859, there were renewed prospects of Italy's unification. All Elizabeth's hopes were pinned on Napoleon III, in whom she unswervingly believed. Robert, as ever, was less credulous, though until the French emperor abandoned the Italian cause when it was half won, taking Savoy and Nice for his reward, he was almost prepared to subscribe

the disappointingly stolid table at Casa Guidi, was
rewarded by far more spectacular phenomena produced
under the inspiration of the American medium Daniel
Home. Home and spiritualism were already the rage
in fashionable society. But at the first séance he attended
Browning asserted that he had caught Home cheating.
The idea of communication with the dead, however,
had seized strongly on Elizabeth's imagination. She had
been enquiring for years from all her friends about
spiritualistic manifestations in London, New York and
Paris; now for the first time she could witness them.
Perhaps after her husband's outburst she was a little less
uncritical, but she did not accept his view of Home. She
was much hurt in fact when he showed that adventurer
the door on the occasion of his calling at Dorset Street.
Her belief was not perhaps dependent on the honesty of
any particular medium. She had no liking for Home as a
man, and indeed wrote later that she was 'disappointed
about him,' conjuring up in the same letter to her sister
the pleasant vision of the conjugal furniture floating
about his room on his bridal night. But she believed
most strongly in the truth of spiritualistic doctrine,
which she held to be a vital proof of the unseen world
offered to a materialistic age. On this matter Robert
and Elizabeth continued to differ; it was perhaps their
only strong difference of opinion in their wedded life.
It was not until after her death that Browning published
his attack upon Home, which he entitled 'Mr. Sludge the
Medium'; and by the time that he wrote it he was prepared to let his victim put up a defence as strong but not
as valid as Blougram's. Some of his readers indeed even
supposed the poem to be stating some sort of case for
the spiritualists, but that it was not.

In Paris, where Elizabeth had been working on her

and all the Anglo-American colony settled in that city; serious work in Rome was impossible.

Back in Florence in the spring of 1854 Browning tried to make up for the time he had wasted in society by setting his poetical house in order. That year they had hoped to come back to England, but lack of money forbade even a summer holiday in the mountains. In the winter that followed Elizabeth had the worst chest attack that she had experienced in Italy; the complaint which had once confined her to her couch had recurred only infrequently since her marriage, but she had always to husband her strength. By the summer of 1855, however, she was well again and anxious once more to visit England. The *Men and Women* was finished but for the dedication, which was written later in their London lodgings. In London once more there were countless social engagements, with Ruskin, Leighton, Carlyle, Kinglake, Forster, the Kemble sisters, Russell Lowell and the Proctors. On one occasion Tennyson and Rossetti called at once, and the Dorset Street lodgings witnessed the meeting of four of the age's chief poets. It was a splendid occasion. Tennyson recited his still unpublished *Maud*, Browning, who was generally shy of public performances, read 'Lippo Lippi,' while Rossetti, in a corner, made a rapid pen and ink sketch of Tennyson, which he presented to Browning as he left. Later Browning sat to him for a portrait. Then when the proofs of *Men and Women* were corrected and London began to feel the first chills of autumn, the Brownings left once more for Paris.

Gay though their summer had been, one incident had come very much to disturb Robert Browning's peace if mind. For in London Elizabeth's interest in spiritualism, which had received such poor sustenance around

bulk of *Men and Women* was written. Company at
Florence was much scantier than in London or Paris.
There were the few American expatriates, chief among
them the Storys. There was Robert Lytton, the novelist's
son, Frederick Tennyson, Miss Blagden, but life in
Florence meant for them both an existence almost
exclusively in each other's company. Here they wrote,
each in a separate room, neither showing the other any
work until it was completed. Here they joined one
another for long and intimate evenings, united in discussion of art and politics and in their worship of their
phenomenal child, nicknamed Penini, whose every
infant saying was recorded for the benefit of their correspondents. 'It was delightful to find ourselves in the
old nest, still warm, of Casa Guidi,' wrote Elizabeth on
her return, 'to sit in our own chairs and sleep in our
own beds . . . You can't think how we have caught up
our ancient traditions just where we left them, and
relapsed into our former soundless, stirless hermit life.
Robert has not passed an evening from home since we
came—just as if we had never known Paris. People come
sometimes to have tea and talk with us, but that's all. . . .'
It was here during the winter that Elizabeth's interest
was first roused by spiritualism. But for a while
experiments were confined to table-turning, and the
tables generally refused to turn for the Brownings and
Lytton or who ever came. Then after a summer at the
Baths of Lucca, the Brownings and the Storys set off to
winter in Rome. Here they met with almost as much
company as in London or Paris, and soon Browning was
sitting to two portrait painters at once. Here they met
Thackeray, the Kemble sisters, the veteran Lockhart[1]

[1] Who took a great fancy to the poet, because he was so unlike 'a damned
literary man.'

turn but simultaneously, lyrical and dramatic, subjective and objective.' Milsand perhaps attributed to his English friend a more conscious purpose than he in fact possessed, but Browning knew how close his friend had come to understanding his true achievement.

After leaving London in 1851, the Brownings had spent part of the winter in Paris, where the first of his *Men and Women* and the introduction to some spurious Shelley letters were composed. It was here that they had first met Milsand, who was writing an article on Elizabeth Browning's poetry, and came to Browning for guidance. This Frenchman had studied art and fallen under Ruskin's influence. Then abandoning the role of painter he had set out to interpret the English critic in France. At the same time he had abandoned Catholicism and fought his way to an independent Protestantism that must have had much in common with Browning's own. After that he had begun writing articles on the English poets, starting with Tennyson and Browning. So it was that the friendship was already half made when the pair first met. It lasted for more than thirty years.

From Paris the Brownings returned to London for the summer of 1852, which they filled with the same round of social engagements as in 1851. Here they met Charles Kingsley, whom they liked despite his 'wild and theoretical' socialism; here Jane Carlyle brought Mazzini to visit them; here Rossetti, William Allingham, and Ruskin called: and here on September 5th Robert stood godfather to Alfred Tennyson's son Hallam. Then by way of Paris and the Mont Cenis they returned to Italy and their Florentine home, which they had left eighteen months before. For the next three years they remained in that country, and it was during those years that the

a degree which compensated for them. Elizabeth was
pleased with the great deal of notice the book aroused,
though she admitted that the reviews contained 'abuse
as well as laudation.' Only the pre-Raphaelites greeted
Men and Women with unmixed enthusiasm. A letter from
Ruskin, indeed, loud in praise of the 'Epistle of Karshish'
arrived on the same day as one from Elizabeth's sister
Henrietta, revealing her secret disgust at what she took
to be the poem's blasphemous implications. Elizabeth
replied to her reassuringly, if a little too firmly, that
'among all the criticisms we have heard, private and
public, such an idea as yours seems to have occured to
no one.' Browning's purpose in writing it, she went on,
had been in the highest degree reverential and Christian.
It was perhaps not for those virtues that William Bell
Scott acclaimed this same poem, putting it on a level
with 'Blougram's Apology' and describing it in a letter
to W. M. Rossetti as 'beyond all inventions he has yet
done.' Browning himself was less flattered by praise
from these rather dubious quarters than by the appreciation of his French friend Joseph Milsand, in an article in
the *Revue Contemporaine*. For whereas most of his English
critics supposed him to be aiming at the utmost objectivity, discussing his *Men and Women* as dramatic characters,
created to speak with voices of their own, Milsand saw
that Browning's inspiration partook of the subjective and
objective alike. He considered that Browning was first
an introspective poet, and only secondarily an artist or
'maker.' 'His explorations,' he had written of earlier
poems, 'are adventures of the intellect; his faculties
expand themselves *within*.' Now in reviewing *Men and
Women* he re-stressed this opinion. 'I am inclined to
think,' he wrote, 'that this constant endeavour has been
to reconcile and combine his talents, so as to be not in

logues Browning rang the changes on his own constituent moods or personalities, embodying each in turn in a character who should hold the stage and, in defending, expounding and pleading his own case, speak in part also for his creator. There was Blougram, the man of intellect who made a virtue of his emotional limitations; Andrea del Sarto, the perfect artist whose creative powers were hampered by emotional shortcomings of another kind; Lippo Lippi, the pagan creator overwhelmed at moments by a melancholy that testified to some deeper experience he was missing; Cleon, another pagan, unable to content himself with the world of art, yet overlooking his one clue to the profound truth he was half in search of; and Karshish, almost distrustful of his scientific detachment when confronted with an event beyond his powers to explain. All are different, yet all share one feature in common: a conviction, an intimation or perhaps no more than an inkling that there is some truth a little beyond their comprehension, the realization of which would alter the whole of their values. It is perhaps his consciousness of just this that Blougram is most anxious to disguise from his prying interviewer. All are different, yet all speak for Browning himself, and testify to his own search for the secret which would be Childe Roland's reward for the dauntless hornblast with which he confronted the Dark Tower, the secret that David knew when in the full outpouring of love and song he attained a moment of true emotional faith.

When the two volumes of *Men and Women* appeared in 1855, the year of Tennyson's far more successful *Maud*, they received a better reception than Browning had yet met with, but still hardly an adequate one. There were the old complaints of his obscurities, though it was admitted that he had grown in power and originality to

Some think, Creation's meant to show him forth:
I say it's meant to hide him all it can,
And that's what all the blessed evil's for.
Its use in Time is to environ us,
Our breath, our drop of dew, with shield enough
Against that sight till we can bear its stress.
Under a vertical sun, the exposed brain
And lidless eye and disemprisoned heart
Less certainly would wither up at once
Than mind, confronted with the truth of him.
But time and earth case-harden us to live;
The feeblest sense is trusted most; the child
Feels God a moment, ichors o'er the place,
Plays on and grows to be a man like us.
With me, faith means perpetual unbelief
Kept quiet like the snake 'neath Michael's foot
Who stands calm just because he feels it writhe . . .
Say I—let doubt occasion still more faith!

This is Browning's own statement of his everyday
fight for conviction; of the mood in which with Roland
he approached the Dark Tower, set the slug-horn to his
lips, but had no sight of whatever grail he was seeking;
of the mood in which the hunter accompanied his
Duchess to the borders of the gipsy country, but brought
back no news of the life there; of the mood in which
Browning himself replied to Robert Buchanan's question
whether he were a Christian with a thunderous 'No.'
It was not the mood of the end of 'Saul.' Browning's
moments of revelation were few; the triangle of love—
creation—faith was seldom completed in a single poem
or a single moment of vision. For him, as for Blougram,
however, evil and doubt existed only in order to occasion
faith. So the temporizing Roman Catholic archbishop,
like each one of Browning's men and women, spoke for
one aspect of the man himself. For in his great mono-

Is—not to fancy what were fair in life
Provided it could be,—but, finding first
What may be, then find how to make it fair
Up to our means . . .

This is a more cautious and tentative position than
Browning's own. But the Bishop, nevertheless, speaks
for his creator in so far as he refers all problems back
ultimately to faith. 'See the world such as it is,' he says,
'you made it not nor I. I mean to take it as it is.' And
as it is, he finds that faith is the principal element in it.
Napoleon could not with comfort to himself have blown
millions up but for 'his crazy trust God knows through
what or in what.' So, faith being a necessary constituent
of life, let it be a reasonable faith. Perhaps Blougram is
understating his case. For, says Browning at the end,
he believed, say, half he spoke.

The rest was the sprightliest of verbal conjuring intended to discomfort his journalistic visitor. Perhaps
Browning means us to assume that the Bishop tempered
the statement of his belief in order to meet Mr. Gigadibs
on his own ground. Yet at the moment when he defines
his attitude to faith the temperature of the poem rises
appreciably from its steady argumentative level, the dia-
lectic swelling to dramatic statement, a certain sign that
the poet was here speaking for himself as well as for his
character. The moment is one in which the Bishop dis-
misses an imaginary objection of his interviewer's, with
an argument foreshadowing the dying St. John's in 'A
Death in the Desert.'

Pure faith indeed—you know not what you ask!
Naked belief in God the Omnipotent,
Omniscient, Omnipresent, sears too much
The sense of conscious creatures to be borne.
It were the seeing him, no flesh shall dare.

> Some future state revealed to us by Zeus,
> Unlimited in capability
> For joy, as this is in desire for joy. . .

But as for the promise of some such state made by the barbarian Jew Paulus, and lately preached upon Cleon's own isle by certain slaves, he cannot trouble himself even to investigate the story, for

> Their doctrine could be held by no sane man.

Bishop Blougram, who holds that doctrine, though with reservations that he does not clearly define, is a very sane man, the sanest perhaps of all the *Men and Women*. He may contain something of Father Prout and, as Browning himself admitted, be intended in part as a portrait of Cardinal Wiseman, the first Roman Catholic Archbishop of Westminster, but he speaks in part also for his creator. For 'Bishop Blougram's Apology' continues the argument of *Christmas Eve and Easter Day*, though now the speaker is far less closely associated with the poet himself than were the two hardly contrasted protagonists of faith in those earlier poems. Browning had, as has been seen, no profound understanding of Catholicism. He saw it, nevertheless, as a creed capable of dealing with the problems of the world in worldly terms. Divorced of its grosser superstitions, to which, the poem suggests, its educated leaders do not subscribe, it represented for him a position to be defended against the theorists of the German lecture halls, and the paying materialism of Blougram's shadowy interlocutor, Gigadibs. Blougram's was at least a teaching 'not so obscured that no truth shines athwart the lies,' but one on a lower level than a man might reach, riding out by the light of his own spark. 'The common problem,' Blougram says,

the likenesses of his patrons and superiors without
thought for the morrow or the hereafter. Yet there are
moments when he too is filled with some other intuition,
that he does not pause to analyse, when

> . . . some warm eve finds me at my saints—
> A laugh, a cry, the business of the world—
> (*Flower o' the peach*,
> *Death for us all, and his own life for each!*)
> And my whole soul revolves, the cup runs over,
> The world and life's too big to pass for a dream,
> And I do these wild things in sheer despite,
> And play the fooleries you catch me at,
> In pure rage!

Such is Lippo Lippi, simple and unregenerate, artist
but no lover, sly, vigorous, humorous and intoxicated
with the vanity of the world, a monk without a vocation,
a painter with a true eye for the prettiest face and a
naïve certainty that

> If you get simple beauty and nought else,
> You get about the best thing God invents.

But if the monkish painter is content to be a pagan,
the pagan Cleon is unsatisfied with the immortality he
can gain through art; his old age is no more tolerable to
him for his paintings, his carvings or the odes he has
made. For what is it, he asks, that will survive him?

> The brazen statue to o'erlook my grave,
> Set on the promontory which I named.
> And that—some supple courtier of my heir
> Shall use its robed and sceptred arm, perhaps,
> To fix the rope to, which best drags it down.

Body and soul will alike perish in death. The prospect
is so horrible that he can at times imagine

They were no part of him, but objective portraits or creations that he could hand over to the public, in the confidence that they would not tell of his joys and his sorrows. But in 'One Word More' he resolved to speak for once in his true person, 'not as Lippo, Roland or Andrea.' A strangely various trio these, for none of his characters betrayed more of Browning's inner experience than Roland, and few came nearer to the status of objective personages existing in their own right than his two painters Fra Lippo Lippi and Andrea del Sarto.

The two blank verse monologues bearing their names stand in the third group of Browning's *Men and Women*, being concerned with the third of his triune qualities, the act of creation, and with questions of character and philosophic beliefs. They are—to use the distinction made in 'Master Hugues of Saxe Gotha'—fugues, to be contrasted with the unstopping of the full organ in 'By the Fireside,' in 'One Word More' and—little though Browning would have acknowledged the fact—in 'Childe Roland.' 'Andrea del Sarto,' 'Fra Lippo Lippi' and 'Cleon' are three variations on the single theme of art's inadequacy as a way of life. The conclusion is overtly stated in 'Cleon' and merely implied in the two Italian pieces. For del Sarto, both as lover and artist, has fallen short of his ideal; lacking any glimpse of the third pole of faith, he has failed to exploit his perfect painter's technique and is content to be deceived by a wife whom he still feebly loves. The poem is as sad in tone as 'Fra Lippo Lippi' is lively. For poor brother Lippi is a creature of a fine earthy humour, with somewhere beneath his monkish cloak the innocent heart of a Pippa. He is the true artist, content to catch whatever he can of the soul by painting the body, to enjoy his 'lights of love,' and catch

but for the biblical strand which was a more or less constant constituent of his more serious style.

'By the Fireside' is the most important of the love poems in *Men and Women*, but there are others devoted to pursuit and wooing, winning and loss, in which the same lyrical note prevails, pieces such as 'A Lovers' Quarrel,' 'The Last Ride Together,' 'Love in a Life,' 'Life in a Love,' concerned with more imaginary situations, snatches often of pure rapture, though not without occasional drops into bathos and sentimentality. For although Browning was not a poet of the highest lyrical attainments except in short flights, and was conscious of the fact, he held that love poetry should be written on a sustained lyrical note, and was willing to strain his voice in order to maintain it. So in effect he states in the dedicatory 'One Word More' with which he presents his book to 'E.B.B.' Every artist, he says, would wish to give to his beloved a work for her eyes alone, performed in a medium that was not his own. Raphael made a century of sonnets for his lady, Dante painted a picture of Beatrice, but he, Robert Browning, will never

> Paint you pictures, no, nor carve you statues,
> Make you music that should all-express me. . .

In this dedication, however, he will give her something more intimate, for her eyes alone.

> Love, you saw me gather men and women,
> Live or dead or fashioned by my fancy,
> Enter each and all, and use their service,
> Speak from every mouth,—the speech, a poem.

This, as Browning saw it, was what he had done in creating his 'Karshish, Cleon, Norbert and the fifty.'

G

in which the Queen lived at peace with her gipsy lover.
Yet he could only hint at its nature by adapting a biblical
phrase for his culminating line.

> Think, when our one soul understands
>   The great Word which makes all things new,
> When earth breaks up and heaven expands,
>   How will the change strike me and you
> In the house not made with hands?

But though that is the poem's central question, 'By
the Fireside' has few verses so abstract and ethereal. It is
in the main a celebration of the beauties of the world
and of human love, rich in observed and affectionate
detail and failing only in one place, in its apostrophe to
'My perfect wife, my Leonor,' a line which partakes of
the same sentimental falsity as that of 'sweepy garment,
vast and white, with a hem that I could recognize,' of
'Christmas Eve.' For when Browning attempted to convey the highest emotion, the deepest experience, each
time he failed. If he had experienced them it was too
fleetingly, with too excited a vision, to allow of his
recording them. So he was reduced to describing the
heights of love or revelation in other men's words, and
sometimes with fatal banality. But in his choice of the
biblical 'house not made with hands,' and even more
magically in describing the Christ of 'A Death in the
Desert,' in words borrowed from the Apocalypse of St.
John:

> With head wool-white, eyes flame, and feet like brass,
> The sword and the seven stars, as I have seen . . .

Browning heightened the emotion of his poem, passing
from his own words to those of the Bible without the
least break; a feat which might not have been possible

which, in their ultimate and metaphysical sense, are
insoluble except in terms of an intuitive and elusive
hope.

'By the Fireside,' perhaps the most personal of
Browning's love poems, containing as it does the portrait
of Elizabeth,

> Reading by fire-light, that great brow
> And the spirit-small hand propping it . . .

looks back from an imaginary middle age on a wooing
transposed to Italy, and set in a mountain landscape
milder than that of the Duke's other country, yet vaguely
recalling it. The actual scene against which Browning
reconstructed his wooing of Elizabeth was copied from
a valley near Florence where they had walked together
a year or two before. The detail is faithfully recorded
in all its intimate desolation:

> Look at the ruined chapel again,
>   Half-way up in the Alpine gorge!
> Is that a tower, I point you plain,
>   Or is it a mill, or an iron-forge
> Breaks solitude in vain?

Like 'The Flight of the Duchess,' this poem is concerned with two contrasted climates. But here they are
not geographical alternatives. Here they are thought of as
man and woman: 'woman's country' and 'earth's male
lands.' What in the earlier poem might appear to be
two aspects of a single mind, the poet's, was here embodied in two people; and the union or reconciliation
required not a flight or escape, but their union, after
Shelley's platonic fashion, to form one soul and pass
beyond life as one. In 'By the Fireside' Browning
glimpsed for a moment, perhaps, that other, magic
country which he had not been able to describe before,

It is through our zig-zags and dodges, he complains, that God's gold is covered beneath the pall of man's usurpature—and experience overlaid by intellectualization.

> So we o'ershroud stars and roses,
>   Cherub and trophy and garland;
> Nothings grow something which quietly closes
>   Heaven's earnest eye: not a glimpse of the far land
> Gets through our comments and glozes.

Far from rejoicing in his philosophical and intellectual complexity—as the Browning society supposed—Robert Browning here, half humorously perhaps, but nevertheless with genuine conviction, wrote the complexities off as mere obscuring cobwebs and comforted himself with the assurance that, nevertheless,

> Truth's golden o'er us although we refuse it.

But 'Master Hugues of Saxe Gotha' is too lightweight a poem to be tortured into yielding so deep a moral; its 'stars and roses' are only by remote inference to be identified with the objects of Browning's quest.

For the symbolism of the quest and the waste land, though profoundly important to Browning, nevertheless plays a part in only a few of his poems. These mark the activity of the poet of *Pauline* continued into middle life, but preoccupied now not with the resolution of adolescent half-rebellion, but with the search for life's secret purpose, a treasure by contrast to which commonplace objects and events seem sordid and brutal. Many more of his poems, however, are concerned with human love, an experience which raises the everyday world to beauty, and shuts out all sight of that desolate plain which leads to the distant mountains. It appears, one might say, to offer at least a provisional solution for problems,

the lying cripple lured him into the waste? This poem has no ambiguities. On the gravestones of an earlier civilization, among the memorials of efforts that have failed, it is possible for Browning, with a ring of certainty that is corroborated by the certain beat of each rhyme, to consign the glories and triumphs of the past to the dust and, in the certainty that 'a girl with eager eyes and yellow hair' will keep her tryst among the ruins, proclaim in his final line that 'Love is best.'

Browning's visits to his 'waste land' were few. The 'Flight of the Duchess' records an escape from it on the plane of fantasy into a country that he wished to describe but could not; 'Christmas Eve' and 'Easter Day' state a false solution of the dilemma he found there; and 'Childe Roland' tells of a journey through its desolation to face an ordeal of which he could picture neither the nature nor the outcome.

In a poem that sprang from far less profound levels of experience than were tapped by the intrusive associations of 'Following the Queen of the Gypsies, O!' or of the fragmentary line from *Lear*, Browning reverted once more to his dilemma, analysing it this time in terms of musical composition; the piece concerns an imaginary composer, Master Hugues of Saxe Gotha. Here the contrast is between the complication of a fugue made up of so many contradictory voices and the full organ blaring out 'the mode Palestrina.' Is all this 'affirming, denying, holding, risposting, subjoining,' the unknown organist asks the ghost of the musician, what he supposes life to be.

> Is it your moral of Life?
>   Such a web, simple and subtle,
> Weave we on earth here in impotent strife,
>   Backward and forward each throwing his shuttle,
> Death ending all with a knife?

                              the plain had given place
          All round to mountains—with such name to grace
        Mere ugly heights and heaps now stolen in view.

The purpose of the quest might seem to be, therefore,
the witnessing of some miracle among the mountains, yet
ultimately the miracle, if miracle there was, was un-
witnessed, and the poet remained in his 'waste land.'
Only on the plans of escape or fantasy could the other
way of living be imagined; in reality it was not the
Judgment but any hope of avoiding or by-passing it that
was a dream.

Associated with 'Childe Roland' by the nearby dates of
their composition are the mysterious 'Women and Roses'
—which seems to recall some failure of a parallel quest—
and the smooth and half sleepy 'Love among the Ruins,'
whose assured, softly chiming rhythms suggest repletion
and rest. But the setting of this last poem, the first of
the three in order of composition, as 'Childe Roland' is
the last, is a landscape rich with memorials of other
and earlier defeats.

            Now,—the single little turret that remains
                On the plains,
            By the caper overrooted, by the gourd
                Overscored,
            While the patching houseleek's head of blossom winks
                Through the chinks—
            Marks the basement whence a tower in ancient time
                Sprang sublime,
            And a burning ring, all round, the chariots traced
                As they raced,
            And the monarch and his minions and his dames
                Viewed the games.

Was it to some such land that Roland was riding when

country into which that dauntless horn-blast may purchase admission. The poem's landscape reveals no hint of beauty even at the last; it is throughout one with the Duke's other country of 'The Flight,' one vast red drear burnt-up plain; but it presents another and far more unexpected parallel. It is into that same land that the Arab physician rode to learn of Lazarus' raising and to hear news of the 'Nazarene physician.'

> I have shed sweat enough, left flesh and bone
> On many a flinty furlong of this land,

says Karshish in the introduction, and at the poem's conclusion he expands his description of the place in which he came upon the sanguine, well-proportioned, fifty-year-old revenant from beyond the grave. 'I met him thus,' he writes:

> I crossed a ridge of short sharp broken hills
> Like an old lion's cheek teeth. Out there came
> A moon made like a face with certain spots
> Multiform, manifold and menacing . . .

The imagery is far less brutal than that of 'Childe Roland' and preserves the microscopic exactness attributed to the scientific Karshish. But the landscape is the same; and it is remarkable, also, that the setting of that other and later poem concerned with the Gospel revelation, 'A Death in the Desert,' is set in country of the same unrelieved desolation, country in which a single goat has nothing to graze on but

> rags of various herb,
> Plantain and quitch, the rocks' shade keeps alive.

The scenery of mountains seems inevitable. For though the quest in 'Childe Roland' began over a plain, at the end and unexpectedly the knight found

deathlike country? But his question finds its own answer. When he arrives, Roland acknowledges a baleful fore-knowledge of the place; there were no other tracks over the plain that he was free to follow.

> Yet half I seemed to recognize some trick
>   Of mischief happened to me, God knows when—
>   In a bad dream perhaps. Here ended, then,
> Progress this way. When, in the very nick
> Of giving up, one time more, came a click
>   As when a trap shuts—you're inside the den!
>
> Burningly it came on me all at once,
>   This was the place! those two hills on the right,
>   Crouched like two bulls locked horn in horn in fight;
> While to the left, a tall scalped mountain . . . Dunce,
> Dotard, a-dozing at the very nonce,
>   After a life spent training for the sight!

Suddenly Childe Roland recognizes the inevitability of his quest, and knows that he has spent his whole life preparing for the ordeal confronting him, an ordeal in which each of the knights before him, his brothers or his former selves, Cuthbert and Giles, and the rest, has been vanquished. Yet have they been vanquished? For, in the poem's final stanza,

> There they stood, ranged along the hill-sides, met
>   To view the last of me, a living frame
>   For one more picture! in a sheet of flame
> I saw them and I knew them all. And yet
> Dauntless the slug-horn to my lips I set
>   And blew. '*Childe Roland to the Dark Tower came.*'

The poem remains half-resolved; its ambiguities are not dispelled. There is no dream-like escape into any land of the gipsies; not so much as a glimpse of a promised

had been able to stand up to the Shelleyan temptation of later days; the stages of the 'Childe Roland' allegory are matched exactly to those of his own history. But each of these comrades—or of his former selves—had fallen into disgrace. Just as there was no return once he had followed the cripple's path, so there was no strength to be gained by returning in spirit to a former state, which to closer view betrayed earlier instances of failure. There was nothing for it but to ride on without hope.

> Better this present than a past like that;
>> Back therefore to my darkening path again!
>> No sound, no sight as far as eye could strain.
> Will the night send a howlet or a bat?
> I asked: when something on the dismal flat
>> Came to arrest my thoughts and change their train.
>
> A sudden little river crossed my path
>> As unexpected as a serpent comes.
>> No sluggish tide congenial to the glooms;
> This, as it frothed by, might have been a bath
> For the fiend's glowing hoof—to see the wrath
>> Of its black eddy bespate with flakes and spumes.

So by fording this murky swift-flowing Styx, fearful every moment of setting a foot on a dead man's cheek, or thrusting a supporting spear in his tangled hair, the knight pushes on into what he vainly hopes may prove a better country, although trodden down by the feet of stragglers who had passed through it before him to face the fight in that 'fell cirque.' Into this arena, in which each in turn must confront his unnamed opponent, lead many footsteps, but out of it come none. 'What penned them there,' asks the knight, 'with all the plain to choose?' Why with apparent free will must each man go compulsively to the same hopeless ordeal in this

however, drawing on far deeper levels of experience, describes the cruelty and ugliness of this country, through
which his Everyman must conduct his search, with
haunting exactness. Browning's frequent return to
themes of brutality and melodramatic disgust, his
startling use of images repulsive in their physical horror,
arose from his deep, though only sporadic, realization
that the soul of unregenerate man presents an extremely
ugly picture. His optimism, for which he was so often
reproached, lay in his belief that a treasure existed and
could be found, by which a man could be saved. Nowhere, indeed, is his imagery so hideously obsessed as
in the description of that country through which the
knight, only half willingly, rode to find that ray of hope
which is not permitted to break in until the poem's last
verse. But here, in all its desolation, is the 'waste land'
that awaits the Judgment's fire:

> As for the grass, it grew as scant as hair
> 　　In leprosy: thin dry blades pricked the mud
> 　　Which underneath looked kneaded up with blood.
> One stiff blind horse, his every bone a-stare,
> Stood stupefied, however he came there:
> 　　Thrust out past service from the devil's stud!
>
> Alive? he might be dead for aught I know,
> 　　With that red gaunt and colloped neck a-strain,
> 　　And shut eyes underneath the rusty mane;
> Seldom went such grotesqueness with such woe;
> I never saw a beast I hated so;
> 　　He must be wicked to deserve such pain.

Roland tries to summon courage by recalling the
happiness of his youth, and the faces of his brothers or
comrades of that time. It was, Browning knew, only
with the strength of his own happy childhood that he

ordeal at the Dark Tower. The lie was not on the cripple's tongue but in Roland's own heart, and it was not so much a lie as a betrayal of his purpose, a desire to avoid that 'ominous tract' and the secret it held. There is obvious relevance in this situation to Browning's former half-hearted rebellion, seen by him still in these same terms of betrayal; his 'lying' wish was for a failure which would excuse him from further endeavours, for a collapse like that of the poet of *Pauline*.

Once the knight had turned despairingly away from 'that hateful cripple,' into the path up which he pointed, resolved deliberately to incur that failure which would bring an end to his search, all possibility of return disappeared.

> For mark! no sooner was I fairly found
>> Pledged to the plain, after a pace or two,
>> Than, pausing to throw backward a last view
> O'er the safe road, 'twas gone; grey plain all round:
> Nothing but plain to the horizon's bound.
>> I might go on; nought else remained to do.

He was now riding through a desolate country, symbolizing some lesser 'dark night of the soul,' where Nature herself was starved and ignoble, through a country of weeds and stones that could only be purged by utter burning. For, in Nature's own words to the knight as he rides through it;

> 'Tis the Last Judgment's fire must cure this place,
>> Calcine its clods and set my prisoners free.

The poet of 'Easter Day' had denied the reality of the Judgment, had woken to find it all a dream, yet with a certainty gained in that dream could confute the sceptic with whom he argued. The poet of 'Childe Roland,'

'Childe Roland' was written in Paris in a single day, January 3rd 1852. 'Love among the Ruins' and 'Women and Roses' had been written on the 1st and 2nd respectively. These are among the few poems of Browning's that can be exactly dated.

The first suggestion for 'Childe Roland' came from a line of Edgar's in *Lear*: 'Child Rowland to the dark tower came,' a line as suggestive as that snatch of a song which had given Browning his inspiration for 'The Flight of the Duchess.' Both poems reach down to the emotional levels at which dualities and congruities are as one. For as the huntsman and the Duke in the earlier poem were but two aspects of the same figure, so the cripple of 'Childe Roland's' opening lines is both a false and a true guide.

> What else should he be set for, with his staff?
> What, save to waylay with his lies, ensnare
> All travellers who might find him posted there,
> And ask the road? I guessed what skull-like laugh
> Would break, what crutch 'gin write my epitaph
> For pastime in the dusty thoroughfare,
>
> If at his counsel I should turn aside
> Into that ominous tract which, all agree,
> Hides the Dark Tower. Yet acquiescingly
> I did turn as he pointed: neither pride
> Nor hope rekindling at the end descried,
> So much as gladness that some end might be.

But what was the cripple's lie? For he was not standing there to waylay travellers, certain of their destination, to some treacherous death in the waste. His lie, if lie it was, was only his means of luring them from a false goal to a true one. For Childe Roland's 'worldwide wandering,' his 'search drawn out thro' years' had been in fact a search for that very secret to be won in the

he can employ the treasure he gained in his short sojourn there. 'We call the treasure knowledge,' explains the Arab Physician, 'knowledge

> Increased beyond the fleshly faculty—
> Heaven opened to a soul while yet on earth,
> Earth forced on a soul's use while seeing heaven:
> The man is witless of the size, the sum,
> The value in proportion of all things,
> Or whether it be little or be much . . .
> The man is apathetic, you deduce?
> Contrariwise, he loves both old and young,
> Able and weak, affects the very brutes
> And birds—how say I? flowers of the field—
> As a wise workman recognizes tools
> In a master's workshop, loving what they make.

Whether his grail be symbolized as a treasure, a rose, or the completed triad of faith, love and creation, or beauty, love and duty, Browning's finest poems are a varied record of the quest for it.

The most important and symbolically the richest of these quest poems is 'Childe Roland to the Dark Tower came,' a piece generally classed with 'The Flight of the Duchess' as pure romance. Mrs. Sutherland Orr in her *Handbook*, however, labels it a moralizing allegory, in contrast to 'The Flight' which she calls a moralizing fairy tale. 'They are both,' she adds, 'a useful type both of Mr. Browning's poetic genius, and of the misunderstanding to which its constantly intellectual employment has exposed him.' The poet of 'Christmas Eve,' in other words, was expected to make plain statements; his public has forgotten the obscurities of *Sordello* and knew nothing of the emotional complexities of *Pauline*. Mrs. Orr, however, knew the nature of his genius better. She was besides in his confidence.

> How soon all worldly wrong would be repaired!
> 　I think how I should view the earth and skies
> And sea, when once again my brow was bared
> 　After thy healing, with such different eyes.
> O world, as God has made it! All is beauty:
> And knowing this, is love, and love is duty.
> 　What further may be sought for or declared?

But, in one of the loveliest poems in *Men and Women*—
'Love among the Ruins'—one finds it conceived of less
intellectually, in terms of pure peace and love in a land
that has grown quiet after the passing of empires. A
much more profound statement, however, of that other
life occurs in 'An Epistle containing the Strange Medical
Experience of Karshish the Arab Physician', a poem in
which an incredulous traveller describes a meeting with
the raised Lazarus—'a Jew, sanguine, proportioned, fifty
years of age,'—and reflects upon the claims of 'the
Nazarene who wrought this cure' to be . . .

> God forgive me! who but God himself,
> Creator and sustainer of the world,
> That came and dwelt in flesh on it awhile!

This 'Epistle,' 'Cleon' and 'A Death in the Desert,' all
three among Browning's very finest achievements, are
attempts to present the miraculous story of Christ with
varying degrees of obliquity, the first two as seen through
the eyes of inquiring pagans, and the third as reflected in
the memory of the dying St. John, the last witness and
the first to foresee the age of mingled hope and doubt that
would come after him. But whereas St. John is waking
for the last time, and speaks with the other-worldly
assurance of one who has almost died, Lazarus has indeed
gone down into the grave and returned. Now he is no
longer attached to the things of the world, but is waiting
patiently to be released into that other country where

'Women and Roses,' though important for its use of the rose symbol and for the statement it just fails to make, is at best an unsatisfactory poem. Mrs. Sutherland Orr speaks of it as the impression of a dream, and both vague and vivid, as such impressions are. The poet dreams of a red rose tree with three roses upon it, one withered, the second full blown and the third still in bud. To him they represent the generations of women dead, living and unborn. Each he endeavours in turn to worship, and each eludes him, for all three 'circle their rose on my rose tree': the phrase is ambiguous. The poet, however, seems to picture himself as in the centre, with the processions of maidens dancing round him, but himself unable to touch them since they are always in motion. The quest for the rose, whether successful or unsuccessful, whether it elude the dreamer of 'Women and Roses' or rise to the spell of John of Halberstadt, symbolizes in fresh form Robert Browning's most urgent preoccupation. For the note of intellectual conviction with which 'Easter Day' closes, the sonorous affirmation of 'Saul' and the Duchess's escape into the gipsy country are none of them earnests of final achievement; in his poetry the quest must be perpetually renewed, possession of the rose is never assured. Browning's was essentially a miraculous view of the world. For he had always the suspicion that life held surprising and magical possibilities for the man who should guess its secret. In three other poems which, like those just cited, appeared in his *Men and Women*, he gives conflicting pictures of what this secret might be. First one finds it in 'The Guardian Angel' described in terms of a healing or, more precisely, of relief from the tortures of an over-active brain. But here he is able to picture this different state of being only imprecisely in terms once more of the triune beauty-love-duty:

> never cared for plants
> Until it happed, a-walking in the fields,
> He noticed all at once that plants could speak . . .

In contrast to Boehme, the representative of this intellectual approach, Browning drew the picture of one John of Halberstadt, a nature mystic, whom he described a as 'magician, botanist and a chymist,' who

> With a 'Look you!' vents a brace of rhymes,
> And in there breaks the sudden rose herself,
> Over us, under, round us every side,
> Nay, in and out the tables and the chairs
> And musty volumes, Boehme's book and all,—
> Buries us with a glory, young once more,
> Pouring heaven into this shut house of life.

The moral is sound enough, though the illustration is strange. But this poem, the first of the *Men and Women*, is important in a further sense. For it is charged with just that symbolism which had been so painfully excluded from its twin predecessor. The rose, in this connection, has the same magic significance for Browning as later it was to have for Yeats. It is the symbol of eternal life, of the renewal of youth and of the triune experience of Love—Creation—Faith that is the burden of 'Saul.' In 'Transcendentalism' the flower is associated with the act of poetic creation; in 'Women and Roses,' a poem far less precise in its allegory, it is linked to the idea of love, and in 'The Heretic's Tragedy' the rose of fire is used in a negative sense, as the symbol of a false consuming faith. for the heretical Templar burns at the stake. In imagery rich in that sense of the horrible of which he was at times a master, Browning describes how

> . . . petal on petal, fierce rays unclose;
> Anther on anther, sharp spikes outstart;
> And with blood for dew, the bosom boils;

Chapter Four

SONG'S OUR ART

'Tis you speak, that's your error. Song's our art:
Whereas you please to speak these naked thoughts
Instead of draping them in sights and sounds.

IN these three lines from the poem 'Transcendentalism.'
Browning proclaimed his abandonment of the false
way up which he had been endeavouring to force a passage
in *Christmas Eve and Easter Day*. Henceforth he would give
up the poetry of argument for the poetry of magic, for-
sake speech for incantation. To that extreme he did not
in fact go; his future poetry was to be poetry of argument,
but not poetry spoken in the first person. Sometimes
only would it be song, but always, at its best, it would
sing more clearly and more tunefully than the halting
verse of those two poems.

'Transcendentalism' is a curious piece, that shows, for
once, the limitations of Browning's reading and understanding. For out of all the possible figures he could have
selected to represent the speaking of naked thoughts he
could not have found one more suitable than the mystical
writer Jakob Boehme. Boehme, according to some
anecdote which the poet had no doubt discovered in his
father's library long ago, was remarkable for his completely negative attitude to the world's beauty, paying no
attention to nature. In fact, Browning tells us, he

F   73

should share his house, and Miss Haworth, his confidante in the days of his theatrical ambitions, quickly won the friendship of Elizabeth to whom she lent some books on mesmerism and Swedenborg, subjects that were later to obtain considerable hold on the poetess's imagination. For the first time too she met her husband's father and sister; her own sisters were constant visitors. But her father's door remained resolutely shut. He returned her in a packet all the letters she had written to him, un-opened. Depression at this, perhaps, and the effect of England upon her health sent the Brownings back to Paris after a couple of months. He, as the visit proved, had retained and perhaps increased his large circle of literary acquaintances; as a poet, however, he stood no higher in public regard than when he had left the country in 1846.

ling, first to Venice, for a fortnight which would have been prolonged had not the place affected Browning's sleep and appetite, then to Padua, Brescia, Milan, across the Gotthard, through Switzerland to Strasburg. They had been uncertain at first whether they would make for London. Certainly they would not be going for the sake of the Exposition, Elizabeth assured Miss Mitford. 'If by any arrangement I could see my sister Arabel in France or on the coast of England, we would persuade Robert's family to meet us there, and not see London at all. Ah, if you knew how abhorrent the thought of England is to *me*! . . . My eyes shut suddenly when my thoughts go that way.' In London was Mr. Barrett, still inflexible, perhaps more inflexible indeed since recently a second daughter had escaped him. In Paris by chance they met the Tennysons, who hearing that they had nowhere to go in England, offered them Chapel House for as long as they liked, with the servants and all that it contained. Robert Browning was deeply touched, but it was not to Twickenham that they went. They took lodgings in Devonshire Street within a few hundred yards of the Wimpole Street house from which Elizabeth Browning had eloped. Their friendship with Tennyson, however, grew stronger. Only the year before Elizabeth Browning had been passed over in his favour, when at Wordsworth's death a successor had been chosen for the Laureateship. Her claims had been quite strenuously advanced; none had been put forth on behalf of her husband. But now all three were united in mutual esteem.

Back in London after five years, the Brownings were welcomed by his old literary friends. Forster gave a dinner in their honour; Rogers invited them both to breakfast; they spent an evening with Carlyle. Arnould too, the friend of Browning's youth, proposed that they

his spirits, the miraculous baby throve and Elizabeth Browning was more active than ever since her girlhood. Once they rode out for a whole long day into the volcanic region of Prato Fiorito, a desolate tract scored with ravines that may have suggested the final landscape of 'Childe Roland.' It was at Lucca that Elizabeth Browning gave her husband the manuscript of those *Sonnets from the Portuguese* which she had written during their courtship and engagement. At Lucca too they met new friends: Charles Lever; the Countess Ossoli, an American woman-writer of pronounced socialist views, whose death in a shipwreck a few months later deeply shocked them both; and Miss Isa Blagden, 'a bright, delicate electric woman,' who was to be a lifelong friend. It was not till after their return to Florence that 'Christmas Eve' and 'Easter Day' were actually written. Outwardly they did not connect in any way with the circumstances of his life. For just at that time his liberal enthusiasms were at their height, so much so that he could hardly tolerate the Countess Ossoli's equally violent socialism, and expressed nothing but antipathy for her heroine George Sand. Moreover he actually refused for some time to make the acquaintance of the tory Mrs. Trollope on the grounds that she had attacked liberalism and the poetry of Victor Hugo. Who would have supposed that inwardly he was taken up with theological broodings?

In the later summer of 1850 Elizabeth Browning fell ill, and in September they moved to Siena, she in a miserably helpless state, as she told her sister, having to be lifted about like a baby, looking ghostly rather than ghastly. The cause appears to have been yet another miscarriage, which she had suffered in July. But soon she had recovered, and they were back in Florence. In the spring of the next year they were once more travel-

summed up their theology perfunctorily but not un-
justly in a manner that offended their author. Not till
his more deeply considered poem *La Saisiaz*, twenty-eight
years later, did Browning attempt again to speak in the
first person of ultimate problems.

The twin poems' setting was English; in it was no
trace of Italy's influence upon him. Nor did they bear any
marks of the happiness he found in his marriage. Perhaps
it was the death of his mother that had called his thoughts
back to England. 'No day has passed since our marriage,'
wrote Elizabeth to her sister-in-law, 'that he has not
fondly talked of her. I know how deep in his dear heart
her memory lies.' These were no facile words of con-
dolence; the poet felt his loss very deeply. A week or
two later his wife was writing that she wished she could
get him to 'go somewhere or do something.' His spirits,
and to some extent his health had given way. He could
not think of returning to Hatcham without extreme pain.
It would break his heart, he wrote, to see his mother's
roses over the wall, and the place where she used to lay
her scissors and gloves. Perhaps he felt no more than
any man would feel; but perhaps his mother's death
had the profounder effect of sending him back from the
Italian present to brood on the old preoccupations of his
adolescence; perhaps it contributed to the failure of his
long contemplated 'poem for the times.'

On March 9th 1849, a month before Sarah Ann
Browning died, Elizabeth, who was now forty-three
and had suffered three miscarriages, bore him a son.
That summer the Brownings left Florence on a sight-
seeing journey along the coast, by the pinewoods and
the Carrara mountains, to the Bay of Spezzia, and settled
for a while at the fashionable summer resort at the Baths
of Lucca. Here they rented a house, Browning recovered

Doomsday had come, and the poet—or his narrator—
read in it his own condemnation, for he had chosen the
world, preferring in his life the finite to the infinite.
Yet how, he pleads, could he have rejected it, for

>   it was hard so soon
> As in a short life, to give up
> Such beauty.

So, not utterly condemned, he was sentenced to
remain in that state of duality which Browning had
symbolically defined in 'The Flight of the Duchess.' For
while he received the gift of all the world he had so
desired, he must enjoy it in the knowledge that its
partial beauty was no more than a pledge of beauty in its
plenitude. 'But since the pledge sufficed thy mood,'
runs his sentence,

> Retain it! plenitude be theirs
> Who looked above.

So Browning might have felt when he knew himself
cast down from the Shelleyan empyrean for his failure
to carry through his Romantic rebellion.

Once in his youth he had known a moment of mingled
terror and revelation, from which he had emerged, in
Pauline, condemned yet treasuring that seed of hope
which had grown to flower in the personal affirmation
of 'Saul.' 'Christmas Eve' and 'Easter Day' together hark
back to this early stage in the development of his faith.
For not since his boyhood had he thought in terms of a
religious choice between free-thought and the chapel.
Such strengths as they have, therefore, they share rather
with *Pauline* than with his mature poetry. From the re-
viewers they had a mixed reception. The critic of the
Athenaeum, indeed, described their verse as doggerel, and

hair-shirt. Browning was incapable of asceticism, for his valuations were coloured at all times by his fundamental belief in earthly love. So much so that when the protagonist of 'Easter Day' is condemned for his attachment to the things of this world, he immediately wakes to discover that his vision of the Judgment has been no more than a dream. Not for a moment could Browning reject the colour and richness and human variety of the temporal scene.

But this dream passage has the same intensity as the scene outside the chapel in 'Christmas Eve.' Indeed Browning, without a hint to his reader that it is finally to prove a dream and no more, sets it upon the same common that his narrator had crossed in the first poem. The coincidence plays no part in the development of 'Easter Day,' though it serves to accentuate the identification of this dreamer with the explorer of many creeds of 'Christmas Eve.' We see him first walking there, brooding only half seriously upon life and the Judgment, when suddenly he is confronted with a vision like that of 'Christmas Eve,' but even more intense. 'I found,' he says, ˙

> Suddenly all the midnight round
> One fire. The dome of heaven had stood
> As made up of a multitude
> Of handbreadth cloudlets, one vast rack
> Of ripples infinite and black,
> From sky to sky. Sudden there went,
> Like horror and astonishment,
> A fierce vindictive scribble of red
> Quick flame across, as if one said
> (The angry scribe of Judgment) 'There—
> Burn it!'

The fierce glory in the night sky was the signal that

At that point the vision ceases to be convincing. For whereas the picture of the night sky suggests one of those states of heightened consciousness such as Wordsworth knew in the presence of nature, something akin too to those experiences which Tennyson called his 'weird seizures,' about the 'sweepy garment, vast and white' there clings no such aura of authenticity. The common outside the meeting house and the cloud-barred sky are lit with the harsh beam of expectancy that belongs to such moments. Clearly Browning was recalling some feeling of imminent revelation he had himself known, perhaps in his childhood. But the culmination is false; the Redeemer 'with his human air' is a lay figure, and with his introduction 'Christmas Eve' drops back to its dull discursive level.

The second of the poems, 'Easter Day', is in intention a dispute concerning the way in which man may

> at last awake
> From life, that insane dream we take
> For waking now.

But no such fundamental inquiry into man's state is, in fact, attempted; the poem is no more than an argument in which a visionary, of no greater depth of experience than the narrator of 'Christmas Eve,' is pitted against a sceptic. Elizabeth Browning complained of the asceticism of this second part. 'Don't think that he has taken to the cilix,' she wrote however, to a friend—'indeed he has not—but it is his way to *see* things as passionately as as other people *feel* them.' Clearly her habitual understanding of her husband's mind had deserted her.

It is difficult to associate that quality with anything Browning wrote. Here indeed his thought is tortured, but it is by the strait-jacket of an alien form, not by a

There was a lull in the rain, a lull
   In the wind too; the moon was risen,
And would have shone out pure and full,
   But for the ramparted cloud-prison,
Block on block built up in the West,
For what purpose the wind knows best,
Who changes his mind continually.
And the empty other half of the sky
Seemed in its silence as if it knew
What, any moment, might look through
A chance gap . . .

The imagery is suddenly clear, and there is a taut urgency about the lines. Here, outside, the poet—or the narrator—finds the ranting sermon less preposterous; the people inside had certainly felt something; 'the zeal was good and the aspiration;' only to the unconvinced was it unconvincing. This passage is, in fact, a premature statement of the whole poem's conclusion. But whilst he thus reasons concerning the relativity of religious belief,

             . . . suddenly
The rain and the wind ceased, and the sky
Received at once the full fruition
Of the moon's consummate apparition.
The black cloud-barricade was riven,
Ruined beneath her feet, and driven
Deep in the West; while, bare and breathless,
   North and South and East lay ready
For a glorious thing that, dauntless, deathless,
   Sprang across them and stood steady.
'Twas a moon-rainbow . . .

And out of the rainbow rose another rainbow, and out of the second

               the sight
Of a sweepy garment, vast and white,
With a hem that I could recognize . . .

based on the free criticism of the Bible. This last, which shook the faith of Arthur Hugh Clough and with which Matthew Arnold struck his compromise, was for Browning even less tempting than Catholicism; yet in the exhausted air of the Bible-critic's lecture-hall too, there dwelt, he admitted, something to find an echo in the Christian soul.

His own choice—or his wife's which for the moment he adopted as his—remained an etiolated version of that Nonconformity from which he had once half-heartedly rebelled, and of which he gives an acid picture in the chapel description with which 'Christmas Eve' opens. For, despite the preaching man's immense stupidity as he 'poured his doctrine forth, full measure'—certainly a childhood memory—Browning found here the true spring 'welling up from underground,' even if 'mingled with the taints of earth.' Therefore, he tepidly decided, here was the message nearest to that gospel of love that he had stated at white heat in 'Saul'. For

> God who registers the cup
>   Of mere cold water, for his sake
> To a disciple rendered up,
>   Disdains not his own thirst to slake
> At the poorest love was ever offered.

If the poem did not rise above such pedestrian Sunday-school moral-mongering, it could be dismissed out of hand as a mere unfortunate attempt to write in a manner foreign to the poet. But after the description of the unprepossessing congregation in a Zion chapel meeting on the Christmas Eve of 'Forty-nine,' its emotional tempo abruptly rises. The narrator rushes out into the evening, having had enough of 'the hot smell and the human noises,' and is confronted by the beauties of the night sky.

All famishing in expectation
Of the main-altar's consummation.

But the poet and narrator remains outside, hesitating
on the threshold stone, and watches the figure of Christ,
whom he has been following, enter there too—as earlier
He had entered into a dissenting house, and as afterwards
He will enter the Göttingen lecture hall of a 'hawk-
nosed, high-cheek-boned' professor—because

> Their faith's heart beats, though her head swims
> Too giddily to guide her limbs,
> Disabled by their palsy-stroke
> From propping mine.

'Christmas Eve' and 'Easter Day,' though intended as
separate poems, must be considered together as marking
two stages in a single quest for religious certainty. As a
whole they are a failure, for their argument is flat and
discursive, their imagery dead, and their verse a loose
shamble. But there are moments when they flare up with
the harsh light of vision, reminiscent of that light which
played over the Duke's wild country in 'The Flight of the
Duchess.' Such moments provide the only beauties in that
long-pondered poem, in which he had proposed to put
aside his men and women and speak out, as Elizabeth did.
For it was her aim to write poetry which would 'rush
into the drawing-rooms and the like, meeting face to
face the Humanity of the Age, and speaking the truth as
I conceive it out plainly.' 'Christmas Eve' is devoted to
corporate religion, 'Easter Day' to the spiritual life of the
individual; in both Browning examines the three alternative creeds competing for the souls of his contemporaries: the Nonconformity of his youth; Catholicism,
which was just beginning to make the first of its spectacular conversions, and a dilute ethical Christianity

happened to be travelling. 'A very singular person,'
Elizabeth Browning wrote of him, perhaps a little
guardedly, 'of whom the world tells a thousand and one
tales, you know. But of whom I shall speak as I find him.
Not very refined in a social sense by any manner of
means,' she went on, 'but a most accomplished scholar—
having seen all the ends of the earth and the men thereof,
and possessing the art of talk and quotation to an
amusing degree.' A few weeks later she was giving her
sister a more circumstantial account of this 'unrefined'
priest. 'And now, will you all believe that Father Prout
has spent *every evening here except one* since I wrote last!
. . . he is our man of the mountain . . . and we think it a
decided gain whenever we can get tea over before he
comes and fixes himself at his smoking post for three
hours at least. As a matter of course the wine is rung
for instantly, with an apparatus for spitting! . . . Poor
Robert has been sorely taxed between his good nature
and detestation of the whole proceeding.' But 'one
likes the human nature of the man,' she concludes.
There can certainly be no doubt that this eccentric
worldling served, on his over frequent visits, as a model
for the pictures Browning was later to draw of Catholic
priests. There is certainly something of Prout in such a
successor to St. Praxed's most scandalous bishop as the
intellectual temporizer Blougram.

In 'Christmas Eve' and 'Easter Day,' Browning attempted to present a picture of Catholicism as a picturesque
survival, not entirely dead at heart. There, in imagination, he penetrates to the centre of that faith, and views
the basilica of St. Peter's alive with worshippers during
the Christmas Eve service; its chancel body and nave so
overcrowded that men are perched on the tombs and
the statues,

in an unsprung carriage along a rough and stony road to a monastery in the Appenines. There Browning was welcomed and allowed to play on the organ of the monastery chapel, upon which Milton was believed to have played two hundred years before. Elizabeth, however, found the Abbot reluctant to entertain a lady, and after five days the pair of English poets departed.

The incident clearly demonstrates Browning's faint comprehension of the Catholic attitude. For despite his frequent choice of Catholic subjects for many of his greatest poems, he had hardly even an average outsider's understanding of Catholicism. No doubt he thought it most unreasonable of the Abbot to turn his wife away. He behaved, unintentionally no doubt, throughout his residence in Italy as if he were living in a Protestant country, whose native rite was no more than an archaic and local anachronism. Perhaps he was encouraged in this attitude by the example of 'Father Prout,' an eccentric and entertaining Irish Jesuit whose true name was Francis Mahony. Browning had met him for the first time at some London dinner table, and Prout was the first person he bumped into when he arrived at Leghorn on his wedding journey. Later, in Florence, the Jesuit turned up at a moment when Elizabeth had an attack of fever and, to the horror of the Italian servant, mixed with his own hands a potion of eggs and port wine, which he persuaded her to drink. This remarkable man was a contributor to *Fraser's Magazine*, and during Pio Nono's short-lived liberal phase acted as Rome correspondent for the radical *Daily News*. His journalistic activities were said to have ruined his hopes of preferment, and he now wandered, with seeming aimlessness, from Florence to Rome and from Rome to Paris, greeting and gossiping with any English families who

Browning had paid a second visit to Italy in the summer of 1844, before the beginning of their correspondence, and found there the same freedom and inspiration he had discovered on his first visit. Already Elizabeth had contemplated a stay in Italy for the benefit of her health. But Browning had first investigated possibilities of work in London; he had even contemplated a post in the reading room of the British Museum. Later, when he was already in Italy, he offered himself, though more out of political sympathy than for the salary he would gain, as secretary to the Embassy which he expected to be opened at Rome. But no minister was appointed; and hopes of Italy's unity were deferred. The cause of Italy was already dear to both the Brownings; to Elizabeth it was an uncritical enthusiasm, but Robert's feelings were not always on the fervent level of his 'Italian in England.' Originally they had planned only to spend the winter abroad. The implacability of Mr. Barrett, however, who refused so much as to open his daughter's letters, persuaded them to stay, and prolong a visit to Florence into a permanent residence there. The small English and American colony in the city welcomed them, and the sociable side of Browning's nature responded to a few new and admiring friends, but for the most part they remained at home, working and rejoicing in each other's company. Elizabeth's small income, left to her by an uncle, and some money which Browning received from home enabled them to exist modestly, though far from uncomfortably. 'In Florence,' wrote Elizabeth, 'for three hundred a year one may live much like the Grand Duchess, and go to the opera in the evening at five pence halfpenny.' Her own health sufficiently improved for her to make long sight-seeing expeditions, riding even, on one occasion,

advertisement shall run,' he replied, 'save and except the avowal of *Paracelsus.*'

The Barrett's departure for a house near Leatherhead was announced for the following Monday, which precipitated the elopement, perhaps by some days. Browning was confusing himself over the times and dates of trains, muddling departures from Southampton with departures from Havre. In the final arrangements Elizabeth seems to have been the more practical of the partners.

In the afternoon of September 19th Elizabeth Barrett Browning stole out of No. 60 Wimpole Street attended by her maid and her dog, while the family were at dinner. Unobserved they walked to Hodgson's the booksellers in Great Marylebone Street, where Robert Browning was waiting. The boxes had been sent ahead, and in a cab they departed for Nine Elms station to catch the five o'clock train for Southampton, and a new life.

From Southampton, by way of Havre to Paris. Then through Orleans, and Avignon to Marseilles, whence by ship to Leghorn and from there to Pisa. The news of the marriage caused some stir in England; for an elopement was an exciting event even though neither of the pair was a romantic or well-known figure. 'So Robert Browning and Miss Barrett have gone off together,' commented the aged Wordsworth. 'I hope they can understand each other. Nobody else can.' 'My daughter should have been thinking of another world,' is the only recorded comment of the bride's father. But there were many well-wishers: Browning's family; Mr. Kenyon, through whose introduction the couple had originally met, and Thomas Carlyle who wrote that 'if ever there was a union indicated by the finger of Heaven itself . . . it seemed to me . . . to be this.'

astonishment that something so unexpected and yet so
inevitable could have taken place.

The elopement of Robert Browning and Elizabeth
Barrett has been so often described that it can here be
briefly passed over. To obtain Mr. Barrett's permission
would have been for ever impossible, and in September
1846 he was about to remove his family into the country,
while No. 60 Wimpole Street was being painted. This
precipitated an arrangement that had been discussed in a
flurry of letters which the lovers exchanged by every post.
'I will do as you wish—understand,' was the final form
of her consent, in the postscript to a note announcing
the migration from London. 'Saturday, Septr. 12. 1846
$\frac{1}{4}$11—11$\frac{1}{4}$ a.m. (91),' Browning scribbled on the
envelope of a letter that had reached him that morning,
the last that Elizabeth Barrett wrote before the wedding,
which took place in Marylebone Church at that hour
and on that day, on the ninety-first of their meetings.
Only Miss Barrett's maid was admitted to the secret—
such was their fear of Mr. Barrett's reprisals against any
member of the family whom they might take into their
confidence. Elizabeth returned to Wimpole Street for
another week whilst packing and final preparations were
completed. During this time Browning did not care to
call, since that would necessitate his asking for his wife
under her maiden name. This did not prevent a daily
exchange of letters, concerning the departure of steam-
ships for the continent, and the exact form of the wedding
notice that would be inserted in the papers on their
departure. 'Robert Browning Esquire, of New Cross,
author of *Paracelsus*, to Elizabeth Barrett, eldest daughter
of Edward Moulton Barrett Esquire of Wimpole Street.
Would you put it so?' she asked, half guessing that he
would demur at the mention of *Paracelsus*. 'So the

position he did define was very close to her own as she had set it down for him in a letter in August 1846. But there is no mention in their correspondence of any new poem actually begun, only of the completion of projects in hand. She in fact encouraged his idleness. For frequently in his letters he complained of headaches and unspecified minor ailments for which Elizabeth could see a certain cure in more walking and less working. So though her admiration of his poems reinforced his belief in his own powers, the immediate effect of their year and a half's wooing was to take him from his work. Indeed, his first publication after the two plays, the small book containing 'Christmas Eve' and 'Easter Day,' did not appear till the end of a four years' silence, in 1850.

The correspondence, though rich during its early months in discussions of poetry and in mutual revelations of character and beliefs, narrows as it proceeds. Soon both were almost exclusively preoccupied with the growth and nature of their love, with arrangements for meetings and with precautions against detection. Their intimacy moved steadily towards a marriage, overcoming obstacles which proved, one after another, imaginary. Her fears of perpetual invalidism, his diffidences, and the menace of her father's interference were less strong than a certainty existing in them both that their relationship was the product of some power stronger than themselves. 'Nothing is my work,' Elizabeth proclaimed. 'Let it be God's work and yours . . . indeed I exclaim to myself about the miracle of it far more even than you can do. It seems to me still a dream how you came here at all . . . the very machinery of it seems miraculous. Why did I receive you and only you? Can I tell? no, not a word.' This is not mere lovers' hyperbole; it is a clear-sighted

and she began to envisage the abandoning of her recluse's life, which she had no doubt adopted, in part at least, in order to protect herself from just such demands as he now made, then her health began to improve. She who had once been exhausted by a half-hour's visit, was able to walk out, to drive out, and to face the prospect of married life on moderate means, very largely hers. For she had a small inherited income, and he little or nothing of his own.

In the spring and summer of their first meetings Robert Browning was finishing the two plays *Luria* and *A Soul's Tragedy*. Then, after many months of apparent idleness, perhaps broken by work on his poem attacking Popes and imaginative religions, he proposed during the next summer, that of 1846, to write 'one last poem . . . a poem to publish or not to publish; but a proper introduction to the afterwork.' For now, he told Elizabeth, his poetry was far from being the completest expression of his being. 'I hate to refer to it,' he wrote, 'or I could tell you why, wherefore . . . *prove* how imperfect . . . how unsatisfactory it must of necessity be. Still, I should not much object, if, such as it is, it were the best, the flower of my life . . . but that is all to come, and through you, mainly, or more certainly.' Browning's dissatisfaction with his work hitherto was excessive; in effect there was no clean break between *Pippa* and the 'afterwork,' the great poetry written during the years of their marriage, between 'The Tomb at St. Praxed's' and 'Fra Lippo Lippi,' or between 'My Last Duchess' and 'The Statue and the Bust.' In 'Christmas Eve' and in 'Easter Day,' however, he very deliberately strayed from the main path of his development in an endeavour to define his religious position. This costly failure was, perhaps, the result of his future wife's influence. Indeed the religious

call the accessories in the story are real though indirect
reflexes of the original idea, and so supersede properly
enough the necessity of its personal appearance, so to
speak. But, as I conceived the poem, it consisted entirely
of the gipsy's description of the life the lady was to lead
with her future gipsy lover—a *real* life, not an unreal one
like that with the Duke. And as I meant to write it, all
their wild adventures would have come out and the in-
significance of the former vegetation have been deducible
only—as the main subject has become now . . .' 'You
are more faithful to your first *idea* than to your first
plan,' was Elizabeth Barrett's shrewd comment.

The early love letters contain many such workshop
secrets, for it was, ostensibly at least, as fellow craftsmen
that they had come together. But discussions of inspiration and technique led easily to more intimate ex-
changes of confidences, and from there to mutual confessions of the value each found in the other, and to the
mutual concern of each for the other's health and happiness. One can see Elizabeth Barrett's initial alarm at the
emotional demands their relationship made of her, and
her almost angry insistence that he should remain, as at
the inception, the more responsible partner. He was too
prone to talk of his 'real inferiority' to herself, and to
indulge in over-wordy self-depreciation. 'For every poor
spark of a Vesuvius or Stromboli in my microcosm,' he
proclaimed, 'there are huge layers of ice and pits of black
cold water.' His protestations that he would wish to
serve her—as the huntsman had served the Duchess in the
poem—without hope of reward, brought from her the
sharp expostulation that the offer might be 'generous in
you—but in me, where were the integrity?' But for her
health, she assured him, she would accept the trust with
which he honoured her. And when her fears diminished,

but with *that* it begins. "Reflection" is exactly what it names itself—a re-presentation, in scattered rays from every angle of incidence, of what first of all became present in a great light, a whole one! So tell me how these lights are born, if you can! But I can tell anybody how to make melodious verses.' He had, he confessed, been at one time impatient of his technique, of his music, and anxious to catch the inspiration nearer its source. As a poet he distrusted the intellectual processes. In his life, hitherto, he had given them too much exercise; a great deal of the self-knowledge of which he boasted was no more than hair-splitting introspection. Nor in his poems did he always draw on deep sources. 'So far differently was I circumstanced of old,' he wrote in this same letter of June 14th 1845, 'that I used rather to go about for a subject of offence to people, writing ugly things in order to warn the ungenial and timorous off my grounds at once.' Such was no doubt the genesis of the 'Soliloquy in the Spanish Cloister,' and perhaps of the two 'Madhouse Cells' as well. But these poems could not have been as successful as they were, had it not been for the residue of nightmare self-reproach which lay at almost as deep a level within him as the purer spring of inspiration.

On another occasion, enlarging on the strange story of the writing of 'The Flight of the Duchess,' Browning revealed with even greater clarity the relative parts played in the conception of his poems by the intellectual plan and the uprush of inspiration. 'It is an odd fact,' he wrote on the subject of the now completed poem, 'yet characteristic of my accomplishings one and all in this kind, that of the poem, the real conception of an evening (two years ago fully), of *that*, not a line is written—though perhaps after all, what I am going to

that he had supposed, to her giving him the prize, the last and best of all. It was a revelation rather of the cleft between Robert Browning's inner conviction which had guided him to Wimpole Street, and an outer affectation of despair which had so far impeded his approach to his fellow men. 'I have made myself almost ridiculous,' he wrote at a still later date, 'by a kind of male prudery with respect to young ladies . . . I was very little inclined to get involved in troubles and troubles for nothing at all. And as for marrying . . .' Perhaps he exaggerated his former restraint and timidity; such early lyrics as 'The Moth's Kiss First' . . . suggest that he did. But chief among the contradictions that are mirrored in 'The Flight of the Duchess' was that between the line of his fate and the line of his intellectual imagination.

Imaginatively, throughout his poetry, he was apt to construct false solutions to his problems. In 'The Flight' he had wished to describe the gipsy country, but had been unable; in *Christmas Eve and Easter Day* he was to build a precarious literary superstructure upon the sound but lowly base of his experience. But in his love for Elizabeth Barrett the imaginative prevision and the ripening of the relationship were as one. Their love was, it must be repeated, the masterpiece he had foreseen. The relative parts played in his life and his writing by the rival forces of heart and head, of inspiration and invention, are clearly revealed in yet another letter to Elizabeth Barrett. 'One should study the mechanical part of the art, as nearly all that there is to be studied,' he wrote, 'for the more one sits and thinks over the creative process, the more it confirms itself as "inspiration," nothing more nor less. Or, at worst, you write down old inspirations, what you remember of them . . .

was to his preconceived pattern that events quite rapidly shaped themselves. For as the huntsman released the Duchess, or as Perseus, in a favourite picture upon Robert Browning senior's walls, released Andromeda, so the poet was preparing himself for that elopement which to Elizabeth Barrett and to her friends would have seemed at the outset beyond her physical capacities. But Browning knew—or acted as if he knew—that his first letter was the beginning of something richer with promise than a mere literary acquaintanceship. 'I do, as I say, love these books, with all my heart,' he wrote of her poetry, 'and I love you too.' It is easy to miss the unexpected ring in these words, now that one is so familiar with the course of events to which they were a prelude. Yet if he was the shaper of this partnership, she fell readily enough into her role, however unsuitable it might then seem to one 'scarcely to be called young now,' as she expressed it. But whereas her age and her invalidism—based certainly on some pulmonary weakness —made her renunciation of any thought of marriage not unreasonable, Browning s initial assumption of a similar resignation is extremely hard to explain. 'Being no longer in the first freshness of life,' he wrote to her in the autumn of 1845, when he had begun to envisage their eventual marriage, 'and having for many years now made up my mind to the impossibility of loving any woman . . . having wondered at this in the beginning, and fought not a little against it, having acquiesced in it at last, and accounted for it all to myself, and become, if anything, rather proud of it than sorry,' he had till then, he claimed 'a mind set in ultimate order, so I fancied, for the few years more.' This was not a mere self-dramatization, a spontaneous reaction to her statement that there were obstacles, though not the financial or paternal obstacles

days. His quickly ripening love for Elizabeth Barrett was in itself that masterpiece which he had seen as his 'First Poem.' In 'Saul' he had expressed the intimate connection he had discovered between love and poetry, and the religious certainty born of the release of their joint powers; in 'The Flight of the Duchess' he had glimpsed that other, gipsy country—represented on earth perhaps by Italy—in which life could be freed from the rack of duality; in *Pippa* he had drawn a symbol of that innocence and womanly compassion—*das Ewig-Weibliche*—that could lead him to it. For only when seen with the eyes of Pippa, of the Duchess, and later of Pompilia in *The Ring and the Book*, could the humdrum shabbiness of everyday existence, the crimes, the meannesses and failures to keep faith—which he saw without him, and reproached himself for finding within him—be redeemed. Now in a supreme human relationship he was to experience that rare ripening into maturity which of the Romantics only Keats had known—and which Keats had discovered only when confronted by imminent and seemingly premature death. From this experience, and from the loss of his wife, which did not bring it to an end, was to be born the greatest of Browning's poetry. But in the year and a half of his wooing he wrote very little indeed.

From his first letter, complimentary, and exploratory at the same time of the possibilities of a meeting, to that first meeting four months later, between an apparently chronic invalid of thirty-nine, and a young man some six years her junior, their intimacy grew rapidly. For both from the outset gave themselves unreservedly to the relationship. Despite Robert Browning's surface timidity, his diffidence in the matter of fixing dates and his repeated apologies for having possibly overtired a woman to whom he was bringing the breath of life, it

Not only were the plays to be dismissed, however, but he was to abandon too the vein of poetry that he had worked to such advantage in his first collection of lyrics and in its successor, now almost ready for the printer. 'These got rid of,' he said of *Luria* and *A Soul's Tragedy*, 'I will do as you bid me and—say first I have some Romances and Lyrics, all dramatic to dispatch, and *then*, I shall stoop of a sudden under and out of this dancing ring of men and women hand in hand, and stand still awhile, should my eyes dazzle, and when that's over, they will be gone and you will be there, *pas vrai*? For, as I think I told you, I always shiver involuntarily when I look—no, glance—at this First Poem of mine to be.'

If it was indeed to be no more than 'a tract for the times,' R. B. a poem took eventual shape as *Christmas Eve and Easter Day*; but if, as the importance he attached to it seemed to convey, Browning was then envisaging a more intimate self-confession, this proposed great work remained unwritten. For seldom in his maturity did he abandon the dramatic method, the presentation of a facet of the truth reflected in the mind of a character chosen for the purpose; and when in his declining years he attempted in *Fifine at the Fair* and *La Saisiaz* to speak directly of his own deepest experience it eluded him. 'They will be gone, and you will be there,' was capable of another construction, and a profounder one, if transferred from the context of poetry into that of the life experience from which the poetry came. 'They' stood not for a class of seemingly objective lyrics, but rather for inner limitations, for the failure to meet with equal friendship offers of affection made in the past, for the last trammels of childhood dependence which, with all his confidence that their severance would not lose him his life, did still prevent his making a break with the old faction, though under the guise of anatomizing his failure to write the poetry he wished to. 'You speak out,' he pronounced. 'I only make men and women speak— give you truth broken into prismatic hues, and fear the pure white light, even if it is in me.' Here, perhaps, he was indicating his reasons for not having written 'R. B., a poem'—that his self-knowledge, acute though it was, remained insufficient, or that he was afraid of it. 'But I am going to try,' he went on; 'so it will be no small comfort to have your company just now, seeing that when you have your men and women aforesaid, you are buried with them, whereas it seems bleak, melancholy work, this talking to the wind (for I have begun)— yet I don't think I shall let *you* hear, after all, the savage things about Popes and imaginative religions that I must say.'

The letter would suggest that Browning was then at work on some early and less tolerant versions of *Christmas Eve and Easter Day*, which were not formally written and published till some five years later. A few weeks afterwards when Elizabeth told him something of a modern poem she was contemplating, he reverted to this subject of speaking out. 'The poem you propose to make for the times,' he says, 'is the *only* poem to be undertaken now by you or anyone that *is* a poet at all; the only reality, only effective piece of service to be rendered God and man; it is what I have been all my life intending to do and now shall be much, much nearer doing, since you will be along with me.' On February 26th 1845, the first day of that spring in the course of which, they both hoped, a meeting between them might be possible, he had taken leave once more of his dramatic ambitions. *Luria* should be his last play: 'there can no good come,' he concluded, 'of keeping this wild company any longer.'

and for the betrayal of the Shelleyan ideal that its collapse had entailed. His friendships and embryonic love affairs had been weakened by the strength and intimacy of his relationship with his parents. He saw the security of his childhood as a precious asset, yet felt that the very firmness of his early hold on life justified—perhaps almost required of him—some undefined but drastic step that might imperil the whole of his future happiness. He was ready for action, he knew not of what kind— for, the past being 'gained, secure and on record,' he was confident that nothing now could 'lose him his life,' even if he were to make a clean break with the 'old days.' For the 'old days' had left one adult side of his nature unsatisfied. We have already seen that his sociability was no more than an outward show, that he visited and entertained his friends more through fear that some 'unknown god'—or goddess—might escape him if he did not, than for the pleasure he took in company; 'I never was without good, kind, generous friends and lovers,' he wrote to Elizabeth many months before they met. 'Perhaps they came at the wrong time—I never wanted them . . . I never deceived myself much, nor called my feelings for people other than they were.' He was prepared, so early, to trust her with the deep knowledge he had acquired of his own character. In casual relationships prone to pose, he treated Elizabeth from the outset with a confessional candour that was called out in him by the rapid maturing of their friendship. It was as if they had known each other before. Preliminary formalities yielded almost immediately to intimate discussion, which was facilitated by the half-illusion that it was their poetry and not their private concerns they were speaking of. But already in his second letter Browning was voicing his self-dissatis-

judgment. 'You persist in making me choose the days,' she grumbled, having made it amply clear that his visits were always welcome to her. 'It is not for me to do it, but for you.'

She found him still divided in mind over the kind of poetry he wanted to write. On the one side he had not given up his ambition to explore further the vein of romantic self-dramatization opened up in those three 'sadly imperfect demonstrations of even mere ability,' to quote his own denigratory verdict, *Pauline*, *Paracelsus* and *Sordello*. He was conscious of great powers of creation within him, but far from certain in what direction they would take him. 'What I have printed gives no knowledge of me,' he had written to Elizabeth Barrett before they met. 'It evidences abilities of various kinds, if you will . . . that I think. But I never have begun, even, what I hope I was born to begin and end—R. B. a poem.' Was it, however, an autobiographical poem that lay within him still unexpressed, or was it that his life had so far failed to take sufficient shape? Certainly he was disappointed with his work and spoke of meaning to begin afresh in deep earnest and without affectation. There is no wilful affectation about any of those first poems, except perhaps *Pauline*; his attitudinizing was no more than the mark of his continued immaturity. Nor were they lacking in earnestness. His long pre-occupation with the theatre had certainly led him to write pieces in which any deep seriousness would have been out of place. But even his plays were never trivial. These strictures upon his work were no more than reflections of a deep sense of unfulfilment. He had reached the age of thirty-two without undergoing any vital experience, and harboured still in the depths of his heart an un-acknowledged guilt for the half-rebellion of his boyhood,

Chapter Three

ALLIANCE OF POETS

'IT is quite startling,' wrote Elizabeth Barrett, three months after her first meeting with Robert Browning, 'quite startling and humiliating, to observe how you combine such large tracts of experience of outer and inner life, of books and men, of the world and the arts of it; curious knowledge as well as general knowledge . . . and deep thinking as well as wide acquisition . . . and you, looking none the older for it all!—yes, and being besides a man of genius and working your faculty and not wasting yourself over a surface or away from an end?' Such was the impression of single-mindedness that Robert Browning made, at thirty-three, upon a woman who by the confined nature of her semi-invalid life had become an acute and ready observer of the few visitors who were admitted to her room. She saw herself as one who could expect nothing more from her active existence, as one who must live through her writing and, vicariously, through the men and women who were her friends. But she found herself outmatched in subtlety by this outwardly fashionable young man whose face betrayed none of the experience vouched for by his poetry and his conversation. 'Read me no more backwards,' she had protested two months before, 'with your Hebrew, putting in your own vowel points without my leave.' He was subtle, yet in a curious way undecided, over-diffident, and unwilling to trust his own

written it anyhow, to get it done, throws rather more light on the reasons for the poem's uneveness. Its symbolism was clearly intractable to the surface intellect, and so it had to be left in an unpolished state, still bearing the mark of technical influences not wholly absorbed. It is however a poem of very much greater intensity than 'The Pied Piper,' and with 'Saul' and *Pippa* stood at the summit of Robert Browning's achievement at the moment of his first meeting with Elizabeth Barrett.

assurance of the reality of a divine law, in 'The Flight of
the Duchess' he conjures up a picture of a life under
magic protectors, that shall lead up, as he himself
attempted to when he wrote his *Parleyings*, to a comprehension before death of 'the outline of the whole.' Both
poems are concerned with the resolution of duality by
the powers of love and creation, but only in 'The Flight of
the Duchess' is the cleft nature of the world of experience
symbolically stated.

Technically, this poem is in the descent rather from
'The Pied Piper' than from any other piece in the earlier
book. Elizabeth Barrett praised it for its 'perfect rhymes,
perfectly new and all clashing together as by natural
attraction.' But clearly she was a little puzzled by what
she called its novelty. It is possible that she did not see
how much, like 'The Pied Piper,' it owed to Hood and
to Barham. At its weakest indeed, it degenerates into the
pure Ingoldsby of such lines as:

> In brief, my friend, set all the devils in hell free
> And turn them out to carouse in a belfry
> And treat the priests to a fifty part canon,
> And then you may guess how that tongue of his ran on.

Elizabeth returned to the poem twice, in later letters,
concluding on the first occasion that its rhythm answered
to Browning's own description of 'speech half asleep or
song half awake'—a phrase more applicable to the poem's
inspiration than to its texture. But reverting once again
to the novelty of its rhythms she decided on the second
occasion that it was 'something like (if like anything)
what the Greeks called pedestrian metre . . . between
metre and prose . . . the difficult rhymes combining too
quite curiously with the easy looseness of the general
measure.' Browning's own statement that he had

ence. All he could do was to tell of her escape, of the
selfless love of the huntsman who contrived it, of the
gipsy queen's prophecy concerning the probation and
fulfilment that awaited her in the land of white magic,
and of the protection that the gipsies could give her in
this world.

> Whether it be thy lot to go,
> For the good of us all, where the haters meet
> In the crowded city's horrible street;
> Or thou step alone through the morass
> Where never sound yet was
> Save the dry quick clap of the stork's bill,
> For the air is still and the water still,
> When the blue breast of the dipping coot
> Dives under, and all is mute.
> So, at the last shall come old age,
> Decrepit as befits that stage;
> How else wouldst thou retire apart
> With the hoarded memories of thy heart,
> And gather all to the very least
> Of the fragments of life's earlier feast,
> Let fall through eagerness to find
> The crowning dainties yet behind?
> Ponder on the entire past
> Laid together thus at last,
> When the twilight helps to fuse
> The first fresh with the faded hues,
> And the outline of the whole,
> As round eve's shades their framework roll,
> Grandly fronts for once thy soul.

'The Flight of the Duchess' was in its inception a poem
of escape, a charm against the powers of death wielded by
the strange Guy Fawkes Day gipsy, with her unearthly
song. But it is more than that. It is the complement of
'Saul.' For whereas in that poem Browning attains an

narrator of the poem his *alter ego*, 'born the day this
present Duke was?' But the dualism of the poem goes
even further. The sick tall Duchess and the queen of
the gipsies, who are the evil and the good geniuses of
the poem's Pippa-like heroine, are again contradictory
aspects of the same figure. It is hardly strange indeed
that Mrs. Sutherland Orr in her *Handbook to Robert
Browning's Works* pronounces the poem to be, like Childe
Roland, 'incompatible with rational explanation and
independent of it.' For it is concerned with contradictions of personality at a very deep level, and its
symbolism is only explicable in psychological terms.

   The poem was in the first place intended to tell 'of
the life the lady was to lead with her future gipsy lover,
a *real* life'; so Browning spoke of the poem to Elizabeth
Barrett. But in the end he 'wrote it anyhow, just to get
it done.' But this is only a rational explanation of the
poem's refusal to take an intellectual shape at variance
with the poet's own profoundest experience. The
Duchess, who embodied his own powers of love and
creation—untried powers of which he was by no means
certain—must be led by the good huntsman, away from
his brother, the wicked—or perhaps only stupid—Duke,
out of the land of worldly contradictions into the land
of pure poetry, the land of the gipsies, who know 'How
love is the only good in the world.' The gipsies represent the secret watchers, the powers that lie dormant
in the depths of our minds capable of guiding us out of
the labyrinth of conflicting desires—which is the Duke's
world of our own restless lives. 'We,' says the gipsy
queen, 'pursue thy whole career.' But to bring the
Duchess to her gipsy lover, to carry his symbolism to
the point of reconciliation, where the two rival worlds
become one, would have overtaxed the poet's experi-

Ours is a great wild country:
>If you climb to our castle's top,
>I don't see where your eye can stop;
For when you've passed the cornfield country,
Where vineyards leave off, flocks are packed,
And sheep-range leads to cattle-tract,
And cattle-tract to open-chase,
And open-chase to the very base
Of the mountain where, at a funeral pace,
Round about, solemn and slow,
One by one, row after row,
Up and up the pine-trees go,
So, like black priests up, and so,
Down the other side again
>To another greater, wilder country,
That's one vast red drear burnt-up plain,
Branched through and through with many a vein
Whence iron's dug, and copper's dealt;
>Look right, look left, look straight before,—
Beneath they mine, above they smelt,
>Copper-ore and iron-ore,
And forge and furnace mould and melt,
>And so on, more and ever more,
Till at the last, for a bounding belt,
>Comes the salt sand hoar of the great sea-shore,
—And the whole is our Duke's country.

Not only was the Duke's country, itself a protagonist in the drama, divided into two contrasting halves, agricultural and industrial, but the Duke himself was the son of parents coming from opposite worlds, the good old Duke and his sick, tall, yellow Duchess, who was 'the daughter of God knows who;' and if the Duke had running in his veins the blood of nobility and of some unknown tribe, he partook also of another duality. He was the twin, though not by parentage, of the huntsman, the Duchess's silent and faithful lover. For was not this

D

Yet for all its half-symbolic, dreamlike opening the poem had, in the half-finished state in which it first appeared, what amounted to a social moral. The Duchess was a pampered Victorian bride, a Pippa, perhaps, trapped into conventional marriage and watched over on the sly by the Duke's witch of a mother. It was not until several months later that a chance remark by a friend, whom Browning had met staying away in Flintshire, set the poem working again. It was Kinglake, the author of *Eothen*, who remarked on that September morning that 'the deer had already begun to break the ice in the pond,' and his words were incorporated in the poem, at the very point where it had been broken off:

> Well, early in autumn, at first winter-warning,
> When the stag had to break with his foot, of a
>   morning,
> A drinking hole out of the fresh tender ice
> That covered the pond . . .

The message of 'The Flight of the Duchess,' as it was completed, is entirely a symbolic one; the social moral slips away into oblivion. For the poem was, in essence, the product of an unnoticed day dream, that twice required the stimulus of a magic and suggestive phrase to bring it to consciousness, and such fantasy can, at times, speak more truly of a man's deep experience than do tales or reasonings that have undergone a more vigorous intellectual sifting.

The landscape of 'The Flight of the Duchess' is neither Italian, nor German, nor English; it is a nightmare country of dualities whose contrasting halves are alike ruled over by the petty Duke. Its nature is described by the huntsman who finally contrives the Duchess's escape from it.

herd boy yearns to pour out for his father—for so Saul seems to him—love beyond the possibilities of earthly love. It is in this complete self-abnegation that to the two components love and song is added that *tertium quid*, the revelation of divine significance. The theme of 'Saul' is central to the whole body of Browning's work, and to his faith in a supernatural reality, not elsewhere and afterwards, but here and immanent in man's two most profound emotions—that are in a sense one—his love and his powers of creation.

While 'Saul,' in its final version at least, flows up from the depths of that understanding of Browning's which is so often and so easily dismissed as a mere superficial optimism, a facile belief in material comfort and automatic progress, another poem which was still incomplete when published in his 1845 collection, speaks more profoundly and less fancifully than 'Cristina' of the force of selfless love which Browning hoped to find in himself when the occasion should call it out. 'The Flight of the Duchess,' however, comes from a deeper level of the imagination than 'Cristina,' from a level indeed in which the poet understood the dangers of duality, of the cleavage between body and spirit and between mind and its object. 'The Flight of the Duchess' had been prompted by the sudden recollection of a song which the poet had heard as a child sung by a gipsy woman one Guy Fawkes day. The poem immediately establishes an atmosphere much more akin to that in which Childe Roland was later to ride than to the imaginary country over which Cristina reigned. 'Following the queen of the Gipsies O' had been the song's simple refrain, but the land of the gipsies the poem conjured up presented, as it had done to the child, a double picture; it was the country of magic both black and white.

black and white than the principle of Italian unification. Human values always obtruded; he had at heart a contempt for politics. 'How exquisitely absurd,' he wrote to Elizabeth towards the end of his wooing, on the subject of Harriet Martineau's ambition to see women in Parliament—'how essentially retrograde a measure! Parliament seems no place for originating, creative minds—but for second-rate minds influenced by and bent on working out the results of these.'

For him the important issues lay on the plane neither of political action nor of supernatural religion, but on those of artistic creation and of love, those two of man's chief activities that seemed to him most closely allied; and nowhere did he express more explicitly the closeness of that relationship, as he saw it, than in the poem 'Saul,' the first nine sections of which appeared in his 1845 collection. It is not, however, till the end of the poem, which was not written till later, that the full significance of David's song emerges. Not till then is it clear that for him, as for Robert Browning his creator, the out-pouring of love in song, the embodiment of emotion in a created thing, leads to an acceptance at a deeper level of insight of the reality of God, not as a supernatural presence, but in his Jewish and Protestant aspect as the supreme lawgiver.

> I have gone the whole round of creation: I saw and I spoke:
> I, a work of God's hand for that purpose, received in my
> brain
> And pronounced on the rest of his handwork—returned
> him again
> His creation's approval or censure: I spoke as I saw:
> I report, as a man may of God's work—all's love, yet all's
> law.

The song is concluded, the king healed and the shep-

Robert Browning, so reticent and uncircumstantial about his statements, that even here, in 'Home Thoughts from Abroad,' in 'Home Thoughts from the Sea,' and in the lines to Nelson's memory which afterwards formed part of the poem 'Nationality in Drinks,' he seemed to speak with the almost anonymous voice of any man who thinks longingly of his country when away from it. In the same way he afterwards presented the picture in reverse, writing of his yearning for Italy when in England, in the poem 'De Gustibus.' Such a capacity for simple, unself-conscious emotion is the mark of a poet who has transcended the need to display himself.

'The Lost Leader,' on the other hand, another poem in this collection, while seeming to apply to an actual situation, is far from faithful to historical fact. For Wordsworth's abandonment of the liberal cause, or even Southey's, could hardly have been attributed to the temptations of 'a handful of silver' or any ribband to stick in a coat. Indeed Browning in his poetry seldom referred simply to contemporary events; nor did the day to day play of politics seriously interest him. When as in this poem, or in the more ambitious *Prince Hohenstiel-Schwangau*, he thought of certain living characters it was not the details or the rights and wrongs of their actions that interested him. He was concerned with their cast of mind, with their essential attitudes, rather than with the chance events of their lives, or their possible effect upon humanity.

Political partisanship played little part in Browning's character. He was certainly an advocate of the repeal of the Corn Laws; in his youth he had proclaimed himself a republican; but in his maturity, though he considered himself a liberal, he could not feel whole-heartedly, as could Elizabeth Barrett, on any subject less

also bore the century's date mark 15—, it was less a
Renaissance picture than a timeless study in failure,
reflecting in part Browning's own ill-success in finding
applause and a public. Perhaps, concludes this unknown
painter, conscious that his works might have obtained as
much praise as a more fortunate rival's—perhaps they
would have suffered too much if they had, at the hands of
those who

> . . . buy and sell our pictures, take and give,
>   Count them for garniture and household-stuff . . .

Soon, indeed, it is clear that Browning has put himself in the place of his character and that the gestures of
the dealers and merchants were copied from those of
nineteenth-century critics, whose prate he had been
forced to listen to, and to whose daily pettiness *Sordello*
and the plays had been exposed. So the unknown
painter, returning to decorate

> These endless cloisters and eternal aisles
>   With the same series, Virgin, Babe and Saint,
> With the same cold calm beautiful regard . . .

consoled himself that at least no merchant trafficked with
his heart. But Browning was now too buoyant and too
vigorous a man to withdraw into the perfectionist
seclusion of an artist content to forego his audience.
'Pictor Ignotus' was the expression of a mere passing
mood.

Browning's first collection contained no poem
written in the first person; in his rejection of *Pauline* he
had turned against the voicing of sentiments which might
be attributed to himself. In the new book, however,
there are three pieces referring to particular situations
and voicing private emotions. Yet so impersonal was

'indeed full of the power of life. . . . and of death.'
Ruskin—by a strange historical confusion—praised its
marvellous apprehension of the medieval spirit. But in
addition to its superscription, "Rome 15—", the signature
of the Renaissance appears in every line. What could be
less medieval than the pagan bishop's claim to have
struck a most un-Christian bargain with his God.

> And have I not Saint Praxed's ear to pray
> Horses for ye, and brown Greek manuscripts,
> And mistresses with great smooth marbly limbs?

he asks his predatory 'nephews,' demanding only in
return a tomb finer than 'Old Gandolf's,' in which he
can

> lie through centuries
> And hear the blessed mutter of the mass,
> And see God made and eaten all day long,
> And feel the steady candle-flame and taste
> Good strong thick stupefying incense-smoke!

'St. Praxed's' is a chip struck from the hard stone of
Sordello. But whilst in its setting the poem recalls
Browning's most ambitious failure, the Bishop himself
is a more highly coloured forerunner of Bishop Blougram,
who was to make equally advantageous terms with his
Maker. 'Well, here am I,' he concluded looking back
on the comfortable grandeur of his life:

> Such were my gains, life bore this fruit to me,
> While writing all the same my articles
> On music, poetry, the fictile vase
> Found at Albano, chess, Anacreon's Greek . . .

There is little to distinguish these two bishops of the
same church except their dates. In the same way the
artist of 'Pictor Ignotus' looks forward to 'Andrea del
Sarto' and to 'Fra Lippo Lippi. But though this piece

Browning family moved away from Camberwell, out into a large three-storeyed farmhouse at Hatcham, a Kentish village long since engulfed in the suburban spread of the city. From here he would take long walks out into the fields, preferably by night when from a neighbouring hill the lights of London could be seen glowing on the northern horizon, walks during which the lines of poems would begin to take shape in his head. In his upstairs study at Hatcham, in the blue shirt that he affected as his working dress, he toiled hopefully upon his plays; but at intervals between his dramatic endeavours and his social engagements he completed that larger batch of lyrical poems which came to him on his night walks, and which he published in 1845.

One cannot give any certain date to the separate poems among these *Dramatic Romances and Lyrics*, though most of them must have been composed during the three years before their publication. There are twenty-six of them, of which at least half a dozen advance, in their own particular genres, beyond the stage attained by the nearest corresponding poems in his earlier collection. 'How they Brought the Good News from Ghent to Aix,' with its persistent galloping rhythms, is more exciting, more graphic and more impetuous than any of the 'Cavalier Tunes' in the previous volume; and 'The Bishop orders his Tomb' carries the dramatic presentation of character and the imaginative reconstruction, not only of Renaissance detail but of a Renaissance attitude to life, considerably beyond the high-water mark of 'My Last Duchess.' Elizabeth Barrett wrote early in their correspondence that 'St. Praxed's' was the finest and most powerful of the poems he had given to Hood[1]—

---

[1] For 'Hood's Magazine', which was supported by various literary men during Hood's fatal illness.

tempted by manifold incitements to treachery, but remains magnificently true to the city of his adoption, even when discredited. It is, of all Browning's plays, the only one that could conceivably be staged today.

His final drama, *A Soul's Tragedy*, is already half-way between a stage play and the internal drama of *Men and Women*. It is entirely concerned with motive, and with the unexpectednesses of human behaviour. Its setting is contemporary and Italian. The first act, in verse, tells of the poetry in the life of one Chiappino, who by a sudden act of heroism takes the blame for an assault on the Provost of a small town in the Papal states, committed by a friend, though partly at his instigation. But the friend's danger proves imaginary, and Chiappino in trying to prolong his heroic gesture becomes once more his old bombastic self; the second act, in prose, reduces the 'soul's tragedy,' if it could be dignified by such a term, to farce. For the Papal legate Ogniben is quite undisturbed by the action of either friend. 'I have known *Four* and twenty leaders of revolts,' he humorously concludes, adding one more to the '*Three* and twenty' he had claimed at his first entrance.

Browning made no further attempts at drama. But his experiments, unsuccessful though they had been, had served one good purpose. They had broken him of the obscurities of *Sordello*. The task of writing lines for Macready or Kean, and for actors whose comprehension was so limited that they supposed 'impeachment' to mean 'poaching,' had forced him to strive—not always successfully, it is true—for clarity even at the expense of writing lines almost entirely devoid of ore. So much he had gained from his otherwise almost fruitless endeavours.

In December 1840, a little before the publication of *Pippa Passes* and when the poet was twenty-eight, the

one of which Browning suspected to have been inspired by Macready himself, gave the actor-manager the excuse for withdrawing *A Blot* after its third performance. 'Macready has used me vilely,' Browning wrote to Domett, and his friendship with Macready lapsed for twenty years from that day, after which interval they met again, each mourning for the loss of a wife, and were reconciled by mutual sympathy.

His next play, *Colombe's Birthday*, Browning submitted to Macready's rival at Covent Garden, Charles Kean, the son of that Edmund Kean whom he had so admired as a boy. Kean tried to keep the piece back for production in the next year, but Browning was impatient, and negotiations were broken off.

Colombe's Birthday is less artificial than *A Blot in the 'Scutcheon*. In its plot and its verse it makes fewer concessions to the low level of contemporary theatrical taste. The heroine, in fact, bears a slight resemblance to Pippa, while the hero voices Browning's conception of love as selfless sacrifice, which he had already sketched in 'Cristina'. But the play was not really conceived for the stage. Nor, indeed, was its successor, *Luria*, in which the poet returned to the historical manner of *The Return of the Druses*. It remained his favourite of all his attempts at drama, but no manager ever considered producing it. Certainly it made no concessions, either in subject or treatment, to the possibilities of a Haymarket or Drury Lane succes.. Browning felt free now, as he had not done in those plays which he had had hopes of seeing staged, to explore motive, to fill in background and to enrich the texture of his verse. *Luria* is set in fifteenth-century Italy, in Florence and in Pisa. It is a study in loyalty, in the loyalty of a Moorish mercenary general, whose character owes more than a little to Othello, and who is

poem on a classical subject, opened for him a second field in which later he was to triumph, though it was followed by nothing more in this vein until his Greek translations of the seventies.

The publication of this little collection of lyrics denoted no weakening of Browning's dramatic ambitions; the poems were few and had been written at intervals over several years. His dearest wish was still to write for Macready a play which should have run at the Haymarket. The piece which came nearest to achieving this success, however, is perhaps the least individual of all his productions, *A Blot in the 'Scutcheon*, which would appear to have been written towards the end of 1841. It is a melodrama of no particular interest, artificial in its situations and even more undistinguished in its verse than *The Return of the Druses*. But its chief weakness lies in its author's sheer inability to construct a play or write dialogue. He was interested not in the clash of personalities, but in complexities of motive. His characters, therefore, when compelled to confront one another, habitually perform what might be called a soliloquy *à deux*. The play's third act opens with Tresham reflecting as he walks down the yew tree avenue towards the light in his sister's window, which is a signal to her lover. After thirty lines given over to his fears that she has disgraced the family name, he hears the midnight bell, and retires behind a tree to give place to a second soliloquist, his sister's lover, coming to keep his assignment and confide his plight to the audience in a mere sixteen lines.

Macready kept the play by him for two years, hoping to find some pretext for breaking his promise to stage it. Finally he decided to go ahead, though with no trust in its success. It was received with apparent favour by the first-night audience, but two very unfavourable reviews,

hotomy of flesh and spirit; it was a woman, not a
fantasy of his own projection, that he sought, when he
wrote:

> 'The moth's kiss, first!
> Kiss me as if you made believe
> You were not sure, this eve,
> How my face, your flower, had pursed
> Its petals up; so, here and there
> You brush it, till I grow aware
> Who wants me, and wide ope I burst.

William Sharp, one of the first of Browning's bio-
graphers, who knew him well in his old age, speaks of
a number of early love affairs; one has certainly a feeling
that his Paulines were no longer fictitious.

Of far greater accomplishment than these love poems,
however, are two pieces in this same first book of lyrics
which already establish Robert Browning in two fields
which throughout his long life he never grew tired of
exploring. The first is 'My Last Duchess,' a study in that
vitality and unscrupulousness, that luxury and love of
art, that cruelty and subtlety, he always associated with
Italy and the Renaissance. The Middle Ages were outside
the range of his understanding, since the idea of Catholic
Christianity was entirely foreign to him. No poet was
more Protestant in outlook. He was quick to sympathize
with the victims of the Church's persecution; he saw
the worldliness of its prelates and scorned its appeal to
superstition; but its religious purpose and its ideal of
moral government were outside his field of vision. He
was therefore always at his happiest when writing of that
age in which faith was overlaid with casuistry and mun-
dane ambition. 'My Last Duchess' leads straight to 'The
Bishop orders his Tomb in St. Praxed's Church,' published three years later. 'Artemis Prologizes,' his first

unlike some of his boyish borrowings from the 'Sun-treader,' remained of lasting significance to him. For Browning, in his union with Elizabeth Barrett, was to live that very experience to which Shelley had restlessly aspired, but in vain. The nature of his early premonitions of this love is most clearly expressed in the second of the 'Queen Worship' series—'Cristina'—which tells of an adoration hopeless but triumphant, conceived in a flash of momentary recognition more significant for the 'I' of the poem than a lifetime of honours and ambition fulfilled:

> Doubt you if, in some such moment,
>   As she fixed me, she felt clearly,
> Ages past the soul existed,
>   Here an age 'tis resting merely,
> And hence fleets again for ages,
>   While the true end, sole and single,
> It stops here for is, this love-way,
>   With some other soul to mingle?
>
> Else it loses what it lived for,
>   And eternally must lose it . . .

The thought of a lovers' first meeting as in effect a 'dèja vu,' an earnest of some previous or extra-temporal existence, might seem merely fanciful, were it not to be fulfilled in the lives of Robert and Elizabeth Browning. But neither this poem nor 'In a Gondola,' the other love poem in his first book of lyrics, is on the high level of achievement of the rest. Clearly too much of what the poet longs for is still imaginative and imprecise. Yet the girl's song from the latter poem has an authenticity that immediately removes Browning from the ranks of the erotic dreamers. It has indeed a surprising sensuality, for Browning never accepted the nineteenth-century's

'Hey up the chimney! Hey after you!'—
The Volscians themselves made an exit less speedy
From Corioli, 'fluttered like doves' by Macready.

From Hood and from Barham Browning derived that
metrical virtuosity which he applied not only to the
Hamelin narrative—but also to the poem 'Waring,'
addressed to his friend Alfred Domett who had now gone
to New Zealand. Here an entire difference of feeling
masks the influence of the two master 'Comics.' But it
is nevertheless present in such apparently careless lines
as these:

> He was prouder then the devil:
> How he must have cursed our revel!
> Ay and many other meetings,
> Indoor visits, outdoor greetings,
> As up and down he paced this London,
> With no work done, but great works undone . . .

Here, however, the influence is almost absorbed, and
the mature Browning rough-cast nearly perfected.

Browning's affection for Domett was deeper than any
he had so far known. Theirs was a friendship which was
to survive long years of separation, and which was
resumed when Domett returned to Europe thirty years
later. But even more important than the warmth of his
affection for his departed friend was Browning's feeling
out towards a love to which he aspired, but of which he
had so far found no more than a premonitory shadow.
Two poems printed under the title 'Queen Worship'
show already the transcendental significances with which
the young poet endowed the idea of the married state.
His romantic platonism owed much, no doubt, to Shelley,
but it was none the less a conception vital to the whole
of his thought concerning human relationships and,

What sort of tricks they mean to play
By way of diversion, who can say,
Of such ferocious and barbarous folk,
Who chuckled, indeed, but never spoke
Of burning Robert the Jäger to coke
Except as a capital practical joke!
Who never thought of Mercy, or heard her,
Or any gentle emotion felt;
But hard as the iron they had to melt,
Sported with Danger and romp'd with Murder!

No one familiar with the *Comic Annuals* will doubt that Hood's example did much to free Browning from conventional forms, and to encourage the tremendous extension of his poetic vocabulary. But the Reverend Harris Barham, the second series of whose *Ingoldsby Legends* appeared in the same year as Browning's *Dramatic Lyrics*, also contributed something to the freedom and daring of 'The Pied Piper's' rhythms, and through them to the rough-cast of the mature Browning's style. The 'Witch's Frolic' runs at the same pace as the rats' helter-skelter rush to their destruction.

On, on to the cellar! away! away!
On, on to the cellar without more delay!
The whole *posse* rush onwards in battle array—
Conceive the dismay of the party so gay,
Old Goody Jones, Goody Price, and Madge Gray,
When the door bursting wide, they descried the allied
Troops, prepared for the onslaught, roll in like a tide,
And the spits, and the tongs, and the pokers beside!—
'Boot and saddle's the word! mount, Cummers, and ride!'—
Alarm was ne'er caused more strong and indigenous
By cats among rats, or a hawk in a pigeon-house;
  Quick from the view
  Away they all flew,
With a yell and a screech and a halliballoo.

than for sense. Now he was master of a free medium in which word-sound certainly guided argument, but in which, far from lulling the ear as in most poetry depending primarily on the music of its words, the metrical devices were used to vary the pace and excitement of the narrative. It is perhaps superfluous to point to the consummate accomplishment of such a passage from 'The Pied Piper' as the one in which the one surviving rat brings home to Rat-land his commentary. But it is important to see what influences Browning was drawing on, to reinvigorate the tired Romanticism which he had inherited. It is too easy to take such familiar lines as these for granted:

> At the first shrill notes of the pipe,
> I heard a sound as of scraping tripe,
> And putting apples, wondrous ripe,
> Into a cider press's gripe:
> And a moving away of pickle-tub-boards,
> And a leaving ajar of conserve-cupboards,
> And a drawing the corks of train-oil-flasks,
> And a breaking the hoops of butter-casks:
> And it seemed as if a voice
> (Sweeter far than by harp or by psaltery
> Is breathed) called out, 'Oh rats, rejoice!
> The world is grown to one vast drysaltery.'

The only contemporary master of such headlong rhythms and of such wealth of rhyme, the only poets then writing with a comparable eye for realistic detail, were Thomas Hood and the Reverend Harris Barham. But they used their medium only for broadly comic purposes; Hood's serious verse is entirely conventional in form. It is most revealing to place beside this impetuous narrative of Browning's, a piece of uncertain mock-romanticism by that master of 'the Comic':

even the most worldly redeemable. Browning had no belief in eternal damnation; Pippa, and later Pompilia, by their purity were capable of saving even such inhuman wretches as Monsignor and Guido Franceschini. But Pippa's creator was not blind to wickedness. In the scene between Ottima and Sebald, which, in Arthur Symons' view, reached the highest level of tragic utterance Browning ever attained, the guilt of their love is expressed in every line, and nowhere more effectively than in their memory of their first secret meetings:

> Buried in woods we lay, you recollect;
> Swift ran the searching tempest overhead;
> And ever and anon some bright white shaft
> Burned thro' the pine-tree roof, here burned and there,
> As if God's messenger thro' the close wood screen
> Plunged and replunged his weapon at a venture,
> Feeling for guilty thee and me: then broke
> The thunder like a whole sea overhead—

Here is the emotional quality of *Pauline* but in more concentrated form, the intensity of 'Porphyria's Lover' without its strained perversity. Browning is now master of an individual line, sometimes rhymed, sometimes unrhymed, less congested than *Sordello*'s. It was with reason that Elizabeth Barrett envied him the writing of this poem, which of all his work she loved best; he himself also valued it above everything else he had produced till then.

Browning's next publication was a collection of sixteen *Dramatic Lyrics*, which contains at least three poems now as well-known as any in the language—'The Soliloquy in the Spanish Cloister,' 'Waring' and 'The Pied Piper of Hamelin.' Yet its most promising feature was the sheer variety of its accomplishment. In his very earliest short poems Browning had cared more for sound

daughter of the priest's elder brother and, as such, heiress to some villas Monsignor expects to revert to him. The plan of the poem is modest and well balanced, and redeemed from sentimentality by Pippa's ironic conviction that the four principal characters are 'Asolo's Four Happiest Ones,' Ottima and Sebald the closest of lovers, Jules and Phene happy on their marriage-day, Luigi and his mother content, and Monsignor—

> —whom they expect from Rome
> To visit Asolo, his brothers' home,
> And say here masses proper to release
> A soul from pain—what storm dares hurt his peace?

As for Pippa herself, on her holiday,

> What shall I please to-day?
> My morn, noon, eve and night—how spend my day?
> Tomorrow I must be Pippa who winds silk,
> The whole year round, to earn just bread and milk:
> But, this one day, I have leave to go
> And play out my fancy's fullest games;
> I may fancy all day—and it shall be so—
> That I taste of the pleasures, am called by the names
> Of the Happiest Four in our Asolo!

This poem was Browning's first completely successful creation, and Pippa the first of his characters to take independent life. For in her he crystallized a personality capable of exorcising that sense of horror and guilt which was his legacy from the half-hearted rebellion of his boyhood. The relationship of the little silk weaver to the guilty lovers foreshadowed, in effect, one aspect of Browning's own attitude to his *Men and Women*, that of the innocent mind which in reflecting evil throws into relief also that vitality and humanity which seem to make

the inspiration he had found in Italy. But, more important still, it introduced a new theme into his writing, the motif of innocence, which contrasts most strongly with the general feeling of self-reproach and the sense of failure that colour *Pauline*, *Paracelsus* and *Sordello*. *Pippa Passes* marks the first stage of Browning's emergence from his Romanticism. In conceiving an image of purity with which to confront the nightmare world of the strange and morbid that he had brought to light in his two 'Madhouse Cells' lyrics—'Johannes Agricola' and 'Porphyria's Lover'—and that recurs even in *Pippa* in the scene between Ottima and Sebald, he had drawn for the first time on the strong and positive side of his own nature.

There could be no greater contrast than that between Porphyria, throttled by her lover with her own hair, or Ottima and Sebald disposing of the body of her murdered husband, on the one side, and Pippa, on the other, the girl from the silk-mills whose holiday it is to live other folks' lives and, by seeing them as more beautiful than they are, by idealizing them for no purpose of her own, to bring benefit to others who do not know of her existence. Pippa is innocence, is poetry. She is the 'third and better-tempered spirit' of Paracelsus's dying speech.

'That little peasant's voice,' breaking in on her one day of holiday, persuades Ottima's lover Sebald to pay the price of his crime, the murder of her husband; prompts the sculptor Jules to accept the bride who has been foisted on him in joke; recalls the patriot Luigi to his duty and awakes the unscrupulous prelate, Monsignor, to the wickedness of the plot which the intendant is proposing to him, to sell Pippa to her death in the brothels of Rome: for unknown to herself, she is the

Victor and King Charles and *The Return of the Druses*. *King Victor and King Charles* was a romantic chronicle play whose plot adhered closely to the anecdote on which it was based. But *The Return of the Druses* was a more ambitious play with an oriental setting, on a subject, in Browning's own words, 'of the most wild and passionate love' rising to extremes of 'self devotement and self-forgetting.' Macready seems to have been against the piece from the start, though had its author possessed a little dramatic ability the plot might have been worked up into quite a colourful melodrama. Certainly Browning did not fail through making concessions to his own taste; he was bent on a stage triumph, and the verse he wrote was plain enough even for the most inexperienced actors. The play's lack of construction, however, was its undoing. Its action is repeatedly held up by soliloquies and asides. Dramatic development is almost entirely lacking. So static is *The Return of the Druses*, indeed, that it is possible to read act five immediately after act one without missing anything of importance. Macready rejected it, as well as the less ambitious *King Victor and King Charles*, as more suitable for the study than the stage. Unfortunately, however, in his endeavour to write plays crude enough for the stage, Browning had produced something too thin and declamatory for any reader.

Fortunately, Robert Browning did not confine himself to attempts at winning stage success. During long walks about the countryside, often taken at night, which he enjoyed as a contrast to his theatrical preoccupations in London, he began to compose a number of lyrics and a long poem conceived in dramatic form though lyrical in texture, which were to excel anything he had so far written. This poem *Pippa Passes*, of 1841, was rich with obscurities, a far better poem than either *Pauline* or *Paracelsus*. Browning wove his texture too tight, but a tautening was necessary. Its failure lies in his incapacity, at that time, to draw with a firm outline.

Perhaps, too, in his pride, and in his disappointment at his failure to find a ready public, he was inclined to be uncompromising, or even to try and shock his reader; perhaps something in him urged him not to make himself plain, to hide his meaning. Writing of society in general to Elizabeth Barrett some years later, he observed: 'For me, I always hated it—have put up with it these six or seven years past, lest by foregoing it I should let some unknown God escape me.' It was perhaps his search for an unknown goddess, foreshadowed in *Pauline*, rather than any love of his fellow men that drew Robert Browning into society.

By the time he wrote that letter he was anxious to make *Sordello* more readable. It had met with blank incomprehension from most who had seen it; even Tennyson, who admired him, made the well-known and often repeated quip that he only understood two lines of it—the opening 'Who will may hear Sordello's story told,' and the final, 'Who would has heard Sordello's story told'— and that these were both lies. Carlyle reported that his wife had read it through without being able to make out whether Sordello was a man or a city or a book. Browning later proposed to Elizabeth that he should clarify the poem by expanding it. She, however, wanted him to draw it together and fortify the connections and associations, but in the end nothing was done. In his 1863 dedication he excused his faults of expression, and claimed that he had written it only for a few.

On his return from Italy, Browning, to the neglect of his poetry, started work on two historical pieces, *King*

thirteenth-century background of the first poem is as
real as the observed nineteenth-century detail of the
second. How deeply significant the creation of Sordello's
world was for Browning may be deduced from the fact
that it is here that his first profoundly individual writing
appears, in lines where the exact eye of a Crabbe, the
emotional force of Shelley, and a compact reasoning
akin to Shakespeare's combine to form something new
in English poetry. It is hard to substantiate this claim
by the choice of a short passage, and it is only in flashes
that poetry emerges from the poem's packed and turgid
detail; but if a few lines must serve for example, let it
be a description early in the second book:

> wide
> Opened the great morass, shot every side
> With flashing water through and through; a-shine,
> Thick-steaming, all-alive. Whose shape divine,
> Quivered i' the farthest rainbow-vapour, glanced
> Athwart the flying herons? He advanced,
> But warily; though Mincio leaped no more,
> Each foot-fall burst up in the marish-floor
> A diamond jet . . .

Here are the beginnings of an original style, and elsewhere in *Sordello* are the first adumbrations of Browning's
characteristic irony.

But the poem is inextricably difficult, a clear proof of
the poet's statement to Domett already quoted, that he
lived by himself. In this state of mind he had made a
solitary three months' journey to Italy, setting out in
April 1838, after the failure of *Strafford*, carrying in his
head this poem whose primary narrative interest to him
had long ago been overlaid by the accretions of secondary
incidents and of introspections concerning the best
method of presentation. Yet *Sordello* is, with all its

evidence that the young man had a dramatist's gifts. *Strafford*, the play he wrote, proved that he had not. Its situations are wooden and its lines undistinguished; it is mere prose chopped to blank verse length. Though not damned on its first presentation, with Macready in the title role, it did not last beyond five performances. Browning swore that he would never write another. But his friendship with Macready and the fascination of the theatre prevented his keeping to his resolution.

For the moment he returned to his poem *Sordello*, which he published in 1840. The Paracelsus in him was far from written out and the new poem is, like its predecessors, a confession of defeat, this time of failure to translate dream into action. In the course of the whole tale the poet Sordello emerges only twice from his subjective world. The stress of the poem, Browning declared in a later preface to it, was 'on the incidents in the development of a soul, little else being worth the study;' which last is as well, for the detail of the story is most obscure, partly owing to a too great allusiveness, and partly because of the abrupt transitions in the narrative. But in one way *Sordello* is an advance on the more diffuse and straightforward *Paracelsus*. Eglamor, the poetic craftsman talented but uninspired, Naddo, the critic, and Salinguerra, the Renaissance chieftain who proves to be Sordello's father, are round characters foreshadowing the great figures in *Men and Women*. The Italian background too is revealed in flashes of lovely detail, more clearly defined than the generalized landscape which occasionally leaps into being behind the larger-than-life figure of *Paracelsus*. *Sordello* was largely written before the poet's first visit to Italy, the impressions of which are more deeply stamped on *Pippa Passes*; but it is no exaggeration to say that the imaginary

match the ruggedness of his thought, which thereby suffers a loosely rhetorical weakening.

Browning's interest in the theatre had begun in his boyhood. The poem *Pauline* is dated 'Richmond, 22 October, 1832,' on which night he had gone with some cousins to the little theatre on Richmond Green, where Edmund Kean, some six months before his death, was playing Richard III. That night, Browning noted in his own copy of his first poem, he conceived the idea of writing it and others. 'I don't know whether I had not made up my mind to *act* as well as to make verses, music and God knows what,—*que de châteaux en Espagne!*'

Meanwhile the poet was making a wider circle of acquaintances; through an old friend he met the actor-manager William Macready, and through him John Forster, the future biographer of Dickens. Forster was writing a life of Strafford, which Browning revised for him during the author's illness, and Macready, as manager of Covent Garden, was championing the true drama against the spectacles and melodramas put on by the other licensed theatre, Drury Lane.

Browning was at that time, in the words of a young woman friend, 'slim and dark and very handsome and, may I hint it? just a trifle of a dandy, addicted to lemon-coloured kid gloves and such things: quite the glass of fashion and the mould of form. But full of ambition, eager for success, eager for fame and, what is more, determined to conquer fame and to achieve success.' To this young man Macready turned to save, if not the English theatre, at least his tenure of Covent Garden. 'He looks and speaks more like a poet than any man I ever saw,' he wrote. But a dramatic presence, though sufficient perhaps to account for the actor-manager's spontaneous invitation to write him a play, was no vision or certainty, unclear to the poet himself and consequently unconvincing to the reader. Yet though the nature of Paracelsus's attainment remains mysterious to the end his final speech does more than merely bring a long and shapeless poem to some sort of conclusion. It adumbrates the course that Browning was himself to pursue in his maturity.

> Let men
> Regard me, and the poet dead long ago
> Who loved too rashly; and shape forth a third
> And better-tempered spirit, warned by both
> As from the over-radiant star too mad
> To drink the life-springs, beamless thence itself—
> And the dark orb which borders the abyss,
> Ingulfed in icy night—might have its course
> A temperate and equidistant world.

'A temperate and equidistant world': so would the intricate landscape of *Men and Women* have appeared, viewed from the cloudy heights on which the young poet dwelt with his Promethean hero. Moreover, as the last quotation suggests, the young Browning half foresaw where his future kingdom lay.

The critics wrote *Paracelsus* down as Shelleyan. Elizabeth Barrett, however, could not accept the verdict of its derivativeness. 'An imitation of Shelley!' she protested in the course of their correspondence, 'when if *Paracelsus* was anything it was the expression of a new mind, as all might see, as *I* saw, let me be proud to remember.' But *Paracelsus*, though certainly the expression of a new mind, was too large and too theoretical in conception. Browning's originality was still unequal to a poem on this scale. Nor was his technique sufficiently developed. The blank verse does not yet bear his characteristic rough-cast texture; it is too smooth to

later poem—and Joseph Arnould. Yet he seems to have remained emotionally isolated and to have found social intercourse difficult, since even as late as 1840 he wrote to Domett on the subject of *Sordello*, 'the fact is I live by myself, write with no better company, and forget that the *lovers* you mention'—the characters in the poem —'are part and parcel of that self, and their choosing to comprehend my comprehensions but an indifferent testimony to their value . . .'

This aloofness is the true subject of the poem. It is in fact the principle constituent of that pride which led to Paracelsus's fall. 'A being knowing not what love is,' he is consumed by a passion for intellectual knowledge, and by a longing to perform some signal deed which will earn him mankind's admiration. But it is his own isolated ambition that the poet is voicing in an exaggerated form when he makes his hero cry:

> I seemed to long
> At once to trample on, yet save mankind,
> To make some unexampled sacrifice
> In their behalf, to wring some wondrous good
> From heaven or earth for them, to perish, winning
> Eternal weal in the act . . .
> Yet never to be mixed with men so much
> As to have part even in my own work, share
> In my own largess . . .

Against this attitude of contemptuous benevolence Festus, Michal and Aprile—the other shadowy characters in the poem—all stand for the power of love. To the young Browning creation and love of his fellow men stood on one side, the scientific pursuit of knowledge on the other; and neither alone was sufficient. It is only after his acknowledgment of this truth that Paracelsus can finally claim, as he lies dying, to have attained some

The central figure of Browning's next poem, *Paracelsus*, written two years later, partakes both of Faust and Prometheus; it is a study in the Romantic sin of intellectual pride—a theme less closely related to the poet's own experience than the Shelleyan enthusiasm of *Pauline*. Though boldly planned, *Paracelsus* is deficient in dramatic development, and its hero's ultimate defeat is so long expected than when it comes it lacks all elements of tragedy. Less mawkish than *Pauline*, this second poem has also less emotional tension; its conception is too patently an intellectual one. Though, unlike its predecessor, it could be reduced to an intelligible abstract, its plot would seem, when baldly stated, to be repeatedly turning back on itself. Nor has this poem any passages as fine as the best of *Pauline*. Browning had abandoned his Romantic style without achieving any compensating individuality. Even the best of *Paracelsus* is, indeed, rather further from the mature Browning idiom than such a descriptive passage from *Pauline* as that quoted at the end of the last chapter. It is reminiscent rather, as Edmund Gosse observed, of the monstrous family of *Festuses*, *Balders* and *Life Dramas*—pretentious works of that day which owed their popularity to a false show of profundity and to an utter flatness of style which made them comprehensible to a newly literate audience incapable of understanding poetry of any complexity. Browning, however, was still not sufficiently plain to rival the masters of that 'Spasmodic' school—Alexander Smith, R. H. Horne and P. J. Bailey. *Paracelsus* found him no readers. The explanation lies in an aloofness in the poet that had not grown less in the two years since the writing of *Pauline*. He had by now made friends with a number of young men with intellectual interests, chief among whom were Alfred Domett—the Waring of a

It is in his attitude to the dead poet that Browning gives us the clue to his own malaise. The sin of which he accused himself, in the person of the poet in *Pauline*, was pride or self-will, and the embodiment of these was Shelley.

The young Browning was at one with his dissenting parents in accepting the Christian ethic, if not the letter of the creed, Nor had he carried through the normal adolescent revolt against their standards and authority. He had, none the less, at the age of fourteen, seized upon 'Mr. Shelley's atheistical poem,' *Queen Mab*, in a box of second-hand books, and for perhaps as much as two years remained 'a professing atheist and a practising vegetarian,' writes Mrs. Orr. Yet this seems to have drawn down no parental disapproval. His mother procured for him the rest of Shelley's works and, on the book-seller's recommendation, some volumes of Keats as well. His careful education at home was not interrupted by this juvenile passion. Mr. Browning approved his son's ambition to make poetry a career. He himself held a clerkship in the Bank of England, then a lucrative post, but he considered that such work might prove too monotonous for his son; and though both the law and diplomacy seemed at times possible careers for young Robert, no one seems to have questioned the suitability of the son's living on at his father's expense, first at Camberwell and later at Hatcham, until at the age of thirty-four he made his runaway marriage with Elizabeth Barrett. Throughout his life his sister Sarianne, who was some years his junior, remained his closest friend.

Browning soon forsook his Shelleyan atheism, and adapted himself to the parental standards, yet there is evidence in *Pauline* that the adjustment was not made without spiritual cost.

nevertheless all contain passages that only a poet of deep, though inchoate, feeling could have written. *Pauline*, in fact, comes near—in parts—to achieving mastery in the field of romantic self-dramatization, which Browning very deliberately eschewed in everything that he wrote thereafter. Its tone is pessimistic. The young poet— he was twenty when he wrote it—monopolizes the poem's foreground, dwarfing his dimly outlined mistress Pauline, till she is no more than a stage property. Its setting is autumn, the verse a weak variant of the measure of 'Alastor,' and the driving force a sense of sin projected upon the imaginary poet, its hero, but clearly at that time dominant in Browning's own mind. This first poem betrays no foreshadowing of the sense of character, the dramatic speech, or the wealth of detail that characterize the later Browning. It is the poetry of mood. But like all Browning's work it is remarkable for a unity of texture, which is unbroken, though the verse falls and rises in its emotional intensity from derivative flatness and self-pity to aggressive self-assertion: contrasting strains which are reconciled only upon a note of general- ized hope, so inconclusive that it is impossible to be certain from the poem whether the young poet is in- tended to have died or survived. '*Pauline* is *the* one of Mr. Browning's longer poems of which no intelligible abstract is possible,' wrote Mrs. Sutherland Orr. One figure, however, does emerge from this shapeless con- fession, that of Shelley, whose example is invoked in a passage which sheds some light on the mind of the young Browning:

> Sun-treader, I believe in God and truth
> And love; and as one just escaped from death
> Would bind himself in bands of friends to feel
> He lives indeed, so, I would lean on thee!

insight into significance. Browning, on the other hand, had no wish to recall sixty-year old events. Everything had led up to the supreme experience of his love for Elizabeth Barrett, and to its counterparts in poetry, *Men and Women* and *The Ring and the Book*. Moreover, from the outset, he had been chary of self-revelations.

> Outside should suffice for evidence:
> And whoso desires to penetrate
> Deeper, must dive by the spirit-sense—
> No optics like yours, at any rate!

So, in the poem 'House,' he warned off the curious for personal ancedote and public introspection. What he sought to recapture in the *Parleyings* was rather former states of mind than the details of far away happenings.

Browning's 'People of Importance' were therefore, in the words of his friend and biographer Mrs. Sutherland Orr, 'men whose works connected themselves with the intellectual sympathies and the imaginative pleasures of his very earliest youth.' 'He had summoned them up,' she wrote, 'not for the sake of drawing their portraits, but that they might help him to draw his own;' and for that purpose none could be fitter than the authors in his father's library at their home in Southampton Street, Camberwell, and the painters in the Dulwich Public Gallery. For Robert Browning's education owed little to school or college. 'Italy was my university,' he would say in later years, when asked whether he had been to Oxford or Cambridge. His tastes and interests were formed, however, long before he visited Italy. They took shape in the years of his precocious reading recalled in the *Parleyings*.

Browning's first three poems, *Pauline*, *Paracelsus*, and *Sordello*, though none of them successful as a whole,

Chapter Two

THE HALF-HEARTED REBEL

IN the spring of 1887, just before his seventy-fifth birthday, Robert Browning published his last book but one, *Parleyings with Certain People of Importance in their Day*. In their day, however, the importance of his people had not been great; it was for their significance to him in his own far-away boyhood that he clothed these scarcely surviving shadows each with a robust and disputatious personality. Bernard de Mandeville, Daniel Bartoli, Christopher Smart, George Bubb Doddington, what were they now but names on the spine of some almost forgotten book or, in Doddington's case, attached to a story of political failure? It was in order to evoke the thoughts and emotions of his own early years that Browning summoned them for parley. The *Parleyings* were his *Dichtung und Wahrheit*, an attempt by calling up pictures from the past to gain a clearer view of his long life's course. This need imaginatively to relive experiences now much more than half a century old was one characteristic—and by no means an isolated one— common to Goethe and Browning; it is perhaps a need common to man, to see his life as a whole before leaving it, and to endeavour to understand, if only dimly, the pattern and purpose of his days. Goethe and Browning, however, adopted widely divergent methods of exploration. *Dichtung und Wahrheit* is an autobiographical reconstruction; facts are arranged in the light of a poetic

By over-daring: far from me be such!
Deep in the hollow, rather, where combine
Tree, shrub and briar to roof with shade and cool
The remnant of some lily-strangled pool,
Edged round with mossy fringing soft and fine.
Smooth lie the bottom slabs, and overhead
Watch elder, bramble, rose, and service-tree
And one beneficent rich barberry
Jewelled all over with fruit-pendents red.

A poet capable of these four passages, carelessly chosen out of his super-abundance, deserves, surely more than any other of the great Victorians, a re-reading and re-assessment. Perhaps the following chapters will do a little towards restoring his reputation, and towards showing the relevance of his poetry to our contemporary scene. For my purpose is to guide readers back to one of the greatest of English poets.

As for Browning's rejoicing in the manifold richness of the visible world, this was present in his poetry from the beginning to the end, from *Pauline*, out of which I draw my next quotation, to the 'Parleying with Gerard de Lairesse' which yields me my last.

> See this our new retreat
> Walled in with a sloped mound of matted shrubs,
> Dark, tangled, old and green, still sloping down
> To a small pool whose waters lie asleep
> Amid the trailing boughs turned water-plants:
> And tall trees overarch to keep us in,
> Breaking the sunbeams into emerald shafts,
> And in the dreamy water one small group
> Of two or three strange trees are got together
> Wondering at all around, as strange beasts herd
> Together far from their own land: all wildness,
> No turf nor moss, for boughs and plants pave all,
> And tongues of bank go shelving in the lymph,
> Where the pale-throated snake reclines his head,
> And old grey stones lie making eddies there,
> The wild-mice cross them dry-shod.

> Noon is the conqueror,—not a spray, nor leaf,
> Nor herb, nor blossom but has rendered up
> Its morning dew: the valley seemed one cup
> Of cloud-smoke, but the vapour's reign was brief,
> Sun-smitten, see, it hangs—the filmy haze—
> Grey-garmenting the herbless mountain-side,
> To soothe the day's sharp glare: while far and wide
> Above unclouded burns the sky, one blaze
> With fierce immitigable blue, no bird
> Ventures to spot by passage. E'en of peaks
> Which still presume there, plain each pale point
>   speaks
> In wan transparency of waste incurred

Spent his life to consummate the Great Work,
Would not we start to see the stuff it touched
Yield not a grain more than the vulgar got
By the old smelting-process years ago?
If this were sad to see in just the sage
Who should profess so much, perform no more,
What is it when suspected in that Power
Who undertook to make and made the world,
Devised and did effect man, body and soul,
Ordained salvation for them both, and yet . . .
Well, is the thing we see, salvation?

          I

Put no such dreadful question to myself,
Within whose circle of experience burns
I must outlive a thing ere know it dead . . .
The central truth, Power, Wisdom, Goodness,—God:

Again, for depth of feeling there is a little known lyric
of the poet's old age, from *Ferishtah's Fancies*, which
shall serve:

Not with my Soul, Love!—bid no Soul like mine
 Lap thee around nor leave the poor sense room!
Soul,—travel-worn, toil-weary,—would confine
 Along with Soul, Soul's gains from glow and gloom,
Captures from soarings high and divings deep.
Spoil-laden Soul, how should such memories sleep?
Take Sense, too—let me love entire and whole—
  Not with my Soul!

Eyes shall meet eyes and find no eyes between,
 Lips feed on lips, no other lips to fear!
No past, no future—so thine arms but screen
 The present from surprise! not there, 'tis here—
Not then, 'tis now:—back, memories that intrude!
Make, Love, the universe our solitude,
And, over all the rest, oblivion roll—
  Sense quenching Soul!

figures of his own time. All of them are to a lesser or greater degree taken up with one of the principal problems of nineteenth-century thought: the question whether art rather than religion is not the highest experience of which man is aware. To this heresy Browning did not subscribe.

But Browning's poems have greater claims on the reader than their mere concern with the problems of their day, and their success in stating these problems without suggesting any premature or facile solution. They are the poems of a mature poet, in whom thought, emotion and sensation are in a state of equipoise. Browning was not predominantly an intellectual poet as was Clough; nor did his work express only his rare intimations of some divine order behind the apparent confusion of earthly life as did Christina Rossetti's; nor did he draw only upon the richness and beauty of the world without, and of its impression upon his senses, as did Alfred Tennyson at his best. In Browning's poetry the three faculties of thought, feeling and sense are brought into play, as can perhaps best be demonstrated by taking some almost random quotations from the body of his work.

First let me choose a piece of close-knit reasoning, in which the Pope in *The Ring and the Book* speculates upon the small effect that Christianity has had upon the world:

> And is this little all that was to be?
> Where is the gloriously-decisive change,
> Metamorphosis the immeasurable
> Of human clay to divine gold, we looked
> Should, in some poor sort, justify its price?
> Had an adept of the mere Rosy Cross[1]

[1] A member of the Rosicrucian Society, practitioners in alchemy (The Great Work).

himself, derived from the quality of her own emotion. She represented a depth of experience greater than theirs that they could not fail to be conscious of, and Browning was able to convey that difference in quality.

It was not that he was a man with first-hand religious experience. He remained a doubter to the end, and if ever he ventured to affirm more than he knew the resulting falsity in his poetry is easy to detect. But Browning, at his best, could express the whole of his experience of love, faith and creative power, which were the three poles upon which his universe hung. He was capable of faithfully recording such flashes of emotion as he had. The nature of his experience, and its relationship to his poetry, it is the business of later chapters to set out.

Browning was a poet of considerable intellectual ingenuity, but he was not a philospher; he makes no general statements about man's place in the world. His reasoning is at its subtlest when he is presenting a case, the case for the cautious yet combative Bishop Blougram, content to believe less than he claimed to, yet firmly convinced of the necessity of belief, or the case of Karshish the Physician, anxious to adhere to a purely scientific standpoint even when confronted with the miracle of Lazarus, which fell outside the province of the scientifically explicable. Both are invented characters in the same sense as is 'The Pied Piper'; yet both stand for elements in Browning's own thought, and in the thought of his age, that could be more succinctly and more completely presented in the form of a poem than in that of a prose argument, worldly-Catholic, positivist or otherwise. Blougram, Karshish, Cleon, Andrea del Sarto, are independent characters, facets of the poet himself and at the same time representative tudes to life. These attitudes were all, no doubt, his own at certain times and under certain circumstances. But he was not interested in them merely on that account. Indeed, as this book will show, he was reluctant to acknowledge that his 'Men and Women' were speaking for himself. Yet of all his critics his French friend Joseph Milsand was the only one whose judgments he whole-heartedly accepted, and Milsand clearly saw the connection between his characters and the various personalities of which he was composed. Indeed Browning tacitly acknowledged the truth of Milsand's argument by the form and nature of his greatest poem, *The Ring and the Book*, in which he succeeded in grouping a number of personages around a central event—as he might a number of his own component personalities around a more permanent self—and thereby presented not only a wide canvas, a canvas as rich and various as that of Frith's *Derby Day*, but one at the same time which conveyed an unity greater than that of a mere group of people all standing at the same place and facing in the same direction. The personages involved in the case of Guido Franceschini are not merely found together on the same day in a Roman court of law. They are not merely witnesses to the same set of facts. Their unity lies in their having, each of them, witnessed a miracle; and the miracle is Pompilia. Never did the great Victorian writers fail so disastrously as when they attempted to present 'a pure woman.' Usually the cause of the trouble was their identification of purity with sexual immaturity. But Pompilia's purity was of a different kind. It lay in her selflessness, first displayed towards her brutal husband and then in the interests of her child. Her transforming effect upon the worldly priest, upon the ageing and still doubting Pope, and finally on her husband and murderer

standards, made with varying degrees of violence by
Wordsworth, Shelley and Byron. Browning came of
middle-class nonconformist stock, and inherited a
liberal background far more difficult to revolt against
than the squirearchical Toryism from which other
Romantics had sprung. Browning, besides, was lucky
in his parents, and fortunate in being allowed to choose
for himself the type of education that suited him. He
was, however, slow in attaining the depths of experience
which poetry requires. Had he died at the age of Shelley
or Keats or even Byron, he would appear today a very
minor figure in the Victorian field, the author of an
obscure narrative poem lit with flashes of brilliant description—*Sordello*; of a promising but uneven verse
drama—*Pippa Passes*; and of a dozen or two fine lyrics
that are none of them word perfect, all of them a little
rough in finish. For, as has been said, Browning was not
an accomplished poet on a small scale. He was an adventurous poet, at his best only when handling large con-
ceptions.

His true poetry, when it came, was the poetry of
maturity, which is, perhaps, one of the reasons why the
present age is reluctant to recognize its worth. For ours
is an intellectually over-ripe but emotionally under-
developed civilization. Browning's poetry is mature in
that he does not self-dramatize; *Pauline*—his earliest
poem and one which despite its beauties he would have
discarded if he could—is the only considerable work in
which 'Robert Browning, poet' monopolizes the foreground. He was not, on the other hand, content to be
a mere objective story-teller, as he had been in 'The Pied
Piper,' which, incidentally, he had composed only to
amuse a sick child. Browning invented characters whom
he could use as his mouthpieces to express various atti-

miracle never took place; society was too widely split by differences in interest and education for the poet to appeal to any but a middle-class audience. But Thomas Hood's apprenticeship to the music hall, his writing of sketches and songs to be presented by the popular comedian Charles Matthews, vastly extended the vocabulary, the metres and the allusiveness of nineteenth-century poetry. This new capital, of which Hood himself lived to make very little use, was taken over by Browning for such a poem as the 'Pied Piper,' and finally developed into a medium capable of expressing far greater psychological accuracy, of referring to far more things in a far less 'poetical' way than any other Victorian poet could achieve. Anyone comparing the nimble argument of *The Ring and the Book* with the conventional narrative flow of *The Idylls of the King* will realize the point of this argument, which I shall develop at length in later chapters. Browning took over from Hood—and incidentally passed on to Ezra Pound and so to our day—rhythms halfway between the spoken and the dramatic—between Charles Matthews' and Shakespeare's, in much the same way as Jules Laforgue, a later and more widely acknowledged ancestor of modern poetry, took elements from the French music halls, nursery rhyme and popular song which have passed from him to T. S. Eliot and so to W. H. Auden, and which still persist in contemporary French poetry.

'The Pied Piper' is an important poem and a very entertaining one, but it is not a great one. Browning did not write great poetry until he had attained emotional maturity, and this he lacked till the years of his marriage. Browning till thirty-five was a minor Romantic, whose single deep experience was his failure to make the Romantic rebellion against religion, society and parental

murder of an innocent woman if the whole of his experience could be summed up in the comforting affirmation that all is right with the world? There is a great deal of evil in the world of *The Ring and the Book*, but three lives are redeemed from their various depths of squalor and sin by the example of Pompilia's suffering and death. The snap judgment which has gone against Browning will not survive a reading of even one chapter of his masterpiece. Besides, do we require all our poets to recommend an early suicide?

Browning has suffered worse even than Spenser at the hands of the anthologist. He has suffered too from the strait-jacket of the printer's double column. Anyone wishing to read him in comfort would do well to use the seventeen volume collected edition, which is still to be picked up cheaply in second-hand bookshops, or to purchase the recent *Reynard* selection, a note of which he will find in my concluding bibliography.

But Browning has one advantage over such comparatively unanthologized poets as Spenser and the mature Milton of *Paradise Lost*: that we have met him in youth. Now both the familiar 'Pied Piper,' and the hardly less familiar 'How they brought the good News from Ghent to Aix,' are poems of tremendous accomplishment. They are, in fact, almost the only poems of their age that tell a story with something of a ballad monger's directness. Rossetti, William Morris and Swinburne tried to revive the ballad form and failed, because the medium was now artificial, and their treatment of it archaic. If a new Robin Hood or Sir Patrick Spens were to be added to the figures of popular imagination, the poet would require a different language, and one closer to the rhythms of the music hall song, or to saloon bar conversation, with which to work the miracle. In fact the

Chapter One

A CLAIM FOR ROBERT BROWNING

No major English poet is worse served by the anthologist than is Robert Browning. He has few perfect lyrics to offer, for primarily he is not a lyric poet at all. His work is always on a bold scale which faces the anthologist with the alternatives of drastically cutting, of omitting, or of including poems that are short but not of his best. Hence the constant inclusion of 'Home Thoughts from the Sea,' of 'The Lost Leader,' and even of that juvenile and unrepresentative horror-poem, 'Porphyria's Lover.' But most damaging of all to Browning's reputation is the too frequent appearance of 'Pippa's Song':

> God's in his heaven—
> All's right with the world!

The contemporary reader finds it hard to forgive Robert Browning the optimism of those two lines. But Pippa speaks for one side of Browning's nature only, voices only his simple belief in a certain primal innocence, of which he made her the symbol. He was, nevertheless, at heart an optimist, though of a far from naïve kind. He certainly believed that there is no virtue in doubt, and that behind the apparent disorder and contradictions of earthly events there is both a meaning and a purpose. But smug or facile he certainly was not. Would his greatest poem be concerned with the callous

I

CONTENTS

FOREWORD

IN striking the balance between 'Man' and 'Book' I have in this study come down deliberately on the side of 'Book', in the first place because the story of Robert Browning's life has been very often told already, and secondly because I have found in his poetry much that seems to me to throw entirely new light on the man. Indeed, by looking once more into the detail of his chief poems from a contemporary standpoint, I believe that I have made some contribution towards a re-estimate of this most seriously underrated of the great Victorians—and that is more than sufficient justification for this book.

My second chapter is based on material from an article on 'The Young Robert Browning,' contributed to *The Cornhill* (No. 975 Summer 1948). I owe my thanks to the proprietors of that journal for permission to make fresh use of it. I have not, however, incorporated it in the form in which it was printed. For in continuing to re-read Browning's poetry, I have had cause to modify some of my previous findings. In that article, as I look back on it, I seem to have been too much concerned with Browning's failure as a Romantic to give proper weight to his tremendous achievement in the field beyond Romanticism. Now, in a complete study, I hope that I have set right my original misjudgment.

J. M. C.

To

EDWARD UPWARD

in friendship

LONGMANS, GREEN AND CO LTD
48 Grosvenor Street, London W.1
Associated companies, branches and representatives
throughout the world

First published in 1952
Second impression 1964

52-14066

PRINTED IN GREAT BRITAIN
BY JOHN DICKENS & CO LTD, NORTHAMPTON

ROBERT
BROWNING

by

J. M. COHEN

LONGMANS

Robert Browning, perhaps the last of the Victorian poets to return to favour, is still imperfectly known. This book, originally written for the MEN AND BOOKS series, attempts to survey the whole of his work, on the basis of a fresh reading and of such new biographical information as has recently appeared. Mr. Cohen's particular interest has been in Browning's attitudes to love and belief and to the multiple nature of truth as demonstrated in 'The Ring and the Book'. He also finds much to praise and comment on in the later poems, both lyrical and narrative. What is attempted is a re-assessment on the basis of the work itself and of the poet's thought expressed in it. Mr. Cohen, however, relates his subject also to the Romantic tradition and to modern poetry since Ezra Pound.

Books are produced in the United States using U.S.-based materials

Books are printed using a revolutionary new process called THINKtech™ that lowers energy usage by 70% and increases overall quality

Books are durable and flexible because of Smyth-sewing

Paper is sourced using environmentally responsible foresting methods and the paper is acid-free

Center Point Large Print
600 Brooks Road / PO Box 1
Thorndike, ME 04986-0001 USA

(207) 568-3717

US & Canada:
1 800 929-9108
www.centerpointlargeprint.com

leaned forward a little. "You are not jealous of Jay," she grinned.

"No."

She laughed again, and she said, "I'm glad you said it, Flint." Then she reached forward with her hands and grasped his head and pulled him toward her. "It's always been you, you big Tennessee fool," she whispered.

She was like the country, Flint MacKeithan was thinking, open and frank with no deception in her, no guile. She would always be so even as the land around was so. He would not want her to change any more than he wanted the land to change. Both were for him—as they were.

"You want to go home," he murmured. "Tom Partridge will take you."

Jennifer Smith was the first one to see them as they came down the trail. She'd walked out to a little knoll a few hundred yards from the camp, and she was watching when they came over a rise.

Flint saw the relief in her eyes as she looked at him, and then she helped Portia into camp, and he saw no more of her until that evening after they'd eaten. He saw her sitting up on the seat of the windwagon, looking at the stars, and he moved away from the fire in front of the Wilde tent.

The starlight was in her eyes as she looked at him, and he put both arms on the wagon, looking down for a moment before looking up at her. He said,

"I didn't kill him."

"I knew you wouldn't." Jennifer smiled.

"How did you know?" Flint asked.

"I know you."

Flint frowned.

"Will he make it?" Jennifer asked.

Flint shrugged. "Moose Clemens says he might with luck, but Bannerman's luck has been bad of late." He paused and he said, "You're still thinking of Bannerman."

The laughter ran through her, then, and she

reins of the gray. Portia Wilde rode. Moose Clemens and Otey Higgins rode on ahead, and Flint could see them topping a rise, looking back to search the surrounding country. Then he heard Portia crying behind him, and he turned around.

She had her head down and she was weeping, shoulders shaking a little.

"You're tired," Flint told her. He remembered the strain she'd been under as they cut down Bannerman's outfit. It had gotten the better of her finally.

"I want to go home," Portia Wilde sobbed. "I want to go all the way home, Flint."

Flint looked across the hills. "You don't like this country?" he asked.

"It's too big," Portia whispered. "It's too wild, too cruel."

Flint looked at it, and it was beautiful; it was free, and a man could look in every direction and believe that it was his. The big sky touched the encircling hills to the north and to the east. The ridge of mountains rose to the west, and beyond them lay Santa Fe. Farther than that lay another vast country—mountains, desert, plain, buffalo country, cattle country, farm country. It was free, still teeming with game, a good country where a man could make his start in life and be somebody—not a lonely Tennessee hunter, living in his shack in the woods.

"I have a rifle," Jay told him.

"A long way back to the states," Flint murmured, "the way you're going, Bannerman."

"It is," Bannerman nodded. He hesitated, and then he said, "I am obliged to you, Flint."

Flint only shrugged. He rose up to the saddle and he waited for Portia Wilde to come over to him, and then he raised her up in front of him.

Bannerman said from the fire, "I might get that rifle from the wagon and put a bullet through you, Flint."

"No," Flint said. "You won't."

They didn't shake hands. They just looked at each other for a moment, and then Flint moved the gray away from the fire and down the trail. From the expression on Bannerman's face he knew that it did not matter too much to him whether he reached the states or not.

There was a vague regret running through Flint as the gray moved down the trail, and he held Portia Wilde in front of him. It was as if he'd beheld a fine and precious jewel, and then had seen that jewel dropped into the mud and soiled, and the dirt would not come off. Yet he remembered the jewel as it had been, as it could have been had it not been dropped.

Two days later they were out of the mountains, still heading down the trail toward the Wilde encampment. Flint walked ahead, holding the

as the back of his hand came in contact with the coals. The gun slipped from his fingers. He managed to get his hand away from the hot ashes now, but he ceased struggling after doing so.

Reaching forward, Flint picked up the gun and tossed it into the bushes. He looked down at Bannerman who lay inert underneath him, looking up at the stars, no expression on his face, and then he got up.

Bannerman sat up, his back toward the wagon and Portia, who'd stepped down and was coming toward the fire now. When Bannerman finally stood up, brushing the dirt from his clothes, not looking at Flint, she said,

"Will you have coffee, Jay?"

"If you please," Jay murmured.

They were in a Boston tearoom now, not here in the wilderness. Portia Wilde poured two cups, and she handed the cups to the men as they stood on each side of the fire. Bannerman still did not look at Flint. When he received the tin cup, however, he turned to Flint, smiling, gay as usual, the old Bannerman.

"To you," he said, "the better man."

"Luck," Flint told him.

They drank up, Portia watching them, saying nothing, and then Flint put the cup down on the rock. He said.

"You have your mare, and you'll find your pistol in the bushes. You have a rifle in that wagon?"

Dropping the rifle, Flint lunged from the saddle as Bannerman stumbled back. The pistol cracked, flame darting from the muzzle, and the shot went over Flint's head. He never learned whether Bannerman had shot high on purpose.

Landing on Bannerman's shoulders, he bore the man to the ground, his left hand circling Bannerman's wrist, holding the gun. They rolled on the ground, Bannerman fighting savagely, and Flint felt the strength of the man, and he knew he could match it, and surpass it.

They rolled over toward the fire, Bannerman lashing out with his free hand, Flint pressing the gun hand down into the dirt, burying his head into Bannerman's chest to avoid those solid, smashing blows Bannerman aimed at his face.

Bannerman threw him off, and they rolled again, and then Flint, with a great effort rolled him back toward the fire, gripping that gun hand, holding it as in a vise, and then slowly he moved the hand toward the glowing ashes on the outer edge of the fire.

Bannerman knew what he was doing, and fought like a wildcat to prevent him, but inch by inch Flint moved the hand, exerting every ounce of strength in his body. He heard Bannerman's breath coming in short, panting gasps, and Bannerman's blows to the top of his head became less vicious.

Then Bannerman let out a short, animal cry

as if he were discussing a pleasant little jaunt across New York State. "We'll cross Texas back to the states."

"Comanche country," Flint told him, "and plenty wild. You'll never make it—not with a woman along."

"I'm taking her," Bannerman said. "Drop the rifle and get off the horse, Flint."

"No," Flint said. "You can't take her, Bannerman. Why do you want her?"

There was almost a note of desperation in Bannerman's voice as he spoke. He said harshly, "I'm taking her, Flint. Dismount."

Flint knew what it was, then. It was not because Bannerman was in love with her, or that he needed her, but she was all he had left of the old life, the old way of life with which he'd broken when he deserted Clayton Wilde. He was reluctant to cut the last string which held them, and he was not thinking clearly any more. He was a desperate man—a man who hadn't slept for days, a disillusioned, embittered man.

Bannerman still held the bridle, the gun leveled on Flint's chest, watching his face, eyes narrowed. Without moving the upper part of his body, and with no expression on his face, Flint's right leg moved. The heel came back hard into the flank of the grey, and the gelding, surprised and frightened by the savage kick, snorted and leaped forward.

Colt gun gleaming dully in his hand. This was a different Bannerman—an unshaven Bannerman, a haggard Bannerman who'd been through his share of hell day by day, hour by hour, seeing his plans of great wealth melting away like snow under a warm sun.

"I need that horse," Bannerman said.

He could still smile, though, and he was smiling now—a cold, calculating smile.

Portia Wilde watched them from the wagon less than ten yards away, very still. The fire crackled and the coffee boiled over the flames, the smell of it coming to Flint's nostrils, making him hungry.

"I need that horse, Flint," Bannerman repeated, and he came around to the front of the gelding, reaching for the bridle, his Colt gun lined on Flint's chest.

Flint made no move. He sat there with the rifle across the pommel, pointing away from Bannerman, and he knew that he could never get it around before Bannerman put a bullet through him.

"Where are you going?" Flint asked him.

Bannerman had his chestnut mare, and he evidently wanted the gray for Portia, which meant that he was taking Portia on with him. He couldn't go on to Santa Fe. Mexican agents, friends of Ortiz, men who knew him, would be waiting if he came in alone.

"Heading due east," Bannerman stated coolly

shoulders hunched a little, face expressionless.

Moving around a bend in the trail he came upon the lone wagon, the fire burning in front of it, and a horse tethered to the wagon. The horse was a chestnut mare—Bannerman's fine animal, and the mare nickered when Flint and the gray came in sight.

He didn't see Bannerman, and he didn't see Portia Wilde. A coffeepot boiled over the flames, and a few strips of bacon had been laid out on a flat rock nearby.

There was a movement inside the wagon as the gray's shoe struck sparks on a rock, and then Portia appeared in the opening. Flint saw her face in the firelight as she stared into the shadows, looking for him, and then her voice reached out, clear, unafraid, "Flint—no."

It was already too late. Off to Flint's left in the brush he heard a gun hammer click, and then Bannerman's cool voice,

"You're covered, Flint. Don't try to use that rifle."

The gray gelding came to a stop, and Flint sat astride the animal, the muzzle of the Hawkins' rifle pointing to his right, away from Bannerman, who was coming out of the shadows. Had it been pointing the other way there was the possibility that he could have gotten off a shot—if he'd wanted to.

Bannerman came out into the firelight, the

"What happens," Moose Clemens asked, "if you don't come back?"

"Come and get him," Flint told the big trapper. "Take Portia Wilde back to Partridge."

He rode off, then, leaving the two men behind him, and he made no effort to conceal himself as he rode straight down the trail in the gathering dusk. The sun dropped behind the ridge of barren peaks to the west, and then the stars glittered through the trees. The coldness came to the mountains, a clear, crisp cold, and the gray snorted several times, its hoofs ringing out occasionally on barren rock.

Occasional broken-down wagons lay just off the trail, the dregs of previous outfits which had come this way. Broken wheels and broken axles lay in the dirt, and shreds of canvas from the downed wagons whipped in the cold breeze coming down out of the pass.

A dead horse lay in the trail, and Flint surmised that it had broken a leg that day, and been shot by one of Bannermen's men. There were no sounds up here but the singing of the wind through the pines.

After a while a crescent moon slid up over the lip of the pass still far ahead, and then Flint saw the yellow flicker of Bannerman's campfire off to the right where the trail wound up through the rock and timber. He rode on slowly, the Hawkins' rifle across the pommel of his saddle,

dream of great wealth which had vanished as all dreams do.

"Bannerman ain't with 'em," Moose Clemens said. "He's still up ahead, Flint, an' alone."

Flint waited until the Westport men had disappeared down the trail, and then he raised into the saddle. He said to Otey and Moose Clemens,

"Wait for me."

Little Otey stared at him. "You goin' ahead?" he asked.

Flint nodded.

"He's dangerous," Otey protested. "He might put a bullet through you, Flint, an' keep goin'."

"I'll be back," Flint said.

Portia was up there with Jay Bannerman, and he had to bring Portia back. Bannerman knew he would be coming down the trail this night, and Bannerman would be waiting, his great scheme petered out in the mountain country here, a line of broken wagons behind him, and broken men headed back to the states. He'd lost the love of a fine woman, and his great opportunity to make a fortune was gone. These things would be preying on his mind like festering wounds in the body of a cougar crouching in the underbrush.

Riding on ahead, Flint MacKeithan did not know what to expect from Bannerman—the friendly smile, the open frankness of the man, or a bullet from the brush, but he had to find out, and he had to find out alone.

The Moose shrugged. "If the Comanches let 'em," he said.

Flint watched the body of men move by and disappear among the trees below. One third of Bannerman's outfit had deserted him, and he wondered what Bannerman would do about that. It was inconceivable that he would go on, hoping to conquer Santa Fe with sixty or seventy odd men.

"He can't go back," Otey said, as if reading Flint's mind.

They moved on up the trail again as it twisted through the trees, up over gray rock which showed the wheel marks of previous outfits, down into ravines where the wagons had to be let down with ropes, and then up again.

They found Bannerman's noonday campsite, and a dozen sullen men sitting around a fire, more deserters headed back for Westport. They skirted the camp, not bothering the men, knowing that they were whipped, and they followed the tracks of the remaining wagons.

"He's licked," Otey Higgins said. "We stopped him, Flint."

They found another broken-down wagon an hour later, and then the rest of the Bannerman party trooping back down the trail, driving the remaining stock before them.

Hidden back among the trees Flint watched them go by, tired, bitter, drawn men who'd had a

the Bannerman camp, whooping like a drunken Apache, firing shots into the dying mess fires, rousing the entire camp.

Bannerman had a flying squadron of men ready to go out after him, but none of them were too anxious to prowl around in the thick shadows beyond the firelight, not sure what they would run into. There was always the possibility that a band of Indians *had* attacked them, and not one man.

Moose Clemens easily avoided the party, circled, and came back to the camp where Flint and Otey Higgins were waiting for him. He said as he went off to sleep, "We got 'em worried, Flint, an' damn tired. Some o' them boys are plenty disgusted now."

"What kin they do?" Otey reflected.

They learned the next day what could be done by the Westport drifters. At high noon as they were following the trail up into the hills, a trail which each hour and each hundred yards became rougher as they moved up into Raton Pass. Hearing a party of horsemen coming toward them, they moved back into the timber to watch, and saw thirty odd men trudging back down the trail, a few of them riding, but the rest walking, driving a dozen oxen ahead of them for food.

Otey Higgins grinned and said, "That bunch has enough, Flint. You think they'll make it back to Westport, Moose?"

Flint studied the man, and then looked at Otey Higgins.

"Fight," he said simply. "Nerves."

"Maybe they'll kill each other off," Otey chuckled. "Then we kin let Bannerman go on all by his lonesome."

As they ascended into the hills the trail became rougher, and at noon they found another abandoned wagon.

That night when the oufit stopped they again sent shots into the cookfires, circling the camp constantly as they fired from the woods and the hills, making it impossible for the Bannerman crew to eat. It was several hours after sunset before they withdrew, making their own camp in the higher hills.

"Be midnight," Otey said, "afore them fellers git up enough nerve to start the fires goin' again. You gonna pay 'em a visit again tonight, Moose, after they git sleepin'?"

Moose looked up at the night sky. "Feel like a howlin' cougar tonight," he said. "Reckon I'll howl a bit after I git a few hours rest."

"Them poor boys didn't rest last night, either," Otey grinned. "Ought to be ashamed o' yoreself, Moose."

"Reckon they should o' stayed in Westport," the Moose observed, "instead o' layin' their bones down here in the wilderness."

That night Moose made another foray against

up ashes from two of the fires, and one bullet tore through a coffeepot on another, scattering men in all directions.

Otey Higgins said as they rode away through the timber. "Now they ain't even gettin' any rest when they eat. That's bad."

That night at two o'clock Moose Clemens rose and made a lone sally against the wagons, imitating a dozen Comanches and Kiowas, as he fired shots into the air and circled the wagons from a distance of a hundred yards. Every man in the Bannerman outfit was awake the remainder of the night, wondering if it really had been a band of wild Comanches now lying hidden in the surrounding hills, waiting for them to lie down and sleep again.

Calmly, Moose rode back to the little camp they'd made in the higher hills to the south. He rolled into his blanket and was settling himself for the night when Otey said thoughtfully, "Ain't you afraid some o' that bunch will track you down, Moose?"

"Hell." The Moose smiled. "Ain't a man in that crew kin tell which way a horse is travelin' by lookin' at its tracks."

They found a dead man at the abandoned campsite the next morning, a man who'd been knifed and who lay in the brush just beyond where the three wagons had stood.

Otey Higgins said, "Hate like hell to shoot a horse, almost like shootin' a brother."

The three Hawkins' rifles spoke and three horses leaped and went down, kicking. They reloaded rapidly and shot; again, dropping two more horses before they ran for their mounts and galloped away in the gathering dusk.

"Five of 'em won't be ridin' tomorrow," Moose Clemens said. He spat disgustedly and said, "Known a lot o' men I'd rather shoot than a horse, but this is war—or to stop a war."

"Four or five days," Otey said, "we kin kill every horse they got. Then we kin ride up, spit right in their eyes, an' ride off again an' laugh at 'em. That right, Flint?"

Flint just nodded. He hadn't liked to give the order to shoot the horses, but it was another way of stopping Bannerman, of putting the pressure on the crew. They were beginning to realize now that there was nothing they could do to stop the three riflemen behind them, and as the food gave out and the rigors of the trail increased, they might become disgusted with the whole business and give it up.

The wagons entered the foothills the following afternoon, and as the Bannerman crew, weary and disgruntled, sat around the fires to eat, three rifles cracked from a growth of low timber on the side of a hill west of the camp. The bullets kicked

either," Otey Higgins stated. "Likely fall apart before he gets another hundred miles, an' they'll never take him through the mountains."

Already, they could see the mountains ahead, the distant ridges, looking almost like clouds on the horizon. It was here that the trail lifted up over Raton Pass, one of the most difficult passages on the entire trip.

Following the slowly moving outfit through the day they came upon one of the wagons which had been abandoned. The rear wheels of the freight wagon had been badly burned the night before, and they'd given way. Bannerman had had the supplies moved to one of the remaining three wagons, or loaded the stuff onto pack animals. The abandoned wagon lay in the trail like a wounded animal trying to rise. It was the symbol of the lost hope, and the cherished dream of Clayton Wilde to liberate a people. That part of it was over, but the evil it had spawned still lingered on, and had to be destroyed.

That afternoon with the sun going down, Flint, Otey and Moose Clemens crouched on the summit of a hill three hundred yards away from the herd of oxen, horses and mules Bannerman had set out to graze. A dozen guards surrounded the herd, indicating that Bannerman realized he had to watch his stock extra careful now.

"How many?" Moose wanted to know.

"Count 'em," Otey said, and the big man climbed up to the rim of the hollow to look.

"Seven burnin' bad," he said when he came back again. "You want to move back a few miles now, Flint, an' make a fire?"

They rode north several miles, camping the remainder of the night near another small stream, a tributary of the Arkansas. Otey Higgins set a pot of coffee over the hot coals, and they roasted a few strips of buffalo meat.

"What about tomorrow?" Moose asked when they'd finished eating.

"We keep after them," Flint said. "Day and night. Maybe we can run off some of the stock tomorrow."

"Like babes in the woods," Moose said and grinned. "Ain't a man in that bunch knows how to take care o' himself in open country."

"Bannerman's no fool," Otey warned. "He has fools with him, but he's no fool."

"Three of us against Bannerman," Moose said. "We'll catch him."

"Caught a wildcat once," Otey murmured. "Don't want to catch another one."

In the morning, from a distant ridge, they watched Bannerman's outfit take the trail—three wagons and the excess cattle and horses.

"Them three wagons ain't in such good shape,

268

"Not bad for a night's work," Otey grinned. "Bannerman lost most o' his food tonight, an' there ain't a hunter in that crowd kin bring him fresh meat when he needs it."

"They still have horses, and oxen to eat," Flint said, "and they have guns. This won't stop him."

"Didn't figure it would," Otey acknowledged. "Just a little nuisance to let him know we're around. Let's find Moose."

They found Moose Clemens back in the hollow where they'd rested earlier in the evening. The giant trapper lay on his blanket, arms outstretched, when they slid down the low embankment, and he said lazily, "Where in hell you been?"

"Warmin' our hands at Bannerman's fires," Otey told him. "You didn't sound like ten Comanches tonight, Moose. It was more like a barrel full o' cougars, an' the barrel rollin' down a hill."

"Have any trouble?" Flint asked him.

"That bunch has a hell of a time shootin' straight in the day time," Moose Clemens chuckled. "Didn't give 'em much of a target an' I kept movin'."

"Bannerman will know who's been after him," Flint said thoughtfully. "It'll be harder the next time."

"Might be harder on him the next time, too," Otey Higgins stated. "All we did tonight, Flint, was burn a few wagons."

"That's enough," Flint yelled. Already, horsemen were swooping back toward the corral, their horses' hoofs pounding the earth.

They went over the chains and out into the deeper grass, running at top speed to get beyond the firelight. Otey, as agile as a rabbit, bounded on ahead of Flint.

Some of the horsemen had swerved around the burning wagons, and although unable to see them in the darkness beyond, and with the burning light of the fires in their eyes, blinding them, were riding in their direction, hoping to intercept them.

Flint slipped the Colt gun out of the holster as he ran soundlessly through the grass. They were a hundred yards from the wagons when two riders pounded out of the night, almost directly at them.

Dropping flat on his stomach, Flint lay there, the horse of one of the riders kicking dirt on him as they shot by. He noticed that Otey Higgins had done the same thing, and when the riders rushed past, they rose to their feet and continued running toward the stream where they'd left the horses.

Behind them they could hear the shouts of excited men trying to put out the flames, and when they reached the two horses and raised up into the saddles they could see six of the wagons burning furiously. Four others were burning, also, but there was the possibility that they would be able to check the fires and save some of them.

He saw the Wilde Conestoga wagon on the other side of the enclosure as they climbed over the chains, and he pointed to it, indicating that Portia probably was in there, and not to touch that wagon. Otey Higgins nodded.

Only one man remained at the wagons. He'd stumbled out of his blankets, dazedly, a heavy sleeper, aroused only after much shooting, and as he walked toward the fire, Otey Higgins moved up behind him, dropping him with a short swing of the Colt gun.

"Work fast," Flint snapped.

They snatched burning brands from the fire and ran toward the nearest wagons. Slashing with his knife, Flint cut huge gashes in the sheets covering the loads, thrust his flaming torch inside, and then ran for another firebrand and another wagon.

He saw Portia climb down from the wagon and watch them as they worked, and he waved a hand to her, motioning for her to get back into the wagon. She understood and she nodded, knowing that they couldn't help her tonight.

He was on his fourth wagon when he heard the cry of alarm from the direction of the stock. By this time two of the wagons were burning briskly, the sun-dried wagon sheets leaping into flame. He noticed that Otey Higgins, also, had four wagons afire, and was running for his fifth, firebrand in hand.

"Burn 'em to hell," Otey whooped.

other after that as the Moose galloped his horse back and forth out beyond the herd. Other guns opened up as the frantic herders fired at shadows, yelling frantically for help.

The Moose continued with his whooping screeches as the crewmen under the wagons leaped out, grabbing at rifles. The fires were kicked into a blaze, and Flint had a glimpse of Jay Bannerman running toward his chestnut mare tied to one of the wagons. Bannerman shouted orders for the men to join him, and he rode at a gallop away from the wagons, rifle in hand.

Men streamed from the wagon corral, running toward the stock, and still Moose Clemens continued his wild whooping, screeching in different keys to give the impression that a number of Indians were in on the raid.

The excited herders shot at everything, yelling for help. Flint stood up and started to walk toward the wagons, Otey Higgins following. He was looking for Portia now, wondering if it would be possible to get her out tonight, and then realizing that it was impossible. After setting some of the wagons afire they would have to make a terrific dash for their horses, and Portia would not be able to keep up with them. The objective tonight, and the days following, was to stop Bannerman, stop his wagons, destroy his supplies, kill or run off his stock. When he was stopped they had Portia.

A hundred yards from the camp they dropped down on their stomachs, wriggling forward through the knee-high grass. Working forward foot by foot they passed one guard fifty yards out from the nearest wagon, passing within fifteen feet of him, crawling up to within a dozen yards of the wagons, where they stopped.

The eleven wagons were drawn up in a quadrangle as usual, wheels interlocked. They could see the huddled shapes under blankets under the wagons and around the smoldering fires. Once a man got up, walked to the fire to kick at it, and then rolled into his blanket again. The fire flared up for a few minutes, the firelight revealing the eleven wagons drawn up around the three mess fires.

Flint pointed with his finger to the wagons to the right of the spot where they crouched. He whispered, "Yours."

They waited now for Moose Clemens somewhere out on the open plains, drawing nearer to the stock. The Moose had promised to give them plenty of time to get up close to the wagons before he went into action. They were ready now.

Five minutes passed, and then ten, and Flint heard Otey Higgins stir restlessly in the grass. A full half hour passed before they heard the first wild Comanche yell, followed by a rifle shot, and then several shots from a pistol.

Blood-curdling yells followed one upon the

from the opposite side of the camp," Flint said. "Bannerman's crew may all rush out to stop the raiders, and then we move into the camp."

"Burn the wagons?" Otey grinned.

"Many as we can," Flint told him.

"Sounds good," Otey laughed. "Might git the whole bunch of 'em, an' then Bannerman will have his oxen an' his horses, but nothin' to pull."

They noticed that the fires at the wagon corral were only red dots now as they'd been permitted to die down. There was no moon tonight, only the stars.

"Good horse-stealin' night," Moose Clemens observed. "Enough light to see, but not to be seen."

"Keep out of their way," Flint cautioned him.

The Moose laughed derisively. "That bunch ain't catchin' me," he said, and then he rode off, disappearing in the shadows.

Otey and Flint swung east, walking their horses slowly, making a wide circuit of the camp. They took their time, giving the Moose plenty of opportunity to locate the grazing stock and make his preparations.

When they were within three hundred yards of the wagon corral, they dismounted, left the horses tied to the willows along a small stream upon which Bannerman had made his camp. They moved forward on foot, watching for the guards outside the camp.

was creating more of a disturbance in his mind now than even Portia Wilde. He found himself thinking of her taunting boldness when they had first met, of the way she had thrown her arms around him and kissed him. Had he avoided her because he was afraid of her or of himself? Had he avoided her because he had wanted to be the pursuer instead of the pursued? He hadn't liked what she had said concerning Bannerman, and even though she'd laughed, he still wondered what her true feelings were concerning the handsome Easterner. But he got consolation from her last words, "I was thinking of you, Flint. Remember that." He wished that this expedition was over, that he could go back to straighten things out with Jennifer.

Otey Higgins said, "Time to ride, Flint."

Flint got up and stretched himself. He said to Moose Clemens, "Reckon you can make as much noise as a dozen Comanches?"

The big trapper grinned. "Maybe ten," he said modestly. "Them damn Injuns kin sure screech when they git started."

"What's up?" Otey asked curiously.

"You move up on the herd," Flint told the Moose. "When you get ready, open up with your gun, whoop like an Indian, and make it sound like a Comanche raid on the stock."

"I'll scare hell out of 'em," the Moose chuckled.

"Otey and I will come up on the wagons

Dismounting, they walked their horses down into a hollow, spread their blankets and lay down, without a fire this night, the starlight illuminating the hollow. They could hear the horses munching grass a few yards away, and they chewed on pieces of buffalo meat they'd cooked at the noonday meal.

Once Flint moved to the rim of the hollow and stared at Bannerman's fires for a while, thinking about the man, and this tremendous risk he was taking. The filibustering expedition had been bad enough, but now Bannerman was lining up with the forces of lawlessness, intent on robbing a whole province if he could. He was a gambler and the stakes were big. For him it meant a life of luxury and ease, or one of niggling poverty completely unacceptable to a man with his upbringing.

Otey Higgins said, "Reckon we kin have a look at his stock in a couple o' hours, Flint."

Flint nodded. He continued to watch the fires for some minutes, and then he went down to the blankets. Both Higgins and Moose Clemens had gone to sleep, and they slept till midnight, both men waking almost simultaneously as if someone had tapped them on the shoulders.

Flint hadn't slept well. Portia Wilde was on his mind, and Jennifer Smith, and Jay Bannerman, and all three were unsettling to him. Whether he wanted to or not he discovered that Jennifer

"That Bannerman," Otey smiled, "is no man's fool. He knows he don't get anywhere without horses an' oxen to pull them wagons. He might have half his crew watchin' the stock at night, an' even a Comanche couldn't git within a half mile of 'em."

Flint could see the logic of this statement. Bannerman did not make too many mistakes, and he would be very careful now that he was nearing his goal.

"How do you figure it, Moose?" he asked.

Moose Clemens puffed on his pipe for a moment. "Have a look at 'em first," he suggested. "See how worried Bannerman is, an' then act. Maybe he is figurin' on somebody comin' after him, an' maybe he ain't."

"Nothin' to worry about," Otey stated, "till we git there. Let's sleep."

They were off before dawn again, still moving parallel with the trail, crossing several small streams over which Bannerman's wagons had to cross farther east.

It was late afternoon when they gradually turned east again, heading back toward the trail. They passed more buffalo, scared a bunch of antelope, and then as the last light left the sky they saw Bannerman's campfires on the horizon, tiny flickering blotches against the darkened sky to the south and west.

to make Jennifer Smith fall in love with him. Possibly he succeeded, too, and that was the reason she did not want him killed.

"Don't be jealous of Bannerman," Jennifer laughed. "I was thinking of you, Flint. Remember that."

They rode off a few minutes later, and looking back Flint saw Jennifer standing with her father watching them. She lifted a hand when he turned.

"They ain't movin' fast," Moose Clemens said. "We should be up with 'em tomorrow."

They left the trail, Clemens taking a route which ran parallel with it, in case Bannerman had sent back a rear guard to watch his back trail. They rode till two hours after sunset, making camp in a buffalo wallow where their tiny fire could not be seen from any direction. They lay back on their blankets after eating, and the Moose took a clay pipe from his sack. He spoke to Flint as he packed it with tobacco, and put a glowing ember on top of the tobacco.

"You figure on runnin' off their stock first, Flint?"

Flint looked at Otey Higgins. "Shouldn't be too hard," he stated.

Little Otey looked up at the night sky and scratched his chin. "If you was Bannerman, Flint, what in hell would you be worryin' about most if you figured somebody might be on your tail?"

"Stock," Flint said.

"Why not?" he asked, thinking of Portia, thinking of the hell ahead of her. "He might try to kill me," he said.

Jennifer shook her head. "Bannerman likes you," she told him. "You know that."

Flint did know it, and it had bothered him even when he'd learned that Jay had gone off with the wagons and with Portia Wilde. He didn't think Bannerman could be stopped short of killing the man, and deep down inside he knew that he didn't want to kill him—even now after what he'd done. He remembered the afternoon Bannerman had spoken to him at the spring, trying to explain in advance why he had to do what he was doing now. He'd saved Bannerman's life on board the General Jackson, and Bannerman had possibly saved his on the ridge with the Osages.

"I hope," Jennifer said slowly, "that it does not come to killing, Flint, because it will bother you all the days of your life."

"Might bother you, too," Flint said, and he stared at her, remembering that she'd been quite friendly with Bannerman on the trip.

Jennifer grinned at him. "You are not jealous of Bannerman, Flint." She chuckled.

"Damn fool statement," Flint said.

"Are you?" she asked.

"No," Flint growled, but he was disturbed, and he didn't like it. Bannerman had had Portia, and there had been no reason for the man trying

Chapter Eighteen

A N HOUR BEFORE dawn the next morning Flint, Moose, and Otey Higgins rode out after buffalo. By ten in the morning they'd bagged three cows, skinned them, and filled their saddlebags, returning to the camp by noon with the fresh meat. They were ready to leave on Bannerman's trail an hour later.

There was no great rush because Bannerman, hampered by the slow-moving wagons, would not make particularly fast time, and three men on horseback could catch up with him within a day or two at the most.

Jennifer came over to the rear of the wagon where Flint was adjusting his saddle blanket just before they rode out. It was the first time she'd spoken to him since Bannerman's departure. She said,

"Take care of yourself, Flint."

"Aim to," Flint nodded, and he looked at her.

"Flint."

He turned around fully to face her, and she said, "I hope you catch him, Flint, but don't let him be killed."

Flint rested one hand on the flank of the gray.

Partridge was in love with Portia. He could tell it from the look in the man's eyes, a look both of suffering and frustration probably caused by the fact that he couldn't be the one to rescue Portia from Bannerman.

Flint now wondered what his true feelings were concerning Portia. Did he want this quiet, blonde girl merely because he had thought her Bannerman's? Did he like the challenge it posed? Did he merely want what he thought he couldn't have, and did he refuse Jennifer because she had thrown herself at him?

He walked over to the fire to join Moose and Otey. Otey said, "Never should o' climbed aboard the General Jackson back in St. Louis. That started it all."

Flint sat down and picked up a sourdough biscuit. He was munching on it when he happened to look toward the Smith windwagon. Jennifer was sitting on the ground, her back against the wagon wheel. The firelight from the small fire in front of the windwagon played on the smooth panels of her face, revealing the gentle curve of her lips and her cheeks. She seemed moody and meditative as though she was trying to quell some inner fight. Flint found himself staring at her. She was an attractive girl, he thought, a damn attractive girl. For some reason he seemed to be really seeing her for the first time.

Tom Partridge sat up again. "You're not thinking of going after them?" he asked.

"We could try," Flint told him, and he was thinking of Portia now, riding beside Jay Bannerman, the deadness inside of her, also.

There were tears in Clayton Wilde's eyes. "I am willing to go, too, gentlemen."

"Three horses," Flint said. "Three riders." To Partridge he said, "Can you get along without us, Tom?"

"Kill me to sit here," Partridge muttered, "but if there's a chance, Flint, go after them. We have supplies, and you are sure that there are no Indians about."

Moose Clemens and Otey Higgins went over to the fire to eat. Clayton Wilde went back to his tent, rubbing his hands together, still in a daze.

Tom Partridge looked at Flint steadily, and then he said, "Bring her back, Flint. Do you hear me?"

Flint nodded.

"It doesn't matter," Partridge said, "if she's for you, or if she's for me. Bring her back, Flint."

"All right," Flint said almost gruffly. Bannerman was out of it now. She no longer was for Bannerman. He'd made his decision, and he had her body, but he didn't have Portia Wilde, and he never would have. Flint wondered how the man hadn't seen that.

It meant that the field had narrowed down to Partridge and himself. Flint had no doubt that

of succeeding in Santa Fe?" Flint asked him.

"The prospects are good," Wilde admitted, "even with his small force. The local government is weak and discontented. We have ascertained that fact. The colony of New Mexico is far removed from Mexico City, and sending even a small army this far north over rugged terrain and mountain country is a hazardous undertaking. With the help of the populace, the discontented element in the New Mexican government, and my agents on the field, Bannerman could succeed."

"Damn this leg," Partridge swore. "Damn—damn this leg!" He lay back on the blankets and put his arm across his eyes.

"Can't go after 'em with twenty-seven men," Otey Higgins observed, "an' three guns, an' three horses."

Flint looked at Moose Clemens. The giant trapper hadn't said much, but he'd been taking in every word.

"What about it, Moose?" Flint asked.

The Moose spat. "Long way to Santa Fe," he observed. "They'll be headin' fer the mountains soon, an' they have to git over Raton Pass. Plenty kin happen."

"What?" Otey asked.

"They kin have their stock run off," the Moose reflected. "Seen two Injuns spook a couple o' hundred head o' horses an' cattle once, an' the outfit never got 'em back, either."

"If you'll tie me on a horse, Flint," he said, "and give me your gun I'll go after him."

Flint just shook his head. He saw Clayton Wilde come out of the tent, an old man, a man who had lost the power to make decisions. His gray hair was mussed, and as he came up he said in a shaking voice, "This is terrible—terrible, gentlemen."

Flint looked around. There were about two dozen men, and the wounded at the camp, all of them dazed by the suddenness of this event. These were the men Wilde, Partridge and Bannerman had brought from the East—the real patriots, and their filibustering expedition was over here in the sand hills on the other side of the Arkansas, only halfway to Santa Fe. Looking into the faces of some of them Flint saw the relief. The big adventure was over, and in a way they were glad.

"He must be stopped," Clayton Wilde mumbled. "We risk a war."

Flint wondered why the man hadn't seen this before, but it was the way with visionaries. They saw their own project crystal clear, but the ramifications were hidden in the mists. The fire had died out of Clayton Wilde, and he was a thin, gray-haired old man.

"I loved Bannerman almost as a son," Wilde was saying. "I cannot understand this, and he has taken my Portia."

"How much chance does Bannerman have

252

subject deftly. "They didn't like it because we been too friendly with the Texans, helpin' 'em out in their fight. There'll be trouble now."

"That Bannerman," Otey Higgins murmured, a trace of reluctant admiration in his voice. "He's smooth an' he's educated, an' he's a nice chap, but he's a damned pirate at heart."

"He shouldn't have taken Portia," Flint said, and then he got up and walked to the fire for another cup of coffee, standing there for a few moments, staring down into the flames, and when he looked up he saw Jennifer Smith watching him from a distance as she spoke with her father. He heard Otey say to Partridge, "Damn him, though, to leave you without hosses an' no guns."

"Not as bad as it looks," Partridge explained. "We have a wagonload of supplies, and Bannerman knew you three would be coming back with guns, and that there are plenty of buffalo in the vicinity to keep us supplied with fresh meat. He suggested we wait for a northbound outfit coming up from Santa Fe, and join them on the way back to Westport."

"He had it all figured," Otey said. "Had it figured way back in Westport. That's why he hired that mangy crew. He knew when the time came he could twist 'em around his finger."

Flint came back to the fire with his coffee, and Partridge looked up at him, the hell in his eyes again.

"If he's successful he takes over the government—and the treasury."

Otey Higgins said softly, "Light's comin' through."

"He'll loot the town," Partridge said. "He'll strip the treasury, take on supplies, and then head east into Texas, and, perhaps, back to the states that way with his gold and silver. He can live like a king, then, the rest of his life in the states, or in Europe."

Moose Clemens said evenly, "It'll bring on a war with the Mexican Government, Tom. They won't take this sittin' down."

Partridge nodded. "Mr. Wilde feels the same way, and he's frantic with grief. I think that bothers him more than the loss of Portia."

Flint started to get up, a tight sensation in his chest. "Portia?" he repeated.

Partridge looked at him steadily, and again Flint saw the hell in the man's eyes. "Bannerman took Portia with him," he said.

Both men looked at each other for a few moments in silence, and Otey Higgins raised his coffee cup to his mouth.

"She didn't go willingly," Flint said, and he waited for the reply, his heart pounding for the moment.

"No," Partridge said.

"Mexican Government has no damn use fer us now," Moose Clemens was saying, changing the

Partridge said bluntly, looking at Flint, "Bannerman pulled out."

Flint heard Moose Clemens curse softly.

"It was Bannerman's idea," Partridge was saying, "for you three men to go on this scouting trip. He wanted you away from the camp. An hour after you were gone he took over with his Westport crew."

Again Flint looked around, wondering about Portia. "Any fighting?" he asked.

Partridge shook his head, jaws tight. "We didn't expect it, and they outnumbered us three to one. Bannerman put a gun on me. His men disarmed the rest of our boys who would have remained loyal. They took eleven wagons, all of our guns and munitions, and went down the trail."

"Down the trail," Flint repeated.

"They're heading for Santa Fe," Partridge said dully. "Bannerman was kind enough to tell me a little of his plans before they rolled away, taking all the stock and our guns so that we couldn't follow them. They're going through with the expedition to Santa Fe. They intend to take over the government with the help of our men down there."

Flint stared at him, unbelievingly. He'd been quite sure that Bannerman was not a liberator in any sense of the word, and that the New Mexicans meant nothing to him.

"He'll pose as a liberator," Partridge explained.

come on. Clayton Wilde's big tent was up, the firelight reflecting on its canvas walls.

"That Westport crowd pulled out," Otey Higgins said suddenly, "an' they took the wagons with 'em. They're headed back home."

"We'd o' passed 'em on the trail," the Moose growled, "or we'd o' seen their tracks headin' north. That bunch didn't go back to Westport."

They rode into the camp, dismounting near the Wilde tent. Tom Partridge still lay where they'd left him, under the lean-to. He was sitting up, watching them, a dull, dead expression on his face. His eyes were dead, too, but he pointed to the coffeepot at the fire and he said, "Drink up, first."

Otey poured coffee into tin cups, and the three of them dropped down on the ground under the lean-to. Flint glanced toward the tent, noticing that Portia Wilde had not come out. Jennifer Smith was still over at the windwagon, talking with her father in low tones.

Moose Clemens lowered his coffee cup, and said laconically, "Reckon you're missin' some wagons, Tom, an' some men."

There were men in the encampment, Flint noticed, all the regulars, the men Bannerman and Wilde had brought out from the east. For the first time he became aware of the fact that Bannerman was not around, and that he had not seen him recently.

Mexicans free themselves, if they've a mind to. Could be they ain't even thought of it."

They rested a half hour after eating, and they continued the lonely ride north and west of the trail, running into the big buffalo herd again, and skirting the herd until they came into the trail a half dozen miles north of the Wilde camp. They'd seen no Indians, and no sign.

The sun had lost its strength as they moved down the trail. It was a red ball hanging over the shallow, muddied waters of the Arkansas as they crossed, and it was gone completely when they sighted the cook's fire at the encampment.

As they swung off the trail, riding up toward the little ridge upon which they'd rolled the wagons the day before, Moose Clemens stopped his horse and stared, jaw dropping. "What in hell!" he gasped.

Flint was staring, also. In the dim light of the big cook's fire they could see only two wagons at the camp—a high-sided freight wagon and the Smith windwagon. The other eleven wagons were gone.

"Maybe," Otey muttered, "we ain't seein' straight. Has to be a dozen wagons there. That's our camp."

Flint pushed the gray gelding ahead fast. The camp was not deserted because he could see figures moving in front of the fire. Closer, he saw Jennifer Smith by the windwagon watching them

247

told him. "Ain't any Comanches within thirty mile o' the trail."

"We'll see," Flint said.

They rode leisurely toward the west over the sand hills, a dry, almost arid land now on this side of the Arkansas, and they saw nothing but occasional clumps of buffalo.

Toward noon they cut the sign of the retreating Comanche band, the Indians who'd attacked them, and Moose Clemens had a long look at the two-day-old traces of unshod ponies.

"Still headin' due west," Moose said, "an' they ain't turnin' back. They got a bellyfull when they hit us."

The sand hills gave way to desert country as they progressed toward the west, and then they moved north back toward the river, crossing it to rest their horses in the shade of the cotton-woods on the north bank, and to eat the midday meal. They'd shot a buffalo cow earlier in the day, taking some of the choice parts along with them.

As they sat under the shade of the big trees overlooking the shallow river, Otey Higgins said, "Been a nice ride so far, but a lonely one."

"We'll head north another eight or ten miles," Flint told him, "and then swing back toward the camp. We should get back before dark."

"Hope by the time we git back," Otey said. "Clayton Wilde's decided to let the New

"North?" Flint said, eyebrows lifting.

"Mr. Wilde is worried about the Kiowas we left behind."

The Moose laughed. "That bunch are back in their tepees," he grinned. "Nothin' to worry about there."

"I told Mr. Wilde that," Partridge said. "He insists on the scout."

When they left Partridge's quarters Otey Higgins clucked softly. "Old Clayton's kind o' worried. He's seein' Injuns all over the country-side. Rather be ridin', though, than sittin' around there tomorrow."

"Wild goose chase," the Moose told him as he rolled into his blanket.

Flint had the same opinion that it was a wild goose chase, and that Clayton Wilde, fearful for his men now, was taking extraordinary precautions to prevent another surprise attack.

They rode out of the camp at dawn after having breakfast in the light of the campfire. The crew-men were still asleep under the wagons as they moved away from the enclosure, passing glum sentries who just stared at them, giving them no greeting.

"Hell of a bunch," Otey Higgins said. "Ain't one o' that Westport crowd wouldn't be happy to see the Comanches take our hair."

"Ain't takin' this cow's hair," Moose Clemens

he shifted his position on the pile of blankets beneath him to make his bandaged leg more comfortable.

Flint had the feeling that the rift had widened between Partridge and Bannerman.

Otey Higgins said when they left Partridge, "This is one hell of a army. Wilde ain't too keen any more about the business. Partridge an' Bannerman, the top men, don't get along, an' most o' the crew is achin' to turn around an' go back. What's gonna happen, Flint?"

"We go on until it stops of its own accord."

Otey grimaced. "Stopped already," he stated. "Stopped dead, I'm thinkin'."

Before they turned in that night Partridge had a few words with them.

"You boys are to make a scout tomorrow," the wagonmaster stated, "looking for Indian sign."

Moose Clemens, finishing a cup of coffee, tossed the dregs away, and said slowly, "Ain't no Injuns around, Tom. We chased 'em to hell an' back."

Partridge frowned. "Bannerman and Mr. Wilde have been discussing the matter," he said. "We'll be camped here at least a few days. They want to make sure there will be no more surprise attacks. You are to make a wide swing to the west and to the north."

group of men discussing some matter outside the corral.

Otey Higgins said, "Better fer a crowd like this that it keeps movin'. You let 'em sit down on their behinds an' they start gettin' ideas in their heads. Ideas ain't good in a crowd like that."

"What can they do?" Flint asked.

Otey shrugged. "Reckon most of 'em got their fill o' fightin', an' they seen what they wanted to see o' the west. They're still four hundred long miles from Santa Fe, an' a hell of a road ahead of 'em. Maybe they're figurin' on startin' back fer Westport."

"Without supplies?" Flint smiled. "Without wagons? We have the wagons."

"Outnumber you three or four to one," Otey Higgins said. "That right?"

"You figure they'll try to take over the outfit?" Flint asked thoughtfully.

"What's all this damned talk about?" Otey countered. "I don't know."

Flint spoke to Tom Partridge about it that night, and Partridge, also, had noticed the undercurrent of trouble in the air.

"I can't count on more than thirty men, including yourself, the Moose and Higgins," Partridge told him, "and if this Westport crowd sticks together they can give us a lot of trouble."

"You tell Bannerman?" Flint asked him.

"He knows about it," Partridge murmured, and

243

Chapter Seventeen

IN THE MORNING they moved the wagons a few miles beyond to a campsite along a willow-lined creek. It was a good site, removed from the dead buffaloes and horses which already had started to swell. They'd buried the dead outside the wagon corral, and then rolled the wagons over the graves a number of times to hide them from the Indians who might try to desecrate the bodies.

The wounded men were placed under lean-tos made with tarpaulins, protecting them from the hot sun, and they were given the best of care by Doc Schoonover, Jennifer Smith, and Portia Wilde.

The stock was driven a half mile from the wagons and set to graze with a strong guard protecting them. After putting the wagons and the camp in order, men sat around in the shade of the wagons, talking in low tones, the Westport men as usual gathering in distinctive groups.

Whenever Flint came near any of them, he noticed immediately that they stopped talking, and he remembered that night when he'd gone out to look at the gray, he'd almost walked into a

"Seven out of a hundred thirty-five," Flint observed.

"I wish," Clayton Wilde said, "I could forget those seven men who died because I brought them out here. If it had not been for me they would have been back in Westport or farther east, happy with their friends and families. Here, they find nameless graves on the open plains."

For a few moments the thin man on the cot was silent, and then he smiled at Flint. "I am obliged to you for stopping it, MacKeithan."

Flint went outside. He found Otey Higgins having a cup of coffee at the mess fire, and he sat down beside the little hunter.

"How is he?" Otey asked, nodding toward the tent.

"Wondering why he came out here," Flint said.

Otey's blue eyes flicked. "He's kind o' catchin' up with us now, ain't he, Flint?"

Flint poured himself a cup of coffee and drank it.

"Allus respect a man who's big enough to change his mind," Otey Higgins said. "Be nice if Wilde called the whole damned thing off an' turned back to Westport."

"Partridge will go with him," Flint said.

"What about Bannerman?"

Flint looked at the ground and then at the tin cup in his hand. He didn't know. He didn't know about Bannerman. No one knew about Bannerman.

Clayton Wilde nodded. He moistened his thin lips, and Flint noticed for the first time how thin he'd become in recent weeks. This arduous trip across the plains had not agreed with him. He'd been frail before he came west, and he was worse now with his injury.

"I understand we had seven of our men killed," Mr. Wilde murmured, "and five others wounded. How many would you say the Indians lost, Flint?"

"Counted thirty-one," Flint told him, "along with Ortiz and Corwin."

"Nearly forty killed," Clayton Wilde said, "and no one knows how many wounded in this fight."

Flint smiled a little. "Out this way," he observed, "they don't count dead Indians."

"They're men," Wilde said slowly. "They have wives; they have children."

Flint didn't say anything to that. He wondered if Wilde realized that the Mexicans whom they'd come down to fight also had wives and children, and were a lot more civilized than the wild Comanches.

"I suppose," Clayton Wilde was saying, "that in war men must die, Flint."

"Reckon that's the way it's been," Flint agreed.

"I had hoped for a bloodless coup in Santa Fe," Mr. Wilde said, "and already we have had men killed."

washing the wounded man's face with a basin of warm water.

She looked over her shoulder when Flint came up, and then she smiled and said, "I haven't thanked you for coming to my rescue during the fight."

"Glad you weren't hurt," Flint told her. "How is your uncle?"

"Resting," Portia said. "He's been badly shaken up, and it will be a while before he is himself again. He's inside the tent if you'd like to see him."

Flint put his head inside the tent and saw Clayton Wilde lying on his camp cot, looking straight up at the ceiling of the tent. When he saw Flint he smiled faintly and said, "Come in a minute, MacKeithan."

Flint went in under the flap. He noticed that Clayton Wilde's face was gray, and the pain was in his eyes. There was something else in his eyes, too, which had not been there before the fight with the Comanches. Wilde had changed. Some of the fire had gone out of him. He'd seen men die this afternoon on the hot plains; he'd heard them scream as they died, and Flint was positive this was a new experience for the Easterner, a man of letters. It had made him sick.

"Portia tells me you pulled me out of the wagon when it went over, Flint," he said.

Flint shrugged. "Nearest to it," he said.

of the corral. Bannerman had been nicked by a bullet, the lead grazing his right temple. He'd wiped the blood away carelessly, but his face was still splotched with it.

He came up to squat in front of Partridge, and he said, "Good fight, Tom. That was clever driving the buffalo at us."

"Nearly whipped us," Partridge agreed. "Another vote of thanks for Moose."

Bannerman made a mark in the sand with a stick. "We can roll into Santa Fe now," he said. "Nothing ahead of us."

"Maybe a Mexican army or two," Moose Clemens told him.

Bannerman shrugged. "One war at a time," he grinned.

"Near had our last one today," Otey Higgins smiled from the fire.

Partridge said to Bannerman, "I am going to suggest to Mr. Wilde that we break camp in the morning and move away from here for a more permanent camp a few miles from here. We'll need to rest these wounded men."

"Good idea," Bannerman agreed. He left and Flint walked over toward the Wilde wagon. He found Portia bending over one of the wounded men who's been laid out on blankets on the ground. The man had had an arrow through his side, but Doc Schoonover had managed to extract the arrow, clean, and bind the wound. Portia was

was a smudge of black gunpowder on her chin.

Some of the stock had broken away in the fight, and Tom Partridge sent out men to bring them back. Other men went to work on the dead buffalo inside the enclosure, skinning them, preparing the meat.

The nearest dead animals outside the wagon enclosure were hauled away, and Moose Clemens said to Tom Partridge, "Gonna have to move these wagons tomorrow, Tom. Be stinkin' like hell around here from the dead buffalo."

The wagonmaster lay under a tarpaulin which had been stretched from one of the wagons. His left leg was bandaged and he rested on his elbows, watching.

"We'll push on a few miles," he agreed, "and then hole up until we can tend to the wounded."

Moose rubbed his jaw thoughtfully. "Figured maybe some o' these boys had enough fightin' to last 'em a while. Big fight's still ahead the way it looks."

Tom Partridge didn't say anything to that, but Flint saw the shadow in his brown eyes.

"That drillin' you gave the boys paid off," Moose said. "Lot of 'em had chicken feet underneath the wagons, but the rest of 'em stood up to it like good mountain men. Couple o' weeks ago every damn one of 'em would have crawled into the wagons."

Flint watched Jay Bannerman making a survey

Flint walked down to the Smith wagon and he found Jennifer sitting on the wagon tongue, the rifle across her knees. She looked at him, her mouth still tight from the tension, and she shook her head.

Windwagon Smith was saying happily, "A great fight, Flint. We chased them right back to the Mexican border."

"How many men did we lose?" Jennifer asked.

"Seven," Flint told her. "Five others hit, but not badly."

He knew that they were fortunate to have gotten out of it so lightly. Only the Wilde wagon had been knocked over by the charging buffalo, and men had righted that, setting it in order, and were now carrying Clayton Wilde into it. His shoulder had been twisted, and Doc Schoonover had bandaged the arm against his side.

"Is he badly hurt?" Jennifer asked, standing up.

"Don't think so," Flint told her.

"I saw the wagon go," Jennifer murmured. "They were fortunate you were close by, Flint."

Flint didn't say anything to that.

"Would you have gone for me, Flint?"

"Yes," Flint said.

She gave him a slow smile and then she walked toward the Wilde wagon to help if she could with the wounded men who were being carried over there for attention by Doc Schoonover. There

Flint leaped from the top of the wagon and ran toward Tom Partridge and Moose Clemens. He saw Portia Wilde running that way, too, and he knew that she'd seen Partridge hit.

Partridge put his head back and stared up at the sky as the Moose broke off the arrow shaft and forced the arrow straight through the leg until the steel head had come out the other side. The sweat poured down Partridge's face, and his jaws were clenched in agony. A tiny trickle of blood coursed down his chin from the lip he'd been biting.

"Ain't no other way," Moose growled. "She missed the bone, Tom, an' you're lucky, but you won't do much ridin' fer a month or two, I'm thinkin'."

Partridge looked up at Flint as Doc Schoonover trotted up to clean and bandage the bad arrow wound.

"All over, Flint?" Partridge asked, still panting.

"They had enough," Flint said. He patted Partridge's shoulder, and left him with Portia and Doc Schoonover. He noticed that Clayton Wilde was sitting up on the wagon, holding an injured shoulder, his face gray with pain.

Flint walked out with Otey Higgins and Moose to look at Corwin. Otey rolled the body over with his foot, squinted and said, "Moose hit him plumb center—right between the eyes."

"Aimed fer his right eye," Moose apologized. "Lot o' dust out there, Flint."

piercing cry, as he was knocked down by the lead bull.

The others went over him, pounding hard, huge heads lowered, sharp hoofs churning Corwin's flesh. When they were past and the dust lifted momentarily, he saw the man lying there like a rag doll, motionless, his face gone.

The Comanches were widening their circle, some of them drawing off, as the crewmen continued to fire. Flint had a glimpse of Jay Bannerman on the other side of the wagon corral, up top of one of the freight wagons, commandeering that section of the corral. Tom Partridge had been covering the west sector. When Flint looked that way he saw Partridge on the ground, a Comanche arrow through his left leg, just above the knee. The wagonmaster sat there, glaring at the arrow, and then big Moose ran up, crouched beside him, shoulders and back toward Flint.

The Comanches were drawing back and Otey Higgins yelled, "We got 'em runnin', boys. Give 'em hell!"

A volley was sent after the retreating Comanches, who withdrew until they were back on the ridge over which the buffalo had come. They sat their ponies on the ridge, holding a council, staring down at the strongly defended wagon train, and then they disappeared below the ridge, and the crewmen broke into wild, frenzied yelling.

Comanche cringed when the lead went home, riding away into the billowing clouds of dust, head lolling.

Another rifleman on top of the wagon to Flint's right was struck, and he rolled and pitched off the wagon, striking the ground with a sickening thud.

The Comanches whirled rapidly around the wagons, firing, dodging, reloading, or sending flights of arrows at the men on top or underneath the wagons. After a while the wagons became pin cushions for their arrows.

Flint spotted Ortiz, the Mexican agent, moving out around the edge of the Indian circle, as the dust lifted for a fraction of a second, and then he heard Moose Clemens' gun crack, and Ortiz fell from the saddle and lay motionless on the churned-up prairie grass.

Moose let out a whoop after that shot, and then Flint saw Lace Corwin sliding by, and he had his rifle ready. His bullet struck Corwin's dapple gray, and the animal collapsed as if its legs had turned to rubber. Corwin sailed forward through the air, struck the ground, and got up, hatless, yellow hair mussed, looking dazed.

Flint heard Portia Wilde's short scream as a dozen big buffalo bulls, stragglers in the stampeding herd, suddenly loomed out of the dust cloud, bearing straight at Corwin.

Corwin tried to run. He took two steps, looking behind him, and then he yelled, a high-pitched,

streaking past. She was supporting her still unconscious uncle with one arm, having taken the gun from his holster.

There were at least two hundred in the band which had attacked them, and they weren't all red. Flint saw a white man out in the attacking force, and then another one, and then he saw Lace Corwin's dapple gray among the varicolored Indian ponies under the cloud of dust.

White gun smoke lifted from the wagons, mingling with the choking yellow dust. At close range Flint opened with his Colt gun, unable to wait for the man behind him to reload. He knocked one Indian from his pony as the Comanche was whirling up toward the wagon in which Portia sat. He saw Portia's gun shoot flame, and another Comanche slid from the saddle, dragged by the tether rope.

A man up on top of the wagon with him died with a Comanche arrow through his throat. He stood up very suddenly, choking, clawing at the feathered shaft, and then he fell.

Most of the buffalo were past now, but straggling groups still thudded by, veering away from the thirty or forty dead buffalo and crippled animals out in front of the wagons.

Flint watched for Lace Corwin to appear again, hoping to get a clear shot at him. He leveled at a buck on a white horse with a black painted face, huge black circles around the eyes, and the

them as they rode. There were no regal head-dresses here, just slim, brown forms, almost part of the animals they rode, riding with a skill Flint had never seen equaled anywhere.

A buck with a yellow and green painted face whirled straight up to the wagon upon which he sat, fitted an arrow to his bow and bent the string. He died before he could release the arrow, a bullet from Otey Higgins' gun on the next wagon striking him in the forehead. He fell backward, the arrow zooming straight up into the air, and as his pony pulled away to the right, he went down and was dragged by the tether rope every Indian had tied around his ankle.

With the buffalo thinning out in front of the wagons, streaming to the right and the left, the Comanches came on, the small hoofs of their ponies drumming the ground, screeching as they fired bullet and arrow at the men on the wagons.

They swirled around the enclosure, riding up to within twenty-five yards of the wagons, firing, dodging behind the necks of their horses, flattening themselves, leaving almost no target.

Flint knocked down a pony, and Otey Higgins shot the rider as the Comanche rolled and leaped to his feet, trying to run. All around the enclosure the guns were popping now. Flint caught a glimpse of Jennifer Smith in the windwagon, crouching, firing coolly, and then he saw Portia Wilde, a pistol in her hand, aiming it at an Indian

get up, a dazed expression on her face when he reached her.

A horse whipped by, making a maddened circle inside the corral, and she staggered, nearly falling again. Lifting her, Flint carried her to the nearest wagon, putting her up on the seat.

Running back to the overturned wagon against which more buffalo were thudding, he crawled inside, picked up the thin form of Clayton Wilde, unconscious among the mass of overturned boxes and crates, and carried him over to the wagon upon which Portia was sitting.

Leaving them up on the seat, Portia supporting her uncle, he climbed back to the roof of the wagon, picked up a rifle and started to shoot again.

Bullets were coming at them now as the Comanches stormed up behind the buffalo. An arrow whistled past Flint's head as he crouched on the wagon. He noticed that the buffalo herd had split, however. The few animals inside the enclosure were shot down and left kicking in the dust, but the main herd was splitting around the mass of dead animals directly in front of the wagon corral.

The Comanches came behind them, whooping, screaming, flattened on the backs of their ponies. They were almost entirely naked, painted hideously for war, unlike the Kiowas who'd called on them. Their long, black hair streamed behind

A horse went down, its belly ripped open by the buffalo's horns, and Tom Partridge roared, "Kill that animal!"

Several guns cracked and the buffalo sank to its knees, but inside, the horses, mules, and oxen were in a frenzy, milling around, seeking to break out of the enclosure.

Another buffalo ripped in between the wagons, and a third followed it, driving straight in among the stock, leaving a path of oxen and horses downed in its tracks. Again the guns sounded and the two buffalo went down, but still they came on, stumbling over dead animals on the ground, lunging into the wagons.

Flint fired until the two guns he was using became hot in his hands. Several times the wagon upon which he crouched shivered as the buffalo slammed into it.

A huge cloud of choking dust drifted over the wagons, covering wagons and buffalo and men, and the Indians beyond. Flint heard Portia Wilde's quick scream, and standing up on top of the freight wagon he saw the Wilde wagon going over on its side.

Dropping his gun, he leaped to the ground inside the enclosure, dodged to avoid being hit by a maddened oxen whirling by, and then raced toward the overturned wagon. He caught a glimpse of Portia on the ground, where she'd been thrown from the seat. She was trying to

Chapter Sixteen

GUNS OPENED UP all along the line as the buffalo tore down at the wagons, driven by the Indians behind them. In the front ranks the huge, ungainly animals started to stumble. As they went down others stumbled over them, falling, getting up again, riding almost up to the wagons before they were shot.

One bull, with blood gushing from its mouth, piled up against one of the wagons and died there, and still they came on with sweaty-faced men shooting at them frantically, reaching back for loaded rifles, shooting again.

The ground in front of the wagons was strewn with their carcasses, struggling, bleeding, striving to rise, and being knocked down and trampled by the animals behind them.

They could hear the screeching and whooping of the Comanches coming on behind the herd, keeping them in a frenzy, firing at them. One bull struck the wagon on which Flint was crouched, shaking it. Another lunged in over the wagon tongue of a second wagon and was in among the stock, rearing, plunging, snorting, sharp horns goring at the frantic animals inside.

flesh, sightless, puffing, the dust swirling into the air behind them. A man next to Flint on top of the wagon started to mumble, and his hands shook as he lifted the rifle.

"Knock 'em down," Moose Clemens bawled above the roar of pounding hoofs.

The nearest animals were less than two hundred yards away, still driving straight at the wagons. Flint lifted his gun. He was sighting it when he saw something else beyond the buffalo, something which flitted between the clouds of dust—a brown, naked body astride a running pinto horse, and then another rider, low on the horse's neck, black hair flying.

"Comanches!" Moose Clemens roared.

The wagonmaster glanced at the wagons. "They'll veer off," he said, "when they see this."

"Damn if I know," the Moose muttered. "Line up twenty, thirty o' the best shots you got in this camp. Put 'em in the wagons facin' this herd, an' have 'em shootin'. Might split the herd that way."

Partridge lined up thirty men. He had Flint, Higgins and the Moose in the line, and men behind them with fresh rifles, ready to reload after they'd shot.

There were four wagons facing the oncoming herd, and one of the wagons was the Wilde outfit with Portia and her uncle inside, looking out. Partridge had given orders for all who weren't shooting to remain in or on top of the wagons in case the buffalo did break through into the corral.

Jennifer Smith and her father were in the windwagon on the opposite side of the corral, and Flint was glad for this. A fifteen hundred pound buffalo smashing into that light wagon, broadside, would send it over on its side, and once down it would be smashed to pieces.

Horses inside the enclosure started to whinny in fright as the buffalo stormed over the ridge upon which Flint had been standing his gray a few minutes before. They came down the slope at a wild gallop, tightly packed, completely covering the ground.

The ground trembled beneath them as they poured over the ridge, a black stream of churning

Flint rode his horse rapidly in circles on the ridge, a sign Moose Clemens had taught him, and Moose and Otey immediately sprinted their horses toward him.

When they came up Flint pointed at the dust cloud. He said to Otey, "Better tell Partridge what we see. We don't know what it is as yet."

"Could be Injuns," the Moose muttered, "an' could be stampedin' buffalo. Hell of a lot of 'em, whatever they are."

Otey Higgins rode away, and Flint and Moose sat astride their horses watching that rapidly moving dust cloud, coming straight toward them. They could hear the rumble of hoofs now, and Flint said, "Stampeding buffalo wouldn't drive into a wagon train, would they?"

"If there's enough of 'em," Moose nodded, "an' they was crazy enough. Damn if I know what started 'em off though—if it is buffalo."

It was buffalo. Both men ascertained that fact a few minutes later when they saw the black humps emerging out of the dust cloud. The ground beneath them started to rumble. It was a big herd, at least several thousand animals, running at top speed.

"Back," Moose Clemens said.

They rode swiftly back toward the wagons, finding Tom Partridge waiting outside the enclosure. Clemens said to him, "Buffalo stampede, Tom. Headin' straight for us."

"Would if they could," the Moose said. "It'll be different when they come. Mark me."

It was different, and they came that day at two o'clock in the afternoon, during the midday stop. It was a peaceful afternoon, and many of the men had crawled under the wagons for a brief nap after eating, and before they yoked the animals and started the journey.

Flint sat astride the gray gelding on a ridge a quarter mile distant from the camp, watching the surrounding country. Otey Higgins and Moose Clemens were on other ridges to the west and the east, all of them having eaten, and then ridden out as sentinels.

The stock was grazing close to the wagons, a strong guard watching them, also. Flint saw a pair of coyotes slink past on the next ridge half a mile away, and then beyond them he saw the dust cloud. It was still a long way off, and it was impossible to see what lay beneath the dust, but it was coming in their direction.

Unhesitatingly, Flint lifted his Colt gun from the saddle, raised the muzzle to the sky, and fired. It was the warning signal to the camp, and immediately he saw the men clambering out from beneath the wagons, racing for their guns. The herders closed in on the stock, driving the animals back toward the wagon corral. Horses which had been picketed outside were led into the corral.

"You don't owe me anything," Jennifer told him grimly.

Thinking of the kiss he'd given her, Flint grinned a little. "Paid you back," he said, and he started to walk away, seeing the color come to her face, knowing that she'd got the point. It was the first time he'd left her as the winner, and it pleased him not a little.

In the morning they moved on, another day of heat and rumbling wagons, of plodding in the dust for the men, the hot sun beating down on them, and no shade. They skirted the vast buffalo herd, and Flint and Moose Clemens brought in a few more pack horses loaded with fresh meat, getting it while they could.

They saw no more smoke signals, indicating that the Kiowas had had their look at them and decided to leave them alone.

"Ain't the Kiowas I'm worried about," Moose Clemens told Flint privately. "Them damned Comanches—friends o' Corwin's. They're the bad boys out this way."

"We'll watch for them," Flint said.

"They got their ways," Clemens went on. "Mean an' clever, an' always different. I know 'em. They ain't ridin' up over a hill, pokin' a gun at you, an' startin' in to shoot. Comanches allus figure somethin' different."

"They can't drop out of the sky." Flint smiled.

have to see the mountains first. You have to get that out of you."

"Lot more than just the mountains," Flint murmured. He wanted to see all of it—Santa Fe, California, the mighty Pacific Ocean, and then maybe Oregon.

"I'd like to see it, too," Jennifer said simply.

Flint looked at the cup. "No place for a woman," he stated.

"I'm not a woman like Portia Wilde."

Flint finished the coffee and handed her the cup. "No," he said, and he saw her lips tighten a little and he knew that he'd said the wrong thing.

"You don't flatter a woman," she snapped.

"That's for Bannerman."

"He's a man," she told him.

"Take him," Flint said.

"Take Portia," Jennifer challenged.

He had to smile because they were fighting again, and it seemed that every time they came together it ended like this. Yet he was not entirely displeased. She had spirit, and never in her life would she be broken. He'd had a horse like her when he'd been quite young, and never had he ridden that horse without taking some bucking first, but it was the finest animal he'd ever owned, and he'd cried like a baby when it had stepped into a pothole, broken a foreleg, and had to be shot.

"Obliged for the coffee," he said.

graduate. He was her type of man if Bannerman failed her.

There was a group of men standing outside the corral, talking in low tones. They stopped speaking when they saw him coming up, and they stood there, waiting until he'd passed on. In the dim light back here he didn't recognize any of them, but was positive they were Westport men. They knew him, too. He was a Wilde man.

When he'd looked at the gray tied to a picket rope, he came back to the corral, passing between the Smith windwagon and the next wagon in line, and he saw Jennifer just putting away the supper dishes. She said, when she saw him coming between the wagons, "Still prowling in the dark?"

"Like to prowl," Flint told her.

"It's in your blood," Jennifer nodded. "You like the night the way a panther does. Do you see well at night, too?"

"What I want to see."

Jennifer looked across the corral toward the wagon where Portia Wilde and Tom Partridge were still talking. She said, "Look the other way, Flint."

"All right," Flint said and scowled. "All right."

"You'll be a good man, Flint, when you settle down. When you get the wildness out of you."

She poured him a cup of coffee from the pot over the fire, and he took it, nodding his thanks. She watched him drink and then she said, "You

"Always too late," Portia murmured. "Do we have a chance of succeeding, Tom?"

"A chance," Partridge nodded. There was a bleak expression on his face as he puffed on the pipe, and Flint realized how small that chance was.

"What about Bannerman?" he asked, getting back to the original subject.

"I don't know," Portia confessed. "I wondered if you had noticed the difference in him."

"If he's lost his zeal," Partridge observed, "it's not because he's afraid. There's no fear in the man."

"He's not afraid," Portia said. "He seems to be torn between two decisions, and he can't make up his mind. It's made him turn in on himself."

"He'll have to come out of it when we near Santa Fe," Partridge said. "We'll need every man—especially the dependable men."

Flint drifted off after a while, leaving Partridge and Portia Wilde by the wagon. As he moved outside the corral, seeing the guards up on the ridges nearby, he thought about Bannerman, and then of Portia and Partridge—and himself. It was a crazy mix-up, and he was on the outer edge of the deal, not even in the game as yet. He'd watched Tom Partridge look at Portia tonight as she spoke, and he'd seen it in the wagonmaster's eyes. Partridge was an easterner, although a soldier. He was a man of education, a West Point

"You are worried, Tom," she said. "I came to cheer you up."

Flint pushed away from the wagon as if to go, but Portia stopped him with a gesture of her hand.

"You needn't leave, Flint," she said.

"Figured I'd look at my gray," Flint told her.

"Your horse can wait. Stay here with us."

Flint settled with his back to the wagon, knowing that she had something to say to them, seeing it in her eyes. She sat down on an upturned box and she said, "I'm worried about Jay."

Flint saw Tom Partridge's lips tighten. "What's he done?" Partridge asked.

Portia shook her head. "He's different. I've sensed the change for some time. He's not the man who came west with us. I have the strangest feeling that he is going to leave us."

Tom Partridge stared. "Leave? Where?"

Portia smiled a little. "Possibly a woman's intuition," she said. "I hope I'm wrong."

"He can't walk away out here in the wilderness," Partridge pointed out. "If he's grown a little cold as far as the expedition is concerned I can understand that. We've had difficulties, and our troubles are only beginning."

Portia Wilde looked at the ground. She said, "Do you think, Tom, that perhaps we've been wrong, right from the beginning?"

Tom Partridge flashed a quick glance at Flint and then he said, "Kind of late for that, Portia."

"I'm damned if I know how Bannerman expects to capture Santa Fe with a bunch who won't even take orders."

"Reckon he expects to capture it," Flint said. "That right?"

Partridge's eyes flicked. "Why do you say that?" he asked.

Flint shrugged. "Bannerman doesn't look like a man who would go for a scheme like this. The odds are too long. Maybe I'm wrong."

"I went for it," Partridge said shortly. "You did."

"Don't bite at me," Flint smiled.

Partridge shook his head. "I'm on edge," he apologized. "Don't mind me, Flint. I'm afraid I'm going to need men like you before this thing is over." He touched a match to his pipe, and then he said, as he drew on the pipe, "Promise me one thing, Flint."

"What is that?" Flint asked.

"See that Portia gets back to Westport if anything happens to her uncle, to Bannerman, and to myself."

"Might happen to me, Tom."

"No," Partridge shook his head. "I think you'll come through it, Flint. Is it a promise?"

Flint nodded his head. He watched Portia come out of the tent and move toward them in the firelight, tall and erect, that gentle smile always on her face.

from the wagons, and away from the warming fires, and stood there, looking a trifle sheepish when they realized that the others weren't following them. Out of the twenty there were no Westport men, recruited when they had been outfitting at the jump-off place.

Jay Bannerman came out of the Wilde tent with Clayton Wilde, looked at Partridge, and then at the few men standing in the firelight. He went over to speak to Partridge, and Flint saw the wagonmaster shake his head grimly.

"Not that they don't need trainin'," Otey Higgins said. "This bunch couldn't lick half as many Kiowa squaws."

"They got a craw full o' trainin'," Moose Clemens said, "an' a belly full o' buffalo steak. That's a bad combination."

The men sat under the wagons or around their mess fires, making no move, talking in low tones, staring at Bannerman and Partridge over near the tent. Bannerman was evidently advising Partridge to give up the idea of the drill tonight, rather than cause any trouble.

Flint watched the wagonmaster nod his head grimly, then walk over and sit down on a wagon tongue, and pack his pipe. He moved over that way himself, a few moments later, and he said to Partridge, "That's the beginning of it."

Tom Partridge looked at him, his brown eyes hard. "Been coming a long time," he admitted.

Partridge had sent out to help them bring in the fresh meat.

That night they camped at Weeping Rock, and Tom Partridge had his first real trouble with his recruits. After a heavy supper of buffalo steaks, the first good meal they'd had since leaving Westport, the men did not want to drill.

Partridge had been having brief drills every evening, acquainting the men with the proper use of firearms, teaching them how to load and fire in unison. The Westport crowd had begun to resent it, and even a few of the Easterners were tiring of this weary march all day, and then the brisk drill in the evening. They'd enlisted to free a people, but as yet all they'd done was march over one sand hill to another, and across innumerable creeks and streams, hauling the wagons when they were stuck, standing guard at night over the stock.

When Partridge gave the order this night to, "Turn out for drill," only a few responded. Flint could see that they'd been talking about it during the day, and tonight they were going to show the wagonmaster that they couldn't be ordered around like cattle.

Otey Higgins, puffing on his pipe at one of the wagons, said to Flint, "Trouble brewin'."

"Turn out," Tom Partridge snapped. "Companies A, B, and C."

They didn't turn out. Twenty men straggled out

shoulders of a horse, their shaggy heads lowered, short, curved horns turned inward.

The cows were smaller, and around them were many calves, skittering like the calves of milk cows. On the outskirts of the huge herd they saw slinking gray shapes—coyotes, always moving, seeking to drag down a stray calf, or an old bull, weakened from age and a thousand fights.

"Pick out the cows," Moose told them. "Better eatin'."

The three rifles boomed and three cows stumbled and fell. The animals nearby dashed away a short distance and then stopped. They stared for some time and then unconcernedly started to graze again.

"Hell's bells!" Otey Higgins whispered. "We kin shoot a million of 'em, Moose."

"They ain't used to guns," Moose told him. "Pick out three more an' that'll be enough to keep our boys fer a few days. We kin allus git more."

They shot three more of the animals, leaving six dead on the ground, and the buffalo nearest to them moved farther away, but continued to graze.

Moose Clemens said to Otey Higgins, "Ride back fer a few pack animals. Flint an' I will start skinnin' these."

"Rather you than me," Otey grinned. He rode off and came back in less than a half hour with a half-dozen pack horses and three more men Tom

Chapter Fifteen

THEY CROSSED THE Arkansas at Buck Island, and on the other side they ran into buffalo. Moving ahead of the wagons again, Flint, Otey, and Moose topped a rise on the trail and then pulled up their mounts.

Flint stared with unbelieving eyes. Otey Higgins said softly, "Land o' Goshen."

The open country ahead of them was black with buffalo, extending to the far horizon—to the south, to the east, to the west.

"A million of 'em," Otey murmured. "Two million of 'em. Reckon they'll mind if we shoot one or two of 'em, Moose?"

"Only ones will mind," Moose grunted, "is the ones that git shot."

They rode on ahead, coming up to windward of the nearest group of grazing buffalo. Moose signaled for them to dismount then, and they moved forward on foot, keeping behind a small ridge. When they reached the ridge they were within a hundred and fifty yards of the nearest animals, and Flint had his first real look at the huge creatures. The bulls stood as high as the

Bannerman until he reached the wagons, and then at a signal from their leader on the big black horse they turned and rode slowly upriver, their ponies kicking up dust as they went.

Otey Higgins wiped the perspiration from his face as he watched them go, and then he said to Flint, "Man ain't got any nerves, Flint."

"That feller," Moose Clemens murmured, "could live through a winter in the Blackfoot country."

It was the highest compliment he could pay Jay Bannerman, and Flint was thinking that Bannerman deserved it.

could see the arrow plainly, steel-tipped, gray goosefeathers on the shaft painted with red and black circles.

"Give it to me," Bannerman said. He kept moving forward, and the buck retreated back into the crowd of horses, pressing against them until he had no more room to maneuver, and then Bannerman was up beside him within reaching distance. He put his hand out and grasped the bow.

Slowly, the Kiowa let the arrow come forward without releasing his grip on the bowstring. He was staring at Bannerman, unsure of himself now, and Bannerman kept tugging at the bow and smiling, and it was the smile more than anything else which disconcerted the Indian.

He released the bow and Bannerman took it away from him, studied it for a moment, and then deliberately drew the ends together with his two hands, a feat of great strength, and bent the bow until it broke.

He was still smiling as he handed the broken bow back to the Kiowa, nodded to him, and turned his horse to ride back. Flint, Otey, and Moose Clemens moved back with him, but still facing the Indians, rifles in readiness. Bannerman rode with his back directly to them and he rode leisurely, dismounting when he reached the wagons.

The Kiowas were silent now, watching

drawn it, and he made no move for it now. He sat there, a few feet from the Kiowa, smiling at him, pointing to the bow, indicating that he wanted it.

Flint stood about ten feet to Bannerman's left, his gun half raised, watching the Indians directly in front of him. Some of them weren't more than a few feet away now, and the smell of them came to him—strong and dank and sour. He saw them staring at Bannerman uncertainly.

Otey Higgins said, "Better get to hell out o' this, Bannerman."

"Give me the bow," Bannerman said to the Kiowa.

The Indian didn't understand the language, but he knew what Bannerman meant. Bannerman moved his horse up closer, and the Kiowa backed away a little, his piebald snorting. Then the Indian lifted the bow, drew back the arrow, and pointed it straight at Bannerman's chest.

A humming sound came from the Kiowas behind him, increasing in volume as Bannerman still moved forward, still smiling, pointing with his finger at the bow. The Indian had but to release the arrow and it would have embedded itself in Bannerman's chest or gone clean through him.

Moose Clemens lifted his rifle and pointed the muzzle at the Kiowa's chest. The Indian saw the move and his mouth started to work a little. He still held the bow up, the arrow drawn back. Flint

211

He started to ride past out toward the Indian band, and Partridge called after him, "Bannerman—Bannerman! Come back here!"

Jay Bannerman kept riding, guiding his horse at an easy walk directly out toward the buck on the piebald horse. Partridge called back to the men inside the corral, "Get those guns up."

The Kiowas had quieted down, and they were watching Bannerman coming toward them. The buck who'd shot the arrow was staring straight at Bannerman, and then he fitted an arrow to his bow and waited, beady eyes expressionless.

Some of the Indians behind him moved forward again as Bannerman drew near with the obvious intention of encircling him. Moose Clement nodded to Flint and to Otey Higgins, and the three hunters walked out, rifles in hand. The Moose gestured with his gun at the riders who'd come forward, indicating that they should stay back.

They stopped when they saw the rifles in the hands of Flint and Otey, and instead of drawing a complete circle around Bannerman and the buck on the piebald, they formed a ragged semicircle.

Bannerman rode his horse directly up to the squat Indian and then pointed with his finger at the bow. The Kiowa stared at him, eyes glittering now. He drew back the arrow experimentally, but he didn't aim it at Bannerman. Bannerman had a gun strapped around his waist, but he hadn't

next day. They'll stick around because they'll think we're afraid of 'em."

"Arrow's shot," Otey Higgins said. "What in hell kin we do, Moose?"

Jay Bannerman said to Moose, "Is it as serious as that, Clemens?"

"Damned serious," the Moose told him.

Like Otey, Flint was wondering what could be done under the circumstances. If they opened fire on the Indians it meant a real fight, and possibly the Kiowas would come back tomorrow, strengthened, to make a real attack on the wagons. The Kiowas were whooping in derision now, and there was almost a grin on the face of the squat buck on the piebald horse. The piebald had a red-stained tail and mane and four red feet. Tiny silver bells hung from the mane, and every time the animal moved the bells tinkled melodiously.

The Kiowas were still yelling, cavorting their horses, moving in closer again, and Flint saw the worry come into Tom Partridge's eyes. The buck on the piebald horse was up in front, shaking his bow, riding back and forth, whooping.

Jay Bannerman turned and walked back to the wagons. Flint watched him untie his chestnut mare and then raise himself into the saddle. When he rode back toward the group outside the wagons Tom Partridge was staring at him curiously.

Bannerman smiled, adjusted his hat, and said, "Have the boys keep me covered, Tom."

"No brothers o' mine," Otey Higgins said. "Coyote's my brother."

Tom Partridge called for one of the men to bring out a small hogshead of tobacco from the wagons. When the tobacco was brought out and placed on the ground in front of the Indians, one of them rode forward, bent down gracefully, and lifted the keg from the ground with one hand.

There was some muttering and occasional whoops of derision from the Indians in the rear at the smallness of the gift, but Moose Clemens said, "Give 'em a finger an' they'll take a hand."

"Or your hair," Otey Higgins put in.

"They're like children," Jay Bannerman started to say. "They make a lot of noise, and they're demanding, but—"

He didn't finish the sentence because an arrow whizzed over their heads, embedding itself in the canvas of the wagon on which Clayton Wilde sat. The arrow struck within two feet of his head, quivering a little as it embedded itself in a box or barrel inside the canvas.

Flint saw a short, squat Indian on a piebald horse up in front of the band lower his bow and then stare at them insolently. He'd shot the arrow. Behind him the other bucks started to whoop, their voices rising and falling and Flint saw Moose Clemens' face grow somber.

"That's bad." Moose scowled. "We let that go an it kin mean plenty o' trouble tomorrow or the

full of buffalo, an' they're supposed to be great buffalo hunters."

"Tell them," Tom Partridge said.

Flint noticed that the Indians back up the river had crowded in close, moving almost imperceptibly, and were now only twenty-five or thirty yards from the wagons. Their horses moved restlessly, and a low, humming sound went through them.

Moose Clemens didn't like this closing in, and his voice boomed as he pointed with his finger at the Indians beyond, and then lifted his gun threateningly. The chief called back over his shoulder, and the bucks to the rear stopped. He made his speech then, and his voice was taunting when he came to the buffalo part of it. When he'd finished he spat and said to Flint, "Got to show 'em you ain't scared of 'em. You show fear an' they'll walk all over you."

"So we give 'em tobacco," Otey Higgins observed.

"A present," the Moose explained. "You allus give presents on the plains."

"Are they askin' like gentlemen?" Otey chuckled.

The chief had spoken to the other braves with him, and he spoke in the Kiowa tongue to Moose.

"He says bring out the tobacco," Moose interpreted. "He is surprised that we have no good gifts for the Kiowa brothers."

could see, being much too big, and he wondered from what *ranchero* south of the Rio Grande this animal had come, and how many men had died in that raid.

Moose Clemens held up his right hand in the sign of peace, and the Indian on the black horse lifted his hand, too. He carried a Hawkins' mountain rifle in one hand, and a buffalo shield in the other, a blending of the two ages of warfare.

"Kiowas," Moose said out of the corner of his mouth.

"Ask them what they want," Tom Partridge said.

The big trapper spoke in the Kiowa tongue, gesticulating with his hands, the six Indians gazing at him, black eyes glittering. Flint saw them look around the corral, at the men behind the wagons, rifles drawn in readiness.

The chief on the black horse spoke in a deep, guttural voice. He spoke briefly, and then he sat very still on the horse as Moose Clemens turned and said, "They want tobacco an' a few mules—fer eatin'."

Flint heard Otey Higgins swallow noisily.

Tom Partridge asked, "What'll I tell them, Moose?"

"Give 'em their damned tobacco," the Moose said and grinned. "Tell 'em to go lump themselves fer the mules. Other side o' the river is

The Indian band came down along the river, riding more slowly as they approached. Flint could see the full headdress on some of them, but most wore their hair in braids with a single eagle feather entwined therein. Only a scattering of them carried rifles, the rest of them having bows and arrows and lances, feathers dangling from the lances.

They were lean, brown-skinned men, unpainted, most of them naked to the waist, with buckskin breeches or breechclouts. They rode beautifully, almost part of the wiry little animals beneath them, and the pounding of two hundred or more horses' hoofs made the ground tremble a little.

Many of them carried buffalo shields with curious designs painted on them, ornamented with bits of metal and tiny bells they'd secured from traders. Some of the horses' manes and tails had bells entwined in them; as they drew close the bells and other accouterment tinkled and jangled noisily.

The whole party drew rein fifty yards from the little knot of men standing in front of the wagons, and then a half dozen of them, evidently chiefs, moved forward, riding slowly, their lean, cruel faces revealing nothing. The man in the lead wore a chain of bear claws around his neck. He rode a coal-black horse with one white foot, and there was a white circle painted on the black's chest. The horse was not an Indian pony, Flint

sun glinting on upraised lances and bits of metal ornamenting rider and mount.

"Hundred an' fifty," the Moose said. "Two hundred, maybe. Good-sized party."

"War party?" Flint said.

Moose Clemens nodded. "No women an' children, no travois. Them boys have been out raidin' after Crow or Cheyenne horses."

Tom Partridge called for the herders to keep the stock close to the wagons. He signaled to Moose Clemens then, and he walked out into the open with the Indian band still galloping straight toward them, whooping, yipping.

"Don't anybody shoot," Moose roared. "Them bucks wanted fight an' you wouldn't be seein' 'em until they was on top o' you."

Flint and Otey Higgins followed the Moose out into the open, guns in hand, and then Jay Bannerman came after them, smoking a cigar, watching the Indians curiously. Clayton Wilde sat up on the seat of his wagon, not a man of combat, ready to take over the reins when Partridge and Bannerman achieved the victory for him in Santa Fe.

Flint noticed that he'd grown thinner on the trip, the heat and the constant travel not agreeing with him, although at all times he was cheerful and optimistic. It was a matter of conjecture whether he realized that there was dissension. Flint did not think that he did.

"Injuns," Moose Clemens said. "Git the women the hell out o' sight."

Otey Higgins said, "So they're payin' us a visit. We ought to shoot 'em to hell when they come up an' then they'll know we mean business."

"Then they come back with a bigger war party," Moose told him. "Could be they're only curious, an' a few presents will send 'em away happy. All we lose then is a little tobacco instead o' scalps."

"Crazy business," Otey persisted. "Comanches an' whites are at war, an' yet the damned Injuns kin ride in an' look over us, see how tough we are, an' then make up their minds if they want to fight or not. We even give 'em presents to keep 'em happy."

"It ain't an official war," Moose said.

"Bullets an' arrows kill just as well," Otey said, "in official wars or any other kind you got."

Tom Partridge made sure that Portia Wilde and Jennifer Smith were inside the wagons under blankets before he drew his men up inside the wagon corral.

"They see a white woman," Moose said without emotion, "an' they'll fight like hell. All Injuns are like that."

"How many of them?" Flint asked him. He leaned against a wagon wheel, rifle in hand, watching the oncoming riders. He could see them quite clearly as they came on, varicolored horses charging out of the dust clouds, the late afternoon

Arkansas River loomed up ahead of them, three quarters of a mile wide, and never more than three or four feet deep, considerably less at the fording places, dotted with grassy islands, its bluffs of sandstone and clay broken down here and there at the fording places.

The men stared at the river as the wagons rolled to a stop. They'd crossed innumerable small creeks and streams, but this was a river—a real river, and eventually, after following it for a while, they would have to cross to the other side.

"Ain't nothin' to cross," Moose Clemens spat out disdainfully. "Some o' you boys ought to see the Columbia up there in Oregon. There's a real river."

The banks of the river were lined with cottonwoods and willows, and again they found some shade as they pulled up late in the afternoon of the seventh day after leaving Council Grove. They'd seen no Indians, only the smoke signals, lazy white streamers lifting into a brassy sky.

They camped with their backs to the river now, giving them protection on one side, and in the morning they moved up along the river, around Big Bend, camping at Walnut Creek.

The wagons were being formed into a quadrangle when they saw the dust cloud moving toward them from the west, upriver. Several of the men yelled "buffalo" and raced for their guns.

scalp, and Otey Higgins rolled his eyes in mock terror.

"Corwin," Flint said, "is a *comanchero*. He's out there."

The big trapper glanced at him and then nodded grimly as they rode along ahead of the wagons. "He's out there," Clemens scowled, "an' there ain't no tellin' what he's up to. Could be he'll persuade his Comanche friends to have a go at us."

That night Tom Partridge posted a double guard, keeping the stock closer to the wagons than usual. They were drawn up in a square now, four wagons on each side, locked together, with the riding horses and the valuable mules picketed close by.

They were careful now when selecting the campsite never to camp on high grass, and always Partridge tried to find a ridge off the trail, giving them high ground for a defense if a defense was necessary. Men were cautioned not to ride away from the wagons in pursuit of game, and never to go unarmed wherever they were.

Daily, they trudged along beside the wagons, the Easterners gradually hardening to the march, and the Westport drifters becoming more sullen if anything as the difficulties increased.

They crossed a number of creeks on the march to the Arkansas—Cottonwood Creek, Turkey Creek, Little Arkansas, Cow Creek, and then the

you kin see. You kin shoot 'em all day, an' if you're careful they won't even run."

"Lot o' meat there," Otey Higgins said and grinned, "or some mountain man's dreamin' like hell."

"Ain't no dream," Moose assured him. "Them buffalo been feedin' the Injuns fer hundreds o' years. Anybody wants to lick the redskins has to kill off the buffalo first."

They saw something else the second day out of Council Grove, and Moose Clemens looked at it with misgivings. Several thin columns of smoke lifted up into the air from points to the south and to the west of them, a long distance off, so far that they were scarcely discernible against the blue of the sky.

"Comanches or Kiowas watchin' us," Moose stated. "First outfit goin' down this summer. They'll have a look at us closer up in a day or two."

"An' they ain't friendly," Otey Higgins murmured.

"Not to them as don't watch 'em every minute of every day an' every night," Moose Clemens said. "Seen 'em ride up to an outfit, beggin' fer gifts. They git their fill o' tobacco an' bread, an' they see how strong an outfit is, Next night the stock is gone, or maybe worse, if it's a small outfit an' they ain't watchin' themselves." He made a motion with his index finger around his

Chapter Fourteen

THE WILDE EXPEDITION remained at the Grove for three days, and on the fourth rolled out alone while the other outfits were still organizing, waiting for more wagons to roll in.

Flint, Moose Clemens, and Otey Higgins rode far ahead of the slowly moving wagons now as they rolled into Indian country. It was a tighter line of march altogether, the wagons keeping close in line, point riders on the flanks, and a rear guard coming up behind the following herd.

The big plains stretched endlessly toward the west, rising and falling, buffalo grass and barren sand hills. Antelope stared at them from the ridges, and the first day out of Council Grove, Flint shot one of the little animals.

They brought in a half dozen the following day, beginning their real work as hunters for the expedition, and the men were grateful for the change from salt pork and bacon. They saw no buffalo as yet, and Moose Clemens informed them that they wouldn't sight the big herds until they'd crossed the Arkansas.

"Millions of 'em," Moose stated, eyes shining at the thought. "Ground's black with 'em far as

"You got his hat," Flint smiled.

"Hell with his hat," Otey said. "Didn't figure he'd have the nerve to head fer Council Grove."

"Nobody to bother him but our outfit," Flint observed. "His crew is here, too, mixed in with the crowd."

"We come close enough to 'em," Otey said, "but we never catch 'em. You ready to go now, Flint?"

They walked back to the camp together, Flint moving slowly, conscious of the fact that he'd been very close to death—the second time at the hands of Lace Corwin.

Vaguely, as he crumpled to the ground, he was aware of the fact that Corwin had unhesitatingly lifted his gun barrel and smashed it down across his skull.

Two more shots, this time from a pistol, came from the woods to the west, and then as Flint crouched on the ground, stupidly, blood beginning to slide down over his eyes from the gashed skull, a gun went off close at hand, the lead digging up dirt inches from his face. He tried to raise himself from the ground, but he could not see, and he did not have the strength. He heard horses running away, and he realized that Ortiz and Corwin were fleeing from the hollow, and that Corwin had probably sent that last shot at him, hoping to drop him before he rode off.

Otey Higgins loped down into the hollow, running like an antelope. Dropping the Kentucky rifle on the ground, he squatted beside Flint, examining the wound with his fingers, and then he applied his bandanna handkerchief to the gash to stop the flow of blood. He said, "Not too deep, but deep enough to cause a little misery. Friends o' yours, Flint?"

"Corwin and the Mexican," Flint told him.

Otey shook his head in disgust. "Had to shoot too damned fast," he scowled. "Just come in sight an' saw him liftin' the barrel o' his Colt. If he'd given me two seconds more, he'd o' been a dead man now."

were lowered, and they seemed to shine as if someone were holding a tiny candle behind them.

"What information?" Ortiz asked.

"Clayton Wilde intends to liberate New Mexico," Flint murmured.

"He don't know a damn thing, Ortiz," Lace Corwin said.

Ortiz nodded. There was a look almost of regret on his brown face as he nodded slightly to Corwin. "That is too bad, *señor*," he said. "Much too bad."

Flint tensed himself for a spring at Corwin's gun. He knew that he'd never make it before Corwin put one and possibly two bullets into him, but there was the possibility his aim would be hurried by the leap for the gun, and the bullets might only graze and not kill. It was a chance, very small, very meager.

Flint lunged toward his right without even looking at Corwin, giving him absolutely no warning. A gun cracked, but it was not Corwin's. Even as he was moving Flint recognized the flat, sharp crack of a Kentucky rifle.

Corwin's hat moved on his head as a ball nicked it. The rifle shot came from the west of the hollow, and the passage of the ball through Corwin's hat disconcerted him for the moment, giving Flint time to come in under the leveled gun. He dived for Corwin's knees, and then the sky fell down on top of him.

"What do you know of Wilde's plans when he nears Santa Fe?" Ortiz asked next.

"Ask him," Flint said again. He felt a cold chill run up and down his back. He was not afraid to die, but dying like this, shot down in cold blood, did not appeal to him. He had come a long way from the Tennessee hills to see the big mountains, and he hadn't seen them as yet.

"No one will notice a gun popping off back here," Ortiz observed. "They will think it is another wild turkey or a squirrel being shot."

"I'll do it now," Corwin grinned. "We're wastin' time, Ortiz."

"Do you know anything?" Ortiz asked him, "which you could impart, *señor*?"

Stalling for time, Flint said, "What's the price for it?"

Ortiz flicked ash from the tip of the *cigarillo*. "That depends, *señor*, upon the value of the information you give to me."

"Wastin' time," Corwin said.

Flint took a step back, wishing now that he'd taken that lone chance he'd had when he held the rifle in his hand. It was too late now. Corwin stood several paces away from him, the gun steady in his hand, knowing that he was contemplating some kind of move, and defying him to make it. There was a cold, confident grin on the yellow-haired man's thin hawk face, and the lust to kill was in his yellow-green eyes. The lids

which according to Moose Clemens, meant that he lived with them occasionally and took Comanche squaws as his wives. He had the smell of an Indian about him, too, the dank, wet-diaper smell, the heavy, almost animal odor of an unwashed body.

Corwin held a Walker-Colt gun in his hand, the hammer pulled back, and he glared at Flint, thin, cracked lips drawn back, his yellowed teeth revealed. They were pointed teeth like an animal's.

"Wilde's hunter," he said to the Mexican. "Ought to sew his damn mouth up with gut like I seen the Kiowas do to a Crow."

Pablo Ortiz still sat on the ground, looking at Flint calmly, puffing on the *cigarillo*. He said, "When is Wilde's party leaving Council Grove?"

"Ask him," Flint muttered.

Ortiz shrugged and smiled, revealing even white teeth in odd contrast to Lace Corwin's. "For a man who is going to die, *señor*," he murmured, "you are not being polite."

He spoke English without an accent, and Flint stared down at him, and then at Lace Corwin, realizing that Ortiz meant what he said. Life meant nothing to these men. Corwin killed for money, and Ortiz out of a sense of high patriotism. He was protecting his country from marauders, and this was war.

When he heard a twig crack behind him, he knew that he'd been right. He didn't turn his head as the man came up behind him, jamming a pistol into the small of his back. He realized that he was very close to death, and the smallest move he made with the rifle in his hand might send a bullet crashing through his back.

"Drop the gun, mister," the man behind him snapped. "You ain't usin' it this afternoon."

Flint hesitated for one moment, feeling the pressure of that pistol barrel against his back, weighing his chances. The man behind him was undoubtedly Corwin himself, and Moose Clemens had informed him that Corwin had no scruples about shooting a man in the back, that he preferred this method.

"Drop it."

Flint dropped the gun, and Lace Corwin came around in front of him, kicking the rifle away. He still wore the black, flat-crowned hat with the broken rim, and the brown leather vest, scuffed and dirty from much wear. His green eyes went over Flint contemptuously as he motioned for him to come forward with the gun.

"Heard you comin'," Corwin said, laughing. "Kin hear a squirrel flick its tail at fifty yards."

"Like an Injun," Flint told him, and the smile left Corwin's face. No man who'd spent much time with the Indians liked to be reminded of that fact. Corwin was a trader with the Comanches,

grove, he heard a gun bang as another hunter fired at a squirrel or turkey.

He walked for fifteen minutes, leaving the beaten path which led through the grove, swinging west now toward the outer fringe of trees. It was here in the little clearings where the trees thinned out that he expected to flush his turkeys, and it was here that he flushed game of another caliber.

Swinging down into a hollow he saw two horses tied to the bushes less than twenty yards away, and a man sitting on the ground, back against a tree, facing him, watching him, a slim, brown Mexican *cigarillo* in his mouth, the smoke of it curling gently upward.

The man on the ground wore a soiled green corduroy vest and tight-fitting fawn-colored Mexican pants, also very soiled. He was thin, sallow-faced with lank black hair and beady black eyes, and he had a crescent scar running from the right side of the mouth to the eye. The man on the ground was Pablo Ortiz, the New Mexican agent.

Ortiz made no move to get up, nor did he grab for the rifle on the ground next to him. He smiled complacently, and Flint knew, then, that he was covered by another gun. He made no attempt to raise his rifle, but he stopped halfway down into the hollow, looking at Ortiz and at the two horses. The extra horse was proof enough that a second man was in the vicinity.

rifle, and then Bannerman revealing part of his soul to him. Bannerman was more than wind and talk and smiles. He was a composite of many things, of many moods, some good and some bad, all of them covered by that mask of affability, and Flint found himself wondering how the man would turn out in the end.

Leaving Jennifer and Delkin in the wagon, he moved toward the wagon in which his own equipment was stored, and he found another shirt, slipping it on. He picked up his rifle, then, and stepped across Council Grove Creek on a fallen log, entering the thick woods beyond. He carried the long-barreled Kentucky rifle instead of the heavier Hawkins' gun because the game here was not buffalo, but wild turkey. Otey Higgins was in this grove somewhere, searching for a flock of them, also.

It was good to be back in the dense woods, and he felt at home as he swung along a trail leading south, away from the creek. Behind him he left the sounds of this big encampment, the bellowing of cattle, the pounding of hammers, the singing, the talking.

Rifle in hand, he walked swiftly over pine needles and dead leaves, watching the birds darting among the branches overhead, listening for the distant gobble of a turkey. He wondered where Otey Higgins had gone, and if he'd had success. Occasionally, at the far end of the big

"Toughing it out?" Flint asked him.

Delkin just grimaced. "Hell," he said.

"Why did you come?" Flint said. He put both arms across the dropboard and looked at the wagon floor.

Delkin laughed, a trace of bitterness in his voice. "Back east it sounded good. Everybody's talking liberty these days. We got ours in this country and it's gone to our heads. We want to liberate the whole world."

"Nobody liberated us," Flint said. "Had a grandfather at Valley Forge."

"Mine was at Bunker Hill," Delkin smiled. "Should have thought of that when Bannerman spoke to me in Boston."

"He's a convincer, Delkin."

Will Delkin looked at him closely. "He is that," he agreed. "He convince you?"

"No," Flint said. "I came."

Jennifer Smith came up to the wagon with a pot of broth she'd made. Flint gave her a hand up, and she said, "Nice to be in the shade again."

Flint watched Portia and Bannerman coming back from the creek, and Bannerman was talking, gesturing a little with his free hand as he carried the pail in the other, and as Flint watched, he thought, He's a convincer.

Then he was a little ashamed of himself, remembering how Bannerman had moved his horse in between himself and the Osage with the

"I do not believe," she said, "that my uncle has any intentions of upsetting the established government of New Mexico, with the exception of those at the head, and breaking away from the Mexican Republic."

"I was joking, Portia."

"You joke too often of this expedition," Portia observed.

"A joke makes for relaxation," Bannerman smiled, and Flint saw him drop his hand which had been around her waist. "If we never smiled, Portia, we would be a sorry lot of liberators."

Portia didn't say anything to that, and Bannerman went to the creek, stooped, and lifted a bucket of water. When he turned he was still in rare good humor and he said, "Now Flint, here, is your kind of man, Portia. He never smiles."

"Damn little to smile about," Flint said. "Stampede, prairie fire, hat shot from my head, and plenty of hell on the other side of the Arkansas." He draped the shirt on a tree out in the sun and then he rubbed his hands on the sides of his pants.

Bannerman said, "Ought to have a woman for that job, Flint."

Flint looked at him. "Everybody marrying me off," he said, and he left them there by the creek, walking back to the wagons, stripped to the waist.

He had a look in at Will Delkin, who was sitting up in the wagon, staring out through the canvas opening.

is hardly the place for an intimate romance—neither the place nor the time."

Flint didn't say it, but he wondered why Bannerman hadn't married her a long time before they started on this expedition, and before it was even planned.

Bannerman was coming down the patch toward them, whistling, carrying a water bucket. He said as he came up,

"Wash day, Flint?"

"Time for it," Flint nodded.

Bannerman came up beside Portia and put an arm around her waist. It was almost a brotherly gesture, and he stood there, holding her lightly, one hand holding the pail, watching Flint, who'd started to scrub again.

Flint didn't look at them. He worked hard on the shirt and then wrung it out. He heard Bannerman say to Portia, "How is Will Delkin making out?"

"Glad for the rest we're getting," Portia said. "It was hard on him jolting over the plains. Jennifer and I fixed up a kind of swinging hammock inside the wagon to offset the shock, but even then he was often in terrible pain."

"When we get to Santa Fe," Bannerman said, "we can make him mayor of one of the smaller towns. He can be a hero."

Flint saw Portia glance at him quickly, and he knew that she didn't like the remark.

man of the broken jug top. He didn't think that she did.

"He's changed a lot since we left Westport," Portia murmured. "I cannot quite account for it, but he's different. I believe I've sensed a change in him since we left Boston."

"You know him well back there?" Flint asked her, careful to keep his voice casual.

"We went to school together as children," Portia told him. She flicked idly at the leaves, and a faraway look came into her eyes, which were now violet and now a lighter shade, almost blue. He realized that she was thinking on those days, comparing them with now, with the turmoil, the fighting, the killing, perhaps, ahead of them, and never any peace.

Flint understood now why they were so intimate. Having known each other since childhood it was conceivable that they could consider themselves engaged without ever having brought the matter out into the light. Taking a deep breath, and starting to scrub the shirt again, Flint said over his shoulder,

"You marrying him?"

Her answer was slow coming, and not too positive when it did come. She said, "I believe so, Flint."

Flint's lips tightened imperceptibly. "He hasn't asked you?"

Portia laughed lightly. "An expedition like this

when he heard someone coming up behind him, and a soft laugh.

When he turned his head he looked into the eyes of Portia Wilde.

"Woman's work, Flint," she laughed.

"Man's outfit," Flint told her. "Don't wash it myself and it'll stay dirty all the way to Santa Fe." He wanted to add "and back" but he didn't because he wasn't sure of coming back.

"You should have a wife," Portia observed. "You would make a good husband, Flint."

Flint looked down into the bucket. "Find the woman," he said.

"What about the Smith girl?" Portia asked him.

"Spitfire," Flint said. "She'd drive a man to drink."

Portia laughed. Her voice was low, musical, and listening to it Flint felt his heart skip a beat. "Maybe you need a spitfire, Flint," she said.

Flint looked up from the bucket. He said, "Reckon I don't, ma'am." He noticed some slight color come to her face and he realized that his remark had gone home. She was flicking idly at a leaf with a small switch in her hand, and very deftly she changed the subject. She said, "What do you think of Jay, Flint?"

"He can take care of himself," Flint said. He looked at her steadily as he said this, and he wondered if she knew Bannerman—the Banner-

drawn by a pair of stout Missouri mules, but with the tall mast brushing the overhead branches.

"All of 'em havin' a good time here," Moose Clemens explained to Flint. "Playin' at politics, just like back in the states. They elect a wagon captain an' a commander o' the guard. There'll be a hell of a lot o' rum tricklin' down dry gullets an' fist fights an' speech makin' an' everybody will be happy. Makes 'em feel independent, but there ain't nobody knows what independence is till he's lived out in the big mountains fer two, three winters, a thousand miles from the nearest courthouse or soldier, an' no law but the law which says a man dies when he don't watch out every minute."

"I'll see it," Flint said.

"Not with that gal up in Wilde's wagon," Moose told him sagely. "The mountains ain't fer her. Other one, maybe so."

Flint didn't say anything to that.

The wagons were drawn up along the creek, the oxen unyoked and taken out to graze on the plains. Tom Partridge set some of the men to unloading the wagons and drying out the tarpaulins. Otey Higgins, hearing that there were wild turkeys in the grove, took his rifle and wandered away, whistling to himself.

Flint got a bucket of water from the creek, stripped off his shirt and soaked the shirt in the bucket. He was washing it vigorously with soap

wild Kiowas, wild Comanches, millions o' buffalo."

There was a blacksmith shop in the grove and teams of oxen and mules were lined up near the shop waiting to be shod. Men wandered under the big trees festooned with grapevines, grateful for this deep shade after the hot days on the trail.

Tom Partridge rolled his dozen wagons up along Council Grove Creek which ran through the middle of the half-mile-wide strip of hardwood timber. The unusually large party of men with his outfit attracted attention in the grove, and Flint saw men staring at them as they moved by.

There were Mexicans and Missourians and Indian hunters working for the outfits, and occasional Negroes and Kanakas, and a few carefree French Canadians. Some women accompanied the outfits, a trader's wife in full skirt of silk or cashmere, some farmers' wives reluctant to let their spouses taste the pleasures of Santa Fe without them. There were black-haired Mexican women, and occasional squaws, wives of the Indian hunters or mountain trappers, somber, silent, dark-eyed, watching everything, saying nothing.

The Indian women stared at Portia Wilde up on the seat of her wagon, golden-haired, smiling, hatless as she came into the grove. They looked at little Jennifer Smith on the seat of the windwagon

Chapter Thirteen

THE WAGON TRAIN reached Council Grove
on a bright sunny afternoon to find a half-
dozen other outfits already there, resting up after
the trip down from Westport. As the wagons
rolled in under the shade of the hardwood trees
in the grove, they could hear the axes ringing on
all sides as men cut down stout hickories to make
spare wagon tongues and axles for the long trip
ahead.

It was a time to wash clothes which had not
been washed since the morning they'd left Westport; it was a time to repair wagons and readjust
loads and renew old acquaintances.

Flint looked at the streamers of wash hanging in
the sun between the big trees—flannel shirts and
drawers and socks and jackets which had started
to become mildewed. He saw many wagons with
their loads on the ground covered with tarpaulins,
the wagons up on jacks, being fitted with new
axles to take the place of those which had proved
too weak for the rugged prairie travel.

Moose Clemens said to Flint as they rode in
under the trees, "Here's where the west begins,
Flint. Other side o' Council Grove, it's wild—

quite sure that he liked her as she'd been before. At least when she was distant she hadn't annoyed him. Now she was annoying him again, and he didn't like it. He didn't like it too well that Bannerman was becoming so friendly with her, either, but he told himself that this was foolishness. It meant nothing to him. He was positive of that.

safe and comfortable while he'd been riding into hot lead. The fact that Bannerman had been talking with Jennifer, he decided, did not concern him.

"Mr. Bannerman thinks well of you, Flint," Jennifer was saying. "He considers you and Moose Clemens the top hands of this crew."

Flint looked at her. "What else did you and Bannerman talk about besides me?" he asked.

Jennifer smiled, and this time she reminded him of the old Jennifer Smith of Westport Landing. It was that same roguish smile, the same pertness which he'd thought she'd lost.

"We talked of the moon and the stars," she said softly. "Of many things."

He knew she was joking with him now as she'd joked before, and in a way he was glad. They would have to be together on this trip for several months, and if they had to be together it was better that they were friendly. "He didn't kiss me," Jennifer said, "yet."

"You could do worse," Flint observed, "than Jay Bannerman."

"You couldn't do too much better," Jennifer said, "than Portia Wilde—even though you'll never have her."

Flint felt his face redden. "Never said I wanted her," he snapped.

"You do," Jennifer told him cheerily.

He moved away from the wagon, then, not

remembered that she'd fought that fire as hard as any of the men, and the smell of smoke was still with her, even though she'd washed the grime from her face and hands.

"I'm all right," Jennifer murmured. "Miss Wilde will take over in the morning." She hesitated and then she said, "Portia is a fine girl, Flint. I like her."

Flint just nodded. He looked at Will Delkin on the blankets.

"She might get along very well in a cabin," Jennifer went on, her face expressionless. "Maybe I was wrong."

"All right," Flint said. "All right." He felt uncomfortable discussing one girl with another.

"I'm glad you came back," Jennifer said. "Bannerman told me it was a rather dangerous mission."

"Bannerman?"

Jennifer nodded. "He thought you could take care of yourself, Flint, but that you didn't have too much support with you if you ran into Corwin's crew."

Flint considered the fact that Bannerman had been chatting here with Jennifer while he had been out riding into a dangerous ambush. Had that first volley from the ridge been inches lower he'd have been a dead man now. He decided, for reasons not quite clear to himself, that he didn't particularly like it that Bannerman had been here to join Portia Wilde over by the injured man, and it was the first intimation Flint had that she was still awake. He watched several of the men lift Delkin into one of the supply wagons, and then after a brief consultation with Portia, Jennifer climbed into the wagon to look after him until morning. It was evident that they'd made an agreement concerning his care.

It was now nearly an hour before dawn with most of the men having had little sleep during the night. Tom Partridge passed on the word that they would postpone the start till near noon tomorrow, resting both men and animals which had been disturbed by the prairie fire.

Before rolling into his blanket for a few hours sleep, Flint stepped over to the wagon in which Delkin lay. When he looked in he saw Jennifer sitting on a box beside the improvised bed. A lantern hung from a crosspiece above.

Will Delkin, a thin, bony man with a hooked nose rocked back and forth on the blankets, moaning a little, his face covered with perspiration. Jennifer was mopping his face with a wet towel. She looked at Flint and nodded impersonally.

"Pretty bad?" Flint asked.

"It was a bad break," Jennifer nodded. "He won't walk any more this trip."

Flint looked at his hands gripping the edge of the dropboard. "You must be tired," he said. He

"We can't leave him to die on the prairie," Partridge observed, his lips tight.

Bannerman was smiling, but it was that hard smile again, and once again Flint sensed the conflict between these two, something which went deeper than their respective feelings for Portia Wilde. It was as if Tom Partridge saw something in Bannerman which other men did not see, and he hated it.

"I had no intention of leaving him on the prairie," Bannerman stated, "but it may be the better part of reason, if we pass a Westport-bound outfit, to transfer him to them."

"He'll rot in Westport," Partridge said quietly. "Who is there to look after him? We're the only friends Delkin has in this part of the country. He was hurt fighting for us. It's our duty to take care of him."

"I did not suggest deserting him," Bannerman observed, and he was still smiling.

Clayton Wilde nodded in agreement. "We will take care of Delkin," he said. "He will receive the best of care. I guarantee that. We have Delkin's interest at heart, Tom."

The odd thought came to Flint that if they'd had poor Delkin's interest at heart they'd have left him in Boston with people he knew and understood rather than taking him down to this wild country from which we might never return.

Jennifer Smith came into the firelight, crossing

Bannerman should make such a statement even in jest.

"Rather ride beside a Comanche buck," Moose Clemens said, "with a bloody scalp on his belt."

Flint sipped his coffee and watched Doc Schoonover, a small, pale man with spectacles, work on the injured Delkin, who'd been placed on a blanket near one of the other fires.

Delkin screamed as Schoonover pulled the leg, resetting the bones. They'd befogged his brain with whisky, but the pain seared through even this palliative.

Over by the tent Portia Wilde lifted a hand to her breast, stood there for a moment, and then walked resolutely over to the group around Delkin. Flint watched her get a basin and towels, and she crouched beside the almost unconscious man, bathing his face as Doc Schoonover set his splints.

Bannerman said, "A man in that condition will slow us down some. He'll have to be carried in one of the wagons for a month or two, probably all the way to Santa Fe."

Tom Partridge started to fill his tin cup from the pot, and without looking at Bannerman he said, "You signed Will Delkin back in Boston, didn't you?"

Bannerman looked at him. "I signed him," he admitted.

again, having had to make a wide circuit of the charred and still smoldering grass.

Tom Partridge was waiting for them as they walked into the firelight. He looked at the improvised stretcher and the man on it, and then frowned.

Flint went over to the fire with him for a cup of coffee, Jay Bannerman and Clayton Wilde joining them. Bannerman said, "You ran into it, Flint."

"They were waiting for us," Flint told him briefly. "Ten of them holed in on a ridge."

"Should o' been more careful," Moose Clemens said bitterly as he squatted down on his haunches, lifting a cup of boiling hot coffee to his mouth. "I know this Corwin. I should o' figgered he'd watch his back trail."

"We lost two men," Flint told Partridge. He saw Portia Wilde standing out in front of her tent, looking in his direction, and he tried to bolster his ego with the thought that she'd waited up for his return.

"Had no real damage here," Partridge said, "thanks to Moose, but it was close. From now on we camp on the grassless ridges even if we have to picket the horses a quarter mile away."

"Then we lose the horses," Bannerman said and smiled faintly. "A man of Corwin's ingenuity should be on our side."

Flint glanced at him, a little surprised that

Fint looked at the silent men standing in the shadows around him, and he knew that, for tonight, they'd already had enough fight. The zest for it had gone out of them, and risking another attack on the ridge would be courting disaster.

"We'll head back for the wagons," Flint said. "That man's leg needs to be set."

They had a surgeon in the company, an Easterner Clayton Wilde had brought out, and he'd been doctoring some of the sick men in the crew.

"Have a hell of a time gettin' him back," Otey reflected. "He ain't ridin' a horse with that leg."

"Fix up a splint with a rifle barrel," Moose told him. "Bind it up tight, an' then rig up a blanket from one o' them dead horses to carry him. It'll be slow business an' it won't be nice fer Delkin, but we'll git him back."

One of the crewmen crawled back to the ambush spot, pulled the saddle blanket from one of the dead mounts, and came back with it. Moose Clemens tore up his shirt into strips, and with the strips of cloth, bound Delkin's broken left leg to his rifle barrel.

They rigged the horse blanket between two of the horses and lifted the injured man into it. He lay there groaning as they started off, two men leading the horses.

They took turns riding and walking, but it was three hours before they reached the wagon corral

The remaining men, dazed by this sudden, deadly fire, had fallen back. They were firing spasmodically, but without too much enthusiasm, awaiting the word to run.

"Reckon they're tougher than we are tonight," Moose Clemens growled. "Better pull in our horns or they'll shoot the hell out of us."

Flint had been thinking the same thing. They were in an exposed spot here with Corwin's crew hidden on the ridge, shooting down at them. He knew, also, that Corwin had better gun hands with him, and just as many guns now. Several of their horses were down, making matters all the worse.

"Pull back," Flint called over his shoulder. He sent a bullet at the flash of a gun, and then he started to retreat himself, running with the gray gelding, crouching low as he ran.

They retreated a hundred yards or so until they'd dipped down into a hollow where the riflemen on the ridge couldn't reach them. Two of the crewmen had helped the man whose horse had fallen on him, and this man was moaning and whimpering as he lay in the grass, twisting from side to side.

"Leg's broke," Otey said. "That's Delkin. Campbell an' Moran are dead."

Moose said, "Like to git up behind that bunch, Flint. We kin give 'em a dose o' their own medicine."

Moose Clemens' big black stopped in its tracks, shivered, and then went down on its front legs. Moose jumped clear, and in the air he bawled, "Cover!"

Before any of the men could dismount or reach for their weapons, a half-dozen more rifles opened up on them at close range. Flint heard a bullet whip over his head, inches above the flat-crowned hat. Another bullet struck a man behind him, and the rider gave a low moan as he slipped from the saddle.

A second man, to Flint's left, screamed as he was hit, and his horse broke away wildly, racing toward the west, the rider eventually sliding down to the grass.

A horse was hit as other guns opened up from the ridge, and the animal went down threshing madly, pinning the rider beneath him. Flint was on the ground in a moment, rifle in hand, kneeling, holding the reins with one hand. Then he slipped the reins up on his shoulder, aimed the rifle at the flash of one of the guns, and pulled the trigger.

Otey Higgins and Moose Clemens were down, too, kneeling and firing, Moose from behind his horse, which had rolled over and lay still.

"Give 'em hell!" Otey yelped.

Reloading the Hawkins' rifle, Flint called back over his shoulder, "Who is down?"

"Campbell," Otey Higgins told him, "Moran, an' Delkin."

the high grass, but occasionally they came out on smooth sand hills where a horse's hoof could be seen quite plainly even at night, and Flint was aware of the fact that the big trapper could practically see in the dark.

They spread out as they rode, and several times Moose Clemens slipped from the saddle to have a closer look at the ground. They struck the trail of the raiders a half hour after they'd swung around the farthest tip of the prairie fire. It was the big trapper who located the hoofprints in the soft earth on the side of a hill, a mile or so back from the edge of the smoldering grass. The riders gathered together.

Flint watched as he dismounted, scurrying around like a big hound for a few moments, and then pushing up into the saddle again.

"How many?" Flint asked.

"Ten of 'em," the Moose said. He pointed toward the south.

Flint glanced back at the silent men behind him and then started to ride in that direction. Otey Higgins called, "Kind o' nice ridin' after them instead o' them after us all the time."

"We ketch up with 'em," Moose murmured, "an' there'll be no more ridin' fer Lace Corwin."

He pushed the horse toward a low ridge dead ahead of them, and as he did so, a shot rang out. Flint saw the flame leap from the muzzle of a rifle less than fifty yards away.

with the same fury as in the center of the crescent with the south wind whipping it into a frenzy.

The gray gelding retreated from the advancing flames, and Flint let the animal run, always bearing toward the east, but making a wide circle. In another five minutes of hard running they swung around the wisps of burning grass on the edge of the semicircle, rode hard toward the southeast, and eventually swung in around the burned grass.

Here they paused for a few minutes, breathing the horses, coughing, wiping the cinders and tears from their smarting eyes.

Otey Higgins said, "Made it, Flint."

"Hate like hell," Moose said, grinning, "to make it that close agin, boys."

Flint pushed up into the saddle. He watched the receding flames toward the north, the burned-over area of smoldering grass, and then he said briefly, "We'll ride."

"Watch fer sign," Moose stated. "If it's Corwin I aim to foller him clean out to the mountains. He'll never try to burn another outfit when we git through with him."

"Didn't catch him, yet," Otey Higgins observed. "We sit here jawin' an' we might have to chase him out to the mountains."

They rode more leisurely now, with Moose Clemens bent in the saddle, peering at the ground. There was little he could see as they rode through

Chapter Twelve

THEY COULD FEEL the heat searing their right sides as they rode. They watched the large fire roar into the smaller one with a strange hissing sound. Yellow flames leaped up into the air all along the main line where the fires had met and then quickly died down.

There were flying sparks, however, carried by the strong wind, hundreds of them swirling through the air, landing on the other side of the burned-out area, and looking back again, Flint saw the crewmen stamping at them.

Otey Higgins yelled at Flint and then clenched his fist and raised it in the victory sign. The backfire had worked, and all along the main line the big prairie fire was leaping onto the smaller fire, destroying itself, making desperate efforts to leap across that small patch of burned-out grass. Here and there it succeeded, but men were waiting with wet blankets, killing these long, snakelike streamers of flame which reached toward the wagons.

Their own race hadn't been won as yet. They were still a hundred yards or so from the fringe of the crescent. Here the grass burned, but not from the south. It was a half mile or more to the outer edge of the crescent, and Flint MacKeithan, riding faster than he'd ever ridden a horse in his life, wondered if they'd make it or be engulfed by those onrushing flames.

to the wagons, moving around restlessly as the smoke sifted through the wagons.

Quickly, Flint picked out nine more men, mostly men from the east, who'd held up well on the trail. He saddled his gray, strapped on his gunbelt, and slid his rifle into the saddle holster.

Burning embers were already dropping around them, igniting dry grass just outside the enclosure. Men with wet blankets leaped at these tiny fires, slapping them out before they could get started.

With Otey and Moose beside him, and the nine crewmen bringing up the rear, Flint raced his horse out of the enclosure, heading east.

The two fire walls seemed to be converging on each other now. Less than twenty-five yards separated the fires as Flint whipped the gray gelding over the patch of burned-out grass near the wagons. The animal kicked up showers of sparks, snorting in fright, the momentum of its drive carrying it over the twenty-odd yards of burned grass almost before the horse could think of stopping.

The other riders followed him, one horse stumbling screaming as it rolled in the still-smoldering grass, but tossing the rider clear. Flint, looking back, saw him rise to his feet and then sprint back toward the wagons.

They were out in the open now, dashing toward the east, with the main fire wall rushing at them

having burned out a section twenty yards across. Moose Clemens yelled, "Everybody keep them blankets ready. Be plenty more sparks crossin' this line when the fire reaches us. Slap out every one of 'em!"

The fire wall was now fifty, now twenty-five yards away from their own thin line of burning grass. Flint was watching it, holding a smoldering blanket in his hands, when Tom Partridge came up to him. Partridge's face was black and tense from his efforts out on the line. He said, "That was started by this Corwin and his crew."

Flint nodded.

"Think you can get through this ring with a dozen men?" Partridge asked him. "I'd say they're still behind the fire, and they won't be looking for trouble from us."

Flint nodded. He noticed that to the east the advancing fire seemed to be thinner, and there was a possibility that they could break through the burned-out grass which they'd fired themselves and swing around the east wing getting behind the main fire.

"Reckon we can try," Flint said.

"Take Higgins and Clemens with you," Partridge told him, "and pick out men you can trust to stick with you."

Flint ran off, calling for Otey and Moose to follow him. Horses which had been picketed outside the enclosure were all inside now, tied

the wagons, leaving a thin line of fire to fight this huge wall advancing on them with almost the speed of a running horse.

Men were everywhere now with wetted-down blankets and tarpaulins, slapping out the flames which the rising wind tried to whip down toward the wagons. Flint caught a glimpse of Jennifer Smith and her father in the mob, slapping frantically at the flames.

Portia was running out with a blanket when Jennifer ran and caught her, motioning for her to go back to the wagons, and pointing at her skirt which would undoubtedly catch fire in a few moments.

Reluctantly, Portia went back to the wagons and she stood by a big water barrel, the top of which had been stove in, wetting blankets, passing them to black-faced gasping men who rushed out to slap at flames which seemed to be springing up everywhere.

Flint and Otey grabbed blankets and rushed out, too, joining the others on the main sector directly in front of the advancing prairie fire. Out there Moose Clemens was a raging giant, dashing here and there, bowling men over in his haste to slap out the flames, roaring, his hat gone from his head, and his flaming red hair reflecting the light of the advancing fire.

There were over fifty men out on the line now, and gradually they brought the fire under control,

torch to the foot-high prairie grass, and then Flint realized what he was doing. They were going to build another fire, burn over a section of the plains in front of this grass fire so that it could not jump to the grass surrounding the wagons.

"Backfire!" Moose Clemens was howling. "Burn it up!"

Tom Partridge ran out from the corral, calling for men to follow him with blankets and tarpaulins. The wagonmaster had grasped the Moose's plan and was ready to beat out flames from these new fires to prevent them from moving toward the wagons.

Twenty or thirty men came out with him as Otey Higgins and Flint raced in opposite directions, dragging their flaming torches through the dry grass, leaving a trail of fire in their wake.

"All around the corral," the Moose roared. "Ring the wagons."

Flint lunged through the grass as fast as he could go, dragging the burning stick behind him. Smoke from the prairie fire drifted over him in huge, choking clouds, blotting out the sky, and as the fire neared them the smoke cloud lowered, choking him. Still a hundred and fifty yards away, he could begin to feel the heat.

He kept running, gasping for breath, making a fifty-yard circle around the corral, and he kept running until he met Otey Higgins coming the other way. They'd completed the circle around

running the stock toward those hills and safety. It was impossible to hitch any of the oxen to the wagons and haul the wagons to safety.

Clayton Wilde came out to talk with Tom Partridge, and he, too, seemed bewildered. Portia stood with him, a dark robe around her, seeming very tall.

"Only thing to do," Otey Higgins muttered, "is git to the hell out o' here, an' quick."

Flint was thinking the same thing and looking at Partridge, wondering why he didn't give the order to abandon the camp and run for safety. In a few minutes it might be too late for even that.

A rider was pounding toward them from the direction of the night herd, and as he came into the firelight Flint recognized the horse as Moose Clemens' big black.

The giant trapper swung out of the saddle, roaring, gesticulating with his huge arms.

"Build a backfire!" he whooped. "Git them boys workin', Tom! We ain't got much time."

"Backfire?" Partridge repeated.

The Moose didn't wait to explain. Grabbing up a burning stick from the cook's fire he raced out on the plains, yelling for Flint and Otey to come with him. Both men hastily picked sticks from the fire and followed him.

Fifty yards from the wagon corral, and with the wall of flame now less than three hundred yards away, Moose Clemens applied his flaming

Otey yelled, "Corwin!" and Flint nodded grimly.

They were camped on a grassy slope up from the spring, and Flint knew that in less than ten minutes those flames would be upon them, ten and fifteen feet high, engulfing the entire corral, burning it to a crisp. The crazed thought came to him that he should run back for his gun under the wagon. He had no idea how to fight this enemy converging on them in a huge semicircle. The little water at the spring could no more stop this wall of flame than a single bullet could stop a herd of stampeding buffalo.

Tom Partridge also seemed stupefied by the sight, and Flint was remembering that Partridge was new to this country, and he'd never had to fight a prairie fire.

Jay Bannerman came out to the group of men standing outside the enclosure, facing the line of fire. Flint saw his face in the reddish light. It was a stunned, unbelieving face. Bannerman could not conceive of the fact that the outfit was to be destroyed in a very few minutes.

Many of the men already had started to run in the direction of the high sand hills to the north, and Partridge did not stop them. The hills were only a few hundred yards away, grassless tops upon which they would find safety, but the wagons were going to be burned.

Off to the west Flint could hear the herders

Moose Clemens spat. "Show me the twenty-five good men," he said.

"Yeah," Otey Higgins murmured.

Flint was to be on the second watch, with Moose Clemens. He slept with the sound of the canvas covering flapping in the wind, the high wind singing across the tops of the wagons, and he awoke with Otey Higgins shaking him, yelling in his ear, "Fire! Fire, Flint!"

A gun banged on the outskirts of the wagon corral, and Flint sat upright. He was conscious of the fact that the wind had increased in velocity. The canvas covering had almost torn loose and flapped more and more wildly. The crescent moon rode high in the sky with clouds racing past it, and then he saw the line of fire, small yellow blotches on the horizon, growing larger with amazing rapidity, blending with each other, and rushing toward the wagon corral.

"Damn grass's on fire," Otey Higgins howled.

Both men rolled out from beneath the wagon. Other guns were banging to awaken the sleeping men. Otey rushed toward the cook's fire, kicked it into life, and threw a few dry chunks of wood on it to bring it into flame.

Men were rolling out from beneath wagons all along the line, sleepy-eyed, staring stupidly at each other as that red line of flame moved toward them across the plains, the wind whipping it into a frenzy.

the Smith wagon was dying out, but Flint could see Jennifer Smith moving around it, putting away cooking utensils. He thought of her, and of Bannerman, wondering if she meant anything to Bannerman, still a little annoyed because Bannerman had showed some interest in her.

He went over to the wagon under which he'd been sleeping with Otey and Moose, and Otey said, "You figure that damn Corwin turned back to Westport, Flint? We ain't seen nothin' of him since he tried to rub you out."

"Could be," Flint told him, but Moose Clemens shook his head. The giant trapper was puffing on a clay pipe as he lay on his elbows on his blankets.

"If he's gittin' paid fer a dirty job," Moose reflected, "he'll stick with it. Chances are this Mexican ain't payin' him till he wrecks our outfit, an' he ain't wrecked it, yet."

"What'll he do now?" Flint asked. "With that small crew he had, he'd have a time running off our stock, and he can't attack the wagons."

"Plenty he kin do," the Moose growled. "Can't name all the things. He's got the mind o' the Comanche, an' a Comanche kin figure more ways to be ornery than any Injun in this country."

"My outfit," Otey Higgins observed, "an' I'd pick out twenty-five good men an' go chase this Corwin if he's on our tail. I'd chase him right into the pit o' hell."

off on another tack. He wondered what it was that Bannerman had approached and then veered away from. Possibly, it could not have been too important.

A wind sprang up as they were eating that night. The wind came from the south, rippling the prairie grass, tugging at the sheets covering the wagons. The night closed down around them. The big cookfire and a few smaller fires inside the wagon enclosure flickered and whipped in the breeze. The sky was clear, however, with no hint of rain, and as the sun went down a crescent moon slid up over the rim of the prairie, bright and golden in color. Off on the ridges the coyotes were howling, and the frogs down at the spring croaked hoarsely.

Tom Partridge had a man hammering down the tent pegs for the Wilde tent, fastening it with extra ropes in case the wind became stronger. The first night guard left the corral to ride out to the herd, and the fires started to die down when the cooking was over. The smell of fried bacon and beans and hot coffee, usually lingering in the vicinity of the cookfire, was wafted away quickly by the strong south wind.

Flint watched Portia Wilde come out of her tent, a shawl around her shoulders, the wind tugging at her skirts. Seeing him near the fire she waved a hand, smiled, and then went into her uncle's tent.

Across the corral the small cookfire in front of

I was a poor boy. Poverty is a degrading thing, Flint. I hate it." He spat the blade of grass away viciously and sat up staring out across the open plains. "My father had money," he said slowly. "He was a very wealthy man, and then he lost most of it in a big land scheme in Ohio. We were people of influence and social standing in Boston, and we had to uphold the family name. I was sent to the best schools and university, my father borrowing or begging for the money, always pretending, always keeping up this sham of wealth we did not possess. At the university I saw real wealth, and I learned to hate those who possessed it. I had to count pennies while they threw the dollars away. Poverty is hell, Flint."

"Never saw it that way," Flint murmured, wondering why Bannerman was telling him these things.

"You were born a backwoodsman," Bannerman said. "You were lucky, Flint." He rose to his feet and put a hand on Flint's shoulder, facing him. He was smiling and affable again, the calm, collected gentleman. "I wanted you to know this, Flint, because I like you and respect you. I want you to understand."

He turned then and walked back up the path, leading the mare, and Flint watched him go, the feeling running through him that Bannerman had intended to say something entirely different to him, but that he'd changed his mind and gone

"You might not have a choice when we reach Santa Fe." Bannerman smiled.

Flint shrugged. "Reckon I'll know about that when we reach Santa Fe," he said. "A long way off."

"Live for today," Bannerman mused. "Tomorrow's a long way off. You are a philosopher, Flint."

Flint made no comment, wondering what Bannerman was driving at in this circuitous fashion.

"You ever stop to consider, Flint, that this is rather a fanciful scheme—the whole plan to free New Mexico from the Mexican Republic?"

"Thought of it," Flint admitted.

"Yet you signed up."

"So did you," Flint told him bluntly.

Jay Bannerman rubbed the back of his neck and looked up at the sky, now turning golden and red. "You were poor," Bannerman said. "You had nothing, and we offered you the opportunity of bettering your condition, and you accepted even though you realized the dangers involved."

"All right," Flint told him.

"I know what it is to be poor," Bannerman said softly. "There is no one more pitiful in this world, Flint, than a poor rich man or a poor rich boy."

Flint looked at him, the surprise showing in his eyes. "You know what it is to be poor?"

"I am a poor man," Bannerman smiled, "as

"More a kitten," Bannerman said and smiled, "than a wildcat. Is that not so, Flint?"

Flint looked at him steadily. "That could be," he said. He wished that Bannerman would stop talking about Jennifer. He had his own woman, probably the most beautiful and talented woman west of the Missouri. That should have been enough for him.

They spoke for a few minutes, and then Smith left, going back to his wagon with a bucket of water. Bannerman sat down on the grass near the spring, watching his horse drink leisurely, and then he said to Flint, who was also preparing to return to the wagons, "What is in this for you, Flint?"

Flint flicked at the grass with a switch. "The expedition?" he asked.

Bannerman nodded. He put a blade of grass in his mouth and started to chew on it like a small boy.

"Came out this way to see the country," Flint told him. "Reckon I'm seeing it. You're paying for it so far."

Bannerman smiled a little. "You didn't come to die in it," he ventured. "Am I not right?"

"Everybody dies," Flint said.

"You ready to die for the New Mexicans?"

Flint rubbed the nose of the gray gelding standing beside him. "I don't aim to die for anybody just yet."

hair. Watching him, Flint had the feeling that Bannerman would have been that polite, that friendly, with an old washerwoman or an ugly Indian squaw. Bannerman was like that with the female sex.

"A fine gentleman," Windwagon Smith commented, looking up the path. "It is a pleasure being on the trail with him."

Flint wondered what the fat man would say if he'd seen Bannerman handle that tough crewman a few nights before, the man who now was blinded in one eye.

Bannerman spoke for a few minutes with Jennifer, and then came down to the spring, nodding to Flint and to Smith, He said genially, "Two more days and we're at Council Grove. It has been a most pleasant journey, gentlemen."

"Very pleasant," Smith nodded. "I am obliged to you and to Mr. Wilde for giving me permission to accompany this outfit."

"Our pleasure," Bannerman told him. "Shall we say that you and your charming daughter have made this trip a little more agreeable?" He glanced at Flint as he said this, and Flint thought he saw the faintest hint of humor in his brown eyes.

"You may say it." Windwagon Smith chuckled. "First time I ever heard anyone say that Jennifer was charming. Usually, they speak of her as a little wildcat."

front wheels of each wagon chained to the rear wheels of the wagon ahead of it. Even though most outfits did not take such precautions until they were on the other side of Council Grove and rolling into real Indian country, Tom Partridge had insisted upon the strictest vigilance.

"Partridge has his reasons," Flint said.

"A good man, Partridge," Windwagon Smith nodded emphatically. "It would appear, however, that he is almost an overcautious man."

Flint smiled a little, saying nothing more on the subject, but he wondered what the chubby little man would say if he knew the real reason for this Santa Fe expedition.

Jennifer came down to take the mules from her father, and she nodded pleasantly to Flint. She'd changed since that night that he'd kissed her. She was polite but not brash as she'd been in the beginning, and Flint noticed that she seldom came near him. It was not that she avoided him, but for one reason or another their paths did not often cross. He tried to tell himself that it was for the better but he did feel some annoyance.

He experienced further irritation when he saw her moving back toward the wagons, leading the mules, and then stopping to chat with Jay Bannerman who was coming down to the spring with his chestnut mare. Bannerman took off his hat and he stood off to one side of the path, smiling, the late sun glinting on his curly brown

Chapter Eleven

FOR THREE DAYS they rolled steadily toward the west and south, the oxen making better time as they were broken to the trail, and the men beginning to harden a little as they trudged beside the wagons. Tom Partridge had organized the men into companies and they marched in military formation, those who were not handling the wagons, and each evening Partridge drilled them in the use of firearms.

Windwagon Smith, who apparently knew nothing of the real reason for the expedition to Santa Fe, spoke to Flint about it late one afternoon, as they were watering the stock in Crazy Woman Spring, a regular stop on the trail.

"I never knew an outfit before," Smith observed, "which found it necessary to practice military maneuvers as protection against wild Indians on the trail. Do you feel that all this training is necessary, MacKeithan? I've always understood the frontiersmen did better against the Comanches and Kiowas than the Army regulars."

Flint watched the gray drink and then he looked back at the wagons drawn up in full corral now, tongues pointed toward the outside, the tent, not even seeing Flint and Otey, who were still back in the shadows near their wagon. He disappeared into the tent and the flap fell behind him.

Otey Higgins took a deep breath, watched the battered crewman rise to his feet, still bleeding profusely, and then he said to Flint, "If that's an Easterner, I'm damn glad I never went East, Flint."

Flint MacKeithan didn't say anything. He stared at the Wilde tent, glowing dully from the lighted lantern inside, and he was thinking that this was the man who would probably marry Portia Wilde. This was the man with whom she'd walked arm in arm on the texas deck of the General Jackson. He wondered if Portia knew this part of him—the wild, cruel, unrestrained Jay Bannerman who could coolly gouge at a man's eye with a jagged jug top.

"How'd they git that tough back East?" Otey murmured.

Flint smiled coldly. "It's not where a man lives that makes him tough," he stated. "It's the man."

"That's one hell of a man," Otey said.

Flint had to agree with him.

and he walked in, swinging his huge right fist for Bannerman's jaw.

Flint MacKeithan gasped and he heard Otey Higgins' short, startled yell as Bannerman took one step forward and jabbed the jagged jug neck straight in the crewman's face.

The scarred man screamed and staggered back, blood gushing from several places on his face at once—from his left eye, from his cheekbone, from his upper lip, red blood which streamed down from his face, dripping off his chin and his jaws.

Bannerman wasn't through, yet. Dropping the jug neck now, he moved in, smashing short, vicious blows to the big fellow's bleeding face, driving him back up against the wagon wheel.

Half-blinded and shocked by the first assault, the scarred man was hardly able to cope with the second. Bannerman, who'd been cool and calm at first, was now a raging tiger, sending terribly hard, brutal punches into the man's face as he was backed against the wheel, wedged there over the hub, unable to fall. He screamed again, jerking himself bodily away from the wheel, and then sprawled on his face in the dirt.

"Bells o' hell!" Otey Higgins whispered.

Bannerman looked at the half-conscious man lying on the ground, and then at the silent, stunned crewmen around the wagon. Nodding politely, he turned and started back toward Clayton Wilde's

hulking shoulders of a roustabout came out of the crowd, moving toward Bannerman slowly. Flint strapped his gunbelt around his waist, and crawled from under the wagon, Otey Higgins following him reluctantly.

"Here we go again," Otey complained. "Ain't our fight, but we're in it."

The man with the scarred face had thick, protruding ears and huge hands, the backs of them covered with hair. He came up to within three feet of Jay Bannerman and he stood there, glaring at the cool Easterner. The light from a nearby fire flickered on his face, making it more ugly than it was. The firelight made his eyes phosphorescent. They seemed to glitter.

Flint heard him say, "You got your nerve, mister."

"Hard liquor is not allowed in this camp," Jay Bannerman said, smiling. "I am sure you are aware of that, my friend."

"Ain't aware o' nothin'," the big crewman snarled.

"You shouldn't o' broken that jug, Bannerman."

"No?" Bannerman smiled again.

"No," the crewman snapped.

"Give me your reason," Bannerman told him. He still stood completely relaxed, holding the broken jug neck in his hand, and Flint was wondering why he did not throw it away.

"Here's a reason, mister," the big fellow said,

figgered." He added softly, "I could be wrong, though."

Jay Bannerman had started to walk up along the line of wagons, the red butt of his cigar glowing like a red eye in the night. He walked without haste, going past the wagon under which Flint and Otey were lying.

The two men who'd been wrestling for possession of the jug were still on the ground, kicking viciously at each other, when Jay Bannerman reached for them. The jug slipped out of the hand of one of the men, and it lay on the ground just out of their reach.

When Bannerman came up he picked up the jug, looked at it quizzically, and then walked to a large rock, the two men on the ground stopping to watch him, jaws gaping.

Very coolly, Bannerman lifted the jug and smashed it on the rock. The other men came out from beneath the wagon and stood up, glaring at him, no one speaking. The two men who'd been fighting got to their feet and dusted themselves off. None of them had had enough drink as yet to be drunken, but they were in an ugly mood, the drink just beginning to whet their appetites.

Bannerman still stood by the rock on which he'd broken the jug, the jagged jug top in his hand, his back toward Flint and Otey.

"Hell be poppin' now," Otey murmured.

A big fellow with a scarred face and the thick,

150

Partridge gits back. No use us goin' to sleep now, Flint."

Flint shook his head. He'd thought once of going over to the group and demanding the jug, but it wasn't his duty as a hunter for the outfit to interfere here. Tom Partridge had been appointed by Wilde and Bannerman to handle the outfit because Partridge had had experience in handling men.

Leaning back on his elbows, Flint watched the dozen-odd men with the jug. In a few minutes the whisky started to make them belligerent. Their loud voices and louder laughter drifted down to the Wilde tent where Clayton Wilde was talking with Jay Bannerman just inside the flap. Portia had already retired for the night.

An argument broke out between two of the men over possession of the jug, and the argument ended in blows, the two Westport drifters rolling out from beneath the wagon, punching each other, kicking, gouging.

Otey said, "Dog eat dog, an' to hell with both dogs."

The loud noise had attracted the attention of Jay Bannerman, and Flint saw him come out of the tent and stare in the direction of the wagon and the carousing crew.

"He won't do nothin'," Otey predicted. "Bannerman ain't the boy to git his hands dirty if he don't have to. Reckon that's the way I got him

Otey Higgins said to him, as he stepped up beside the two hunters and watched the drill again, "Looks like you just bearded the old she bear in her den."

"Never mind," Flint said.

"Never mind, nothin'," Otey chuckled. "Reckon that's why I'm here with this outfit goin' nowhere an' gettin' there fast."

Flint's gray eyes moved to Portia Wilde, still sitting out in front of the tent with Bannerman and her uncle. That strange, a little perplexed, and disturbed expression was still on her face. He tried to imagine her in a log cabin in the foothills of the big mountains. The mental picture was slow in coming.

The weary men put down the rifles after a while, the Westport recruits cursing as they crawled under their wagons. Flint saw a group of them take a whisky jug out from beneath a blanket and start passing it around, this in open defiance of Tom Partridge's orders that there would be no drinking once the outfit got on the trail. Partridge had ridden out to the grazing herd with Moose Clemens to check on the guards. Again, a double guard had been set to watch the stock, and another guard to watch the wagons, Partridge taking no chances now that they knew Corwin and his desperados were in the vicinity.

Otey Higgins, sitting on his blankets under one of the wagons, said to Flint, "Be hell to pay when

wealthy one, with education. I mean nothing to her."

"You haven't answered the question, Flint."

"It's a damn fool question," Flint snapped.

"Do you think you could be happy with her, Flint? Do you think she could be happy with you—living in a log cabin with dirty children swarming around?"

Flint gulped. "What—?" he started to splutter.

"Don't ever kiss me like that again," Jennifer Smith said. "Not ever."

She walked away from him then, and he could see her dim shape in the shadows, moving out toward some of the picketed animals. He walked on, stumbling over another picket rope, cursing, and then going on until he was standing beside the gray gelding, stroking its neck. He stood there for some time, the anger running through him, more angry with himself than he was with Jennifer Smith, and then, as he started back toward the fire after checking the tether rope, he found himself more angered at Jennifer's remarks concerning Portia Wilde. She *could* live in a log cabin, and her children would be *clean,* and she could accept the hardships as well as any girl, if she wanted to, if she loved a man sufficiently.

The odd thought came to him as he stepped between two wagons and walked toward the drilling men. She was capable of these things, but would she be happy?

he was eighteen he'd kissed a Creek girl and that had been her response.

He still held her, but her arms were at her sides, and she made no move to lift them. She said slowly, "What was that for, Flint?"

Flint released her. He stepped back and he was frowning now. He said, "Pay you back."

It was a stupid and immature reply and he knew it, but there was nothing else he could say at the moment. He was a MacKeithan again, and the Cherokee had fled to the hills, and he was alone and embarrassed, knowing that he'd done wrong.

"That is no answer," Jennifer Smith said.

"I kissed you," Flint growled. "A man kisses a woman."

"You would rather have kissed Portia Wilde," Jennifer told him. "Is that not right?"

It was ridiculous to deny it. He knew it and she knew it. She'd known it that first afternoon in Westport when she'd looked at Portia smiling in the carriage, and she'd seen the expression on Flint's face as he stood on the walk—gazing up at her.

Flint looked away. He took a deep breath and then he looked up at the sky, wondering why she had to talk this way after she'd kissed him first.

"It's true, isn't it?" Jennifer asked him.

"I'm a hunter," Flint said with a trace of bitterness. "Miss Wilde is an Eastern girl, a fairly

realized that this was her way, the little defense mechanism she'd set up. She had to joke about everything in order to conceal her real emotions.

"I'm obliged anyway," Flint MacKeithan said, and he took a step closer until he was almost touching her. She was standing back against the wagon, and he thought he saw the surprise come into her face. She looked up at him, lips parted slightly, eyes wide.

The blood of the cautious MacKeithans warred against the Cherokee in him, but the Cherokee predominated. At the other end of the camp they could hear Tom Partridge's hard, brittle voice as he drilled the raw recruits in the manual of arms, but here they were alone in the shadows with an occasional horse moving at the end of a picket rope, a coyote lifting its mournful cry to the night sky.

Flint MacKeithan put his arms around the girl, drawing her to him hard, and then he kissed her just as hard, and when he lifted his head finally he said, almost as an apology, "That was to pay you back."

He was a little disturbed and unsure of himself now because she had not responded the way he'd thought she would. She'd accepted his kiss and she hadn't tried to break away from him. She'd accepted it the way an Indian squaw would accept a kiss, stolidly, without emotion, possibly wondering a little at a white man's ways. When

She stood there, looking straight at him. She was hatless tonight, and her dark hair was fluffed a bit by the night breeze. "Going out to look at my mules," she explained.

Flint ran his tongue across his lips, and then he remembered how she'd kissed him that night in the grove along the Missouri. He remembered that he hadn't asked for that nor had he made any advances. The kiss had disturbed him then, as the remembrance of it was disturbing him now. He'd been kissed by a woman then, not by a girl, and by a woman to whom he'd had an appeal.

Standing there so very close to her now, looking down into her small, oval face, pale in the star-light, and with the starlight in her dark eyes, the Indian strain in him came to the fore. He was a man, and a man needed a woman, and Portia Wilde was still as far away as those distant stars, maybe never for him. Jennifer Smith was here, a frontier girl with the freedom of the border in her. She'd kissed him but she'd probably kissed other men, and it meant nothing.

His voice was not steady as he spoke. He said, "Reckon I didn't thank you for coming out after me this afternoon. That Corwin and his crew would have had my scalp."

"We were looking for stray animals, too," Jennifer said, "not just stray Tennessee hunters."

She was smiling a little as she spoke, and he

he was here to stay. Moose Clemens had been telling him of the faraway mountains and the vast buffalo herds grazing on the other side of the Arkansas, of bears standing higher than the heads of horses, of vast grazing land where a man with a few head of cattle could in a very short time become a rancher of means.

He wanted to see the country and then he wanted to settle down, and when he settled he was going to need someone in his house—someone who loved the country as he did, and who would be willing to tough it out in the lean days and the good. Even though he knew how foolish it was, the thought kept persisting that there was a girl with this outfit—a girl with golden hair and calm violet eyes, a girl who could shoot with a gun and ride a horse, a girl unafraid even here in a strange and dangerous country. He'd watched her with the Osages on the ridge, and there had been no fear in her, where another Eastern girl would have fainted at the sight of them.

Stepping over a picket rope, Flint swung around the wagon tongue of one of the parked freight wagons, and then nearly bumped into a small dark figure coming the other way. In the starlight he recognized Jennifer Smith, and he said rather gruffly, "Be safer for you to stay near the fires. This is a rough crowd, and there aren't too many women around."

"I can take care of myself," Jennifer told him.

few yards from Clayton Wilde and his niece, and Bannerman had a cigar in his mouth, his legs crossed and arms folded on his chest. His hat was pulled low over his eyes, and Flint could only see the lower part of his face in the firelight as the men drilled. There was no expression around his mouth.

Again, Flint found himself wondering about this cool, courageous Easterner, second in command of this expedition which might lead to the death of all of them. Bannerman did not seem like a man who would throw his life away recklessly. If he were to die he liked good odds, as on the ridge with the Osages. On the ridge it had been a fifty-fifty chance that the Indian with the rifle would use it. Flint MacKeithan did not like to think of the odds on this Santa Fe filibustering expedition.

When another squad took the place of the first, Flint moved out of the firelight, walking back behind the corral of wagons to have a look at the gray he'd picketed close by.

Off to the west he could hear a coyote howling on a ridge, a weird, ghostly sound, different from the deeper cry of wolves he'd heard in the Tennessee hills.

He liked this vast country with its enormous bowl of a sky filled with stars, and the clean, fresh night air, unlike the damp air of the hills. He liked it better than the hills and he knew

support from this bunch. The Westport crowd likely won't even shoot a gun, an' the others might break an' run if it comes to a fight. Other way around, it might not be so bad. Government down in Santa Fe is weaker than a day-old colt. If the army officers are bribed to walk out of it, there might not even be a fight. This mob marches up to the governor's palace an' they stick a gun in Governor Armiijo's belly. That's all the fightin' there might be."

"What about the Mexico City government?" Flint wanted to know.

Moose spat again. "There's the rub," he murmured. "Maybe they won't take this serious an' maybe they will. If they're marchin' a battalion up from Mexico City now with some o' their best cavalry, we're rollin' right into the pit o' hell, boys. I'm thinkin' o' that funeral pyre. Burnin' dead men don't smell good. I smelled 'em."

"Run across some live men didn't smell too good, either." Otey Higgins grinned.

"You won't laugh," Moose Clemens told him, "when they hoist the red flag and sound the *deguello*."

"What in hell is that?" Otey wanted to know.

"No quarter," the big trapper stated. "They sounded it at the Alamo when Travis wouldn't give up. It ain't a pretty sound to hear when you're on the other end of it."

Jay Bannerman was sitting on a camp stool a

beginning to form in her mind concerning the propriety of her uncle's actions.

He, of course, was posing as a liberator, but guns in the hands of liberators were just as deadly as guns in the hands of cutthroats and border ruffians. Blood had to be spilled in order to achieve Clayton Wilde's objective, and Portia Wilde, while not as squeamish as other Eastern women, still had not seen men die.

Otey Higgins and Moose Clemens stood with Flint just outside the firelight watching one of the squads, and then the Moose spat and said, "Damn easy firin' at air with no cartridges in them rifles, an' nobody shootin' back at you. I wonder how many o' them boys will stand there that easy with a line o' Mexican regulars comin' at 'em lances shinin' in the sun."

"You had 'em come at you, Moose?" Otey asked.

The giant looked at him. "I was all through the Texan War," he stated quietly. "Damn near got into the Alamo, too, but them Mexicans had it surrounded so's a flea couldn't crawl through. I seen the funeral pyre when they burned Travis an' his boys after shootin' 'em to hell."

"What chance does this little outfit have?" Flint asked him in a low voice.

Moose shrugged. "Mr. Wilde's talkin' big about the support he'll git down in Santa Fe," he said. "One thing I'll say. He ain't gettin' too much

the stars beginning to come out, few of the men even bothered to set up the tarpaulin shelters, content to crawl under the wagons or sleep in their blankets out in the open.

That evening, when the meal was over, Tom Partridge gave the expedition its first military lesson, not marching because the men had marched all afternoon and were tired, but a lesson in the proper handling of firearms.

He divided the company up into squads, giving each of them rifles from the boxes in one of the wagons, and then teaching them how to load, fire, and reload in unison.

Clayton Wilde watched from a camp stool in front of his tent, approval on his thin, hatchet face. Portia stood behind him, and as Flint watched one squadron going through the motions, he thought he saw the first signs of worry come into the dark eyes of this golden-haired girl.

Up until this night they'd been planning an expedition to New Mexico, and it was to be a glorious, soul-stirring affair with the New Mexicans cheering them on, and liberty and happiness in store for the underprivileged. Back East, it had all sounded wonderful, and it was like a game to be played, but now she was watching grim-faced men with rifles in their hands, and this was no longer a game. Men were going to die. She was becoming aware of that fact now, and it frightened her. Possibly, the first faint doubt was

Chapter Ten

FLINT WAS ASLEEP atop the second wagon in line when they pulled away from Willow Fork that afternoon. The hot sun blazed down on him, but he scarcely felt it or noticed it. Otey Higgins and Moose Clemens were asleep on top of other wagons in the line, neither of them having had much sleep the previous night, either.

The other men of the expedition trudged along sullenly, as usual, many of them half tempted to turn back, and Flint's last thought before he went to sleep was Why didn't they? He noticed that Tom Partridge had point riders out in front of the line of slowly moving wagons, and a rear guard was watching the spare animals.

It was six o'clock in the evening and still plenty of light in the sky when they rolled off the trail at Snake Spring. Flint climbed down from the wagon to help unyoke some of the oxen and then drive them out to graze. They'd made fifteen miles that afternoon, which was good time, and the night was clear.

Miraculously, the mud and water had dried up on the plains a few hours after the sun rose, and it was a dry, comfortable camp that night. With

girl, too, a girl for whom he would have gladly died, only she didn't know about how he felt, and there was a very strong possibility that she never would.

"We are pulling out of here in an hour," Clayton Wilde said. "I suggest that you catch up on your sleep on top of one of the wagons, MacKeithan. The other herders will be doing the same."

He went off with Bannerman, and Tom Partridge rode his horse out to the ox herd to get them started. Portia sat down on an upturned box across the fire, watching Flint quizzically. She said finally, "We really were worried about you, Flint."

"Me," Flint murmured, "or the oxen?"

"You, of course," Portia laughed lightly. "We can always buy more oxen. We could have sent back to Westport for them."

"Reckon you can always get more recruits, too," Flint told her.

"We can only get one Flint MacKeithan," Portia Wilde said, smiling, "and we are very proud to have you."

Flint saw Jennifer Smith stepping down from the windwagon on the other side of the semi-circle. They'd just rolled the light wagon up from the creek bottom where they'd stopped it.

Jennifer saw them across the enclosure, but she looked away quickly, and then went into her tent.

Portia Wilde said softly, "She's a very fine girl, Flint."

Flint kept on eating. He nodded slightly but didn't say anything. The food had lost much of its taste for him. He was speaking to a very nice

Tom Partridge and Jay Bannerman came out to meet him, both men smiling, pleased at his return and the return of the stock.

Bannerman said, "You had us worried, Flint."

Flint dismounted. Over his tin cup of black coffee and plate of bacon and beans, he told them of the encounter with Corwin's outfit.

"You didn't see Ortiz?" Bannerman asked.

"I recognized only Corwin," Flint told him. "Ortiz may have been with them, though."

"Or he may have been back in Westport," Bannerman said and scowled, "rounding up an even bigger crew to take after us. I'm afraid we haven't seen the last of him."

Flint watched Portia Wilde and her uncle walking over, and both of them greeted him warmly, Clayton Wilde shaking his hand, thanking him for bringing in the stampeded cattle.

"We owe the success of this expedition," Mr. Wilde told him sincerely, "to the efforts and zeal of men like yourself, MacKeithan."

"Some day," Jay Bannerman said with a grin, "the New Mexicans might erect a monument to you, Flint, out of gratitude."

Flint looked at him over the coffee cup. It was a joke, and even Portia was smiling a little. He noticed, however, that Tom Partridge wasn't smiling. The wagonmaster stood a little behind Bannerman and he was looking at the man intently, a shadow in his hazel eyes.

"I'm obliged," Flint said to her, and she nodded.

"Them oxen must o' run like hell last night," Moose Clemens observed. "How many you bringin' in?"

"Thirty-three," Flint told him.

"We lost two, all told," Moose stated, "which ain't bad fer a night like last night. Partridge was worried, though, about this band. If we'd o' lost them, he'd been in a fix."

Windwagon Smith was all smiles. He ordered the sail hoisted again, and in a few moments they were gliding across the plains, running parallel with the trail. Watching it from the rear, Flint could spot its good points and its weaknesses. The light wagon could really make time, but it had to avoid every rock or rut in its path or else the light wheels would be smashed from the impact. Also, when the summit of a low grade blocked off some of the breeze, the wagon immediately slowed down, and Flint could not picture a large, heavily loaded freight wagon being propelled by this force. He wondered if the astute Mr. Smith mentioned these facts when boasting about his windwagon to the public.

When they neared the camp, Smith pulled out wide again, away from the grazing ox herd so as not to frighten them, and Flint rode straight into the camp, noticing that the stock he'd been running back had joined the others on the grazing ground.

Windwagon Smith guide his wagon up along the trail and then veer away, knowing that it would smash to pieces if it hit those deep ruts at the rate of speed with which it was moving.

Jennifer had picked up a rifle now, and she, too, was firing at the raiders. When Flint opened up with his pistol, they had enough. At a signal from Corwin, riding a big dapple-gray animal, they headed north again.

Flint watched the windwagon come around, Jennifer manipulating the big sail cleverly. They came into the breeze, tacking nicely, Jennifer letting the sail flap down loosely as they drew near Flint, and her father applying a wheel brake, bringing the wagon to an easy stop.

Otey waved his rifle as Flint rode up to them. "Chased 'em off," he said jubilantly. "What in hell you think o' this contraption now, Flint?"

Flint looked at Jennifer Smith sitting silently on the wagon side, looking at him. He said, "You saved that bunch of stock and maybe my life."

"Corwin with that bunch?" Moose growled. "Thought I saw that devil."

"His crowd," Flint nodded. "They jumped me when I was running the stock back to the camp."

"Had us worried," Otey told him. "Everybody else come in early this mornin', but not you. Miss Jennifer's idea usin' the windwagon. She figured we'd cover a lot more ground lookin' for you, an' she was right."

right side of the trail and he had the satisfaction of seeing this rider's horse stumble and go down, the rider jumping clear, rolling as he hit the ground. Then he started to move up through the moving oxen, ready to break clear, and it was then that he saw the windwagon bearing down toward them soundlessly, it's broad, square sail puffed out, moving faster than a running horse.

The well-greased wheels whipped through the low grass over a flat stretch of open plain, veering off toward the right as it neared the trail, and heading straight for the riders coming up on that side.

At a distance of two hundred yards, Flint could see four people in the wagon. The roly-poly Smith was at the rudder handle in the rear, guiding the strange craft. Jennifer was up in the bow with two men—one of them the gigantic Moose Clemens, a rifle in his hands, and the other man—smaller, also red-haired—Otey Higgins.

Moose's rifle cracked, and one of Corwin's men lurched from the saddle. They'd pulled up and were staring at the wagon in consternation as Flint, grinning, left the trail too and crossed to intercept the wagon, the oxen continuing down the trail toward the camp.

Otey Higgins opened up with his rifle, sending a bullet whistling over the heads of the riders. They'd all stopped now and had moved across to the opposite side of the trail. Flint watched

slow-moving oxen he could make it to the Wilde camp, but it meant that he'd lose the valuable stock after all his efforts to save them the previous night.

Glancing behind him, he saw the dozen men throwing saddles on the horses, ripping up picket stakes, and he gained precious minutes and precious yards as they did so.

When they eventually pounded out on the trail he was nearly a mile ahead of them, the oxen still moving fast, but beginning to pant, and Flint was finding it more difficult all the time to keep them going. He fired his gun into the air, riding up close behind the laggards, and then reloaded as he rode after them, but when he looked over his shoulder he could see Corwin's crew closing the gap rapidly.

He figured that he was still five or six miles from the Wilde camp, too far for them to hear his shots and come to the rescue. Corwin's crew opened fire on him when they were a hundred and fifty yards behind, and turning in the saddle, he sent two bullets back at them, forcing the leaders to slow down a little.

They started to spread out, then, leaving the trail, forming a fan of riders, coming up on either side of his moving herd, and he realized that he had to make his decision very shortly—either to leave the oxen or be riddled with bullets.

He fired another shot at a rider coming up on the

he came abreast of their camp he lifted a hand laconically, hoping they wouldn't recognize him or the stock he was driving. Other Santa Fe-bound outfits were on this trail, and he hoped they would assume he was from some other outfit which had lost stock during the storm and was now running them back.

He was sure that Corwin would recognize him if he stopped to talk, and if Pablo Ortiz, the Mexican agent, was with the outfit, he undoubtedly would remember him and deal with him accordingly.

Corwin called something to him and started to walk toward the trail. Flint waved again and kept going, trying to pretend that he'd only been hailed. Corwin called sharply, and this time Flint heard him distinctly.

"Hold up," Corwin ordered.

Again Flint waved back, but when he saw Corwin turn and give an order to the men with him and then slip a gun from his holster and send a shot in his direction, Flint took out his own Walker-Colt, fired once at Corwin, again into the air to start the oxen moving at a rapid run, and galloped down the trail.

Corwin's men were running for their picketed horses as Flint rode on grimly, yelling at the moving oxen, knowing that in a very short time Corwin and his crew would be on top of him. There was a good possibility that if he left the

He picked up two other steers on the way, lone animals which had become lost during the night, adding them to his string.

An hour or so before noon, still heading due south, he hit the trail, the deep-rutted wagon tracks, a full eight inches below the surface of the surrounding plains, heading south and west.

It was easier keeping the stock in line now, since they preferred moving along the beaten path. Remembering this section of the trail from the previous day's travel, Flint figured that they were another hour's drive from the camp. He hadn't eaten since the wet supper they'd had early in the evening, and it was nearly noon now. He pushed on steadily, anxious to reach the camp, and it was then that he saw the party of men camped on a small ridge a hundred yards up off the trail.

He came upon them quite suddenly as he pushed the herd of oxen over a summit. There were a dozen of them, without wagons, their horses picketed on the plains behind them, and all of the men standing near a small, smokeless cookfire, staring straight at him.

Even at the distance Flint recognized one of the men immediately, standing a little apart from the others—a man with a brown leather vest, black, flat-crowned hat, broken at the brim, a man with yellow hair, and green eyes—Lace Corwin.

Hunching his shoulders, Flint rode on, and as

quarter of a mile away as he sat his horse on the edge of a small grove. He was wet to the skin and hungry, but there was nothing to do about food now.

Dismounting, he unsaddled the gray, spread the blanket and the saddle in the sun to dry, and then entered the grove. In ten minutes he'd found sufficient dry wood to start a fire, and then stripping his wet clothes from his body, he hung them on sticks in front of the fire, drying them thoroughly before putting them on again.

He felt much better an hour later after he'd saddled the gray and was riding slowly out toward the grazing oxen. He was in a country of high plains, riding through hock-high grass. Occasional groves broke the monotony of the rolling, grassy country. Far to the west were a series of sand hills, barren and lifeless. He saw no game, no signs of life.

The oxen were reluctant to move after their long run of the previous night, and Flint had a little difficulty getting them started toward the south. The sun was blazing hot and the sky clear blue as they started the long trek back. The buzzing of insects and the croak of frogs in old buffalo hollows, now rain-filled, pervaded the air.

Flint jogged along steadily, breaking the gray to the right and then to the left, urging on the plodding oxen who wanted to graze and to rest.

Chapter Nine

IT SEEMED TO Flint that he'd ridden for several hours, the first breakneck gallop eventually turning into a long, steady, mile-consuming jog, before the oxen slowed down. Several times he'd tried to turn them, but in doing so, always lost the group which persistently refused to follow the leaders, and after a while he gave it up and was content to ride with them, waiting until their strength gave out and the fear in them subsided.

The rain stopped toward morning, and there were only occasional deep rumbles of thunder to the west when the first gray light came into the sky. He counted thirty-one animals in the group he'd been following, which was almost a third of the herd, and he was glad now that he'd stayed with them. With one-third of the oxen gone, the Wilde expedition would have been severely handicapped.

When the sun came up he was considerably north of the trail. He did not know how many miles, but he realized it would be well after noon before he could get the stock back to the wagon corral. They were grazing calmly on the plains a

he'd been trying to turn, and he realized that it was almost useless. The only alternative lay in keeping with the animals running north, riding with them until they became exhausted, and then running them back to the encampment in the morning when the storm was over. It meant a long night in the saddle and in the rain, with always the possibility of a deep draw opening up in front of them as they plunged through the night, and death at the bottom of the draw.

Flint MacKeithan tried to think of more pleasant things as he rode the gray gelding at top speed across the plains. He thought of Portia Wilde back in her tent at the encampment, and occasionally he thought of Jennifer Smith, who'd cried because he'd treated her unkindly.

hills. Here the entire sky was revealed, miles upon miles of it, and the lightning ripped across it in jagged streaks.

A bolt struck a nearby cottonwood, snapping off the top half of the tree, toppling it to the ground, and there was the smell of sulphur and burning wood in the air. Flint's gray bucked when the lightning struck less than fifty yards from where he sat watching the herd. A number of oxen also tried to break away from the huddle, but they were driven back, and then a bolt struck the center of the mass of animals.

There was a blinding, crackling flash of light, blending with the bang of the thunder, and then the herd was off, scattering in all directions, as Otey Higgins had predicted. A fear-crazed bull whipped past Flint, horns grazing the horse. Other animals were plunging toward him, and he had to jerk the gray around to avoid being struck. The gray gelding started to run, too, racing along with some of the stock heading north.

The other herders were yelling, firing guns to turn back the maddened animals. In the rain Flint saw the flash of their guns. Spurring the gray, he pulled up ahead of the oxen which had broken to his side of the circle, trying to turn them toward the left, thus eventually running them back in the direction from which they'd come.

As he turned some animals, another came up on his right, swinging away from the group

more and more nervous as the night wore on and the storm grew worse.

Ordinarily, two or three men would have been out with a herd this small, but Tom Partridge was taking no chances that they'd bolt and end up in a ravine or run back to Westport.

The eight men on assignment rode 'round and 'round the herd, passing and repassing each other in the dim light with the thunder sounding like a cannonade and the lightning rippling across the blackened sky.

The bolts were coming closer and closer, several times striking hills and ridges in the vicinity, and Flint waited for the moment when a bolt would smash into that huddled mass of oxen. It seemed almost inevitable.

Otey Higgins said once, "Thing surprises me is that they ain't run off already. Reckon if I were an ox, I'd be headin' back to Westport fast as my legs could carry me, an' for more reasons than one."

Flint just smiled and kept riding, driving back drifters from the herd when they started to wander, calling to them in low tones to reassure them. The thunder and the lightning seemed to be coming all around them now, and he realized that at last they were in the center of the storm.

The lightning was awe inspiring, seeming to flash from one end of the sky to the other, unlike anything Flint had seen back in the Tennessee

124

back in Westport, and we'll start this trip all over again."

"What happens," Otey asked, "if them damn critters all start runnin' in different directions, which is what they'll likely do."

"Watch for the leaders," Partridge repeated. "If you have to split up and follow different groups, do so. It'll be easier rounding them up in the morning."

The eight men rode away from the encampment, each having had a cup of hot coffee from the pot boiling over the flickering flames. They rode out with the rain beating down on them, their horses' hoofs sloshing in the mud, making sucking sounds as the hoofs came up. A peal of thunder close by set the horse of a herdsman to bucking, and he had difficulty retaining his seat.

The stock had been taken about a mile from the encampment, and Flint, as chief herdsman for his group of guards, located the grim, thoroughly wet, and disgusted guards on duty, relieving them.

The man to whom he spoke rode off grumbling, cursing to himself. There were over a hundred head of oxen in the herd, most of the riding horses and mules having been picketed close to the wagons because of the storm. They were restless, unable to sleep tonight, and when the lightning flashed Flint could see them, huddled close together, bellowing occasionally, growing

He fell asleep with the steady patter of the rain on the canvas overhead and the sound of the wind in the willows along the small creek near which they'd camped. He was still thinking of Jennifer Smith, and the tears in her eyes, when Otey shook him by the shoulder.

"Time to git up, Flint."

Flint sat up immediately, kicking off his blanket. It was still raining, and the rumble of thunder was heavier. Lightning skipped across the hills to the west, not just the glow of it in the sky, but the real thing, and Otey said, "Reckon we're in fer it, Flint."

Flint put on his hat and then slipped into a Mexican serape which was part of his equipment, especially for nights like this. The serape went over his shoulders like a cape and would shed some of the rain.

Otey Higgins wore a similar coat, and they plodded out to where they'd tied their horses earlier in the evening. There were a half-dozen men going out with them to relieve the herdsmen on duty tonight. Flint found them with Tom Partridge out in front of the Wilde tent, and the wagonmaster gave them their instructions.

"If they bolt," Partridge said, his face just a blur in the darkness and the falling rain, "go after the leaders and try to turn them. If you get them to running in a circle they'll tire themselves out. If you can't turn them, they won't stop until they're

up the guards for the night watch. Flint drew the midnight-to-three watch, along with Otey Higgins, Partridge wanting some of the most dependable men out with the stock during those critical hours.

As they stood around the cookfire or squatted under the tarpaulin shelters, the rain came down harder than ever, turning the sandy stretch of ground on which they'd camped into a morass. Across the encampment, Flint could see the flickering fire in front of the windwagon.

Jay Bannerman was in the large tent with Clayton Wilde and Portia, having taken food to them. The rain pelted down on the canvas wagon covers, rolling off the Osnaburg sheets in rivulets, rolling off the tarpaulin shelters. Off in the distance they could still hear the roll of thunder, the western sky lighting up occasionally with the lightning flashes, but the main storm seemed to be coming no closer.

"We'll git it," Otey Higgins said glumly just before they turned in under one of the lean-tos, "soon's you an' I go out, Flint. Then we'll have to ride like hell out there in the dark, chasin' them crazy critters."

Already, just before he fell asleep, Flint could hear some of the cattle bawling nervously after a particularly heavy roll, and he wondered what would happen if it really started to crack and spit close at hand.

girl at all. "Reckon I spoke out of turn," Flint apologized.

"Why do you dislike me so?" Jennifer whispered. They'd stopped in front of her tent, and the firelight was playing on her face now. Her face was wet, but Flint could see now that it wasn't all rain.

Flustered, Flint said quickly, "Never said I disliked you, Jennifer."

"You have," Jennifer Smith told him slowly, "from the first day you saw me on the wind-wagon. I wonder if you'd seen me first instead of—" She stopped, blinking her eyes for a moment, and then she ducked in under the flap of her tent.

Walking back toward the cookfire, Flint met Moose Clemens coming up, unmindful of the rain, the water dripping from his red beard.

"Trouble up here, Flint?" he growled.

"Not any more," Flint told him, and he was thinking about Jennifer Smith. She'd been crying, and it disturbed him.

"Hell of a bunch," Moose said grimly. "Ain't twenty-five men in the whole outfit you kin depend upon. We'll set watches tonight to keep the stock from runnin' off, an' half of 'em will crawl back to the wagons an' to hell with the stock."

Flint nodded. He watched Tom Partridge ride in, and then the wagonmaster started to line

face. It was the first time he'd angered her. She stood there with the chunk of wood in her hand, glaring at him.

"Woman's got no right hittin' a man over the head with a club," the crewman growled. "It ain't ladylike."

"She's young," Flint said, and this time he saw Windwagon Smith grin a little at his daughter's discomfiture.

The crewman moved off with his horse and his picket rope, and Flint turned to go, too. He heard Jennifer coming up beside him, touching his arm.

"Just a minute, Mr. MacKeithan," she said stiffly. "I am not young."

Flint shrugged. "Figured you were," he said. He looked down at her. She, too, had a blanket around her shoulders to keep off the rain and she looked small, almost pathetic in the dim evening light, her face wet with rain.

"I've taken care of myself and my father for nearly three years now," Jennifer said slowly. "I am not a child, Mr. MacKeithan."

She'd always called him Flint before, and his formal name sounded strange in her mouth.

"All right," Flint murmured, and he was a little ashamed of belittling her, not thinking that it would make such an impression. He was surprised that she was showing such emotion because he hadn't thought she was an emotional

said thickly, "How the hell many wagon captains we got around here, mister?"

Tom Partridge had left with the herdsmen and was out of the camp for a few minutes. Flint had seen Bannerman at the other end of the camp helping to set up Portia Wilde's tent. He hadn't seen the trouble brewing.

Flint said quietly, "Who had his picket stakes in first?"

"I did," Windwagon Smith snapped. "This fellow wants me to move."

"He ain't even a member o' this outfit," the yellow-haired man growled. "Why in hell should he get the best grass fer his damn mules?"

"Mr. Wilde gave him permission to travel with us," Flint stated. "Talk to Bannerman if you want an argument."

"All I'm wantin'," the man snapped, "is grass for my ridin' horse."

"Plenty of grass up on the ridge," Flint said, pointing his finger. "Move your animal."

The yellow-haired man didn't want a fight. Most men in Westport had seen or heard of Flint's epic fight with Moose Clemens, and they didn't want to sample his hard fists. Backing down now, he had to save face so he said gruffly, "That girl's too free with her club, MacKeithan. She's runnin' into trouble around here."

Flint nodded. "Reckon you're right there," he agreed and he saw the anger come into Jennifer's

Yanking hard, Flint jerked him from under the lean-to, sending him slithering across the mud. When he tried to scramble to his feet, slipping and cursing, Flint put a boot against his left shoulder and shoved hard, sending him over on his face. Covered with mud now, he righted himself and glared at Flint uncertainly, a fairly big man himself, but not as big as Flint.

"All right," Flint said softly. "Come and get it."

The crewman didn't come. He muttered something under his breath as he stood there in the falling rain, his face and clothes muddy, and then he crawled under the lean-to again.

Jennifer Smith had watched Flint for a moment as she got up on her feet, and then she'd retrieved her club and was advancing on the yellow-haired man who was still kicking the stake loose. Flint followed her, giving the silent men under the lean-to a hard look as he went by.

He saw her poke the yellow-haired man in the back with the chunk of wood, and when he turned around she brought the club down across his head, knocking him to his knees.

He got up, reeling a little, but only temporarily stunned, and as he started toward Jennifer, who'd stepped over to her father's side, Flint came in between them, putting a hand against the man's chest.

The yellow-haired man glared at him and then

to be having an altercation with one of the men from the other wagons, who was picketing a riding horse in the same vicinity.

The argument seemed to be getting quite loud, and Flint saw Jennifer look up from the fire. He started to walk that way, knowing that the men were in a bad mood tonight, and that it might go hard with the roly-poly Windwagon Smith if one of them lost his temper.

Other men, sitting under the lean-tos near the Smith wagon, were watching and grinning as the voices became louder. Evidently, the crewman wanted Smith to move one of his pickets, and the fat man refused to do so, having staked out his animals first, on good grass.

As Flint neared the scene he saw the crewman, a big, red-faced fellow with a shock of yellow hair, kick at one of Smith's stakes, loosening it. The fat man was pointing a finger at him, his voice rising in anger as he protested.

Jennifer left the fire and started that way, a chunk of firewood in her hand. As she moved past one of the lean-tos, another man stuck his boot out, tripping her. She went down heavily on the now muddy ground, the stick falling from her hands.

Before she could recover, the man under the lean-to had reached out and grasped her arms, pinioning them to her sides. He was grinning as Flint came up and grasped him by the left boot.

little hunter grinned. "They pretty rough on you, Flint?"

"Reckon they'll make trouble," Flint told him, "if you let them."

"Wait'll we hit real Indian country," Otey said. "Them Comanches an' Kiowas are wild as hell, Moose tells me."

Flint picketed the gray gelding close to one of the wagons, in case he would need the animal during the night. The men were setting up tarpaulins out from the sides of some of the wagons, forming lean-tos under which they would sleep that night. The two tents for Clayton Wilde and his niece were thrown up, and Flint saw Clayton Wilde in the larger tent, seated at a camp table, writing by lantern light.

The rain came just as the cook got his big fire going, and the raindrops sizzled in the flames. Glum, dispirited men sat under the tarpaulins or stretched on blankets under the wagons, almost too tired to eat, and the cook fussed around the fire, cursing the falling rain, a blanket around his shoulders, hat pulled low on his face, as he manipulated his big pots.

The dozen wagons had been arranged in horseshoe form tonight, set fairly close together. Smith's windwagon was on the outer edge of the semicircle, and Flint saw Jennifer getting supper over a small fire. Her father was picketing the two mules behind the wagon, and he seemed

Chapter Eight

THEY CAMPED AT Willow Fork that night, thirty-five miles from Westport Landing, with the thunderheads building up in the west, and the dank smell of rain in the air. An hour or so before sunset the sun had become hazy. A stillness came to the open plains as the breeze died down, and off in the distance they could hear the faint rumble of thunder.

Tom Partridge said disgustedly to Flint, "I'd been hoping for a few days of clear weather to get this outfit accustomed to the trail. If this storm hits us during the night, we might have every head of stock racing back to Westport before morning."

"Might miss us," Flint mused. He watched the men driving the stock out to graze and he noticed that Partridge had assigned dependable herders to the job—men from the Eastern battalion. The other men slumped to the ground as soon as the wagons stopped and the oxen were unyoked.

Otey Higgins had been assigned to head the first watch on the herd, and before he rode out he had a few words with Flint.

"Heard you had a run-in with the Osages." The

persons. He was the smooth, pleasant, polite, and courageous Easterner whom everyone liked and respected, and he was the Bannerman who rode at his side now, ruefully considering the unnecessary death he'd narrowly missed. He was a man who had plans—elaborate plans.

and all six whirled their ponies and rode away in the direction from which they'd come.

Jay Bannerman took a cigar from his shirt pocket and put it in his mouth. He said, "A little too close for comfort. Glad you came up, Flint."

"Never go without a gun in this part of the country," Flint said, scowling, "especially when you're escorting a woman."

"I needn't be told that twice," Bannerman said dryly. He had his cigar going now and he started to puff on it as they turned and rode after Portia who'd stopped and was waiting for them on the next ridge. He didn't speak again until they were within a hundred yards of the waiting girl, and then he said meditatively, "That would have been a strange freak of fate, Flint, if I'd been left up on that ridge with a half-dozen Indian arrows in me, after all the elaborate plans I've made for the future."

Flint glanced at him, surprising a very solemn expression on his handsome face. A few moments ago he'd had the deepest respect for this man who'd walked his horse directly up to a dangerous savage with a gun in his hands and the itch to kill. Now, staring directly at a girl whose life he'd endangered because of his carelessness, he was not concerned about her, but about his own fate and his own plans.

The more he knew Jay Bannerman, the more he realized that Bannerman was not one, but two

the rifle moved to get around him, Bannerman moved his mare, too, keeping always in between Flint and the rifle.

The Hawkins gun was a single-shot affair, whereas Flint's Walker-Colt could shoot six times. The Osages knew that; they knew the value of that pistol at close range, and this was close range.

"Like playing a game of chess," Bannerman grinned. "You're the king and I'm a pawn out in front of you, protecting you. They have to kill me to get at you."

The cool, cold courage of the man impressed Flint. Bannerman was an Easterner, a foolish one this afternoon, riding out without a gun, but he was displaying a brand of courage any frontiersman would envy.

They could both hear the hoofbeats of Portia's mount receding in the distance. They watched the Osages who'd seen her go, and who wanted very much to take that splendid little sorrel she'd been riding.

"Don't go after her," Flint said. "The first man who rides that way will be dead."

If they didn't understand his language, they knew what he meant by the inflection of his voice and the slight gesture he made with the gun. For several long moments the six of them stared at him, and then the buck whose arm Flint had nearly broken said something in guttural tones,

he slammed the barrel down across the forearm of the Osage.

The Indian let out a quick yelp of pain, dropped the reins, and backed his pony away rapidly. Without looking at Portia, Flint said over his shoulder, "Start riding back toward the wagon train, Miss Wilde. If any of them try to follow you, I'll shoot them."

He had his gun lined on the chest of the fellow who'd held the horse, even though he noticed that two of the others had fitted arrows to their bows and were watching him like hawks. The man with the Hawkins' rifle, the only real gun in the outfit, had retreated a few more paces, the big gun held across his chest.

Watching him, Flint realized they were not beaten as yet. If the buck threw up that gun and put a bullet through him, they could riddle Bannerman with arrows, ride after Portia Wilde, overtake her long before she could get near the slowly moving wagon train, and be gone with three horses, not to mention three scalps. He wondered if these Osages, part wild, part civilized, still took scalps when they could get away with it.

Jay Bannerman foiled any move the Osage with the rifle could make. Calmly, he moved his chestnut mare in between Flint and the Hawkins' rifle, and he sat there, smiling at the Indian, arms folded across his chest. When the buck with

and a single eagle feather in it. Only two of the six carried guns, and one of the guns was an old flintlock, which probably missed fire half the time. The others carried bows.

They were undoubtedly Osages, the Indians Moose had warned Flint about, friendly enough in the presence of a large band of white men, but treacherous where only one or two were concerned.

Without a word Flint moved around toward the Indian who was holding Portia's mount. Coming up beside him, he pointed toward the reins, indicating that the buck should let go.

The Osage stared at him, black eyes glittering. He wore a cheap gold medallion about his neck, along with a string of blue beads, and he seemed to be the tallest of the six and the leader.

Bannerman said evenly, "They evidently want our horses, Flint."

"Let go," Flint said to the Osage, looking him straight in the eye.

The Indian knew what he meant and he probably even spoke a few words of English. He said nothing, but his right hand still gripped the reins. Flint had had a fleeting look at Portia before he spoke to the Indian. She was a little paler than usual but apparently unperturbed.

The other five bucks started to close in around Flint, and he knew that he had to act very quickly or not at all. Lifting the Colt gun very suddenly,

outfit, and not so-called friendly Indians hanging around on the outskirts of the trail, begging, and stealing occasional horses and mules.

He watched the two groups converge, and he put the gray to a full gallop now as he dipped down into a hollow out of sight of the riders ahead. When he came up out of the indentation he was within a half mile of the group on the ridge summit ahead.

They were Indians. The horses they rode were varicolored-browns splashed with white, black ponies with white faces and legs. There were six of them and they formed a semicircle around Bannerman and Portia.

Sliding his Colt from the holster, Flint came on as fast as he could and he saw one of the Indians come away from the group to stare at him. He saw something he did not like; another Indian was grasping the reins of Portia Wilde's mount. The animal, frightened by the smell of the Indian, was trying to break away, and Portia was having difficulty remaining in the saddle.

Flint came up the grade at top speed, swinging around the lone Indian who'd left the group. The six who'd stopped Bannerman and the girl were unlike any Indians he'd seen around West-port. Two of them wore men's trousers, but the other four were in buckskin—buckskin shirts and fringed leggings. They were lean, brown men, with thin hawk faces, lank black hair, braided,

Pulling up the gray, Flint stared for several moments. This was not Indian country, but there were occasional friendly Indians to be met on the open plains west of Westport. There were Osages and Delawares, and some Shawnee reservation Indians, but Moose Clemens had stated emphatically that no man was safe among any Indians, friendly or otherwise, if he didn't carry a gun. Many a lone rider had disappeared in this territory because he'd ridden a good horse and because he'd failed to carry a firearm, believing that he were safe.

"Seen many a good boy rubbed out by a friendly Osage," Moose had growled. "Make sure you're carryin' a gun, Flint."

Flint was quite sure Jay Bannerman hadn't worn a gun when he went off with Portia Wilde. They'd both been riding good horses, and if those half-dozen dots moving toward them were Osages, it could mean trouble.

Glancing back toward the wagons a half mile behind him, Flint kicked the gray into action, a little angered that Bannerman had been so foolish as to take a woman almost out of sight of the wagon train. He noticed that Bannerman and Portia had stopped and were watching the oncoming riders, probably unable to identify them as yet, and thinking they were white men.

Riding hard now, Flint MacKeithan hoped fervently that they were white men from another

"You mean by kissing him?" Jennifer grinned.

Flint glared at her. "You kiss everybody you meet?" he snapped.

"Every handsome man who will stand still," Jennifer chuckled. "Don't think you were the first one."

"I don't," Flint growled. "Try it on Bannerman."

"Thinking about it," Jennifer said and laughed lightly. "He is very handsome. I would say even more so than you."

Flint just looked at her and then urged the gray ahead. He was still riding at the head of the column when Bannerman and Portia came up, Portia on a little sorrel, riding side saddle, and riding very easily. They were both laughing and chatting gaily as they swept by him, Bannerman lifting a hand in greeting.

For some time Flint watched them enviously as they moved up a slope and down the other side. For the hundredth time he wondered if he were a fool, following in Bannerman's wake. This beautiful girl with the violet eyes, a girl who could ride and shoot a gun and who feared nothing was not for him.

He watched them ride on ahead until they were almost out of sight of the wagon train, two dots moving on the horizon, and then he saw a number of smaller dots, at least a dozen in number, moving toward them from the west.

wagons. As he passed the Wilde wagon Portia looked out at him. She was wearing a sun bonnet and a gray traveling dress, and as usual she looked cool and calm. Flint said to her, "Pretty hot in there, Miss Wilde."

"I don't mind it," Portia answered. "Tomorrow, I believe I shall ride one of the horses."

Bannerman swung up along the other side of the wagon and he said gallantly, "I'll bring you up a saddled horse now, Portia, if you'd care to try it. These Western horses are not like the gentled Eastern mounts."

"I accept your challenge." Portia laughed gaily.

Flint rode on as Bannerman swung back toward the herd. As he passed Smith's windwagon he saw Jennifer getting ready to crack the whip, the two mules being in the traces. Her father, evidently, was inside the wagon sleeping.

"Everything all right here?" Flint asked her gruffly. He hadn't quite forgotten that kiss she'd given him, an unsolicited kiss, and during the few days they'd been in camp, he'd deliberately stayed away from her. His previous opinion of her remained the same. She was brash, unladylike, entirely too forward.

Jennifer said, "It's a long trail to Santa Fe. I was wondering if you would speak to me before we reached there."

Flint frowned. "You have a way of crossing a man."

these boys are scrappin' an' we ain't ten miles from Westport. There's eight hundred miles to go, an' storm an' dust an' desert an' Injuns an' stampedes ahead of us, not to mention what we got waitin' fer us when we reach Santa Fe."

"You want to follow those men?" Flint asked him.

Higgins laughed. "Reckon I'm a curious man," he said. "Kind o' curious to see how this thing works out. Like to keep the hair on my head, if I kin, an' I don't want to be killed so dead that I can't enjoy myself any more, but I'm curious, Flint."

The reluctant crewmen were bringing in the harnessed oxen now, and Moose was having a little difficulty with a fat, greasy-faced man who'd gone to sleep under a wagon after eating a prodigious quantity of bacon and sourdough bread.

"Roll out!" Moose roared. "Roll out, you monkey's uncle."

The other Westport men watched him grimly, bitterly, as he grasped the fat man by the boots and jerked him out into the open, sending him reeling across the grass.

"Ain't a real man in this crew," Clemens growled when he came over to Flint and Otey. "If they ever even git to Santa Fe, I'll eat a mule's head."

Flint mounted and rode up along the string of

an army, Bannerman, in the strictest sense of the word. None of these men have signed papers of any kind."

Jay Bannerman was still smiling pleasantly, but his brown eyes were lighter in color, and Flint could see that he was a man who did not like to be crossed. "I believe," he purred, "that I made it clear to these men that they were recruits in an army, and that they were expected to stand by us all the way."

"If you'd made it that clear," Partridge retorted, "they may not have agreed to come in the first place."

"Are you implying, Mr. Partridge, that I signed these men under false pretenses?"

Flint saw Otey Higgins grinning as he lay back against the rock.

Partridge got up from the wagon tongue on which he'd been sitting. "I make no implications," he said stiffly. "It is apparent that the men have left. To men of that caliber, I say good riddance."

Bannerman bowed, still smiling, and walked away. Flint saw him talking with Clayton Wilde a few moments later. Tom Partridge, his jaws set angrily, started to rout out the men from under the shade of the wagons.

Otey Higgins got up, scratching himself, still grinning. He said softly, "Reckon it ain't all peaches an' cream even up at the top, Flint. Here

in the groves along the river. The hot midday sun beat down on them. Flies buzzed around, biting, making life even more miserable, and Flint was not too surprised when, after the men had eaten, a dozen of them suddenly stood up and started to walk back up the trail in the direction of Westport.

He was reaching for his gun when Tom Partridge said quietly, "Let them go, Flint. It's better that they leave now rather than in a week or so, after we've had to feed them all that time."

Otey Higgins, sitting across from Flint, his head against a rock, spat and said, "Kind of a small army to be fightin' the Mexican Government, ain't it, Flint? Wonder how many will be left when we reach Santa Fe."

Neither Flint nor Tom Partridge said anything. Jay Bannerman came up, staring after the departing men. He said to the wagonmaster, "Are those men deserting, Tom?"

"Pulling out," Partridge nodded. "It's tougher than they thought it would be."

"You're not stopping them?" Bannerman queried.

Partridge looked at him, his hazel eyes narrowed a little. "No," he said.

"Isn't that unusual?" Bannerman smiled. "Isn't a deserter usually followed and brought to trial in the Army?"

Partridge's lips tightened a little. "This is not

dressed in white men's clothes, cultivating small patches of soil, staring at them thoughtfully as they rolled by, and then they were on the open plains with the horizon all around them, a sea of waving grass, the blue sky flecked with white clouds, prairie hens scuttering out of their path, and myriads of larks wheeling and diving above them.

There was little game this close to civilization, and Flint didn't bother to look for any. According to Moose, it would be several days as yet before they would spot anything to shoot—a deer or an antelope.

At high noon Partridge called a halt for the midday rest. Oxen, still yoked, were let out of the traces and permitted to graze nearby. Dull-eyed men, dead with fatigue and unaccustomed to this steady march for hours, the liquor fumes now vanished, threw themselves on the ground in the scant shade of the wagons, waiting for the cook to get his fire started and his huge pans of bacon sizzling.

Flint noticed that the Easterners, about thirty in number, gathered up near Clayton Wilde's wagon. These men had remained in camp the previous night, preparing for the dawn journey, and while they were greenhorns on the trail, they'd held up much better than the Westport crowd.

There was no shade here as there had been back

which, while it made a greenhorn look like a frontiersman, stiffened after the first rain and chaffed the skin.

Bannerman rode up beside Flint at the head of the column, smiling, lifting a hand to him. "Off at last," he said. "Luck on the trail, Flint."

"Might need it," Flint observed, glancing over his shoulder at the straggling line of wagons and the men plodding stolidly beside them. Many of the expedition members had gone into Westport the previous night for a last fling, and they'd had little sleep. Gray-faced, bleary-eyed, they walked beside the rumbling wagons, and Flint was thinking grimly that it was a sorry liberating army. Unless Tom Partridge were able to whip them into military shape before they reached Santa Fe, one platoon of Mexican regulars would send them scurrying over the plains like so many rabbits.

"You do not share our optimism," Bannerman said and laughed. "Think of Washington's men at Valley Forge."

Flint thought of them, remembering that the men at Valley Forge were fighting for their own homes and their own safety and prosperity. He wondered what many of these Westport drifters were fighting for, if anything. He even wondered if they *would* fight!

During the first few hours of the trip, they passed the shacks and hovels of Indian farmers

a large red and blue painted Conestoga, not the usual trail freight wagon. Six mules pulled the Conestoga, and Wilde himself handled the reins. He seemed quite expert at it, but Flint was sure he'd learned the art more from a book than experience.

There was no particular order in this early march, the line of wagons being strung out loosely. Until they passed Council Grove, one hundred and forty-odd miles to the south and west, there was no danger from Indian attack, and there was no need to send out point riders.

Partridge, however, had suggested to Flint that he occasionally move up or to the sides of the slowly moving column in case there was a party of white raiders in the vicinity, intent on running off the trailing herd.

"If Corwin and Ortiz are coming after us," Partridge had said to Flint, "they won't risk a direct attack on a party as large as ours. I am worried about nuisance raids, especially at night, stock run off, a wagon burned, supplies lost. That can hamper us badly."

Jay Bannerman sat astride a chestnut mare, riding the animal with the ease of a man who'd spent his lifetime in the saddle. He was dressed for the trail, broad-rimmed hat, flannel shirt, hickory pants, and boots. Unlike some of the other Easterners, he hadn't made the mistake of purchasing a gaudy, fringed buckskin shirt,

Chapter Seven

FIVE DAYS LATER, the Wilde expedition left Westport with one hundred and thirty-eight men, twelve heavily-loaded wagons, extra oxen and horses coming along in the rear. They rolled away from the encampment at dawn after much confusion, Tom Partridge running from one wagon to the other, seeing that the oxen were properly harnessed.

Moose Clemens helped him, and Otey Higgins drove one of the wagons until another crew-man could be broken in on the job. Flint rode a big gray gelding which had been provided for his hunting. There were other horses in the herd following for Higgins and Moose.

Windwagon Smith's light wagon, drawn by two mules, was at the head of the column. (Tom Partridge had requested that he not use his sail, for fear that it would spook the oxen in the traces, causing even more confusion.)

Flint, riding past in the dim gray light, saw Jennifer Smith handling the reins, cracking her whip at the two mules, as they rolled out on the open plains.

Clayton Wilde's wagon was second in line,

looked at Flint, and said, "You knock him down, mister?"

"No," Flint said. "I was too late."

The new man, lank, lean, thin-shouldered, glanced around at the silent fellows behind him, the two drunks staring stony-eyed, swaying. He said, "What in hell kind of deal we get into here, boys?"

Flint MacKeithan smiled a little. In a way, he'd been wondering along those lines, himself.

water bucket near the fire and came back to pour the contents full into the face of the unconscious man.

When he turned around to replace the bucket he saw Jay Bannerman coming into the firelight, a half dozen men following him, unkempt, poorly-dressed fellows, two of them staggering, obviously very drunk. They looked stupidly at the man on the ground and then at Flint.

Bannerman asked pleasantly, "Having a little trouble here, Flint?" He was smiling, but there was a peculiar glint in his brown eyes which Flint had never seen there before.

"Ask Partridge," Flint told him.

"My pleasure," Bannerman murmured. He took off his high beaver as he walked toward the group by the smaller tent, and Flint watched him flick a speck of dust from the pearl-gray hat. He wondered if Bannerman would be wearing that hat on the trail. It was an odd thought and a ludicrous one. He was quite sure that on the trail Jay Bannerman would quickly prove himself an expert horseman, an adept shot, and a first-class Santa Fe trailman. There was no real reason for this conclusion, but it persisted. Bannerman was that kind of man.

One of the new crewmen edged over to look down at the barrel-chested man who was beginning to stir on the ground, blinking his eyes. The new man tugged at his chin thoughtfully,

when they'd tried to go back to sleep after the quick raid on the wagons. Flint hadn't even seen them around when the shooting was going on, and he assumed that they'd taken cover under the wagons at the far end of the encampment.

One man, a short, thick-set, barrel-chested fellow with a bullet-shaped head, seemed to be doing most of the complaining. He was muttering under his breath as they drove in the tent pegs, and several times he swore aloud when he stumbled over a taut guy rope as he moved around the tent.

As he came around to the front of the tent, Partridge said to him casually, "We will have no swearing in the presence of Miss Wilde, my friend."

The crewman turned and looked at him, an evil grin spreading across his wide, ugly face.

"Worth havin' Miss Wilde along," he chuckled, "even if we can't swear. Ain't that so, Mr. Partridge?"

Tom Partridge's answer was a hard swinging blow to the jaw which dropped the crewman as if he'd been stoned. He lay there looking up at the night sky, arms and legs outstretched, motionless. Partridge said to Flint, "Would you be kind enough to throw a pail of water over that man, Mr. MacKeithan?"

Then he walked over toward Clayton Wilde and Portia, and Flint, smiling, picked up the

the men in camp rather than carousing in town."

Flint nodded. "Will all your men be recruited by then?" he asked.

"We'll have them," Partridge answered grimly. "A town like Westport is always filled with drifters who'll make a stab at anything as long as they have full stomachs. The other outfits won't bother with them unless they can put up their own stake. We're taking almost anyone, but I do wish Bannerman would be a little more careful in his selection. It seems, almost, as if he's picking out the poorest of the lot."

"Have a hard time getting good men for a trip like this," Flint remarked. "Reckon Bannerman's doing the best he can. You tell a man there's a good chance of his being cut up or shot up for some Mexican citizens who don't give a damn about him, and he'll think twice."

Tom Partridge nodded. "We have brought some high-spirited men from the East," he stated. "Personal friends of Clayton Wilde's. They mean well and they'll be loyal, but they're not frontiersmen. They've never used a gun and they've never seen an Indian. I intend to drill them en route to Santa Fe, but you can't make a soldier out of a civilian in a few months."

Flint watched the men setting up the tent. There were four of them, and they were border riff-raff Jay Bannerman had sent in that afternoon. Partridge had routed them out of their blankets

it'll be safer traveling with a large party of men."

"One woman should be enough for any outfit on the trail," Flint said gloomily.

Jennifer laughed. She was standing directly in front of him and she whispered, "Which woman, Flint?"

Before he could say anything she reached up, put her hands around his neck, and kissed him. As she ducked under the flap of the tent she called back over her shoulder. "You'll never get that from Portia Wilde, Flint."

Flint walked back toward the cookfire, red-faced, scowling, but a little disturbed, too. He'd been kissed by a woman, not a schoolgirl. He told himself that Jennifer Smith was too forward, that she was not a lady. Then he remembered that she didn't pretend to be a lady. She'd been living on the frontier a number of years now and she was a frontier girl. Frontier girls were different—very different.

Back at the Wilde campsite, he found Tom Partridge directing some of the crew as they hauled a spare tent out of one of the wagons and set it up. Portia and her uncle sat near the fire, and Clayton Wilde, in good spirits now, was having another cup of coffee.

Partridge said to Flint, in low tones, "Mr. Wilde has decided to leave Westport in a few days, or as soon as the new wagons come off the packet. He believes we'll be safer on the trail with all

coming up to his shoulder, but he remembered how she'd handled that rifle and shot a man.

They walked under the trees, back toward the Smith camp, and Jennifer said to him, "Are you from Tennessee, Flint?"

"Tennessee."

"We're from Pennsylvania," Jennifer told him. "The hill country. I love hills, Flint. Father owned a general store in one of the small towns ninety miles from Philadelphia. He wasn't much of a storekeeper, any more than he is a windwagon salesman. He was too busy with his great plans, and Mother had to keep him in line."

"Now you keep him in line," Flint said. "Where is he tonight?"

"In town," Jennifer said, laughing lightly, "trying to sell his windwagon proposition to Westport townsmen."

"You think it'll work?" Flint asked her.

Jennifer shrugged. "It's a good toy and it keeps Father happy. It may do some good, but I don't think it'll ever haul heavy loads or pull trailers as Father claims. It'll never take the place of oxen or mules."

They had reached the tent next to the windwagon and they stopped there. Flint touched his hat. "We're obliged to you," he said, "for your help in running that crew off."

"We're part of the outfit now," Jennifer observed. "Father wants to reach Santa Fe, and

told him. "Now we have been forewarned, Tom, so we shall be more careful. If they struck at us in camp, it means that this same band of desperados will be on our trail when we leave. We shall have to take every precaution to secure our wagons and our livestock."

"They won't get away with it again," Partridge promised.

He and Portia then assisted Clayton Wilde toward the smaller tent, where he would stay until they were able to rig another shelter for him. Flint watched them go as he stood by the fire, clicking the empty cartridges from the gun cylinder. He was aware that Jennifer Smith was watching him across the fire, sitting on a box there, hat pushed back, the firelight playing on the soft contours of her face.

She said, "You knocked me down, mister."

"Didn't see you," Flint told her gruffly.

"You saw her." Jennifer smiled, nodding toward the small tent.

Flint just looked at her, and then he shoved the Colt into its holster. "Walk you back to your tent," he said stiffly. "Reckon I can do that much."

"You'd rather it were she, though." Jennifer grinned and got up immediately, coming around the fire.

Flint MacKeithan took a deep breath but said nothing. She was very small at his side, not even

the shooting broke out. The message was a lie, of course."

Clayton Wilde sat up, and Jennifer Smith went over to the cookfire where the coffeepot was always warming. She brought him a cup of hot coffee in a tin cup, and when she handed it to him he said, "The Smith girl, of course. Daughter of the windwagon man. I am very much obliged to you."

"It appears," Tom Partridge said, smiling, "that it was Miss Smith's rifle that prevented the raiders from burning more than one wagon."

Clayton Wilde was assisted to his feet by Flint and Portia. He stood there, sipping the coffee, watching the wagon still burning brightly in the grove. The tent fire had already died down.

"Damage—one wagon and one tent," Mr. Wilde murmured. "Not bad at all."

"I recognized one of them," Flint told him. "A man in town goes by the name of Lace Corwin. He has a bad reputation in Westport and along the trail."

Clayton Wilde glanced at Tom Partridge and then he shrugged. "They have plenty of money to hire cutthroats. It was Ortiz, of course, and it means, Tom, that we will have to start setting guards even here in Westport."

Partridge nodded soberly. "My fault," he admitted. "I should have foreseen this."

"No man can see around a corner," Mr. Wilde

gash on the right temple, not very deep, and already Wilde was struggling to sit up, blinking his eyes.

Partridge came up with a bucket of water and they bathed the cut, Portia then going to her own tent to bring out bandaging material. Through it all Flint noticed that she was calm, almost unperturbed, and then he remembered that bullet she'd fired at his head. He'd felt the breath of that piece of lead, and he realized that he'd been inches from dying.

Portia looked up at him and smiled as she worked on the bandage, stopping the flow of blood. She said, "I did not mean to kill you, Flint. I wasn't sure who you were and I deliberately shot wide of the mark to stop you."

Flint only stared at her, and Tom Partridge said casually, "Portia is an excellent shot with rifle and pistol, Flint. She has been practicing with both those weapons for more than a year back East, preparing for this trip."

"I see," Flint murmured. He looked over at Jennifer Smith, sitting calmly on a box, watching the fire die down. Then he said to Tom Partridge, almost accusingly, "Reckon I wouldn't have left the camp if I'd known you were going, too."

"It was a ruse," Partridge explained. "A man stopped in here with a message that the wagon-master for the outfit farther upriver wanted to talk with me. I wasn't gone ten minutes when

man, missing him, and Corwin disappeared among the trees. Flint stopped short, aghast, when Portia Wilde, kneeling before her uncle on the ground, calmly lifted a Colt gun, similar to his own, and fired a shot straight at his head.

"Wait!" Flint called, ducking.

He came on more slowly then but she held the gun on him until she'd recognized him. Then she lowered the muzzle and said quite calmly, "My uncle has been hurt, but, I believe, not too badly."

Another man came running out of the wood then, gun in hand, and Flint recognized him as Tom Partridge. Partridge's face was gray.

"You all right, Portia?" he asked quickly.

"Uncle was clubbed," the girl explained, "as he came out of the tent right after you left. I fired several shots at them and they ran, but some of them had already set fire to the rear of the tent and they were beginning to burn the wagons when Flint, here, and someone else opened fire on them."

Jennifer Smith was coming into the light of the burning tent now, and Flint nodded toward her.

"She was in it before I came up," he admitted. "They got one wagon, but they couldn't get to the others."

"There were at least a half dozen in the group," Portia said, as Flint bent down to examine Clayton Wilde's head wound. It was a simple

to her feet after she'd been sent headlong into the bushes.

"You big ox!" she snapped. "You made me miss him."

Flint blinked at her. She was reloading the rifle rapidly, expertly. "Who—?" he started to say. Then he saw Portia Wilde kneeling over someone on the ground close by the burning tent and he said no more. Another dark figure was running toward a loaded wagon on the outskirts of the camp, and he fired twice at this man, seeing him stumble, right himself, and then lurch away among the trees, dropping the firebrand he'd been carrying.

As he ran toward the tent he heard Jennifer Smith's rifle crack again, the bullet whistling over his head, aimed at a man who'd been climbing to the top of one of the parked wagons. The raider dropped to the ground, clutching at his arm.

Flint broke out into the clear about fifteen yards from the Wilde tent, now a mass of flames. He saw a man running around the tent, heading toward the deeper woods behind, and he had a fairly good glimpse of him—a thin man with a broken, twisted nose, wearing a leather vest and a flat-crowned black hat with a broken rim. This was the man Moose Clemens had shouldered into the road earlier in the evening—Lace Corwin.

Lifting his gun, Flint got off one shot at the

Chapter Six

RUNNING AT TOP SPEED through the trees, dodging the overhanging branches, Flint slipped the Walker-Colt .44 gun from the holster at his side. Jay Bannerman had furnished him with the gun, and it was a deadly weapon, comparatively new to the frontier, a six-shot weapon with a revolving barrel.

He noticed that most of the shooting seemed to be coming from the direction of the Wilde tent and he raced that way, rounding Smith's parked windwagon, the sailless mast rising up among the trees around it. He didn't see Smith, nor did he see Jennifer, but a small cookfire was glowing close by their little tent.

As he tore through the underbrush he saw, a fraction of a second too late, a small kneeling figure, rifle raised, the barrel of it lined on a man who was running toward one of the wagons with a lighted torch. The rifle cracked as Flint stumbled into the shooter, the bullet missing the mark, but chasing the man with the firebrand back into the shadows.

In the dim light from the burning tent, Flint righted himself and watched Jennifer Smith leap

Flint passed the deserted lumber mill and moved up toward the Wilde camp. There, too, the cook's fire was burning brightly—very brightly. Flint stared at it thoughtfully as he walked through the woods, and then suddenly he broke into a run. The fire was not a cook's fire; it was something else going up in flames, the flames reaching up toward the lower limbs of the giant trees along the river. It was a tent—the tent in which Clayton Wilde had spoken to him that afternoon!

As he ran, he saw red flames leaping up into the air from one of the wagons, and then a gun banged. Another gun opened up from the opposite side of the encampment, a heavier-gauged gun, one shot following the other, evenly spaced. The Wilde camp was being raided.

When Otey looked at Flint, he shook his head. "See you back at the wagons."

"She won't walk tonight." Otey Higgins grinned at him. "Ain't no texas deck up along that river."

Flint watched the two of them disappear into the nearest saloon, and then he sat down on a barrel head back in the shadows against one of the buildings and watched the crowd go by, watching for the scar-faced Mexican who'd tried to kill him earlier that day.

An hour passed before he gave it up and headed back along the river. Campfires were burning all along the water front now, the yellow light illuminating the white-topped Conestoga and Pittsburgh wagons drawn up under the trees.

When he passed the encampment of a group of Oregon-bound emigrants he heard a baby crying in the night, and two dogs bounded out to bark at him. The camps of the Santa Fe-bound traders were different—all men, experienced teamsters and bullwhackers, some of them rolling in under their wagons or sleeping on top of the loads if the wagons were already loaded and covered.

Where there were many campfires for the emigrants, one for each family, the Santa Fe crews had one large cookfire which burned brightly, and around which a white-aproned cook bustled with his array of pots and pans.

It was nearly nine o'clock in the evening when

"Friend o' yours?" Otey grinned impudently.

"He's the one broke into a cache o' mine up on the Green River," Moose growled. "Can't prove it, but he's the one. Whole winter's trappin' gone to hell. If I could prove it, I'd skin him alive."

When Lace Corwin came abreast of them, Moose, on the outside, swung his big shoulder, catching the yellow-haired man in the chest and sending him spinning out into the road. Corwin staggered, righted himself, smiled, and kept walking, not even looking at the giant trapper.

"Just to let him know I'm on to him," Moose growled.

"Some night," Otey told him, "he'll stick a knife between your ribs, Moose, an' then you'll know he's on to you."

"He would," Moose admitted, "if he could."

They passed the various saloons, Flint looking in over the doors, always on the alert for the scar-faced Mexican agent. When they'd walked from one end of town to the other and started to retrace their steps, he'd seen nothing of the man.

"He's holed up," Otey stated. "You ain't seein' him until he sees you, Flint."

"You boys want to walk the streets," Moose told them, "you're welcome. This child has to do a little drinkin' 'fore we set out for Santa Fe."

Otey said promptly, "Reckon you'll need a little help, Moose. I'll go with you."

blacksmiths' hammers were still ringing, and the freight wagons rolling through the streets, but not with the same fervor as earlier in the day.

The saloons were more crowded and the eating houses jammed. They found a little lunchroom at the far end of town and were able to get a good meal of fried potatoes, ham, and eggs.

When they came out of the lunchroom Flint spotted Jay Bannerman talking with a man at the head of an adjoining alley. Bannerman had his back toward them, and they could see the man he'd buttonholed, a tough, hard-faced individual who looked as if he'd just been thrown off a river boat, and who would cut a man's throat for ten dollars.

"Another border ruffian," Otey murmured. "Wonder how much they'll be payin' a feller like that to start a war agin' the Mexican Republic."

"Comin' this way," Moose said, "is the biggest damn cutthroat from Westport to Santa Fe an' down to Mexico City. Take a good look at him, Flint. The name is Lace Corwin."

Flint watched the man coming toward them, a thin man with a wedge of a face and yellowish hair. He had green eyes, the color of dirty pond water, and a broken nose twisted to the left.

"Cache stealer," Moose rasped. "Squaw man, dealer with the Comanches. He'd steal the pennies off a dead man's eyes, an' then claim he was short changed."

"Might run across that Mexican chap again, Flint," Otey remarked.

That was Flint's main purpose in returning to town. Ortiz was still in Westport, hiding out, but he might show himself in the evening.

There were only a few men at the camp when they left, the others having headed back to Westport and the evening's amusements. No guard had been set, the only Indians in the vicinity being friendly.

The few livestock Bannerman had been able to purchase were out on the plains with the common herd, guarded by specially assigned herdsmen. Bannerman himself had gone into Westport to spend the evening there and to beat his drum for recruits.

Flint saw Windwagon Smith and Jennifer rigging up a small tent next to the wagon, and Jennifer grinned and waved a hand to them as they walked on. Otey Higgins waved back, but Flint just stared straight ahead.

Otey grinned and said, "Can't be that you're mad at that gal, Flint."

"She talks too much," Flint snapped.

"Not to me," Otey chuckled. "Could be she likes you."

Flint disdained to reply.

They found the town jammed with men, coming in from the various encampments for the same reason as themselves. At five in the afternoon the

Flint shrugged. "Reckon we might have a chance," he stated, "a long one."

"Yet you are going," Partridge told him. He put the filled pipe in his mouth but he did not light it, and then he put his back against the tree, rubbing it gently.

"You are going, too," Flint countered.

Tom Partridge looked down at the ground. "I gave up a commission in the Army," he said slowly, "to sign up with Clayton Wilde's expedition. A man, perhaps, does strange things in his lifetime. I hope I shall be forgiven for this action if it is a mistake."

"Reckon you like the New Mexicans," Flint murmured.

Tom Partridge smiled broadly now. "At least," he admitted, "as much as you do, MacKeithan." He held out his hand and said, "Again, I'm glad to have you with us. We have too few men of your caliber in this outfit."

Flint shook his hand, warming toward the man. Tom Partridge had fallen in love with a fine, intelligent, warm-hearted, sincere woman. If she were mistaken he intended to go down the line with her, sacrificing his own career and future.

After telling Bannerman that the two hunters had decided to accompany the expedition, Flint walked back to town with Otey Higgins and Moose Clemens.

and started through the woods. Seeing Flint and the two hunters, however, he slowed down, and Flint stood up, quite sure that the man wanted to talk to him.

"That feller," Otey Higgins said softly, "seems like the only chap in this crew knows what he's doin'. He ain't got bees buzzin' around in his bonnet."

Flint left the two hunters and walked over to Tom Partridge, who was stuffing his pipe with tobacco. Partridge was as big a man as himself, though not as broad in the shoulders. He wore a gray flannel shirt, boots, and a flat-crowned border hat, but Flint couldn't get over his first impression that Partridge had been an Army man at some time.

Partridge said quietly, "How did your friends take it, MacKeithan?"

"They'll come along," Flint told him. He saw the faint smile playing around the corners of Partridge's wide, thin-lipped mouth, and there was some small, almost sardonic humor in his hazel eyes.

"I am a little curious to know their personal reactions to our expedition," he said.

"They think it's a damn fool idea," Flint told him promptly, and he saw quick approval of his honesty come into Partridge's eyes.

"And what is your opinion?" Partridge murmured, watching him closely.

anybody get out of it?" he countered, "aside from a Mexican lance in his belly an' a hole in the ground where they'll put him, if they bother to bury him, which ain't likely."

"There'll be a woman along on this trip, too," Flint said.

Otey Higgins looked at him. "More likely two," he stated.

Flint stared at him. "Two?" he repeated.

"This Windwagon Smith had a little talk with Mr. Wilde 'fore you got here," Otey Higgins explained. "Seems he's damned anxious to git to Santa Fe, an' Mr. Wilde kind o' liked the windwagon. Figures it might do pretty well on the open plains. Heard him tell Smith he could string along with the outfit, but that he'd have to git himself a pair o' mules to keep up when there wasn't no wind."

Flint kicked at the dirt disgustedly but didn't say anything.

"That little gal will be comin' along," Otey murmured, "least as far as Santa Fe. She ain't Portia Wilde, Flint, an' I don't reckon she walks in the moonlight, but there ain't too many like her on the frontier."

"One," Flint told him grimly, "is too many for me."

He saw Tom Partridge, the wagonmaster, talking with one of the teamsters over near the crew's cookfire, and then Partridge left the fire

better than yours." He grinned. "Count me in, Flint."

Moose Clemens nodded too. "Reckon I'll go along," he said. "Gonna be two fools, might just as well be three."

"Noticed somethin' about this outfit already," Otey Higgins stated as he examined Moose Clemens' new Hawkins' rifle, a big heavy gun, brass-mounted, with a buffalo inscribed on the stock.

"What about the crew?" Flint asked.

"Two bunches of 'em," Otey said. "Seems like the one bunch is a lot o' Easterners sent out here in advance by Mr. Wilde, an' the others look like border riff-raff, goin' along fer the ride an' to see how much they kin get out of it."

Flint frowned. He looked around the clearing, having taken no particular notice of the dozens of men in the area. There were thirty or forty men at the camp, some of them busying themselves around the wagons, others just sitting on the ground, sleeping or playing cards. The card players did seem like a rough lot, and he wondered that they'd consented to go along on a dangerous expedition like this with small reward for their efforts. These men were not visionaries like Clayton Wilde.

Moose Clemens said, "An' what in hell kin they get out of it, Higgins?"

Otey Higgins shook his head. "What kin

"We had a drink in town," Flint told him briefly. "Moose Clemens wants to come along on this trip."

"He's welcome," Otey grinned. "Allus like a big man in front o' me when the Comanches start shootin' arrows."

The three of them sat down on an upturned tree at the edge of the clearing, and Flint told them the purpose of Clayton Wilde's expedition. He saw little Otey Higgins' eyes widen as he listened, and even Moose Clemens, ordinarily phlegmatic, muttered several times under his breath before Flint finished.

"They want the three of us as members of the outfit," Flint told them. "We're to liberate New Mexico."

"What in hell for?" Otey asked. "They ain't never done nothin' fer us."

Flint shrugged. "That's the deal," he stated. "If you don't go for it, all we ask is that you don't tell anybody about it."

"Gonna run into a lot o' hell down there," Moose Clemens growled. "Them fellers runnin' the government ain't gonna just walk away. It could be they'll bring up soldiers from Mexico City if they figure they can't stop us, themselves."

"What are you doin' about it, Flint?" Otey said thoughtfully.

"I'm signed up," Flint told him.

The little hunter shrugged. "My hide ain't any

came up, and Flint said to her sardonically, "Reckon this grove is too small for both of us."

Jennifer Smith smiled at him, her brown eyes twinkling. She was very cool, unperturbed. She said softly, "I wanted to tell you that you were wasting your time."

"Where?" Flint growled.

"Now there are two of them," Jennifer observed. "A woman like that draws men the way honey draws the bees. What chance do you have?"

"Did I ask you?" Flint snapped. He started to brush past her, and she left the tree and fell in at his side, walking briskly with him as they moved toward the windwagon at the edge of the grove.

"Two things I've noticed about men," Jennifer said and smiled. "One is that they're always wrong, and the other is that they'll never admit it."

"You sound," Flint growled, "as if you'd had a lot of experience with men."

Jennifer stopped walking suddenly and she got behind Flint. "Here is one," she said grimly, "I don't want to see too often."

Flint saw Moose Clemens coming up, a new rifle under his arm, and a broad grin on his face.

"Ain't nothin' to worry about, little girl," the big trapper boomed. "Comin' to see a friend o' mine."

He walked off with Flint, leaving Jennifer staring after them. Flint waved a hand to Otey Higgins, and the little man joined them, looking at Moose curiously.

the impression that Bannerman and Partridge were not particularly friendly beneath the surface. He attributed this to the fact that both men were in love with the same woman.

Bannerman said to Partridge, "The supplies coming in, Tom?"

"We're pretty well organized," Partridge told him. "I need two more wagons, but they are coming in on the next steamboat, due within a few days."

"Good," Bannerman nodded. "We're all anxious to get on the trail." He said to Flint, "What about your hunter friends, Flint?"

"I'll talk to them now," Flint said. He'd already got Clayton Wilde's permission to speak to Otey Higgins and Moose Clemens about joining the party officially.

As he touched his hat to Portia Wilde and moved away from the fire, he saw Jennifer Smith strolling among the wagons, watching the men loading. He was quite sure that she'd been watching the group at the cook's fire, and as he came away she changed her direction and moved to intercept him.

Flint scowled, increasing his speed to reach Otey Higgins and Windwagon Smith, who were still at the windwagon, but Jennifer, smiling, walked still faster, so that when he came out from under the trees she was still in front of him.

She waited with her back against a tree as he

As they stood there by the fire, he saw the tall man who'd met the party at the boat coming toward them from one of the wagons, and Flint had a better look at him now. He was tall, a little taller than Bannerman and heavier in the shoulders, a fine-looking man in his early thirties, with a plain, almost severe face. He had the bearing of an Army man, and Flint was quite sure he'd done some military service in the past.

As he came up, Portia said to him, "Tom, meet Flint MacKeithan. He has just signed with the expedition."

Flint shook the man's hand, finding it warm, friendly, very strong. Tom Partridge had hazel eyes to go with his nut-brown hair. He said, "Glad to have you with us, MacKeithan."

"Tom will be wagonmaster on this trip to Santa Fe," Portia was saying. "He has already been south several times and he knows the route."

"A rough road?" Flint asked him.

Partridge shrugged his big shoulders. "Safe enough for a party our size, barring a big Indian raid on the livestock or a buffalo stampede or a prairie fire or—" He stopped because Portia was smiling at him, and Jay Bannerman was coming out of Clayton Wilde's tent, walking up to them.

"Everybody acquainted?" he asked genially, and immediately Flint was warmed by the man's presence. He noticed, though, that Tom Partridge's manner changed slightly, and he got

concerning the New Mexican province was secondhand.

"You figure on going along this trip?" Flint asked.

"My uncle needs me."

"Be dangerous," Flint observed. "There'll be shooting sooner or later."

The tall girl shrugged. "I am not afraid to die," she said, "if I have to."

Flint picked up his empty coffee cup and studied it for a moment. "How long you and your uncle had this in mind?" he asked.

"My uncle has been planning the expedition for two years," Portia told him. "He's had advance agents in Westport and in Santa Fe for nearly a year now, making preparations. Have you met Tom Partridge?"

"Not yet," Flint said. "He the man met you at the boat?"

Portia nodded. "Tom has been our greatest blessing, aside from Jay himself."

"Bannerman with you from the beginning?" Flint wanted to know.

"Almost a year now," Portia said. "He has a wonderful mind for organization. He's done most of the recruiting for uncle back East, and will continue in Westport."

"Easy man to get along with," Flint murmured, remembering how impressed he had been at his first meeting with Jay Bannerman.

Chapter Five

PASSING THE COOKFIRE after coming out of Clayton Wilde's tent, Flint saw the flap of Portia's tent open, and then she came out, walking directly toward him, and he surmised that she wanted to speak with him. She was wearing a green corduroy jacket now most becoming with her blonde hair. There were large golden buttons on the jacket, and her hands were in its pockets as she came up. She looked very slim and athletic, and Flint's gray eyes lighted up as he watched her.

"Did my uncle speak with you, Flint?" she asked.

"I'm signed up," he stated; and he saw the pleasure come into her eyes and he was glad that he'd made the decision, even though it was very possibly the wrong one.

"I'm glad," Portia Wilde said. "I'm sure you will be a great help to us, Flint. These poor, impoverished people need us."

Flint didn't say anything to that, but he was quite sure Clayton Wilde's niece, like himself, had never been closer than two thousand miles to Santa Fe, and all the information they had

There was, also, the matter of Portia. It was already established that she would accompany the expedition. What happened to her if it proved a failure—if her uncle and Bannerman were killed?

"Reckon I'll go along," Flint heard himself saying.

He saw Bannerman smile at him faintly, approvingly, as he said this, and he wondered if Bannerman knew the real reason for his acceptance. He thought Jay Bannerman did.

"Originally," Wilde said, "we hired you and your friend as hunters to supply our party with fresh meat on the long journey to Santa Fe. You were to be released from your contract when we neared the capital city. Now I am inviting you to join our army of liberation as a full-fledged member. We can offer you no great monetary reward. You will be well paid, of course, as long as you continue with us, but you would be well paid with any outfit leaving for Santa Fe or Oregon, with considerably less danger entailed. Would you care to make a decision now, Mr. MacKeithan?"

Flint looked at him, and then at Jay Bannerman, now standing behind Clayton Wilde's chair, the cigar in his mouth. Flint rubbed his big hands together and looked down at the hard-packed dirt floor of the tent.

He had no particular desire to free a land of New Mexicans who neither knew him, cared about him, or as far as he knew had requested him to come down to free them from misrule, but he'd come west because life in the Tennessee hills had become too tame and the game was disappearing. This was adventure on a grand scale, and there was the possibility that they would accomplish their purpose and deliver to the United States another state contiguous to it, whose peoples would be immensely benefited after generations of oppression.

we would like it to be. Rumors have already gone out that an American expedition is being formed, and back East we have been spied upon by an agent of the New Mexican government, a Señor Pablo Ortiz."

"The gentleman with the scar," Bannerman said, behind Flint.

"Ortiz and his confederates," Wilde continued, "have already made an attempt upon the life of Mr. Bannerman, my second in command. They will strike again and they will make every attempt to stop us before we reach Santa Fe. They may even try to prevent us from leaving Westport."

And when you get there, Flint thought uneasily, they'll be waiting for you with guns and cannon and sharp Mexican lances.

"We will not be stopped," Clayton Wilde said grimly. "We have the right on our side, and the right shall prevail. We will be victorious, as the Texans were victorious in their gallant fight, and I shall live to see the day when both New Mexico and Texas are states of the United States of America."

Jay Bannerman came around in front of them then, still puffing on the cigar, his handsome face expressionless. He looked down at Flint as if waiting for him to make a comment on this amazing revelation, but before Flint could think of anything to say Clayton Wilde made the proposal.

United States as an additional state. It is my aim, MacKeithan, to give to the poor people of New Mexico—the Indians, the mixed bloods, the good people of that colony—the independence the Texans fought for and achieved. I feel that the time is ripe for revolt."

Flint was staring at the tall, thin, bony man as he spoke, immediately grasping the fact that Clayton Wilde and Jay Bannerman were filibusters, aiming by force to free a nation of people now under the yoke.

"Our force," Wilde was saying, his voice beginning to ring out, "may seem very small for an expedition of this nature, but we are not depending only upon ourselves for the success of our venture. I have ascertained through associates already on the field that the New Mexicans are ready for revolt, and that they need only a leader to fan the fire which has been smoldering all these years. We are counting upon support from the local populace of Santa Fe and the surrounding areas when our hundred and fifty brave Americans strike for the independence of that country."

Flint heard Jay Bannerman's footsteps behind him as Bannerman paced the tent. He smelled Bannerman's cigar, the rich aroma filling the tent. Then he listened again to Clayton Wilde.

"Much to our regret," Wilde went on, "our expedition to Santa Fe is not so secret a matter as

in the tent, and then he said, "Tell me about it, MacKeithan."

Flint told him of his sighting the Mexican on the street, following him into the saloon, and then, later, up the stairs. When he finished, Clayton Wilde drummed with his fingers for a few moments on the table and then stood up, taking a turn around the tent. When he came back to his chair he sat down, leaned forward a little and said, "I believe it is time, MacKeithan, that we acquainted you with a few facts concerning the nature of our expedition to Santa Fe."

"Been itching to know," Flint admitted.

Clayton Wilde leaned forward on the chair. He said, "We came west on board the General Jackson with fifty men. In Westport we are at this moment recruiting one hundred more men to accompany us to Santa Fe. We are not going there with the intention of trading with the New Mexicans."

"Figured that," Flint said. He glanced at Jay Bannerman, who'd moved to another part of the tent, half turned away, and was lighting a cigar.

"For centuries," Clayton Wilde went on, "New Mexico has been a far distant colony of old Spain and now of the Mexican Republic, and always, under both governments, it has been dominated by corrupt politicians. Six years ago, Texas was also a province of the Mexican Republic. She is now an independent nation seeking entry to the

"You make friends of your enemies, Flint," she remarked. "That is a good policy."

"This man told me," Flint went on, "that our outfit is headed for trouble. That's the rumor along the Santa Fe trail."

Jay Bannerman lifted his eyebrows, and his brown eyes were quizzical.

"It is time," he said, "that we acquainted you with a few facts, Flint. Will you come inside?"

Flint followed him into the tent as Portia Wilde walked to another smaller tent which had been set up for her. They found Clayton Wilde at a folding table, surrounded as usual by books and papers. He was scribbling furiously on a sheet of paper as they came in, and Jay Bannerman waited until he'd finished.

Clayton Wilde looked up at them, and Flint noticed how deeply lined his face was. The peculiar turquoise eyes were red-rimmed from much reading and work under poor light. Wilde evidently was a man who drove himself to the point of complete exhaustion and still carried on.

He nodded and smiled at Flint, extending a long-fingered, bony hand, and then he said, "It was a splendid fight, MacKeithan. I congratulate you on your victory."

"Flint has news for us," Jay Bannerman stated. "It seems Señor Ortiz is in town, Mr. Wilde."

Clayton Wilde looked at Bannerman and then at Flint. He motioned them to camp chairs

the wagons. As he came around a wagon tongue he saw Jay Bannerman and Portia Wilde having a cup of coffee near the cook's fire, and Bannerman waved for him to join them.

Flint came up, touching his hat to Portia. He noticed that she'd taken off her bonnet and her golden hair gleamed in the bright afternoon sunshine. She smiled at him and poured a cup of coffee, handing it to him.

"Seeing the town?" Bannerman asked.

"Seeing somebody we both know," Flint told him. "A Mexican with a scar on his face whom we last saw on the General Jackson."

Jay Bannerman frowned and then looked at Portia Wilde. "He's in town?" Bannerman asked.

"Threw a knife at me in the Santa Fe saloon," Flint said. "He went through a window and I lost him."

Jay Bannermen said wryly to Portia Wilde, "They haven't forgotten us, Portia." To Flint he said, "Will you step inside with me, Flint? I'm sure Mr. Wilde will want to speak with you."

Flint finished his coffee and put the tin cup on the flat rock near the fire. He said, "Wanted to talk to him about another hunter who'd like to come along with us."

"Who?" Bannerman asked.

"The big redhead I was fighting in the street this afternoon," Flint stated and he saw Portia Wilde smiling at him.

encampment after another, Flint MacKeithan did not like to dwell upon this fact.

Momentarily, however, he forgot it as he passed the Judson lumber mill and drew near the dozen wagons drawn up in a grove beyond. He saw Windwagon Smith's vehicle on the edge of the grove, a dozen men standing around it, studying it curiously, and then as he walked under the trees he saw Jennifer Smith, sitting on a log, watching him come up. Otey Higgins was still up on the wagon with Smith, grinning broadly, already a confirmed plains' sailor.

Flint nodded briefly to the dark-haired girl on the log, and he was passing by with the intention of looking up Jay Bannerman when Jennifer Smith said coolly, "I don't blame you for falling in love with her, Flint MacKeithan. I had a good look at her here and she is the most beautiful and the most gracious woman I have ever seen."

Flint stopped, his face red. "You babble on," he said grimly, "like a schoolgirl."

"I am nearly eighteen." Jennifer smiled at him. "I should have been married, already."

"Would that you were," Flint told her, "but not to me."

She looked at him and her brown eyes started to twinkle. "You would not make a bad husband," she observed. "I'll consider you."

Flint heard her light laughter as he strode on toward the big tent which had been set up among

"Above Judson's Mill," Flint told him. "Clayton Wilde's camp."

They were passing out through the bat-wing doors, and Moose stopped on the porch and stared at Flint curiously.

"Clayton Wilde?" he repeated.

Flint nodded. "Know him?" he asked.

Moose Clemens shook his head. "Man hears talk on the trail," he murmured. "Never laid eyes on this Wilde chap, but there's talk among the mountain men an' the boys who hunt fer Santa Fe trail outfits."

"What's the talk?" Flint asked.

"It ain't healthy to ride with Wilde's outfit," Moose Clemens told him. "Ain't nobody knows why, but the talk is that it ain't healthy. That outfit's runnin' into a hell of a lot o' trouble."

After the mountain man left him, Flint moved down the walk slowly, a frown on his face. He had little doubt that Moose Clemens was right and that trouble was coming to the Clayton Wilde outfit. A trapper like Moose, moving up and down the Santa Fe Trail and roaming through Santa Fe, Taos, and other Spanish settlement towns heard rumors, and the man who discounted such rumors was a fool.

Portia Wilde was going along with this outfit to Santa Fe, and it meant that her life would be endangered as well as the lives of the others. Walking up along the river, passing one wagon

minutes—in a stable, a back alley, the back room of a saloon or boardinghouse.

Coming out into the corridor again, he saw Moose Clemens yanking the knife from the plaster and looking at it curiously. Moose said softly, "Reckon you got enemies, mister. This thing is sharp."

Flint took the knife from his hand. It was a bone-handled affair, slim, deadly, very sharp; a throwing knife, the blade at least six inches long. If it had struck him in the chest he was positive he would be dead now, or dying.

"Never liked no damn knife throwers," Moose Clemens was saying. "You git a look at him?"

"I know him," Flint nodded grimly, and he knew that the next time he ran into the sallow-faced Mexican with the scar, it would be the last time for one of them.

As they went downstairs Moose said thought-fully, "You workin' south with an outfit, mister?"

"I'm signed up," Flint told him.

"Reckon you kin put in a word fer me?" Moose asked him. "Guarantee to bring in more meat than any three hunters north o' Taos."

"Come out to the camp with me," Flint invited. "I'll talk to the head man."

"Meet you up there," the big trapper said. "I'm sellin' my pet bear to a storekeeper in town fer a new Hawkins' rifle an' some ball an' powder. Where is yore camp?"

that he could see the Mexican and his associate when they came out.

He'd decided on the first plan and he was moving toward the door nearest him when the other one, farther down the hall, suddenly opened and the slim Mexican stepped out into the corridor.

Flint didn't see the knife in his hand until the Mexican suddenly raised his right arm. The knife sang through the air a fraction of a second later, coming straight toward Flint's chest.

For one moment Flint was hypnotized, and then he fell to the floor as if he'd been hit by a sledge-hammer, the knife grazing his left shoulder as he went down and embedding itself in the plaster of the wall behind him.

The Mexican leaped back into the room, slamming the door behind him. Scrambling to his feet, Flint charged down the corridor, hitting the closed door with his shoulder, tearing it from its hinges as he tumbled inside.

He stumbled forward as he came into the room, and as he fell he caught a glimpse of the Mexican slipping through the open window to the shed roof outside.

When he reached the window, his assailant was already gone. He could hear him running up the alley to the main street, and he realized it was useless to chase the man now. In a crowded town like Westport a man could lose himself in a few

"Nothin'," the bartender told him. "Card rooms for private games. Reckon they're empty now."

Laying a coin on the bar to pay for the big trapper's bottle, Flint pushed away from the bar. "See you in Santa Fe," he said.

"Ain't got an outfit to go with, yet," Moose Clemens told him. "Have to git back to Taos, though, for the fall an' winter trappin'. I'll be there, mister."

Flint started up the steps to the second floor, leaving the giant redhead at the bar. He went up leisurely, wondering what he would find on the next floor. He had little doubt that the Mexican had gone upstairs to meet someone privately in these empty card rooms. He had to know who that man was if he wanted to protect Clayton Wilde.

At the head of the stairs he stopped. There was a narrow corridor with a half-dozen doors opening on it, several of the doors open, revealing empty card tables, still strewn with playing cards, dirty glasses, and empty bottles. An old man was pushing a broom around in one of the rooms, whistling a song tunelessly.

Two of the doors were closed, and the Mexican had undoubtedly gone into one of the two. Flint hesitated, wondering if the best policy would be to barge into one of the rooms, pretending that he'd thought it empty, or if he should step into one of the empty rooms, leaving the door open so

The big trapper did not need a second invitation. Picking up the nearly filled liquor bottle, he tilted it to his mouth and didn't stop drinking until it was empty. When he put the bottle down he said thoughtfully, "Reckon I needed that one, mister." Then he held out a huge hand to Flint and said, "Moose Clemens, the original ring-tailed panther, an' I kin lick any man livin' from the Rio Grande to the Hudson Bay country, exceptin' you."

"You could have licked me, too," Flint assured him. "That girl stamped on your toes and I had the advantage."

"Damn that girl," Moose Clemens chuckled. "Yesterday, she cracked my knuckles with the whipstock when I got too close to that wind-wagon. Figured I'd teach her a lesson."

"Wish you had," Flint scowled. "Reckon she needs it, Moose."

Moose Clemens looked at him curiously. "Hell of a business," he said. "First you fight for her like a young bull an' then you chase her off."

"Didn't fight for her," Flint stated.

Big Moose Clemens just looked at him and shook his head, mystified. Flint watched the scar-faced Mexican push away from the bar suddenly, after paying for his drink, and start up the flight of red-carpeted stairs to the second floor, disappearing out of sight.

Flint hooked a finger at the bartender, and when the man came over he said, "What's upstairs?"

58

bartender took it down, sliding a glass in front of him.

"Headin' for Santa Fe?" he asked.

"That could be," Flint said and nodded.

"Or Oregon?"

"That could be, too," Flint told him, and he noticed that the Mexican was listening as he pretended to fondle his liquor glass.

"Santa Fe's the town for excitement," the bartender observed. "Wine, women, an' plenty o' hell for everybody. Plenty o' traders come back after two or three trips with enough to last 'em the rest of their lives."

Flint nodded without comment. He poured the drink, and then he saw the giant trapper, Moose Clemens, coming through the doors, his face puffed and bruised, swollen out of shape. He didn't notice Flint at the bar until he was almost on top of him, and then, seeing him, he started to turn away, looking uncomfortable.

"Moose," Flint said.

When the redhead stopped, Flint pushed the bottle toward him. "On me," he said. "The toughest fighting man east of the Rockies."

Moose Clemens stared at him uncertainly and then tugged at his red beard.

"Toughest of 'em all," he admitted, "till I run agin' you, Jack."

"You need a big one," Flint told him. "Finish it up, Moose."

steering rudder in the rear. A breeze struck the big sail, billowing it out, and the wagon started to move up the street, the crowd parting to give it room.

A teamster heading their way, with half a dozen mules in the traces, had his hands full when the mules shied away from the strange vehicle. He was still cursing violently as the windwagon slipped past him and veered out on the open plains, where the breeze caught the sail fully. It disappeared over a hillock, moving at a good rate of speed, and Flint, watching until it was out of sight, turned and walked up the street to the Santa Fe saloon.

At this early hour of the afternoon the barroom was only sparsely filled. Two bartenders chatted at one end of the bar. A man played solitaire at a card table, and several drinkers stood at the bar, talking in low tones.

The Mexican with the scarred face stood at the far end of the bar, alone, nursing his drink. His dark eyes swiveled to Flint as Flint pushed through the bat-wing doors, and then he turned back to his drink again, but Flint noticed that he watched him in the bar mirror.

One of the bartenders moved down along the bar, grinning at Flint, and he said, "Man that whips Moose Clemens deserves a drink on the house. What'll it be, mister?"

Flint pointed to a bottle on the shelf, and the

He scowled and said, "You go along, Otey."

He was wondering how the Mexican had reached Westport so soon after going over the side, and then he remembered that the General Jackson had been tied up along the river for half a day while the engineers repaired a loose piston, and that a man going overland along the Missouri could oftentimes make faster time than the boat which had to follow every snakelike bend of the river. The Mexican had beaten them to Westport and could this moment be planning another assault on Bannerman, or on Clayton Wilde.

He'd promised Portia that he would do all that he could to protect her uncle from attack. The sallow-faced Mexican undoubtedly was a menace and had to be watched.

Otey Higgins was looking at Flint curiously, knowing that he had a reason for not going along, a little disturbed because he did not know what it was.

"You don't want to go, Flint?" Otey said dubiously.

"See you at the encampment," Flint told him. He was anxious to leave now so that the Mexican wouldn't elude him.

Windwagon Smith had already climbed into the wagon, and a grinning crowd gathered again as he hoisted the sail, Jennifer helping him. After Otey Higgins climbed in apprehensively, the fat man kicked loose the brake and stepped to the

shall navigate the open plains like ships at sea."

They were standing in front of the windwagon now, and Otey Higgins was examining the rudder arrangement critically. Windwagon Smith said breezily, "Would you gentlemen care to test the windwagon? We can run up to Blue Creek and back in less than an hour."

Otey Higgins scratched his head and looked at Flint dubiously. "Reckon I ain't no sailor," he murmured, "but I sure would like to see how this contraption runs. How about you, Flint?"

"Some other time," Flint told him. He'd just seen someone go by on the walk—a slim, sallow-skinned man with a crescent scar on his cheek—the Mexican who'd tried to stab Jay Bannerman on board the General Jackson, and then leaped overboard into the river when Flint had pursued him down to the main deck.

The slim Mexican had taken no particular notice of them as he went by, turning in at the Santa Fe saloon, and Flint was positive the man did not recognize him. He'd been in buckskins and it had been night when they'd had their slight scuffle on the texas deck of the boat. The Mexican had not seen his face at all and would not know him.

Jennifer Smith was saying almost tauntingly, "You do not trust the windwagon, Mr. MacKeithan?"

Flint looked at her. "Try it some other time."

Chapter Four

WHEN THEY CAME out of the saloon a half hour later, Jennifer Smith still trudged at Flint's side, walking with that same easy swagger which he decided was distinctly not ladylike. She hadn't had anything to drink at the bar; she'd listened to the conversation of her father and Flint and Otey Higgins, taking no part in it but smiling a little when Windwagon Smith related pompously that if he couldn't find financial support in Westport he intended to take his invention down to Santa Fe and speak with the New Mexican governor.

Flint realized, then, the relationship between these two. The fat man was bubbling with grand ideas, and his daughter went along with him, a settling influence, helping him out of scrapes. He'd learned that Smith's wife had died when Jennifer was still a child, and they'd traveled together ever since, the attachment between them being very strong.

"Yes, sir," Windwagon Smith was saying as they walked, "the windwagon will revolutionize travel in the far West. I hope I shall live to see the day when giant wagons, pulling smaller trailers,

and he stopped to say stiffly, "Reckon a saloon is no place for a lady. You'd better wait outside, ma'am."

"I'm not a lady," Jennifer Smith said promptly. "At least not like your lady of the carriage."

"She's not my lady," Flint growled.

"The way you looked at her," Jennifer Smith said, "one would think so."

"How did I look at her?" Flint asked, quite sure that he did not like this girl at all, and that it probably would have served her right to let Moose Clemens toss her around a little.

"You looked like a calf bellowing for its mother," Jennifer Smith answered.

Flint just glared at her, and then turned and stepped up to the bar. He wondered what foolish impulse had sent him into a fight with the big trapper to defend this slip of a girl who apparently could take very good care of herself, and who within five minutes of the fight had started to insult him. He told himself that he did not care for these Western girls who walked into saloons and who carried themselves like men.

looking straight at him, and then at Jennifer Smith at his side. If she had seen the fight, a particularly bloody one, it did not seem to have affected her. She was still calm and unperturbed, a slight smile on her face as she looked at him.

Very definitely now, Flint wished this small, dark-haired girl had not followed him up on the walk. He noticed that she was watching him closely, having seen him look at the carriage out in the street. She said softly, "Are they friends of yours?"

"Reckon I know them," Flint growled.

The carriage had started to move forward now, several men having dragged the inert Moose Clemens out of the way. Jay Bannerman waved his cigar to Flint, and Portia Wilde lifted a gloved hand in greeting.

At that moment Windwagon Smith reached him and he grabbed Flint's hand, pumping it vigorously.

"We are much obliged to you, sir," the fat man wheezed. "May I have the pleasure of buying you a drink?"

Otey Higgins said promptly, "A pleasure both ways, mister."

Flint nodded, assuming that by entering the saloon they would be temporarily rid of this dark-haired girl with the cool brown eyes. As they pushed in through the doors, he was a little exasperated to find her still at his heels

to the point of the chin, and Moose Clemens dropped to the ground as if he'd been shot. He lay there on his back, arms and legs extended, not a muscle in his body moving.

Flint looked at his bruised knuckles and then walked over to Jennifer Smith. She handed his hat to him and said softly, "I'm obliged, mister."

"All right," Flint said gruffly. He put on the hat, nodded to Otey Higgins, and then started to push his way through the yelling, cheering crowd. When he reached the boardwalk he found that Jennifer Smith was still with him, having followed in his wake. Her father was pushing through the crowd, sweating, smiling, waving a hand at Flint.

"Wait," he called. "Wait, young man."

Flint looked down at the girl, a slight frown on his face, and then he looked out over the crowd and he saw the Dearborn carriage which Portia Wilde, her uncle, and Jay Bannerman had climbed into on the wharf. They were sitting in the carriage, and the carriage was blocked by the crowd in the middle of the street. Evidently, they'd been driving around the town and their way had been blocked by the fight in the middle of the street. Flint got the impression that they'd been there for some time, which meant that they'd witnessed the fight with the big trapper.

Bannerman was smoking a cigar. Clayton Wilde was smiling broadly, and Portia Wilde was

in to slash at the big trapper's face with his fists. He hit Clemens hard, cutting open his cheek, but the giant did not seem to mind. He kept leaping in, face distorted, big hands reaching for Flint, and Flint knew that if the big man closed with him, he was finished.

It was a fight between a panther and a lumbering bear, with the panther slashing and the bear constantly trying to move in for the death hug.

Otey Higgins called from the inner edge of the circle, "Hit him in the belly, Flint. Wastin' your time on his face."

Flint had already come to that conclusion. When Clemens rushed him again he stepped in, driving his right fist deep into the giant's stomach. Moose Clemens' mouth opened and his face changed color. He stood there, gasping for breath, clutching his stomach, and then Flint hit him four times on the chin and then another terrific blow in the stomach, above his clutching hands.

Still the giant trapper wouldn't go down. He stumbled forward, face exposed and bleeding, holding his stomach, and Flint hit him again on the side of the face, ripping the flesh, sending the blood cascading down his cheek.

"One more good one, Flint," Otey Higgins called.

Flint hit him the good one, a swinging blow

Then Jennifer Smith stamped hard on his toe with the heel of her boot as she scrambled to her feet. The giant let out a whoop, bent over double, and then Flint slashed out at him again, a downward blow which knocked Moose Clemens into the dust of the road.

All around them, men were yelling, "Fight! Fight!" They moved in closer.

Flint backed away then to let the giant get to his feet. He saw Jennifer Smith staring at him curiously.

"I'll hold your hat, mister," she said.

Flint handed it to her without a word. He watched Moose Clemens get to his feet without haste and then start to dust himself off.

"Wagh," the giant said. He wasn't even looking at Flint, who was waiting and watching a few yards away, the circle closing around the two of them. For one moment Flint thought the fight was over but, when he looked into Moose Clemens' tough blue eyes he realized that it had only begun.

"I'm a ring-tailed panther," Moose whooped. "I'm a horned buffler rootin' the dust."

He jumped up into the air, clapping his hands, crowing like a rooster, and then he lunged in at Flint, with the crowd howling excitedly. He was wide open, trying to grasp Flint around the waist and throw him to the ground.

Flint eluded him, backing away, and then leaped

was as red as his beard, a bright rust color, and he had pale blue eyes.

The giant trapper bowled over two spectators as he made his final lunge toward the wagon, reaching up and wrapping his powerful arms around Jennifer Smith.

The girl let out a quick yell as she was jerked off the wagon, her arms pinned to her side. When her boots hit the dust of the road she started to fight and squirm energetically, kicking back at Moose Clemens' shins with her boots.

The crowd didn't like it, but no one intervened. Otey Higgins looked at Flint and then said softly "He's a big one, Flint, an' you got a nice job. Ain't no sense ridin' down to Santa Fe with only one ear an' maybe an eye missin'."

Flint was already pushing off the boardwalk, going through the crowd. He saw Windwagon Smith leaning over the wagon guard, pointing a chubby finger at the giant trapper.

"I'll have the law on you!" the chubby man shouted. "You set that girl down."

Moose Clemens set Jennifer Smith down hard in the road and then he laughed uproariously. Flint came up behind him, touched him on the shoulder, and as he turned around, swung with all his strength at the giant's chin. His fist felt as if it had collided with a doorjamb.

Moose Clemens roared, "What's this—what's this?"

was brown-skinned, brown-eyed, and Flint had to admit, rather pretty.

"You see that," Otey Higgins muttered. "Hit him right over the head an' put him away."

"They don't bother Windwagon Smith too much when Jenny's around." The man next to them chuckled. "She'll handle 'em."

Flint MacKeithan had another look at Jennifer Smith, noticing that she had a rather small, uptilted nose, and that her mouth was well-shaped. He frowned, though, thinking of how she'd struck the drunk over the head with the whipstock. He could not imagine Portia Wilde doing a thing like that.

"Reckon we seen enough," Otey Higgins said. "Have a drink, Flint, an' then we'll move on up to that camp along the river."

The man next to them said suddenly, "Gonna miss the fun, boys. Here comes big Moose Clemens. He got his fingers rapped yesterday by Jenny Smith."

Flint turned and saw the giant mountain man with the bear moving along the walk in the direction of the wagon. As he watched, he saw Moose Clemens chain the bear to a post and then start to push his way through the crowd, coming up behind Jennifer Smith. The giant was grinning, a toothy, slavering grin. He was at least six feet, four inches tall and must have weighed fully two hundred and thirty pounds. His hair

"Reckon Jennifer kin take care o' herself," their new friend said and grinned. "Wouldn't be surprised she kind o' took care o' her father, too."

Flint MacKeithan discovered that fact a few moments later. A drunk staggered out of the Comanche Saloon across the way, pushed through the crowd, and came up to the wagon, gripping the wagon wheel directly in front of Windwagon Smith as the fat man continued with his talk.

"Want a ride," he growled. "Hoist up that damn sail, Smith. I'll try her out."

"Not now," the fat man said pleasantly. "Another demonstration tomorrow morning, sir."

"Now," the drunk told him flatly. He started to climb up the wheel, and then Windwagon Smith stepped back to let his daughter pass in front of him. Flint saw the short whipstock in her hand but he didn't really believe she would use it.

The drunk let out a whoop of pain as the whipstock came down across his knuckles just as he was pulling himself up over the wagon guard. He let out a groan as the whipstock cracked him across the skull and he fell back into the arms of the nearest listeners, who lowered him to the ground and promptly forgot about him.

"Hurray fer Jenny Smith!" a man yelled from the porch of the Comanche Saloon.

Jennifer Smith smiled and sat down again. She

A man next to him turned his head and said, "She really rolls, mister, but he's got a light wagon there an' no load in it. I ain't sayin' how far or how fast she'll go with a couple thousand pound o' trade goods loaded on. I ain't sayin' she'll go at all."

Flint glanced at the boy sitting on the wagon guard, and then he looked at the fat man, and then his eyes moved back very quickly to the boy. Otey Higgins said it for him because Otey had also been looking at the boy.

"That ain't a boy," Otey murmured. "Reckon that there's a girl, Flint."

"Windwagon Smith's daughter, Jennifer," the man next to them explained. "She helps her father run the contraption. Damn if I'd ride on it, though. She goes like hell out on the open plains. Buffalo catch sight o' that rig an' they'll all run clean into the Pacific Ocean."

Flint was staring at Jennifer Smith up on the wagon. She was short and dark and slender, dressed in tight-fitting jacket and a man's jeans. He'd never before seen a woman in man's clothes and at first was shocked. However, Jennifer Smith made a very fetching figure as she sat easily on the wagon guard, legs crossed, smiling at her father and then looking out over the crowd.

"No place fer a woman to be," Otey Higgins said vehemently. "That fat feller ought to be ashamed o' hisself."

numerous as ships at sea. There is no upkeep. You need not break in mules nor oxen. It can roll twenty-four hours a day and it needs no rest. A wagon constructed along the lines that I will design can take a full cargo to Santa Fe in three weeks, where it takes the best teamsters in the country nearly two months. Gentlemen—"

"What if there ain't no wind, Smith?" a man in the crowd yelled good-naturedly.

The fat man smiled. "Always a wind out on the open plains, gentlemen," he stated.

"How do you get it over Raton Pass, Smith?" another man jibed.

"We take the desert route," Smith informed him. "The windwagon is not designed for mountain travel. I have already demonstrated to you the speed and maneuverability of this device. I am interested now in forming an organization of financially solvent Westport citizens who will put up the capital and buy shares in the corporation which will manufacture windwagons on a large scale."

A bartender yelled over the doors of his saloon, "How much you got to put into the corporation, Smith?"

The fat man ignored the question and went on talking, asking for financial backers to step forward and be counted.

Otey Higgins whispered to Flint, "He says he had it goin', Flint. You believe that?"

"Reckon hell's poppin' here day an' night," Otey grinned. "The way I want it, though, Flint."

Flint was staring down the street at the huge crowd gathered at the main intersection. The crowd was surrounding a light wagon—the strangest wagon Flint had ever laid eyes on. There were no horses in the traces and the wagon tongue was drawn up and rigged in such a way that it could be used as a steering rudder.

There was a mast on the wagon, a single main-mast with the sail drawn and folded now. A short, roly-poly man with an apple face was standing up in the prow of this unusual contraption, addressing the crowd. A boy sat nonchalantly on the wagon guard, looking out over the crowd.

Otey Higgins pulled up short on seeing the wagon, blue eyes popping. "That ain't a wagon with a sail on it, Flint?" he asked.

Flint smiled, saying, "Reckon that's what it is, but I'll lay ten to one odds it won't work."

They came up on the outskirts of the crowd and they could hear the short fat man going at a great rate, gesticulating with both hands as he explained in great detail the merits of his "wind-wagon."

"The greatest invention since man first per-fected the principle of the wheel." The fat man smiled expansively. "We shall all live to see the day, gentlemen, when windwagons will be moving across these great American plains as

Otey Higgins came over, tugging on his chin thoughtfully. The little hunter said, "Now we got another job, Flint. Who in hell is tryin' to kill a man like Clayton Wilde, an' why?"

"Same bunch tried to kill Bannerman on board this boat," Flint murmured. "Why—we don't know."

They left the General Jackson a few minutes later, mingling with the crowd on the wharf. The hatches already were being broken open, and roustabouts were swarming over the boat, ready to unload.

Flint saw Clayton Wilde, his niece, and Jay Bannerman standing near a Dearborn carriage on a side street, talking with an erect, broad-shouldered man in dark, civilian clothing, but who carried himself like an Army man.

After a while they got into the carriage and drove away, upriver, and Otey Higgins said, "Must be one o' Wilde's advance men come up here on an earlier boat to git things in order."

They walked through the crowded streets, dodging the innumerable wagons and carriages which seemed to be moving in every direction at once. Men pushed in and out of the bat-wing doors of saloons; hammers pounded in a half-dozen blacksmith shops. A big red-bearded mountain man came down the boardwalk with a brown bear on a chain, and both Flint and Otey Higgins gave the animal a wide berth.

"Yet he is taking one hundred and fifty men down to Santa Fe."

"I cannot tell you why," Portia Wilde said. "My uncle or Mr. Bannerman will advise you when they are ready, if they advise you at all."

The passengers were going across the planks now, and Jay Bannerman was coming up the steps from the main deck, having left Clayton Wilde below. He touched his hat to Portia and nodded pleasantly to Flint. Again, he was immaculately dressed, pearl-gray claw-hammer coat with the high beaver, a white silk shirt with maroon cravat. His boots were polished to a mirror-like shine and they gleamed in the sunlight.

He said to Portia, "Getting acquainted with our hunter, Portia?"

"I have asked Mr. MacKeithan to keep an eye on Uncle," Portia explained. "You know his danger, Jay."

Jay Bannerman nodded soberly. "I am sure we can count on Flint's help," he said. "I had intended to speak to him." To Flint, he said, "You will find our wagons and our encampment up above Judson's Mill. "I believe a large tent is being set up to accommodate Mr. Wilde and Portia. We expect to be in Westport a week or two before we shall have sufficient wagons and supplies to take the trail."

"We'll be there," Flint said, and he watched them go down the stairs together.

life, every moment he is in Westport, is in grave danger. I would appreciate it if you would remain near him as much as you can to—to prevent any accidents."

Flint looked at her steadily. "Kind of like to know what I'm to watch out for," he said. "Be easier to keep an eye on him."

The girl frowned a little. "At this time," she stated, "I cannot tell you. I am afraid only that he will be shot down by an assassin. It is tremendously important that my uncle reach Santa Fe this summer. You can help ensure his safety."

Flint nodded. "Do what I can, ma'am," he told her.

"I can ask no more," Portia Wilde smiled. "It is good to have men who can be trusted. We will need many like you before we reach Santa Fe."

"You going to Santa Fe?" Flint asked.

She nodded. "I am my uncle's secretary. He needs me."

"Hear it can be a dangerous trip," Flint stated. "Reckon there won't be too many women moving out on the trail this spring."

"That is not important," Portia Wilde said. "I must go."

Flint looked toward the shore. "Your uncle is not a trader," he said. "He is not taking trade goods to Santa Fe."

"No," Portia admitted. "His business is not trading."

advance men in Westport purchasing wagons and supplies.

Portia Wilde came out of the cabin a few moments later, a steward carrying several carpetbags and a portmanteau. As she walked toward the stairs she saw Flint standing over near the awning.

Flint touched his hat to her. He'd seen her since their first meeting in the cabin but he hadn't spoken with her, and he was a little surprised now to see her say a few words to the steward and then walk directly toward him.

Again she was wearing the gray traveling costume with a green bonnet to match. Her golden hair was done in a bun at the nape of her neck, and was very becoming.

Otey Higgins got up from his chair when he saw her approaching, and he touched his hat clumsily. Then he moved back to the rail out of hearing.

Portia Wilde said, "Mr. MacKeithan, before you leave this boat I must ask a favor."

Flint stood there with his hat in his hand and waited.

"You are a member of this expedition," Portia Wilde told him. "I believe my uncle has already paid you a month's wages in advance."

"Reckon he's been good to us, ma'am," Flint nodded. "We'll stand by him."

"I must tell you," Portia said slowly, "that his

scene below, and then he yawned and said, "Hell of a sight, ain't it, Flint? Must be five thousand people in this town, an' four thousand of 'em gettin' ready to take the trail—either to Santa Fe or to Oregon. Them Injuns out on the plains gonna look twice when these outfits hit the trail."

They'd had their first look at the western plains that morning too, as the General Jackson came around a bend in the river, moving up toward Westport, and both men had been silent for several long moments as they stared at the terrific expanse of open, rolling grass country. To men accustomed to the dense woods, the hills, and the mountains of Tennessee, this flat land upon which a man could spot an antelope at two miles or more was almost terrifying. It was like the sea—a sea of grass stretching to the horizon, undulating, birds wheeling above it, white fleecy clouds drifting past.

"Reckon a man kin move around out there," Otey Higgins had said thoughtfully.

As the General Jackson's ropes were cast ashore and the packet snubbed against the dock, Flint saw Clayton Wilde come out of his cabin with Jay Bannerman, talking earnestly, a heavy leather saddlebag under his arm, bulging with papers.

Bannerman had already instructed Flint that the members of their party were to meet in a grove above Judson's Mill, Clayton Wilde having had

Fox Indians in white men's clothing, watching the oncoming steamer.

Blank-faced emigrants, farmers from Illinois and Indiana, stood with Santa Fe traders in their black frock coats and mountain trappers just arrived from Santa Fe and the shining mountains.

Big Conestoga and Pittsburgh wagons were everywhere, lined up along the dock, taking on cargoes, being rolled off tied-up packets, new wagons, bright and gleaming in their red and blue paint, with bright yellow wheels giving them a rakish tilt.

Huge cargoes of merchandise—cotton goods, cutlery, ironware, foodstuffs—lay on the dock covered with tarpaulins, waiting to be loaded aboard the wagons, the largest wagons Flint had ever seen. Oxen and mules were pulling most of the wagons, six and eight teams to the wagon, straining to get away from the dock and out into the groves where the wagon trains were being formed for the first leg of the journey down to Council Grove.

From midriver Flint had seen some of these temporary encampments, smoke curling up from a hundred campfires, white-topped wagons parked under the trees, teamsters and bull-whackers breaking in fresh oxen and mules.

Otey Higgins, also wearing a new outfit, (his worn and patched buckskins thrown into the river) sprawled in a deck chair watching the

Chapter Three

WEARING A NEW hickory shirt, a flat-crowned felt hat, and blue jeans which Jay Bannerman had provided for him on board, Flint stood in front of the guardrail on the texas as the General Jackson nudged into the dock at Westport Landing, the pilot cleverly maneuvering the sidewheeler in between the two other packets already tied up.

A big crowd had come down to watch the steamer move into its berth after they'd blown the whistle far downriver. Flint stared out over the motley collection of board houses, log huts, false-front buildings, and occasional tents which formed the river port of Westport Landing. Several hundred people were down at the dock, a good cross section of the town. Flint spotted dark Spaniards with tall peaked sombreros leaning against warehouse walls, checked ponchos wrapped around them.

Tough roustabouts were already congregating at the dock to unload the General Jackson. Wealthy merchants in their high beavers and swallow-tail coats stood next to swarthy Delaware or Sac or

face with a handkerchief and then looked at Flint. Flint was watching Portia Wilde coming toward them with a tray and three filled wine glasses on it.

She said, smiling, "To the success of our expedition, gentlemen."

The three men drank, and then Jay Bannerman arranged for Flint and Otey to take a small cabin near the sternwheel. He left them immediately, and Otey sat down on the edge of his bunk to stare at Flint. The little redhead said slowly, "What in hell have we got into, Flint, boy?"

Flint shrugged. "It's a job," he stated. "Reckon I'd like to see Santa Fe."

"He ain't a trader," Otey pointed out, "not that Clayton Wilde. You've seen traders in St. Louis an' aboard this boat, Flint. He ain't goin' down to Santa Fe to trade an' make money."

"No," Flint admitted. Clayton Wilde was definitely not a trader, nor did Jay Bannerman seem to be a man in business for profit.

"Hundred an' fifty odd men goin' down to Santa Fe," Otey Higgins muttered. "What in hell for?"

Flint shrugged. "We'll find out." He smiled, and he was wondering if the party to Santa Fe would include one girl—a girl with golden hair and violet eyes.

of your needs. You will need arms, clothing, blankets—"

"We have our Kentucky rifles," Otey Higgins interposed. "Best damned gun on the frontier, Mr. Wilde."

Clayton Wilde smiled a little and put both hands into his pockets as he stared down at the floor. "You are new to this country, Higgins," he stated. "I am new, also, but I have taken great pains to ascertain facts which it is needful to know. Mr. Bannerman will supply you in Westport with the latest Hawkins' mountain rifles, a heavy-bore gun, thirty-two balls to the pound. Your Kentucky rifles, Mr. Higgins, will only tickle a fifteen-hundred-pound buffalo. You have seen buffalo, Mr. Higgins?"

"No, sir," Otey gulped.

"Neither have I," Mr. Wilde said and grinned, "but I have read every available document on that interesting subject and I believe I speak with authority. A Kentucky rifle, however admirable a weapon, will not bring down a buffalo, gentlemen."

"Yes, sir," Otey Higgins murmured.

Clayton Wilde turned to pick up a letter on the table, and then Jay Bannerman touched Flint's arm, nodding toward the door. As they were leaving, Mr. Wilde said over his shoulder, "A pleasure meeting you, gentlemen. Good hunting."

Back in the other room, Otey Higgins wiped his

He had a deeply lined face, a hatchet-shaped head with a mop of unruly gray hair. His eyes were turquoise in color, deep-set, very intense, the most peculiar eyes Flint had ever seen. They were the eyes of a man who saw things other men did not see—the eyes of a visionary.

"Mr. Clayton Wilde," Jay Bannerman murmured. "These gentlemen desire to join our expedition as hunters, Mr. Wilde."

He introduced them, and Clayton Wilde shook their hands, smiling again. The hand he extended to Flint was thin, blue-veined, bony.

"We are indeed happy to have you," Clayton Wilde told them. He had a deep voice which seemed to fill the room. It was the voice of a man who was accustomed to speaking to large audiences.

"I have not acquainted our friends with the nature of our expedition," Jay Bannerman said, looking straight at Clayton Wilde, "other than to inform them that our destination is Santa Fe, and that they will be expected to keep our party in fresh meat when game is available."

Mr. Wilde nodded soberly. He looked at Flint and Otey Higgins sharply, as if sizing them up, and his lips were pursed as if he were about to say something, and then he changed his mind.

"If the pay and the conditions suit you, gentlemen," he said, "Mr. Bannerman will handle all

MacKeithan," Portia Wilde told him. "I am sure my uncle will see you immediately."

She shook hands with the astounded Otey Higgins, too, commenting on the color of Otey's hair, leaving him grinning and pleased, and then she disappeared into the next room of the large, double cabin.

Otey Higgins murmured, "A nice girl, Mr. Bannerman."

Flint didn't say anything, but he looked at the smiling Bannerman, who was leaning against the wall, very cool, very poised, in every sense a gentleman, with background and education and wealth, and he wondered how he could have been so foolish as to think he could give Bannerman competition where Portia Wilde was concerned.

Portia came out, dressed in white this noon, with a blue sash around her waist. She said, smiling, "My uncle will be happy to see you now, gentlemen."

Bannerman pushed away from the wall, nodding to Flint and to Otey Higgins. He walked in through the open door, and Flint followed him.

The second room of the suite was considerably smaller than the first. It contained a bunk and a side table and chairs. A tall, angular, gray-haired man had been sitting at the side table, a batch of papers, documents, and books on the table in front of him. He got up when they entered, smiling his welcome.

golden hair, and her eyes were violet in color, not the light blue Flint MacKeithan had fancied they would be.

She was looking straight at him, past Jay Bannerman, and smiling a little. It was the same beautiful, cool, and serene face, the perfectly shaped nose and mouth, the skin clear and white, but the nose slightly sunburned, indicating that she'd been out on the texas in the daytime as well as at night. It was the only distinctly human touch to her, and Flint found himself rather entranced by that sunburned nose.

Bannerman stepped aside. He nodded to Flint and Otey and he said, "Two gentlemen whom we may sign up for our expedition, Portia. Is your uncle busy?"

"You may come in," Portia said. Her voice was as Flint had imagined it would be—low, but not throaty, clear and distinct, definitely Eastern, the voice of a highly educated girl.

Flint did not expect Bannerman to introduce them, but he did, mentioning their names. He introduced the golden-haired girl as Portia Wilde. She came forward when Bannerman nodded to her, extending her hand to Flint, another wholly unexpected gesture.

Swallowing and red-faced, Flint took the extended hand, finding it warm and friendly. He mumbled his pleasure at meeting her.

"We are glad to have you with us, Mr.

two hundred paces, with the tail switchin'."

Jay Bannerman smiled and touched a match to his cigar. It was an expensive cigar and it gave off a rich aroma.

"I am with an expedition going down to Santa Fe," he stated. "We can use a few hunters to keep us supplied with fresh meat. Would you be interested in such a proposition?"

Flint looked at Otey Higgins, and then nodded. "Reckon we came out here to latch on with an outfit," he said.

"Our expedition," Bannerman was saying, "will pay your fare to Westport Landing, and a salary of thirty dollars a month and found to keep us in fresh meat—when fresh meat is available."

"How many men with your party?" Flint asked him.

Jay Bannerman pursed his lips, the cigar in his hand and then he flicked ash from the cigar.

"We'll say one hundred and fifty. Possibly more."

Otey Higgins whistled a little. "Pretty big outfit," he murmured. "You runnin' it, Mr. Bannerman?"

Bannerman shook his head. "I should like to have you meet the head of our expedition," he said, "in the adjoining cabin."

Flint and Otey Higgins followed him out to the deck and waited while he knocked on the door of the next cabin. It was opened by the girl with the

Flint shrugged again. "Reckon one's as good as the other," he said and he glanced at Otey Higgins. Otey nodded without comment.

Both men knew that the trail to Oregon was the emigrant trail—farmers fanning out from the East and the Middlewest to work the rich, black soil of the new Oregon Territory. The Santa Fe Trail on the other hand was the trade trail, a two-way trail with traders hauling huge cargoes of manufactured goods, pots and pans, blankets, down to the Mexican province of New Mexico, and then returning with buffalo robes, beaver skins, and rich metals.

Back in St. Louis they'd heard men tell of the huge profits to be made carrying trade goods down to Santa Fe; they'd heard other enticing stories of the brown-skinned, black-eyed Mexican *señoritas* who welcomed the Yankee traders with open arms. It was a long and a tough trail down to the New Mexican capital, eight hundred miles of open plain and dry desert and mountains and rivers to cross, with always the threat of Indian attacks and prairie fires and buffalo stampedes. They'd said in St. Louis that it took a man to haul wagons down to Santa Fe and then bring them back.

Jay Bannerman was saying, "I understand you Tennesseans are pretty good with a rifle."

Otey Higgins grinned. "Any one of us," he chuckled, "kin shoot a fly off a cow's tail at

and Bannerman got up from the bed, took a turn around the room, and then came to a stop before the small window which looked out on the deck. He said to Flint, "You didn't get a look at the man who went over the side last night?"

"Saw him," Flint said, "briefly. Looked like a Mexican or Spaniard. Dark hair, sallow face—"

"A scar," Jay Bannerman said softly, "running up from the right side of the mouth?"

Flint looked at him, realizing now that the men who'd tried to kill Bannerman had not been ordinary footpads after his wallet or valuables.

Jay Bannerman had his back to the window now, and he said no more on the subject. When Flint finished washing and was drying his face on a clean towel, Bannerman said to him, "What is in Westport Landing for you, MacKeithan?"

Flint shrugged. "Not much back in Tennessee, either," he observed. "New country beyond the Missouri. Figured I'd like to see it."

Jay Bannerman put a cigar in his mouth but he didn't light it. He was facing the two men now, watching them steadily, and then he said to Otey Higgins, "What about you, my friend?"

"Like to see them shinin' mountains," Otey said, "with the snow on 'em in the summertime. Want to chase a buffalo an' watch him fall."

"Heading for Oregon?" Bannerman asked, "or Santa Fe? Trails run in both directions from Westport."

dresser, and Bannerman pointed to it carelessly. He said as he sat down on the edge of the bed, "You might like to wash the blood from your faces and make yourselves presentable."

"Who we meetin'?" Otey Higgins asked, grinning, "the President of the United States."

Bannerman smiled. He had level brown eyes and rather long eyelashes and he was the handsomest man Flint had ever seen, and yet there was nothing feminine about him. He'd handled the husky mate very easily. His hands were smooth, uncalloused, and not too big, but they were strong hands, and the width of his shoulders, and his height, almost as tall as Flint himself, would make another man think twice before tackling him.

"Not the President," Bannerman said evenly, "of the United States, gentlemen."

Flint walked over to the dresser and poured some water into the basin, and he knew that Bannerman was watching him as he sat on the edge of the bed.

"You are the man who routed the two who tried to assault me last night," Bannerman stated.

Flint glanced at him and nodded. "Reckon so."

"I'm obliged," Bannerman murmured.

"We're even," Flint told him, and Bannerman smiled a little.

"The name," the tall man introduced himself, "is Jay Bannerman, from Boston."

Both Flint and Otey gave him their names,

Mr. Bannerman," he protested. "Pair o' damned drifters. Country's full of 'em."

"I will assume full responsibility for them," Bannerman repeated. He stepped up to Flint and said quietly, "Are you able to walk?"

Flint nodded. The few moments of respite had enabled him to recover. The numbness was leaving his arms and shoulders, although he still felt weak.

"Please come along with me, gentlemen," Bannerman said.

"A pleasure." Otey Higgins grinned as he followed Bannerman toward the main staircase which led up to the texas. "Never did like the company down here in the first place."

Flint watched Bannerman lift the chain across the staircase, and then the three of them went up the steps to the texas deck, the passengers up above watching them curiously.

Bannerman walked without haste toward the line of cabins, his high beaver on the side of his head, hands in his pockets, the claw-hammer coat thrown open. When he reached the cabin he opened the door, motioning for them to go in.

It was the first time Flint had seen the inside of a riverboat cabin. The room was small, but tastefully furnished, a built-in bed in one corner, table and chairs, an overhead light, rugs on the floor, the wall panels painted a light blue.

A white water pitcher and basin stood on the

Otey Higgins, who was still backed into the corner.

Flint tried to lift his arms to protect himself, but the mate brushed his hands aside and lashed out viciously with another blow to Flint's face. Flint sagged against the bales, dazed, the blood dripping from his cut cheek. He saw Otey Higgins go down again, one of the crewmen kicking at him, the crowd yelling incoherently.

The mate was lifting his fist to swing it again into Flint's face when his hand was caught and he was spun around by someone who'd come up from behind.

Flint MacKeithan had a good look at the tall young man with the curling brown hair who'd walked the deck the previous evening with the golden-haired girl—the man whose life he'd saved when the footpads attacked him.

"That'll be all," the passenger said quietly.

"Ain't paid their fare," the mate growled. "Damned stowaways. We're teachin' 'em a lesson, Mr. Bannerman."

The two crewmen who'd been working over Otey Higgins left off, and little Otey scrambled to his feet, none the worse for wear, still grinning, but with his left eye swelling up.

"You may inform the purser," Mr. Bannerman said evenly, "that I am paying their fare and that I will be responsible for these two men."

The mate stared at him. "They ain't worth it,

rear, driving him forward against a high crate, stunning him when his head struck the crate.

Flint met the mate's second charge with a flurry of hard blows to the head, dropping him to his knees. Since he was moving forward when he was punching, he stumbled over the man, and the crewman assisting the mate brought a fist down across the back of his neck as he fell.

The blow paralyzed Flint and he fell awkwardly on hands and knees. The crewman immediately brought his knee up into Flint's face, sending him over on his back.

Otey Higgins had left the crewman he'd attacked, but the tough mate was on his feet now, too, and the two of them backed the little redhead into a corner where he fought gamely, but futilely, trying to work his way out of the cul-de-sac where he could use his great speed of foot.

Flint, still dazed, the upper part of his body numb from that vicious blow to the back of his neck, saw Otey go down and get up again, and he tried desperately to get back into the fight. He managed to climb to his feet and stumble in their direction, but then the mate, seeing him coming, whirled, grinning bloodily, and hit him squarely on the jaw, sending him reeling against some stacked bales.

As Flint stood there, helpless, the mate moved toward him, fists cocked. One of the crewmen who'd been on the floor was up now, going after

23

Flint moved back like a big cat, very light on his feet, carrying his hundred and ninety pounds as if he were fifty pounds lighter. He was hatless and his black hair gleamed in the bright sun. He watched the three men coming toward him, no fear in his gray eyes, big hands loose at his sides.

Out of the corner of his eye he saw one of the crewmen leap at little Otey Higgins, or at least at the spot where the redhead had been a fraction of a second before.

With incredible swiftness, Otey had moved out of the way, trailing one foot over which the crewman stumbled and pitched forward head-long. As he landed flat on his face, little Higgins went up into the air like a ballet dancer, landing with both feet and all of his weight on the crewman's back. He let out a wild Indian whoop as his feet came down, driving the air out of the man's chest, leaving him stunned and breathless on the deck.

The mate, thinking that Flint's momentary retreat was a sign of fear, lunged in at him. Flint met him with a swinging blow to the face, the hard fist catching the mate full in the mouth, splitting his lips. The blow stopped the chunky man temporarily, but he came on again, blood cascading down over his flannel shirt.

The two crewmen with him came at Flint from either side, but Otey Higgins sidetracked one of them by running into him at high speed from the

He moved forward again, making the club whistle in his hand, and then Flint slipped the hunting knife from his belt. He said slowly, "Never like to use this on a man, but I will if you don't put that club down, mister."

The mate hesitated, looking at the knife, frowning, and then one of the wealthy passengers on the texas called down, "Give the boy a break. There are four of you against one."

Otey Higgins said with an injured air, "Two of us, mister. I ain't over the side, yet."

The main-deck passengers, a tough crowd of teamsters, roustabouts, and frontiersmen, took up the cue, also, and began to demand that the mate drop the club and go at it with his fists. While he didn't particularly relish the idea, he was a man with pride in his fists, and he had a reputation aboard this boat.

Flint watched him toss the club aside and then he placed his hunting knife on a barrel top nearby, moving out into the open space where he could maneuver a little.

Otey Higgins spat on his hands and said softly, "Here goes nothin'. Broken heads or not, we go over the side, but if I'm to have my choice I'll go over in one piece."

"Get 'em," the mate said briefly, and then he rushed forward, swinging heavy, freckled fists. Two men came behind him, and the third man moved in at Otey Higgins.

was shorter than Flint but heavier in the waist.

Otey Higgins said to him placatingly, "Reckon we're willin' to work our way up to Westport, mister."

The mate grinned. "Kind o' late talkin' o' work, ain't you, friend?" he asked, "more than halfway to Westport?"

"Habit o' mine," Otey murmured, "mentionin' work when the time fer work is over."

"Take the little one, Ben," the mate said to the crewman on his left. "An', if you was to break that club, remember that we got twenty cords o' firewood on board this boat. Wood is cheap."

"I have only one head, though," Otey Higgins told him, "an' it don't work well when it's broke."

Flint rubbed his big hands on his buckskins. He saw the crowd gathering on the main deck, and then the passengers above on the texas became aware of this little altercation below, and many of them were moving toward the guardrail, grinning in anticipation, grateful for this break in the monotony of a river voyage.

"We're willing to work," Flint said evenly, "to pay for our passage. We'll help unload when this boat ties up at Westport."

The mate shook his head. "Too late," he grinned. "You boys are goin' over the side an' you ain't goin' easy. Reckon we're gonna teach you drifters a lesson they'll hear about from Westport clean down to New Orleans."

Chapter Two

I**T WAS HIGH NOON** the next day, and still a hundred and fifty miles from Westport Landing, when the second mate and three crewmen kicked away the crates concealing their hiding place.

"Come out an' get it, boys," the mate grinned. "You been livin' off the fat o' the land long enough now."

Flint looked at him as he crawled out through the little opening, a dozen or so main-deck passengers watching him apprehensively. The mate took a firmer grip on the short, thick club in his hand and eyed Flint speculatively. Then he said to one of the crewmen with him, "Might need a little help with this one, Sam."

Flint straightened up, blinking in the bright sunlight. He said softly, "Need more than Sam to help you, mister."

Otey Higgins crawled out of the hiding place, grumbling in disgust that someone had informed on them, and vowing that he'd cut the gentleman's ears off when he found out.

The second mate had a flat face with a blunt, red nose and a pair of tough, pale blue eyes. He

texas every night. Then again maybe you was licked right from the start. I don't know."

Flint MacKeithan tilted the wine bottle to his mouth and he looked up at the sky as he drank. He didn't know, either, but it was something to think about. A man with time on his hands could spend much of it in speculation on such a matter.

deck gathered around the body of the man he'd knocked unconscious. He saw the brown-haired young man with the high beaver come up from the main deck to join this group. The boat captain was there, and a number of excited passengers, and Flint MacKeithan lay on top of the Pittsburgh wagon, a wry smile on his face.

He's still alive, lady, he thought, for you.

Otey Higgins joined him after a while, clutching a half-filled bottle of wine as he came up to the top of the freight wagon.

"Had mine," he said. "This is fer you, Flint, an' you earned it,"

"How?" Flint said, smiling.

"All the excitement around here," Otey grinned. "One man with a bashed-in skull an' another overboard, it was easy enough fer a man o' my talents to locate a bottle o' wine that wasn't bein' drunk at the moment. An' all because o' you."

"You saw it?" Flint murmured.

"Saw you comin' down them stairs like a bat out o' hell," Otey observed, "an' when I heard that one of 'em had a busted head, I figured you was in on it right from the beginnin'. What happened?"

Flint told him briefly, and when he'd finished Otey Higgins lay on his back, crossing one leg over the other. He said casually, "If that feller was floatin' in the river right now, Flint, you might o' had a chance with that angel walkin' the

17

Flint went after him until he'd reached the railing, and then he saw the man plunge over the side into the water. As he watched, the swimmer's face came into the patch of red light from the open firebox door, and he saw it clearly, a thin, sallow Mexican face, lank black hair plastered on his brow, and a crescent scar running up from the right corner of his mouth, reaching almost to the right eye.

Sleepers on the main deck were getting up, some of them cursing because they'd been stepped on either by Flint or by the Mexican he'd been pursuing. The second mate was pushing his way through the crowd, a thick-chested man in seaman's cap, with a barrel-like body and a roll to his walk. Flint had seen him a number of times as he lay under tarpaulins or peered out from under the den they'd made by moving a number of crates and barrels.

It was still dark on the main deck, but a number of lanterns were being lighted, and the second mate was bawling, "Bring a light here. Bring a light!"

Flint moved away from the low guardrail, made a circuit of the main deck, passing around the capstans, and then came back to the wagon upon which he'd been lying. He scrambled up to the top and lay down, scarcely breathing hard even after the exertions of the past few minutes.

He could see the knot of men on the texas

back of the man with the knife, bearing him to the deck, and then he reached out with his free hand, grasping the second man by the coat and yanking him down hard so that he hit the deck with a bang.

The man under him, however, was small and wiry and as slippery as a rat. He was trying to squirm around so that he could slash at Flint with the knife.

Grinning, Flint grasped the knife hand, ground the knuckles against the hard deck, and then when the knife slipped from the footpad's bruised and bleeding fingers, he grasped the man's hair, lifted his head, and banged it down against the deck.

He felt the body go limp beneath him, and he rolled off, making a grab at the second man, who'd scrambled to his feet and was darting toward the staircase which led to the main deck. His hand missed the fellow's coat, and as he started in pursuit down the steps, he heard the young man with the cigar coming after them, calling loudly, and then the bull-like voice of the second mate from the saloon roared, "What's that—what's that?"

The footpad hit the chain stretched across the stairway, tumbled over it, recovered, and darted around the wagons, the half-aroused sleepers on the deck, and the piles of crates, boxes, and barrels which had overflowed the capacity of the hold.

patches of light from the saloon windows, that warned Flint of impending danger to the young man on the texas.

He came up on his knees on top of the wagon, and then he stood up, still in the deep shadows. The young man with the cigar was richly dressed, and undoubtedly he would have a fat wallet and valuables on his person. The riverboats always had their quota of footpads and undesirables moving up from St. Louis to the cities. In a very few moments the young man who'd walked so gaily with the young lady might find himself in the river, his throat cut, and his valuables gone— unless someone intervened.

Flint reached down, feeling the cold, smooth barrel of the Kentucky rifle on the canvas, and then he straightened up again, his right hand caressing the hunting knife in his belt, before he stepped across to the next wagon in the line on the deck.

He moved across two big freight wagons lashed to the deck side by side before he reached the guardrail of the texas. He was swinging up over the railing, still in the shadows, when the two footpads started their rush at the cigar smoker under the awning. He saw a knife flash in the hand of one of the two men, and then he lunged forward, at the same time calling a sharp warning to the unsuspecting victim.

With one long, catlike bound he landed on the

When he'd finished the last of the bread he lay back again on his elbows, watching the red glow of light reflected on the water from the open door of the engine room; the smell of the river coming to him strongly, dank and cool, mingled with the stable odor from the mule pens in one corner of the deck.

He saw a cigar butt, glowing red, moving along the darkened walls of the cabin, and then the cigar smoker came out into the moonlight. Flint recognized him as the young man who'd walked with the golden-haired girl. He was alone now, evidently taking a final stroll around the deck, finishing his cigar before turning in for the night.

He had his hands in his pockets, the claw-hammer coat thrown back, and the cigar tilted toward the night sky as he walked, and Flint watched him, wondering who he was, what his business was upriver, and how he'd become acquainted with the girl.

The tall young man paused under the darkened awning which was spread across a portion of the texas during the daytime as protection from the sun's rays. He stood there in the bow, staring upriver, and then Flint MacKeithan sat up very quickly, all his senses alert.

Two shadows were stealing up along the guard-rail of the texas, moving toward that awning, coming up behind the young man with the cigar. It was the way they moved, keeping out of the

one of the wagons on the deck had let them eat with him.

The second-class passengers were living like cattle on the main deck, living with their animals, their horses and mules and crates of chickens, bedding down on the deck or under their wagons at night, all of them headed for the frontier—settlers, teamsters, Spaniards headed back to Santa Fe, hunters, like himself, moving over the land like so many restless ants.

On the texas deck, eating in the ornate saloon, living in the luxurious cabins, the wealthy passengers lived a life apart, a heavy chain across the main staircase separating them from the rabble below. Each day rich merchants and Santa Fe traders paraded on the texas in their high beavers and swallow-tail coats, in their ruffled shirts and fancy embroidered vests. The girl with the golden hair and the young man in the high beaver were of this class, and Flint MacKeithan wondered how it would be to walk that deck, and to walk it with a girl on his arm, a girl with golden hair and the face of a Greek goddess.

Otey Higgins said, "Man kin choke eatin' dry bread. See if there's any wine layin' around, Flint."

He was gone, then, as swiftly and as soundlessly as he'd come, and Flint sat on top of the wagon, munching on the bread, wondering if he'd see the girl again tonight.

Flint smiled faintly. As far as Otey was concerned the affair was over, but he, Flint MacKeithan, did not think so. He had the strange feeling that some day he would meet this girl with the golden hair—he, a Tennessee backwoodsman in buckskins with empty pockets, with the second mate on the General Jackson trying to ferret him out and throw him into the river.

The packet surged slowly upstream against the current, white wood smoke gushing from its twin stacks. Up through the wagon Flint could feel the heartbeat of its engines as they churned toward the west—the still open frontier, the vast country which extended toward the distant mountains.

Like Otey Higgins he had no plans, but there was a restlessness running through him. He'd heard stories of the country west of the river, the huge buffalo herds staggering the imagination, the wild Indians riding the high plains, the long trail to Santa Fe, the capital of the Mexican province. He wanted to go everywhere and to see everything, and that would take a long time— probably a lifetime.

"Eat," Otey Higgins said, pressing a hunk of the bread into Flint's hand. "Nothin' like eatin' to make you forget. Stole this out o' the cook's galley."

Flint ate the bread. It was fresh and it was good, and he was hungry because he hadn't eaten since noon, when a tall Missouri teamster in charge of

beaver hat, which he took off when he came up to the girl on the deck. His white, ruffled shirt was spotless; the pearl gray vest flower-embroidered. The gray claw-hammer coat fit him perfectly, accentuating the width of his shoulders and the slimness of his hips.

Staring at him, Flint MacKeithan realized with growing and painful envy that this man was the perfect match for the girl with the golden hair. He was a fine-looking young man, probably in his middle twenties. When he smiled at the girl he revealed a set of perfect white teeth. There was a deep cleft in his chin, and his nose was straight, a classic Roman nose.

"Reckon that's the way it is," Otey Higgins murmured. "You meet a girl an' fall in love with her, an' then somebody else comes along an' it's all over, an' you don't even know her name an' you ain't ever spoken to her. That's hell, Flint."

The tall young man had taken the girl by the arm and they were walking together now, moving past the saloon windows. Flint could see her looking up at him, smiling as she spoke. This was not a chance meeting between two strangers. These people knew each other, and intimately, and that revelation was not a pleasant one to Flint.

He watched the couple pass out of sight, and then he heard Otey Higgins say complacently, "You et, Flint?"

"Here she comes," Flint said softly. He came up on his elbows again to watch as the girl with the golden hair recrossed the deck to their side, moving through a patch of moonlight in full sight of them.

Even Otey Higgins was silent as they watched her, and then the red-haired little man with the squinting blue eyes and the prow of a nose said thoughtfully, "You picked one, Flint, but I ain't sayin' you wouldn't o' been smarter to find yourself a hill girl, or even a Comanche squaw out on them plains we're headed for. This one ain't fer you, boy."

"You learn her name?" Flint murmured.

"Hell," Otey scowled. "I ain't goin' up on that texas deck. Too many officers up there, Flint."

"I'll learn who she is," Flint said with conviction, "before this boat docks at Westport Landing."

"The second mate learns who you are," Otey smiled, "an' you ain't even goin' to Westport, my friend." He sat up straight and Flint heard him start to gnaw on a piece of bread he'd filched, borrowed, or bought from another passenger on this main deck. Then he said laconically, "Reckon you got yourself a rival, Flint. Who in hell is this comin' up?"

The girl passenger had been joined by a man—a young man with curly, nut-brown hair, well-built, immaculately dressed. He wore a pearl gray, high

9

girl to reappear on the far side of the texas as she made her way down toward the cabins, and then he said to Otey Higgins, "A man can watch, Otey."

"Watchin' makes you want," Otey reflected philosophically, "an' wantin' what you can't ever have makes you miserable, boy. Forget about it, an' start thinkin' o' that tough second mate aboard this floatin' palace. He's thinkin' o' you plenty an' he's thinkin' o' me, an' he's figurin' on bouncin' our heads together when he finds us out."

Flint put his head back on the canvas for a moment, stretching his long frame like a big cat. He wasn't worried about the mate even though both of them had come aboard the General Jackson back in St. Louis without having bothered about steamboat tickets. They'd slipped across taut hawser lines holding the packet to the wharf, and then they'd lost themselves immediately in the crowd on the main deck, but now evidently it was being winded about that two stowaways were aboard, and the second mate was making his search.

"Two hundred people aboard this packet," Otey Higgins complained, "an' here they're worryin' themselves sick about a pair o' lone hunters from the Tennessee hills jest because they ain't paid their fare. We'll pay it on the way back—a hundred years from now, Flint."

Without turning his head, Flint murmured, "Reckon you missed her, Otey."

Only one man on the western frontier in the year 1842, as far as Flint MacKeithan knew, could have climbed to the top of a Pittsburgh wagon, making as little noise. That man was Otey Higgins, fellow Tennessean; the small, lithe, light-footed, light-hearted Otey whom he'd met on a lumber raft moving down the Ohio weeks before, and who, like himself, was headed for the western frontier, footloose and fancy free, knowing only one thing—that when the neighbors crowded to within a half mile of his log shelter, it was time to move.

"Still watchin' the queen o' the river?" Otey said and laughed softly. "Reckon that's Helen o' Troy herself, movin' like a sunbeam across the texas deck. What'll it get you, Flint?"

Flint shrugged and smiled. He lay there on the wagon top, a big man, solid in the shoulders, slim in the waist, black hair beginning to curl at the neck of his buckskin shirt. There was a faraway look in his gray Scotsman's eyes. He had the high cheekbones of an Indian and the same deep coloring, and he had the nose of an Indian, too, sharp and straight, a throwback to the single Cherokee ancestor in his strain, but his mouth was wide and the jaws solid—the jaws of a MacKeithan from the heather hills of Scotland.

He lay there, waiting for the golden-haired

stacks. She'd moved past him on the texas not more than twenty-five feet away and he'd had a good look at her, hatless, her golden hair fluffed a little by the breeze, a tall girl in gray traveling costume, long, full skirt, a white scarf around her shoulders.

She had the kind of face that a man looked at once and then remembered all the days of his life, even after he'd married someone else and was sitting in front of his house with his children around him. It was a serene face, a face which went well with the moonlight. She had a high brow and a perfect nose, the eyes set well apart. Flint was not sure, but he was willing to bet his long rifle that her eyes were blue—the blue of a mountain lake on a clear spring morning.

He watched her move under the awning spread across a portion of the texas deck in the bow, and then come out on the other side, walking slowly, head erect, her face to the river breeze. She was alone there on the texas, most of the other cabin passengers having gone to bed. A card game or two was going on in the saloon, and Flint could hear the low hum of talk occasionally through the open windows.

Then he heard something else, a light, rustling sound, a faint scraping of the canvas sheet to his left, almost as if a rat were passing over it, and then a faint sigh as someone stretched out on the canvas beside him.

Chapter One

THE WAY Flint MacKeithan had it figured out, a Tennessee mountain man needed three things to make him happy and to keep him that way. He needed a good long rifle in the hoop of his arm, a sharp hunting knife in his belt, and plenty of land all around him so that he could take a deep breath and stretch his arms without fear of knocking another man's eye out.

That, of course, did not take into consideration the strangely disquieting factor of a girl with golden hair, which the moonlight made alive, promenading on the texas deck of this Missouri River sidewheeler, General Jackson, at eleven o'clock in the evening as they steamed up toward Westport Landing, jump-off spot for the Santa Fe Trail.

This was the third night Flint had watched as he lay on the rough Osnaburg sheet tied down across the load of a big Pittsburgh wagon lashed to the deck of the General Jackson. The first night that she'd come out into the full moonlight he'd thought she was an angel, and he'd come up on his elbows to stare at her, open-mouthed, as he lay in the shadows cast by the steamer's huge

ON TO
SANTA FE

William Heuman

CENTER POINT LARGE PRINT
THORNDIKE, MAINE

Also by William Heuman and available from
Center Point Large Print:

Heller from Texas

**This Large Print Book carries the
Seal of Approval of N.A.V.H.**

Center Point
Large Print

ON TO
SANTA FE